The Other Mrs Walker

MARY PAULSON-ELLIS

The Other Mrs Walker

MANTLE

First published 2016 by Mantle
an imprint of Pan Macmillan
20 New Wharf Road, London N1 9RR
Associated companies throughout the world
www.panmacmillan.com

ISBN 978-1-4472-9390-3

1 3 5 7 9 8 6 4 2

A CIP catalogue record for this book is available from the British Library.

Printed and bound by CPI Group (UK) Ltd, Croydon, CR0 4YY

Visit www.panmacmillan.com to read more about all our books
and to buy them. You will also find features, author interviews and
news of any author events, and you can sign up for e-newsletters
so that you're always first to hear about our new releases.

For Audrey, with love

And my mother, with thanks

Oh my darling,
Oh my darling,
Oh my darling, Clementine,
Thou art lost and gone forever,
Dreadful sorry, Clementine.

19th-century American folk ballad

PROLOGUE

Christmas in Edinburgh, 2010

She died like this – with her shoes on and nylons wrinkling at the knee. The glass she was holding fell to the floor, the last of its contents trickling out with the last of her breath. The liquid glinted in the moonlight, winking a last goodnight before seeping away too – down through the fibres of the carpet, down through the rough and dusty floorboards, down to the ceiling of the flat below. It evaporated as it went, leaving nothing but a stain. And that smell. Whisky. The water of life. But not for her. Not any more.

In a drawer she left a Brazil nut with the Ten Commandments etched in its shell. On a mantelpiece a ridge of dust where once a photograph had stood. In a wardrobe she left an emerald dress, sequins scattered along the hem. On a blue plate an orange, full of holes now like her bones and her brain.

Everything was faded. Tea towels in drawers. Nets at the windows. The newspaper wrapped around her middle underneath her clothes. In the bathroom ice grew on the wrong side of the glass. In the crockery cupboard none of the plates matched any of the bowls. Outside, the street was faded too and the faces of the passers-by all gone to ash in the unrelenting cold. Inside, her fridge contained a single tin of peas.

She died like this – with a name wedged under her fingernails, scratching at her arms and her face, trying to remember. With a drift of hair, red at the tips and white at the roots. With bombs going off like bells in her ear. And that call, *Help me!* as plaster showered her head, splinters of wood, of metal and of glass flying through the silence as she called out again.

'Help me!'

Catching the thought as it scuttled through her brain, *This could be it.* But it wasn't. For this was it now. The glass slipping from her fingers. The tiny amber trickle. The liquid seeping down through the carpet to the ceiling of the flat below.

And somehow she'd always known that she would end like this. In a small square room, in a small square flat. In a small square box, perhaps. Cardboard, with a sticker on the outside. And a name.

What was that name? Lost, along with everything else she'd ever owned.

She hoped then, as the liquid seeped away, that she had not cursed God too often. For somebody had to say it, didn't they? *Ashes to ashes. Dust to dust.* Otherwise where would she be as they lowered her deep into the earth, or lit her up with those blue jets of gas? She knew she'd prefer it, that blaze of hot air. But still, as her breath trickled out, she did wonder if she might not deserve the damp embrace of heavy Edinburgh clay.

PART ONE

The Orange

EDINBURGH EVENING NEWS
2 January 2011

SECOND COLDEST WINTER ON RECORD
Experts from the Met Office today confirmed that Edinburgh is in the grip of the second coldest winter on record. Roads throughout the city have been made treacherous by sheets of solid ice.

ICE
'We urge householders to help by digging out the pavement in front of their homes,' said a spokesperson for Edinburgh City Council. The council has been attacked for failing to keep the thoroughfares clear.

NEIGHBOURS
National charity, Age Scotland, asked city residents to look out for the most needy at this time. 'Check on your elderly neighbours to make sure they are keeping warm.'

The cold weather is set to continue for at least the rest of the month.

2011

Margaret Penny came home on the spin of a coin. Heads to the north, tails to somewhere else – over the hills and far away, perhaps. Or a place much further than that. Six twenty-five a.m. on the second day of the New Year, and she arrived back in the Athens of the North to grey skies, grey buildings, grey pavements all encased in ice. And the people too.

She woke as the engine of the overnight bus juddered to a halt, hair all this way and that, head sticky with lurid, panicked dreaming. She gathered up all she had left – a small holdall and a red, stolen coat – and stumbled from the warm confines of the bus as though from a womb. The exit steps were narrow. She stumbled as she went down, stepping as though into air, straight into a gutter full of slurry.

'Shit!'

But cold and viscous. Ruining the only pair of shoes she had left.

It was a rebirth of sorts.

'All right, hen!' Margaret Penny's companion of the night and of the dawn and of the early, early morning that had never seemed to end, tumbled down the steps behind her and cracked open yet another tin of Special. 'Happy New Year!' He had reached his promised land. Edinburgh (along with the rest of Scotland) had one more day to party before work, and life, resumed.

Spume sprayed towards Margaret in an arc, flecks of

foam spattering her stolen coat. The man cheered, swinging his can up in a salutation of sorts, a tangle of dark hair
and sparkling lager droplets scattering hither and thither.
Everything to celebrate. Nothing to regret. After thirty
years, Margaret Penny was home.

Her mother, Barbara, lived in a modern block of maisonette flats on the north side of the city. Seven or eight
pounds in a taxi at that time of the morning. Double at
that time of year. It was nothing compared to London
prices, but half of all the money Margaret had left. Edinburgh never had been afraid to charge more than one was
expecting. She decided to walk.

The grey streets were deserted. Six forty-five a.m., and
it was as though the whole of Edinburgh was sleeping or
dead. Not a light in any of the tall windows. No one exer-
cising their dog. Nothing but street lights surrounded by
sodium halos in the murky morning air and plumes of
steam rising from central-heating vents like ghosts.

Margaret slid and cursed her way down the hill from the
bus station, gripping at whatever she could find to aid her
descent. Railings and traffic-light poles, litter bins studded
with the glacial remains of a million cigarettes smoked to
the last. The ice here really was treacherous, thick and
impacted, the air pinching at her lungs. She wished she'd
stolen a pair of gloves to go with the coat, or a scarf at least;
something to cover the bare extremities of her flesh – hands
and throat, ears and fingers, frozen already like the very tips
of the Alps. Margaret had forgotten how cold Scotland
could be. And how godforsaken too.

Down at the bottom of the long hill at last, she stag-
gered into the residents' parking bay at The Court, almost

colliding with the back end of a large black car as it revved
and skidded its way out. The car threw up a spray of grit
and slush that spattered across the hem of Margaret's coat
too. 'For God's sake!' she shouted, but the vehicle was
already escaping, up and out onto the main road, disappearing in a cloud of toxic exhaust. Half an hour in
Edinburgh and Margaret was already covered in dirt.

She climbed the concrete steps to Barbara's front door
like a foundling come home in the hope that her past was
just a mistake. But when the door finally edged open in
response to her third, insistent ring, Margaret realized that
the new dawn she hoped for was unlikely to happen here.
Her mother had got old. Much, much older than Margaret
had imagined. With a face already marked by the pallor of
a corpse.

'What are you doing here?' It wasn't the usual mother–
daughter greeting.

'I thought I'd help you bring in the New Year.'

'It's already happened.'

All spoken with the chain still on the door.

'I brought rum.' Margaret held up the quarter-bottle she
had carried all the way from the south. A peace offering,
perhaps, the promise of better things to come. Or, more
likely, because Barbara had always taught her daughter
that at moments like these it was best to Be Prepared.

The dark liquid glinted in the stair lighting. Through
the narrow crack in the door Barbara's pupils glinted too
as she eyed the bottle, while Margaret eyed her mother
in return. Old. Definitely old. And something else. But
there wasn't time for Margaret to be sure, for the door was
closing, then opening again. Without the chain this time.

Seven a.m., and crammed into Barbara's miniature hallway, Margaret opened her assault. 'That was a nice welcome for the season of good cheer.' She couldn't help herself. Attack, the best form of defence. Just like her mother, contrariness was buried in her bones.

'I thought you were one of those do-gooders.' Barbara was wearing a quilted dressing gown in a shade of something that had once been pink.

'A Jehovah's Witness?' Margaret had never known her mother to be religious. More interested in rum and biscuits than the chance to save her soul.

In her right hand Barbara gripped a grey NHS stick. 'I already belong to them,' she said.

This wasn't the kind of homecoming Margaret had expected. A sudden conversion to God in all his many guises. 'I thought you were Church of Scotland. That one round the corner.'

Barbara sniffed, a faint whistle rising from her chest. 'And all the rest.'

'The rest?'

'Episcopal. Catholic. Evangelical. Friends,' Barbara recited as though she was in church right there and then.

'Friends?'

Barbara leaned into her stick, lungs wheezing. 'Quaker, like in that film with that Indiana man.'

'I think that's Amish.'

'Whatever.'

Only two minutes in the flat and Margaret wasn't performing well. Her neck felt sweaty. She hadn't even taken off her coat. 'So you're a member of more than one congregation?'

'All of them, more or less.'

'But you don't believe in God.'

'How do you know.'

It wasn't a question and there was nothing Margaret could say in reply. Ten years, maybe more. Very few phone calls. Couldn't remember the last time she had turned up for Christmas or New Year. After all, her mother was old now, well over seventy. Maybe she'd had a sudden conversion. A kind of Road to Damascus experience, like Margaret's own Beginning of the End. It would be typical to have come home for her mid-life crisis, only to discover that her mother's end-of-life crisis was well under way. Margaret clutched tighter at the neck of the quarter-bottle. Who Dares Wins. Or something like that. But, of course, her mother got in first.

'So, are you going to pour me a glass out of that bottle? Or do I have to do it myself like everything else around here?'

Margaret Penny hadn't planned to come back to Edinburgh any more than Edinburgh had been expecting her to return.

But . . .

Home is where the heart is.

Isn't that what they say?

Especially a heart that has been beaten, pummelled and cut into tiny pieces before being left to fester on a life-support machine.

She'd abandoned the life she once had in London by tossing it into a skip sometime between Christmas and New Year. All the things that were no use to her any more discarded over landfill – black suits and blouses with furls down the front, tights the colour of skin, garlic presses, smart dresses, folders in variegated shades. Also a juice machine she'd hankered after once but never even used.

It was around the same time that the life Margaret thought she was living also got rid of her. A job lost without so much as a by your leave. A bank account emptied like bathwater down a drain. No savings to fall back on. No real friends to fall back on either. Various debit, credit and other types of card that turned out to have no money (or loyalty) attached. Finally a visit from the bailiffs to announce that the flat she had rented for all of these years had somehow been repossessed.

Thirty years in the great metropolis vanished like snow sliding from a hotplate. And all because of an encounter with an ashen-haired lady who laid out photographs on a small, stained table in Margaret's local coffee shop. A man Margaret imagined was hers at the time. And next to him two silver-haired children in crumpled Technicolor. The life Margaret had always wanted.

Except . . .

It turned out to have belonged to someone else all along.

Her mother's lucky coronation penny appeared just when Margaret needed it most. Nothing to celebrate, everything to regret, down on the cold kitchen tiles of a flat that was no longer hers, toasting the end with a bottle of cheap wine gone sour. The penny rolled from between two kitchen units, a small missive from the past teetering into view. Margaret crawled after it. The tiles were hard and unforgiving, left bruises on her knees. But Margaret didn't care. Here was something unexpected, just when she had been anticipating the worst.

The penny was old-fashioned, smelling of metal and of earth, a dull glint of bronze in the low winter light. On one side Britannia wielded her trident. On the other a king who should never have been a king gazed out. Heads to the north, tails to the south. Or somewhere much further than that. Margaret spun the coin without considering what might come next. Disaster, or the broaching of a new reef. Let the king decide.

So he did.

She departed with nothing but a small blue holdall (four pairs knickers, spare bra, two pairs tights. Also a toothbrush and a bottle of tinted moisturizer down to the last few smears). She left behind a man with hair the colour of wet slate standing in the middle of a London living room, walls painted the colour of the sun. And stole a coat because . . . well . . . she turned out to be good at that. Also a photograph of two silver-haired children because one never did know when it might prove useful to have a family of one's own.

There was a certain satisfaction to it, not owning anything and not being owned. But it didn't leave Margaret many options. Just a ticket on the first bus north and a flat in a former Edinburgh council block – living room, kitchen, bedroom, box room full of junk and that tiny square of beige her mother called the hall. Home. It wasn't where Margaret's heart was. But at least it was somewhere to run.

*

A quart of rum drunk to the last lick. Television turned up full. Chips eaten from the knee. It wasn't the best New Year's celebration Margaret Penny had ever had. But it certainly wasn't the worst.

She and her mother covered all the normal topics in three minutes, give or take.

Weather.

'Some people have sons and daughters to help them clear their paths.'

Health.

'You'll have seen the stick.'

Friends.

'All busy with their families at this time of year.'

Before getting to the matter in hand.

'I was wondering if I could stay for a while.' Margaret crumpled the last of her chip paper, vinegar and a slick of grease under her fingernails reminding her of how short a distance she had travelled over the past thirty years.

'So you're here for a holiday then?' Barbara dribbled the last of the rum onto her tongue.

Margaret couldn't tell if her mother thought a holiday was a good idea or not. Decided to hedge her bets. 'Yes. Sort of.'

'What's that supposed to mean?'

A vacation. A visit. A three-day trip. Looking for love. Or (in the likely absence of that) money to aid a quick exit for when the time came. But Margaret couldn't think which answer might be best, so she avoided one altogether. 'It would just be for a week or two,' she said. 'Maybe a month.'

Silence.

Barbara stared at the television screen with the intent gaze of a newborn, frills peeking out at throat and cuffs from beneath her all-consuming dressing gown. Margaret couldn't tell if her mother was considering her request to become a house guest or pretending to ignore it. Or whether (perhaps more likely) she needed a hearing aid. It was like being interrogated, but without the other side saying a thing. But just when she was resigned to heading out once more into the freezing Edinburgh night, Barbara switched the television off with an abrupt flick of her wrist and said, 'You can take the box room.'

'Sorry?'

'It'll need clearing.'

It was amazing, really, when Margaret thought about it later, how easy it had been.

That night Margaret Penny lay on an inflatable lilo on her mother's box-room floor, turning and turning in a failed attempt to get warm. The stolen coat, red as a massacre, covered her body. Outside the temperature was well below freezing. Inside, the box room was inhabited by a deep-seated chill. Whichever way she turned, one elbow, one ankle, one hand or hip bone was forever outside in the cold. Margaret was certain she could see her own breath hanging above her like some sort of miasmic shroud.

'I don't have visitors to stay often.'

That was how Barbara had put it as she handed over the only spare blanket she seemed to own. Small and square, with a satin trim around the edge, all gone to rot now, the blanket had been more suited to a baby than a grown woman already well established in the middle of her life. But Margaret took it all the same. Beggars couldn't be choosers. Besides, her mother was like a book with no words. Impossible to read.

After Barbara went to bed, still grumbling about having her New Year plans disrupted, Margaret spent half an hour clearing a space on the box-room floor. Head against one wall, feet nearly touching the next, it was a sort of mini ground zero well suited to this stage of her life. It took her a while to resuscitate the lilo (the only mattress available, it seemed), giving the blue-and-yellow plastic the kiss of life while she practically expired. As she brushed her teeth in the freezing bathroom, peering through a gap in the window onto tarmac glimmering with frost, she wished someone would give her the kiss of life too. There were no windows in the box room. No emergency exits of any kind.

Her mother had been right. The room did need clearing. It was entirely filled with junk. A whole life laid out in front of Margaret, not on a small, stained coffee table this time, but piled up wall to wall. A heater with a broken dial that gave off a burning smell when Margaret tried to turn it on. A clothes horse stripped of all its plastic coating. An iron with a frayed flex. An ancient wardrobe full of ancient clothes. A small brown painting, dirty in more ways than one. And a grubby china cherub, chipped and fractured, one arm severed long before.

So here it lay. All the junk Margaret had spent thirty years trying to escape. Yet here she was again, too. Forty-seven, soon to be fifty. No children she could point to as an achievement. No grandparents or siblings. Not even any pets. And now she was back in Edinburgh. Land of grey buildings. Land of tall chimneys. Land of secrets that everyone knew but pretended they did not. It wasn't what she'd planned, aged forty-seven, to be coming home empty-handed apart from a stolen coat and a bottle of rum. But then Margaret wasn't really sure what she had planned exactly. When she tried to imagine, nothing came to mind.

Except . . .

In the clutter of the box room, deep in the dark of an Edinburgh night, Margaret Penny felt something trapped beneath her hip. Squashed. Misshapen. Rather like her. The last of her Christmas clementines, borrowed from a market stall in London as a final reminder of the south.

Margaret shifted, grasping hold of the small fruit as it rolled free from the pocket of her coat. She raised it towards her mouth in the blackness. Somewhere out in the frozen wastelands of the city a drunk man was dancing, lager sparkling like a constellation in his hair. But here, in the cold and inky pitch of her mother's box room, Margaret Penny was tasting the sun.

He came home and it rolled from his jacket sleeve – a small orange sun appearing like magic out of the dirty tweed.

'Daddy, Daddy, Daddy.' The small girl waiting for him in the corridor of their cold London home jumped up from the bottom stair, clapping her hands together over and over. 'Give it to me. Give it to me.'

'What's it worth, lass?' Alfred Walker held the treasure out of the little girl's reach, high in the sky of the hall. He was laughing, like he always did, in a way that made everyone want to join in.

The girl pouted, her tumbling, twirling hair all stuck to her rosy little cheeks. 'Daddy,' she said, as though she were forty, not four, hands held flat against her clean Christmas frock. She was looking at him with those startling eyes: first one thing, then another. Difficult to resist.

'Oh, you're killin' me.' Alfred groaned and made as though to stab his chest, a clenched fist hard against his waistcoat buttons.

'Give it to me then,' the little girl replied.

From upstairs the beginning of a long moan stretched out to meet them, rising and rising, then falling and falling, then rising again; taking everything in the house with it, from the lids on the pantry jars to the cherub with the missing thumb that decorated the parlour mantelpiece. The child and her father looked at each other, his fist still clenched against his chest, her small hands pressed together now as though in urgent prayer.

Then Alfred lowered his hand. 'It won't be long now,' he said, sliding the orange back into his jacket pocket, treasure swallowed by the dark.

In the scullery through the back, Alfred splashed water from the cold tap straight onto his forearms and his wrists. 'Have you thought of names yet?' he asked.

The little girl shook her head.

He splashed water straight onto his face and his hair. 'What, can you not think of any?'

The little girl turned her startling eyes to the floor.

Alfred pulled back from the thick earthenware sink and shook his head – a wild dog-like shake that sent tiny droplets raining down on every surface. When he looked up the girl was standing in front of him, her dress all speckled, holding out a towel that was all speckled too.

'Thanks, darling.' Alfred wiped all around his face, his ears, his neck. When he tossed the towel down there was dirt all across its weave. He pulled out a chair and sat. 'We got your name from the song.'

The little girl wriggled onto a chair next to him.

'Oh my darling.' He put out a hand to touch her slippery hair. 'But if you can't think of anything we'll just have to call them after me and your ma.' Alfred laughed then. That laugh which made everyone want to join in. The girl covered her mouth with her hand. But she was frowning this time.

Upstairs another moan started on its long journey. Alfred raised his eyes to the ceiling. 'No time to waste,' he said, getting up from his chair.

The girl slid off her chair too.

Alfred went to the doorway and looked out into the hall: nothing but a thin slit of yellow at the top of the stairs. 'Onwards and upwards,' he murmured, lacing his fingers together and cracking all the bones.

'Daddy.'

Four small fingers and a thumb touched the edge of his tweed jacket.

'What is it?' Alfred's hand was already on the wooden banister.

'Happy Christmas.'

'Oh aye!' Alfred stepped back into the hall patting at both his pockets. 'How could I forget?' For a moment his eyes danced, then one of his hands vanished into the tweed, appearing again a moment later with a small orange resting in the centre of his palm. 'Happy Christmas.'

The girl reached out to touch.

But Alfred held something else out with his other hand this time. 'To celebrate the babies when they come,' he said. 'Heads for one of each. Tails for neither.' He laughed as the penny flipped in the air, a slow turn at the apex, both of them watching, before its sudden drop.

The coin fell with a clink and a clatter, then rolled away, teetering into the darkness. The little girl didn't scrabble to follow, down on her bare knees amongst the dust. Instead she reached out once more to curl four small fingers and a thumb around the orange, holding on tight this time until Alfred took his hand away.

The little girl watched as Alfred took the stairs two at a time, right to the top, waiting for him to disappear into the shadows. Then she ate the whole thing before he could come back down. Didn't wait for it to be peeled or segmented. Or to sit at a table. Instead she tore through the orange flesh with her sharp little teeth, squatting on the bare floorboards, biting and gnawing and sucking until there was sticky juice running all down her chin.

Clementine. That was what they called her.

Upstairs it was a boy and a girl. Named for their parents, all smiles now. Mrs Sprat, the midwife (though she wasn't married now and never would be) moved around the room from one baby to the next, sorting a washbasin here, tidying a bundle of cloths there. 'What a racket,' she muttered. But she didn't mean the newborns, who were as sunny in their first moments as they would be in their last. She wiped her way around the stump of a severed umbilical cord, frowning at the slew of garments strewn about the floor. A good sweep out, that was what this house needed. And some sense drummed into them all. She swabbed around a small penis and two tiny testicles pressed high in their sac. And that husband, choosing to watch! Well, where would it end?

The first baby wriggled and squirmed in the midwife's arms, twisting his head as though to find something he had lost. Mrs Sprat held him in hands like two sides of a vice as she wrapped his jerking limbs inside a cotton square. And all that banshee screaming from the wife. Really, it was enough to make you want plugs for your ears. The midwife placed the boy into a waiting basket, tucking a blanket with a bright satin trim all around. She'd have to have a word with the matron about coming to this part of town again.

In the wide double bed Alfred's wife, Dorothea, lay back, hair scattered all this way and that. Alfred perched by her side stroking the top of Dorothea's head over and over. 'Oh my darling,' he murmured.

'Pass me my hairbrush, will you.' Dorothea's hair was her favourite feature. She brushed it every morning and every night. And sometimes in between too.

Alfred reached to the bedside cabinet and handed Dorothea a brush with a handle made of bone. Dorothea began to stroke, slowly, from the very crown of her head right down to the very tips. 'Are they chirruping?' she asked.

Alfred got up from the bed and went to lean over the basket. 'Aye,' he said. 'One of them at least.'

'Have they all their necessary digits?'

'Ten fingers. Ten toes. Twice.' And he laughed.

'Hair?'

'Well, the boy has, that's for certain.' Alfred reached down into the basket and held up a tiny bundle for Dorothea to see. The blanket fell. The cotton square came untucked. A miniature pink heel dangled. Alfred scooped it back up, rolling his eyes at where the midwife stood in the corner, her square back turned. Dorothea giggled. Mrs Sprat hunched lower over her task.

'And what about Clemmie?' Dorothea twirled the hairbrush once in her hand then began from the crown again.

'She's sucking away on that orange.'

'Did she choose a name?'

'No.'

'I knew she wouldn't.'

'Why's that?' Alfred lifted his head away from his new son and looked at his wife.

'Because . . .' Dorothea was concentrating on the pale ends of her hair now. 'She doesn't want them.'

'Don't be daft,' Alfred turned back to the basket. 'She'll love them.'

'Oh, no,' said Dorothea. 'She told me.'

'Well, she's stuck with them now, either way.' Alfred and Dorothea both looked up, startled.

'She speaks,' said Alfred.

The midwife's cheeks reddened as she thrust a second bundle towards him. 'Here's the other one.'

Dorothea put the hairbrush to her lips so the midwife would not see her smile. Then she held out a tiny pair of silver scissors to Alfred. 'Cut me a piece of them, will you, so that I don't forget.'

An hour later Alfred stood in the centre of the bedroom, a small baby balanced on either arm. 'We shall call them Little Alfie and Little Dottie.' He looked like a man who had eaten a very satisfactory dinner.

'Dotty, like me,' said Dorothea, hair spread out across her shoulders like a shawl. Then she laughed. The kind of laugh that made people turn to look, then look away. The midwife, who had returned to the bedroom to pack her bag, did just that.

Alfred laughed too. 'Aye,' he said. 'Like two wee chips off two big blocks.'

'Like two peas in a pod, more like.' They both looked at the midwife again. She was dressed in her cap and her cape now, ready to exit.

'She speaks again.'

'Alfred . . .' Dorothea gave a little shake of her gleaming head.

'Madam,' said Alfred to the midwife. 'Allow me to assist you from the premises.' He placed the two bundles into the basket, top to tail, and tucked the blanket with the bright satin trim all around them once again. Then he advanced towards the bedroom door holding out his hand. The midwife clutched her bag tighter to her chest. She was reluctant to pass it over, but good manners prevailed.

Downstairs there was no sign of Clementine. Just six orange pips sucked dry and left in a little pile on the bare floorboards of the hall. Alfred stepped over the pips as though they did not exist. 'Well, goodbye,' he said, one hand holding open the front door. 'And Happy Christmas.'

The midwife was already out on the step. 'Oh, yes.' She put a hand to her cap. She'd forgotten all about that.

'Your bag.'

'Oh.' Mrs Sprat turned back. She'd forgotten about that too. Whatever was it with this family that got her all mixed up? 'And a Happy Christmas to you too.'

But the door was closing already. Midwife outside in the cold December air. All five of the Walker family together in the warm.

'Oh,' Mrs Sprat said again, though there was no one to hear her. Then she set off down the frosty London street, a little skid here, a little skitter there, almost a tumble. They're mad, she thought as she clutched at her bag, fingers already numb from the slow creep of snow. She fumbled inside the pockets of her cape for her thick blue gloves. But they had vanished, replaced by several pieces of sticky orange peel.

2011

There were five of them altogether. A priest. Three mourners. And a dead person folded into a wooden box.

Praise Be.

RIP.

And anything else appropriate for a funeral where nobody knew the deceased. Margaret Penny had only been in Edinburgh for a few days and already she was consorting with the dead. It seemed a fitting epitaph for the failure of her life to rise to much beyond the cradle or the grave.

The call had come the day before and it was Margaret who answered. Barbara seemed strangely reluctant to pick up her own phone.

'Hello?'

'Hello.' A light voice. Male. Unexpected. 'Is Mrs Penny in?'

'Can I ask who's calling?'

'It's Mr Wingrove. The assistant from West Leith Parish.'

'West Leith?' Episcopal. Catholic. Evangelical. Friends. Barbara hadn't mentioned that particular congregation in her litany of churchgoing to date.

Across the room, from the depths of her armchair, her mother made furious gesticulations with her stick, as though outraged that Margaret would even contemplate lifting the receiver, let alone getting into a conversation with whoever was on the line. Barbara's hair had not been brushed all day. Little flecks of spittle were gathering on her chin. And just for a moment there was that expression. The one Margaret had seen when Barbara first opened her front door.

Margaret turned slightly to avoid her mother's insistent glare. 'I'm afraid she's indisposed at the moment. Can I take a message?'

'Yes, could you tell her she's next up on the rota. For tomorrow afternoon.'

'The rota?'

The way her mother explained it later, being an official mourner to the 'indigent' was almost a full-time job.

The crematorium chapel was small and empty, three rows of chairs diagonally placed, a big curtain drawn across one wall. There was a plinth at the front covered in a blue velvet cloth and a lectern for whoever might preside, but there was no sign of human activity. Not even from the dead. From the doorway, Margaret peered in towards the gloom. The only light came from a few narrow windows positioned very high up in the bare concrete wall. It was rather like her mother's box room. No chance of gazing out over green pastures while the last rites were relayed.

'Shall we go in?' she said, breath blooming in the frigid air. Sleet was falling (again) as it had ever since Margaret had returned to Edinburgh, casual stinging drops that clung to her red, stolen coat in little icy clumps. It was official now. Edinburgh was in the grip of the second coldest winter on record. All the city's surfaces turned into a deadly rink. Still, Margaret didn't see why they had to stand outside getting chilblains. The guest of honour was dead, after all. He wouldn't know if someone else got to his party first.

Barbara stubbed at the frozen ground with the rubber tip of her grey NHS stick. 'No,' she wheezed. 'That would never do.'

'Why not?' Margaret said.

'Because.'

And there really wasn't an answer to that. Barbara always had been a person who knew when right was right and wrong was (always) wrong. Only that morning over breakfast, small strands of mini Shredded Wheat clinging unnoticed to the front of her quilted gown, she had apprised Margaret as to all the day's rules.

Don't smile.

Don't mention the deceased.

Don't talk about anything other than the weather.

Funerals, Margaret had realized then, were just like being a child again. The Edinburgh of her girlhood returned to feed on her bones. She had resisted leaning over to pluck the wheaty strands from her mother's chest. It wasn't her responsibility to make Barbara look good. Besides, she hadn't touched her mother for years. And certainly never like that.

Instead, now, Margaret just turned up the collar of her coat and folded in the lapels to cover the bare triangle of her throat. She still hadn't found a scarf to wear, despite a quick rummage in the box-room wardrobe to see what she could see. Nothing of any use but a pair of ancient wool gloves in navy, holes at the fingertips, and a blouse in a distressing shade of fawn. When she'd first opened the wardrobe Margaret had wondered what might happen if she stepped inside rather than pulling something out, disappearing forever into a crush of starch and mildew, a forest of oversized coats and dresses flattened between thin plastic sheets. But needless to say, her mother had got there first.

'Aren't you ready yet?' Barbara's great bulk appeared in the box-room doorway, blocking out what little light there was.

'Yes,' Margaret replied. 'Just coming.' And pulled out the first few items that came to hand. A calf-length corduroy skirt to match the navy gloves and that terrible blouse in fawn.

Barbara turned out to be wearing a woollen coat the colour of wet sand and a lilac hat more suited to a summer wedding than a funeral on a dark January day. As they'd clambered into the waiting taxi, the driver levering Barbara from behind, Margaret had glimpsed something else too. A flap of summer jacket the colour of a Hebridean sea. 'Shouldn't we be wearing black?' she had asked as they settled themselves onto the back seat.

'I am,' said Barbara gesturing with her stick to a flower made of black net wilting above her lilac brim. Then, as the taxi engine whined and revved, she'd rummaged in a stiff-sided handbag and taken out a plastic Rainmate with which to top the lot. 'Be prepared,' she said.

Now, as they stood waiting for the entrance of the deceased, Margaret conjured a vision of her own demise, Barbara celebrating in a turquoise two-piece, one glassful of rum segueing into the next. There was no denying it, her mother looked happy. But what would Margaret wear if it were the other way around – Barbara dead on a slab, all oozing flesh and badly applied rouge? For there was nothing suitable in her current wardrobe, reduced as it was to a holdall-shaped succinctness (four pairs knickers, spare bra, toothbrush, two pairs tights, etc.). Maybe she would have to borrow the lilac hat. Though would it count as borrowing if her mother was dead? After all, once Barbara succumbed for good to whatever had taken up residence in her chest, all she possessed could be Margaret's. That dirty china cherub in place of a shiny juice machine. Margaret laughed then, a hollow little sound.

'What's so funny?' Next to her Barbara was hunched beneath her plastic headgear, a woman who always expected the worst.

'Nothing.'

'Well then.'

And it was all Margaret could do not to squeal as the rubber tip of Barbara's grey NHS stick pressed down hard onto the surface of one of her inappropriate shoes.

Five minutes later, just as Margaret was contemplating rebellion, a priest appeared, hands held wide as though in a gesture of praise. 'Ah, Mrs Penny.'

But it wasn't Margaret he was welcoming into the flock.

Barbara shuffled forwards, eyes shining suddenly in the pale January light. For one horrified moment Margaret thought her mother was going to embrace the holy man, kiss him right there on the chapel steps. Surely Church of Scotland hadn't gone as far as that in all the years she had been away?

But the priest simply bowed towards Barbara as she

approached, clasping her two hands inside his own as though paying obeisance to a queen. 'How wonderful to see you again,' he said. 'So kind of you to come.'

Must not know about the Catholics, thought Margaret, folding her lapels back down to make herself presentable. Or the Episcopals. Or the Friends. Then again, perhaps he did and simply ignored the implications. That would be the Edinburgh Way.

As she bared her throat to the chill Edinburgh winds, Margaret noticed that her mother appeared to be whispering some sort of incantation into the priest's ear. He nodded and rose from his stoop, turning towards Margaret instead. 'And Margaret.' The priest was tall suddenly, staring straight into her eyes. 'The prodigal daughter.'

That wasn't a question.

'Yes,' Margaret said.

Barbara inclined her head towards the priest. 'Reverend McKilty.'

Margaret almost laughed. Then she remembered her mother's instruction. 'Pleased to meet you,' she said. 'It's a pity about the weather.' She saw how the priest's eyes glinted, reflecting for a moment her own.

Inside the chapel they didn't sit in the front row of chairs. Instead Barbara indicated to Margaret with her stick that they should sit at the back. 'Have to save the front row for the family,' she wheezed.

'What family?' whispered Margaret. 'I thought the whole point was that there weren't any.'

'You can never tell.'

Margaret squeezed in beside Barbara, two rows of empty chapel chairs in front (all with better legroom) and wondered how many other funerals her mother had attended without knowing anything about the deceased. As usual, Barbara wasn't giving anything away. Instead she sat immobile, staring straight ahead at the plinth, chest letting out small gasps and pants.

The priest ignored them too, hanging around at the door, clasping and unclasping his hands as though he was waiting for someone else to arrive. Holding out for the spectre at the feast, perhaps, some sort of distant cousin. Or maybe a long-lost daughter materializing from out of the famous Edinburgh mist. Then again, it could be that they were all just waiting on the dead person. For even if the deceased was without relatives or cash ('It's called indigent, Margaret. Please try to remember'), their body was presumably a prerequisite for their own funeral. At least that was what Margaret surmised.

In fact it was a small woman with no hat, carrying a bouquet of weeping snowdrops, who was the cause of the hold-up.

'Mrs Maclure,' the priest murmured as the latecomer rushed through the chapel door.

'So sorry, so sorry, so sorry,' the little woman murmured, nodding and bowing to the chapel floor as she slipped into a chair on the other side of the aisle.

'Who's that?' Margaret whispered to her mother.

Barbara looked ahead, gaze rigid, lungs giving out a small accordion-like moan. 'She's the other one on the rota.'

'Obviously, but what's her . . .'

'Shhhh!'

Everyone in the chapel (all three of them) turned their

heads towards Margaret, waiting with silent frowns for her to shut up. Margaret subsided into silence. Trouble. That was what her mother always used to call her. Nothing but trouble right from the start.

A priest. A dead person. And three official mourners who just happened to top the rota when the day for the burning came. It wasn't an excessive event. In fact the whole thing only took around fifteen minutes, including the coming in and the going out. Reverend McKilty intoned. Mrs Maclure sniffed. Barbara sat like a totem propped up throughout by her grey NHS stick. There were no flowers. No hymns. No order of service. Just a few words, a reading from the Bible and a dead man called John. It wasn't exactly an elaborate send-off for what was once a life.

Margaret sat through it all trying not to fiddle with the coronation penny safe in the pocket of her stolen coat. *Find a penny, pick it up, all day long you'll have good luck.* That was what her mother used to say. And like everyone else Margaret Penny had always assumed luck would be on her side, until it turned out she had no luck at all. The coin had been the first sign that something might change. Heads to the north. Tails to somewhere much further than that. But was that luck, she wondered now, so much as random chance? Heads or tails. Could have gone either way. She turned the coin in her pocket, once, then twice, as the priest declared the dead man dead. Margaret knew that she was missing something in her life. Perhaps if she flipped the penny again, she might find out what.

As the priest announced *ashes to ashes* and the coffin began its final shuddery descent into fiery oblivion (or at least the crematorium holding bay), Margaret tried to picture someone she knew lying inside so as to call up the requisite emotion. Somebody ought to cry, or look like they might, for it to be a proper funeral.

There was her mother, of course, the only one of Margaret's relatives to get anywhere near the grave. In fact, the only relative Margaret had ever known, full stop. That lilac hat. Those lips wet with rum. And all that junk just waiting to be passed on. But despite the whistles rising from Barbara's chest now, Margaret was certain that her mother would be around for some time yet. So she thought instead of a man with hair the colour of wet slate, the person who had made the middle of Margaret's life seem like a new dawn, until it turned out to be the beginning of the end instead. Margaret knew she could cry an ocean for him, twice over. But she was determined that she would not.

There was her own future self, of course, thirty years hence, lying stranded in the box room of a flat where the carpets matched the walls. Found frozen to the mattress like a bad dream, three months too late, no friends, no savings, no prospects. Ex-Directory just like her mother. Nothing but the faintest hint of rum to sweeten her goodbye.

But in the end it was the photograph that did it. Lost now. Vanished. Just like Margaret's previous life: nothing but a memory pulled from the depths of a chest of drawers one evening when Margaret was still a child herself. Two anonymous twins in black and white, sleeping behind a cold rectangle of glass.

'Who are they?' she had asked her mother, though

she'd known even then that she had been digging where she ought not.

'None of your business.' Barbara had leaned across from her ironing and snatched the photograph away. 'Put it back and don't touch.' Barbara never had been big on family history, either her own or other people's.

'But what are they doing?' Margaret had persisted.

'They're dead, of course.'

Afterwards, gathered outside for what passed for a wake, Mrs Maclure enquired as to Barbara's general and spiritual health. 'We didn't hear from you on your birthday.' (That small celebration misfortunate enough to fall just before Christmas.) Margaret realized she had forgotten. She hadn't celebrated Barbara's birthday for years, and nor, as far as Margaret knew, had her mother.

'And we missed you at the Christmas service.'

Barbara whistled and panted, leaning heavily on her stick. 'I haven't been out much this year,' she said, voice tuned to full mourning mode. 'Death follows me around.' And Margaret saw it again – that look behind her mother's eyes when she'd first peered out through a crack in the door. Fear. That was what Margaret had seen. As though whoever might be waiting could only mean one thing.

'Oh, I know just how you feel, dear.' Mrs Maclure still clasped the weeping snowdrops even though the coffin had been dispatched. 'This is the third time I've been up here already this year.'

Christ, thought Margaret. It's only the second week of January.

Barbara stood a little straighter now. 'Are the others not available?'

'Oh no, dear,' said Mrs Maclure. 'It's just . . . there's been a rush on. Cold weather. Backed up at the mortuary.'

'Why haven't I been informed?'

'You didn't seem to be answering your phone, dear. I've tried you several times.' Mrs Maclure bobbed and bowed as though she was the one who ought to be apologizing.

The crescendo of wheezes that had been rising in protest from Barbara's chest subsided somewhat. 'Been busy,' she muttered, stumping with her stick at the ground. Though Margaret couldn't imagine with what.

Mrs Maclure turned to Margaret instead. 'And what about you, dear? Will you be joining the rota?'

'Oh no, I'm not . . .' Coming to Edinburgh was one thing. Being required to consort with the actual dead on a regular basis, quite something else.

'We always need a helping hand.' Mrs Maclure's eyes shone black in the shadow cast by the chapel door. 'To help with the abandoned.'

'Well, maybe . . .' Head frozen to the mattress. The sweet kiss of rum.

'Good.' Mrs Maclure smiled, revealing surprisingly long canines for a woman who was so slight in other ways. 'Never do know when it might be your turn.'

Margaret instantly regretted what she might have put herself in the way of. A life amongst the indigent of Edinburgh wasn't exactly her idea of a future. 'I may not have much time, though,' she said, just to leave her options open. 'I'll have to get a job.'

'What?' Barbara's eyes boggled all of a sudden. 'I thought you weren't staying.'

'Well, I . . .'

'Really?' Mrs Maclure hesitated for a moment, head cocked as though she saw yet another opportunity coming her way. 'I may be able to help with that.' And she brushed up against Margaret's red coat for a moment, as though some agreement had passed between them.

Margaret sucked in a lungful of chilly January air and wondered what exactly she might have signed up for. She had forgotten all about this in her years down in London. The Edinburgh Way of getting things done.

Margaret left her mother and Mrs Maclure to chat over the finer details of the official mourners to the indigent rota and went in search of the taxi she had ordered for their return trip. Up behind the crematorium chapel she watched as a black car peeled away from a row of hearses and disappeared down the long driveway towards the road. The car looked just like the one that had revved and skidded its way out of the residents' parking bay at The Court only a few days before. She searched for any distinguishing features.

Except . . .

She was at a crematorium. All the cars were black.

In the taxi on the way home, slithering and bumping across the brooding town, Margaret asked her mother, 'If you don't want death following you around, why are you on the rota?'

'Somebody's got to do it.' Barbara touched her lilac hat, the black flower a little crushed now from all the excitement.

'Isn't it a bit like being an ambulance chaser?'

'At least we're doing something useful.'

Margaret didn't respond to that. Neither of them had been inclined to confession since she had returned, despite her mother's conversion to the religious way of things. Still, Barbara seemed to have read Margaret from the inside to the out.

'But you don't believe in ghosts, do you?' Margaret persisted.

'Of course not, don't be ridiculous.'

Yet there it was again – that tiny, brief unmasking – just as when Barbara first opened the front door to Margaret's insistent ring. Margaret turned to look out at the frozen city through a swirl of condensation. The black monoliths of Edinburgh were passing: castle (ancient); volcano (dead); finance quarter (wounded). A whole world stilled beneath a globe of ice. Dead parents. Dead grandparents. Two dead children pressed behind cold glass. No wonder her mother was morbid if that was the only legacy she had to bequeath. The taxi turned into the grey streets of the New Town, bouncing across the frozen setts as it picked up speed.

'By the way – ' Barbara poked with her stick at Margaret's calf this time – 'she's not married. Never has been.'

'Who?'

'Mrs Maclure, of course.'

'Why is she "Mrs" then?'

'It's an Edinburgh thing.'

Say one thing, mean another.

They both clutched at their seats as the taxi swerved

around a corner, back end swinging out in a big, sliding curve.

'Has she always been on the rota?' Margaret asked.

'She knows where all the bodies are buried.' Barbara's chest gave off a small whistle at the joke. 'Used to work for the council. Amongst other things.' Then she said, 'Did you read the note she gave you?'

'What note?'

Yet there it was. In the pocket of Margaret's coat, nestled up against a lucky coronation penny and a stiff piece of orange peel. Paper ripped from a small pad and folded into four. Margaret unfolded the note as the taxi jerked to a halt. The message was scribbled alongside a phone number.

LOST, it said. *CAN YOU HELP?*

1935

Six years gone, and the house was the same, the hall was the same, the tweed jacket was the same, but with patches now and tears and frays, all sorts of bits gone shiny and worn. No small orange sun rolling from the sleeve.

Alfred Walker came stamping in the front door on a cloud of frosty air, bare boards squeaking beneath his heavy boots. 'Has it happened yet?'

Clementine was in her usual place, crouched knees to chin on the bottom step of the long, narrow stair. She was ten now, her Christmas frock long gone. She didn't bother to get up, just shook her head to let her father know the state of things.

Alfred sighed, rubbing a dirty thumb across his forehead. 'I'd better go up then.' He skirted his daughter, making no attempt to touch her, and took the steps one by one, still in his dirty coat with his dirty neck and his dirty hands.

Clementine watched Alfred go, her hands no longer rosy, her hair no longer twirled, her dress grey with so much washing, covered by a cardigan held together with darns. Alfred's tread was leaden on the rough wooden floorboards as he made his way up, anything he might have had in his pocket going with him into the dark. Clementine waited until her father's big, hunched shape merged with the shadows at the top. Then she got up and went along the passageway into the kitchen to sit at the table all on her own. If there was any magic left, it had disappeared years ago. Besides, ten-year-old Clementine didn't believe in such things. Not any more.

Upstairs Alfred stood at the bottom of the wide double bed, cracking his dirty knuckles and picking at his dirty fingernails with his teeth.

'Do you mind,' said Mrs Sprat, pushing past with a cloth and a bowl.

'Excuse me,' said Alfred, shifting slightly, black lines of grime embedded in his thumbs.

'Excuse me.' The midwife pushed past him again, the water in her bowl lurching like a drunk man, thin pink stain rolling around the rim. Mrs Sprat could smell the whisky oozing from Alfred. She thought the neighbours could probably smell it too.

Dorothea lay in the bed, flesh all mottled and damp. Her hair was tangled and matted. Her breathing harsh. The smell of meat left out too long oozed from her insides. Alfred stared at his wife's swollen belly, large above a sea of stained sheets. Her feet were straining at the ankles, pressing against the wooden bars. There was blood smeared on the inside of her thighs. And she was making that sound again. A low, urgent grunting.

Between Dorothea's legs a small slick of black appeared for a moment, then subsided. She groaned, the long deep groan of a woman two days in labour. The midwife pushed Alfred aside with a sharp prod of her elbow. He stepped back. Let it be a boy, he thought. Everything would be all right if only it were a son.

*

Downstairs Clementine shifted amongst the packets and jars in the pantry. She liked the cool feel of the long, narrow space. Flagstones. Painted wooden shelves. A meat safe with a wire mesh front. She lifted the covers from some of the large jars. Took a broken biscuit from the bottom of the barrel. Stuck the tip of one finger into a jug of cream.

On the shelf was a pie, its edges fluted. Also a bowl of floury cooked potatoes and a bottle of stout. Clementine pushed one or two of the potatoes around, their skins already split and peeling. Then she pulled the stout towards her, removing the stopper and breathing in its thick, musty scent. The smell made Clementine's head swirl. She sniffed again. Then she leaned forward and placed both lips over the thick glass rim. Her saliva slid down the inside of the bottle's neck, pooling for a moment on the top of the dark liquid before sinking. Stout, Clementine knew, was Alfred's favourite. Not including whisky, of course. The water of life.

In the parlour, where she was not allowed, Clementine ran a finger along each surface. The table that used to be polished. The rough green curtains, all dusty now along the hem. Christmas this year would be non-existent. The baby was early. Nothing was prepared. Her mother had been upstairs in bed making that horrible grunting sound for days now, the midwife coming and going and coming again. The women from the street had been coming and going too. Pies. Cold potatoes. Bottles of stout. And somewhere a paper bag full of oranges, if only Clementine knew where to look. They hadn't even retrieved the old pram from the coal cellar where it lay abandoned, all covered in soot.

Of course, Dorothea had been in bed for much longer than two days. Months, even. More than a year. Working her way through a drawerful of nightgowns, cotton and flannel, frills at throat and wrist. Sitting by her mother's bedside each morning before school, Clementine had counted, hairbrush in hand, brushing and brushing and brushing. The strands of Dorothea's hair rose like cobwebs, clinging to Clementine's cardigan or attaching themselves to her skin. But Clementine didn't care. She was just waiting for Dorothea to say her name once more.

On the mantelpiece in the parlour the china cherub was still on display, all plump flesh and rosy cheeks. Clementine stood up on tiptoe now and touched her finger to the little white mark where the cherub's thumb used to be. What would it be like to lose a thumb? She tucked her own thumb to her palm and waggled her four remaining fingers. Her hand looked odd when she turned it over. Like a mistake. She'd seen old men in the street with mistakes for hands when she was younger. Missing fingers and stumps for thumbs, sometimes missing arms or legs too. War wounds, her mother used to call them. But the men had been too old to be fighting in a war. Clementine crossed the road to avoid them if she could.

The cherub was forlorn and neglected, dust gathered along the edges of all its pretty flowers. There should be holly poking out of it now that it was Christmas, small sprigs cut from the tree in the cemetery. Clementine used to go with Alfred to collect it, dragging the prickly branches home inside an old sheet. Together they would cover the mantelpiece and the tops of all the mirrors, Alfred lifting Clementine to the high places in his thick, stocky arms. When they were finished there would be red berries scattered across the house like a thousand miniature rubies. One year her father even strung up mistletoe with its tiny moonlike fruit. Then he had made Clementine kiss him, small lips pressed to a face full of prickles, the smell of earth and coal dust as she pushed her nose into his flesh.

But Clementine knew that the holly would not be cut this year, even though the bushes were covered in a maze of scarlet berries sparkling in the frost. She had gone to look on her way home from school, stood up close against the forest of stiff green leaves until she felt them pressing through her skirt. She'd even held a finger to one green spike until it pierced her skin. A tiny crimson berry all of her own, growing on the tip.

She rose now on her toes and pressed the little puncture wound against the cherub's sliced-off thumb. A sharp prick of pain. A tiny thrill. And the sound of footsteps on the stairs.

'Clementine!'

Clementine took her finger away and curled it up inside her cardigan sleeve. It was the midwife calling, fat and argumentative. Clementine had seen her with those bowls of water stained pink, sluicing them out in the scullery, bare forearms all florid. Clementine never wanted to have arms like those and she would make sure that she did not.

She crouched between the table and the empty fire-place, making herself small so as not to be seen. There was a photograph there, hanging against the dark wallpaper. In it two children slept, their faces surrounded by curls, their lips two pouts. It smelled of dust here and of mice droppings scattered along the edge of the skirting board. Clementine waited and listened. She touched a fingertip to the photograph, one child after the other, felt the glass hard and cold on her wound once more. Then she took her finger away.

Upstairs it wasn't a boy, but Ruby. Ruby with her eyes so bright, squeezed out from between her mother's reluctant thighs. Another little girl to join the older one downstairs, pushed out on a gush of fluid, ready to greet the world.

Alfred smiled down at the small, writhing thing. Why was it not a son? He put a hand out to touch the child's wrinkled face, those tiny clenched fists. There was a smear of blood beneath the baby's eye and he wiped at it with his thumb, his nail black against the child's bright skin.

'If you don't mind.' Mrs Sprat pushed in with her towel and her cloths, scooping the baby up and handling it this way and that as though it was a pat of butter needing to be shaped. She cut through the thick, pulsing cord.

Alfred looked at Dorothea. There was sweat all along her lip. Her eyes were like hollows surrounded by bone. 'Is she all right?'

'Yes,' said the midwife, wrapping the baby in a tight muslin square.

'I mean my wife.' Alfred moved to the top of the bed and laid a hand on Dorothea's hair, soaked now and dark.

'She'll be fine.' The midwife didn't even look up. 'Now what's this one to be called?'

But Alfred didn't reply, for Dorothea was arching back in the bed, neck all taut. 'Dorothea?'

The grunting began again, urgent and guttural, right in Alfred's ear. The midwife turned from the basket and came straight to the side of the bed, bending low over Dorothea's stomach. 'There's another one coming.'

'Another one?' Alfred stood for a moment staring at the midwife. Then at Dorothea as she turned and writhed in the bed. Both of them were surprised. Twins again. One more spin of the dice for a boy. Alfred picked up his wife's hand, grey against his own stained fingers. 'Dorothea?'

Dorothea rolled her eyes towards him then back, dark irises surrounded by white like a cow destined for slaughter. Her hair was stuck to her neck with sweat. She gripped at Alfred's hand until he thought all his bones would crack. The grunting began again from deep inside her throat, her knees rigid, feet thrashing at the sheet.

'Is she all right?' Alfred tried to prise his fingers away as Dorothea crushed them tighter.

But the midwife just pushed him aside as all of a sudden Dorothea let go. Her head flopped back. Her neck all slack. A long groan unwinding from her mouth as out came the next one, floppy and bloody, lying on the sheet like the afterbirth from a calf.

Alfred stared at the strange creature, blue, almost pickled, curled on a sheet all stained with faeces and blood. Let it be a boy, he thought. The midwife rolled the baby over and wiped at its face. She unspooled the cord from its neck, picked it up by its ankles and dangled it over the bed.

'It's a girl,' she said.

Then she delivered the slap.

Later that same night ten-year-old Clementine looked down into the frayed basket, blanket with a satin trim tucked all around. 'Hello, babies,' she murmured. 'Hello.' In one hand she was holding the china cherub. In the other the remains of an orange, nothing now but a small pile of peel.

Two babies stared up at her with unfocused eyes. Clementine hummed as she placed the china cherub on a table by the side of the basket. The babies had feet like the cherub, smooth and pink. Clementine imagined bathing their fat little bodies in the big tin bowl, lowering their wobbling heads down, down amongst the suds, small bubbles popping from their mouths like fish.

She reached into the basket and touched her finger to each of the babies' fluttering eyelids – one, two, three, four. The babies blinked at her in surprise, small limbs jerking. One of them has eyes like mine, Clementine thought, as she retrieved six little orange pips from her pocket and pushed them down the side of the crib. Difficult to resist.

'Two again,' sighed the midwife as she set about packing up her bag. Some women have all the troubles. She had already washed her arms in the scullery sink and scoured out all the bowls. And they weren't bonny either, not like the last time. Well, one of them at least. The midwife rolled down her sleeves and buttoned her white cuffs. They weren't even the same. As different as chalk was from cheese compared to the ones that had gone before. It really was a pity.

Alfred was talking to Dorothea, who lay limp as a discarded fish skin in the crumple of the bed. 'Can you think of a name, Dotty? We need another name.'

'A name,' Dorothea murmured.

'Aye, for the other one.'

They'd only agreed on Ruby if it was a girl, named for Dorothea's grandmother, long gone now. But Dorothea wasn't even really in the room now. She was back inside a dream of another time instead, a lady with burnished hair whispering to her from a bright screen.

Say it, darling, just say it.

The prickle of smoke in her eyes and that jacket, rough and smelling of coal dust, pressed up against her face.

Say it, darling, and I'll be yours.

Alfred turned to look at the midwife. 'What's your name?'

'Barbara.' The midwife was already putting on her thick blue coat.

'Barbara then.'

The midwife's cheeks didn't even flush when he said it. There were a lot of Barbaras on this patch already. All seconds or thirds. Sometimes even fourths. She grunted in Alfred's direction as she did up her buttons. Some form of acknowledgement was required.

'Aye,' said Alfred. 'That'll do.' He turned to the bed. 'Barbara Walker,' he said, touching Dorothea's hand where it lay, grey and slack, on the cover.

But Dorothea was gone, dancing somewhere across a strip of moonlit floor with a man's rough face tight against her hair, her long, gleaming hair. *Say it, darling, just say my name.*

'Dorothea?'

By the time the midwife was ready to leave, Alfred was gripping the railings at the end of his wife's bed, knuckles as white as Dorothea's hair would become, voice thick with despair. 'What'll I do?' he kept saying. 'What'll I do?'

'Yes,' said the midwife, as though she'd seen it all before (which she had).

'I don't know what to do.' Alfred looked up at the midwife, then around the room at his limp wife and his oldest child in her darned cardigan. Then at his two new daughters lying in a basket covered by a blanket with a torn satin trim. How was it his life had come to this, he thought, sweeping his arm out in a fury of bemusement, clipping the china cherub and sending it to disaster along with them all.

The cherub fell to the floorboards with a bump and a roll, little mouth pursed in surprise. *Oh!* One of its flowers cracked and split. One arm snapped off snip-snap above the elbow, the severed limb skittering somewhere into the dark. Alfred threw his hands to his head and cursed. The midwife stopped buttoning up her cuffs. Dorothea lay in the bed, oblivious. Clementine stared at the small china arm wedged between two floorboards beneath her parents' bed.

'Christ!' said Alfred.

'Say my name,' said Dorothea.

'I'll put the word out,' said the midwife (and she did).

But Clementine didn't say a thing.

The midwife let herself out of the front door this time. She never had got the matron to reassign her, even though she'd asked a thousand times. Five years' hard labour as far as she was concerned. She slid a little on the icy ground as she hurried away. Why was it, she wondered as she picked her way along the slippery street, that the pretty children never got named for her? Still, that first baby – the midwife gave a little shiver inside her thick coat. She had those strange eyes, just like the older sister. Startling, in an unwelcome kind of way.

Mrs Sprat came to the end of the street, collar up against the threat of snow. In her pocket were six little orange pips, retrieved from down the side of the babies' basket. Just waiting to choke the poor little things, God bless them and protect their little souls (which blessing Mrs Sprat knew they would need). As she turned the corner, soon to be swallowed herself by the gathering gloom, the midwife cast up a little prayer to whoever might be listening. *Never let me have to return to the Walker house again.*

2011

The Office for Lost People was impossible to find. It took Margaret several goes before she arrived at the correct place, lurking in a dip behind the railway station in the dead centre of town. Snow towered in man-made drifts each side of the entrance as she picked her way in. She was still wearing her inappropriate shoes, not having found a suitable substitute in the box room. Though it seemed unlikely, Barbara's feet turned out to be much smaller than her own.

The building was several storeys high, a palace of glass encasing a labyrinth of open-plan offices radiating towards the windows on every single floor. *Receptionist. Personal Assistant. Manager of Administration.* After thirty years grinding the mill of paperwork, Margaret understood the black hole that an office complex could become.

Beneath her red, stolen coat the funeral outfit prevailed – fawn blouse and a corduroy skirt falling to mid calf, with the addition of a cardigan wrestled from a bin bag, brown and baggy at the pockets, the sleeves much longer than Margaret's arms and hands combined. The clothes weren't pretty, or even becoming, but at that moment they were all Margaret had that might be suitable. Even so, as she made her way towards this palace of death, she decided to keep her coat on.

'This lady's for you, Janie.' The girl who escorted Margaret up through layer upon layer of open plan couldn't have been more thinly clad if she had been living on a beach. A diaphanous blouse, almost transparent. Fishnets with holes ripped in them. A skirt that barely skimmed the very tops of her thighs. And yet she was suitably dressed in a way that Margaret wasn't. For the Office for Lost People turned out to be as hot as a furnace, rather like the one into which its clients were eventually despatched. The girl had black lines drawn onto her face instead of eyebrows and three miniature silver skulls in her ear. Perfect for Bereavement Services. That was what Margaret thought.

Janie Gribble, Funerals Officer (amongst other things), was wearing an angora wool sweater in a shade that could only be described as 'bubblegum', with nails and lips to match. She looked as though she belonged in Births rather than being responsible for burning a whole city's worth of bodies to clinker month after month. She conducted an interview, if one could call it that, just to prove that here too in Edinburgh some sort of process prevailed.

'Tell me a little about yourself, Margaret.'

'Well . . .' Margaret looked at the delicate gold chain undulating across Janie's breastbone and began to regret the discarding of her previous life over London landfill. A black suit and a shirt with ruffles down the front might have worked wonders here. 'I used to work in finance,' she said, tucking both feet out of sight to hide the salty tidemarks rising inexorably across the toes.

Janie Gribble frowned, a small crease on the smooth sea of her forehead. 'Finance?'

Expense accounts. Bonuses. Three-course lunches. A black car with windows designed for one-way viewing only. After which, champagne in the bath. Margaret knew that finance was no longer the recommendation it had once been. But what else could she say? She coughed instead, the cough of the apologist. 'Spreadsheets. Memos. Data management.' All gone now.

'And your particular skills?' Across the desk the gold chain settled into the dip at the base of Janie's throat, a small, glittering target.

'Well . . .' Margaret gave a little shrug. Where to begin?

A tendency to kleptomania. Life-and-death decisions made on the spin of a coin. Then there was her ability to keep drinking when everyone else had stopped. No wonder her old job had ended in the way that it had – abruptly, with a solicitor's letter attached.

Margaret flicked her tongue over her front teeth in case of red wine stains. She'd put away a whole bottle yesterday evening courtesy of the leftovers from a twenty-pound note unfurled from the pocket of a drunk man who'd leaned up against her on the overnight bus. Who Dares Wins. Although Margaret knew even then that in the grand game of life she had dared and lost. She'd hidden the evidence in the bottom of the box-room wardrobe, having discovered Barbara's own forest of empty bottles taking up the space beneath the kitchen sink. Then, as she lay on the plastic lilo in the darkness, she'd pondered what else she might share with her mother besides the ability to drink.

Janie gave a little cough, polite but insistent, and Margaret touched her own throat for a moment. Sacking because of threats to the boss, not to mention money siphoned away due to a lifestyle which had always been beyond her, were not the kind of items on a CV that Margaret wanted broadcast. So she decided to go with the answer she had always given her mother when Barbara's questions about what she got up to in London became too persistent to ignore. 'I'm very good at admin,' she said. Her whole life reduced to a five-letter word. And an abbreviated one at that.

It turned out to be the right answer, however. 'Excellent.' Janie glanced at the form in her hand. 'We're looking for someone who is good with paperwork.' She put a large tick in a box. 'And you know Mrs Maclure?'

'Mrs Maclure?' Margaret crossed and recrossed her legs, sweaty now behind the knees.

'I thought . . .' The small crease appeared again.

Margaret understood at once. 'Oh yes,' she said. 'A friend of my mother's.'

Janie beamed. Neat teeth, no red wine stains. 'Everyone seems to know Mrs Maclure, don't they.'

It wasn't a question. It was the Edinburgh Way once more.

Back at home, Margaret tried to explain to her mother. 'I'll be a sort of investigator.'

'What's that when it's at home?'

'A sort of assistant.'

'What, wiping bums and that?'

'A sort of finder of families for dead people.' The only way Margaret could describe it that made any sense. 'For people who've died on their own without any relatives to take them on.'

'Aye, well, there'll be a lot of that nowadays. All those old people left to rot.' Barbara tipped back the last of her rum and glared at Margaret through the bottom of her glass. 'Who's your client, anyway?'

'Confidential.' There had to be at least one thing Margaret could keep to herself now that she was living back at home.

'Have it your own way.'

And Margaret was determined that she would. But she held out an olive branch anyway. This was the first proper conversation she'd had with Barbara since she'd returned. 'I have to clarify a couple of facts, that's all. Date of birth etc.'

'So it's a short-term thing then.'

'Yes, well . . .' A quick exit or a new mattress. Margaret hadn't yet decided which might be the more desirable.

'It's just, I might need the room,' Barbara mumbled into her glass. She seemed as keen as Margaret that no new roots be put down any time soon.

'That's fine.' Margaret tried not to be offended that the mother she hadn't seen for years seemed so keen to have her out. 'It shouldn't take me long to track down any next of kin.'

And there it was again, that tiny wraith flitting across Barbara's face like a spirit hurrying from its grave.

'Children. Brothers or sisters. Cousins. That kind of thing.'

Barbara had never had any next of kin herself, other than Margaret of course. 'Adopted,' she once said. 'Dead before you were born.' As though that explained the total absence of any sort of family records, either the living or the paperwork kind.

'It's for the money,' Margaret said. 'Someone has to pay.'

'Aye well, every penny counts.' Barbara lifted her glass

to her mouth even though it was empty. 'And what happens if you don't find any next of kin?'

Margaret couldn't help but notice how her mother's fingers trembled on the tumbler. 'Then the council will sort it. Decide whether to bury or burn.'

Janie was overburdened. 'There's a bit of a waiting list.'

Lots of bodies. Festive season. Mortuary stacked high.

'The basic searches have been done and now we just need a quick result.'

All the paperwork backed up because of snow, because of ice, because of too many days off over Christmas and New Year. Because of general lackadaisical attitudes. Because of illness caused by inebriation or cold. The inability of a person to come through from Glasgow. The person from Glasgow having got trapped up north. Or just the inconsideration of lots of lonely people dying at this time of year.

'The police can't help, *there's been a murder.*' Janie grinned then, a brief parting of frosted bubblegum lips.

'Sorry?' It was Margaret's turn to frown now.

'*Taggart.*' For a moment Janie sparkled under the modulated strip lights.

But Margaret had been south for too long. 'I don't . . .'

'Oh, never mind.' Janie turned and tapped something into her keyboard. 'It's just that everyone is very, very busy at this time of year.'

More for less, thought Margaret. 'I understand,' she said. The usual post-Christmas, post-New Year glut of cutbacks, holidays and cold weather. Just like any other job, in any other town.

'You'll be attached to the Crown Office via us – a sort of temporary arrangement. They ask us sometimes, when no one else can help. Between you and me, they fear another Mrs Johnson.'

'Mrs Johnson?'

A spot of pink appeared in the very centre of each of Janie's cheeks, bright amongst the pastel shades. She hurried on. 'There is no salary, or benefits of any kind. The cuts, you know. We're all on a pay freeze.'

'Of course,' said Margaret. Who wasn't on a pay freeze, so much as a pay Armageddon.

'We'll pay on receipt of an invoice for services rendered.' Janie tapped on her front teeth with a biro. 'But no expenses.' She was particularly firm on that.

Margaret nodded. Hard times indeed.

'Who was Mrs Johnson?' Margaret called after her mother, who had levered herself out of her chair and disappeared into the kitchen.

'Mrs who?' Barbara clattered away in the cupboards.

'Johnson,' Margaret shouted above the din.

'Oh, her.' Barbara shuffled back into the living room clutching her glass with three fingers of rum now sloshing up the sides. 'She's dead.'

'I gathered that.'

'For five years.' Barbara lowered herself into the armchair again, thighs touching armrests on both sides. She was still wearing the quilted dressing gown, threads dragging from the hem.

'What do you mean?'

'When they found her. She'd been dead for five years.'

Frozen to the mattress, nothing but a few strands of hair spread out where once her head had been.

'She'd turned into a mummy.'

'A what?'

'You heard.'

And Margaret revised her vision to include leathery hands and feet, the stiff creep of blackened skin. 'How did they know it was five years then?' she said.

'Most recent post through the door and the oldest. Counted the years in between.' Barbara sucked some rum up between her teeth. 'It's amazing what you can learn from junk.'

Which perhaps explained why nothing in Barbara's box room had ever been thrown out.

'What about her neighbours?' Margaret said. 'Didn't they miss her?'

'The florist downstairs mentioned that she hadn't seen her for a while.'

'And the electricity? Or her council tax?'

'Direct debit.' Barbara put her tumbler down on the table by her chair and picked up the remote control. 'That's what happens when you automate.'

So Edinburgh had hidden depths after all. As neglectful and careless as any other sort of town, despite its elegant facade.

'Did you go to her funeral?'

'No,' said Barbara. 'It was before my time.'

Margaret tried to imagine any time that had been before her mother, but could not.

'Anyway – ' Barbara shifted in her seat – 'they didn't have the rota then.'

'Why not?'
'It got set up later.'
'Because of Mrs Johnson?'
'I suppose.'

Outside after the interview (a drop of five floors in a silent lift to the slush of a car park she didn't recognize from when she'd gone in) Margaret understood that it all came down to money. The pursuit of it. The need of it. The loss of it. The lack. She'd looked up the word 'indigent' at the local library before she went to the interview.

A needy person.

That was what it said. Which seemed to Margaret rather a good description of herself.

Somebody had to pay, even when you were dead, and it wasn't going to be the state if the state could find someone else. *Every penny counts.* Wasn't that what Barbara always said? Especially when there were no pennies left. Austerity Britain. Margaret had been feeling its chilly winds blowing through her bones for some time now.

Down in the hidden car park amongst wet piles of ice, Margaret opened up the slim brown folder Janie Gribble had given her along with the job. The folder was empty except for a three-page police report saying nothing untoward had happened and a letter from Janie confirming payment of an invoice for services rendered should Margaret get a result. The amount wasn't exactly a fortune. But it was enough for a quick exit should a quick exit be required. For a moment the prospect of London rose before Margaret like a flame. Then she saw again the look that had crossed Barbara's face when she realized it was

Margaret at her front door rather than some other spectre. Relief. Of a sort. If only for a second. So perhaps there was a reason why the lucky coronation penny had fallen to heads after all.

Margaret's client turned out to be an old lady too. One more of the neglected, the lonely, the misplaced, the lost. Margaret's heart gave a small pitter-patter of recognition. She felt an affinity with her client already and they hadn't even met.

There was nothing in the folder to suggest why her client had exited in the way that she had. In a solitary room, in a solitary flat. Hair stuck to the back of an arm-chair. In fact there was nothing in the folder that gave any indication of who Margaret's client was at all.

'All we need to confirm is Full Name . . .' Janie had said.

Nothing to say when she was born.

'. . . Date of Birth.'

Where she came from.

'. . . Place of Birth, if possible.'

Or what she believed in.

'Religion. Plus any family, of course.'

All Margaret had was a surname, *Walker*, and an appendage, *Mrs*, that might or might not have been correct. Mrs Walker. Once here. Now gone. Lost to the second coldest winter on record.

Janie had signed Margaret's offer letter with bubbles over the *i*s instead of dots. 'What we want is paperwork.' She had been very particular about that. 'Everything else is irrelevant.' She held out the folder to Margaret by way of dismissal.

'But where should I start?' Margaret asked.

'You should start in the mortuary,' Janie said. 'They uncover all sorts there.'

1933

The party was to be in the garden if the weather was fine. 'Thirty-three, like the year. A grand age to be.' Eight-year-old Clementine watched as her mother laughed, hair like pale fire lifting in the breeze.

'What if it's wet?' said Alfred, pausing for a moment in his task of shovelling dirt.

'We'll pray for sun.' Dorothea bent to her fledgling flowers, wilting and flat. Yet another failed attempt to conjure magic from the shallow river-gravel beds.

Clementine looked up to the grey sky from her own small patch of earth, gritty and full of broken bits of china. She had prayed once before, at the christening of the twins over three years ago. Little Alfie and little Dottie, draped in linen and lace, knitted bootees tied with white ribbons around their soft white flesh. 'Oh, how lovely they are,' all the guests had murmured. 'Bright as the promise of a new day,' before they had knelt to pray too.

Down on small round knees, crouched in a pew, Clementine had prayed for shoes with button fastenings. 'Please, Lord, please.' Though she had known, even then, that she should have been praying for the souls of the twins. It hadn't worked, anyway. Three years on, and she was still confined to boots.

At the end of the service, as if to make up for her bad thoughts, Clementine had stayed in her pew staring up at the chapel window when everyone else had been gathered around the twins.

'Little angels!'

'Little dolls!'

High at the front, all criss-crossed with trails of lead, the window had been a blaze of emerald and gold and red. Clementine couldn't help but notice that in the glass all the children went barefoot. *Suffer little children*, it said, *to come unto me.* But as far as Clementine could tell, the children seemed happy enough.

The priest came by, picking up hymn books. 'It's pretty, eh?' Reached out to place a hand on the top of Clementine's head.

Clementine slid sideways, out from under his touch. 'Where are they going?' Her voice rose like a small bird's into the cool arc of the empty chapel.

'Why, child . . .' the priest had said. 'To the promised land, of course.'

Outside now in the back garden of the tall, narrow house, the first spot of rain fell onto the bare curve of Clementine's neck. Alfred turned his face to the heavy sky, dirty hands on dirty hips. 'I'm going in,' he said. 'To light the stove.'

'All right,' said Dorothea, abandoning the flowers she had cherished only a moment before. 'I'll come with you.'

Clementine looked back at the dark patch of ground that was meant to be hers and drew a rough pattern into the earth with a broken twig. A stick girl in a triangular skirt. *Oh my darling.* Then she scratched the picture out. She watched her parents disappear through the back door, Dorothea's long fingers slipped inside Alfred's fist. Clementine knew she could remain in the garden for as long as she liked, crouching in the mud. Even if she ended up filthy. Feet and hands all black. Her parents never did instruct her, unless it concerned the twins.

Another drop of rain fell from the heavens, a dark stain on Clementine's pale head. She touched a finger to where it had landed.

Upstairs she knew the twins would be stirring, ready to rouse like two daisies cleansed by a shower of spring rain. Two faces bleary with sleep and the warmth of a shared blanket peering out from a high window, rubbing their faces on the backs of plump hands. Fingers tapping and scraping at the glass. 'Clemmie! Clemmie! Clemmie!' Ready to crawl and to clutch. To run pitter-patter all over the house in their soft leather shoes.

But Clementine could run too. From the front door to the back. From the top floor to the cellar. From one bedroom to another. Away, away, away. From stubby, grasping fingers and little pitter-patter feet. To hide in the cool passageway of the pantry with its meat safe and its jars. In the scullery with its copper. And the coal-hole under the street. There she would crouch in the dark, black dust clinging to the hem of her skirt, listening for two pairs of feet as they pitter-pattered outside. Calling to them in a whisper, 'This way, this way!' Watching for eight fat fingers and two fat thumbs to come crawling around the edge of a door. Then leaping out, shrieking like the devil she knew herself to be, before running off once more as they tumbled into the grime.

In the garden she would leave them lying on the small patch of manicured grass, while she disappeared. Two toddlers with golden hair, rolling on the lawn. She had taught them to count. *One. Two. Three. Four.* All the way to a thousand. Just like Alfred had once taught her. She'd hide amongst the undergrowth, surrounded by the crawl of insects and the tickle of long grass, silent and still, until they couldn't wait any longer. Then they'd come running. 'Clemmie! Clemmie! Clemmie!' Trying to find her latest den.

'Clementine. The twins are up.' Dorothea's call had an edge to it, like the blade of a pair of silver scissors. She had been in a bad temper for weeks now, brushing and brushing her hair as if to brush it all out. Clementine had no idea what she had done wrong.

She crouched down further in her current favourite nest, knees to chin, hidden from all who might try to search. The far end of the garden was an overgrown, jungly sort of place, a wasteland of couch grass and brambles, tangles of ancient raspberry canes and a single forbidden tree. Here, Clementine hollowed out one secret place after another. Nests fashioned from dead grasses. Hidey-holes dug from the earth. She buried treasure in amongst the nettles. Dorothea's bobby pins. Alfred's waistcoat buttons. A small china arm rescued from between two floorboards beneath her parents' bed. Also a knitted bootee laced with white ribbons, buried deep in the dirt.

The rain began to spatter, dripping from the leaves on the trees above, sliding from the bushes, tall grasses bent low in the wet.

'Clementine!' Alfred shouted from the back door, throat rough with ash from the laying of the fire. 'Come and play with your brother and sister when you're told.'

But still Clementine waited, down in a hunch, counting

as Alfred had taught her. *One elephant, two elephant*, all the way to a thousand. It always took them a long time to search.

The day of the party, the sun shone. Clementine had been praying for good weather every day for a week. This time it had worked.

Out in the garden there was a table covered by a cloth and every piece of Dorothea's favourite tea set, white and gold; a teapot garlanded with small china flowers dancing around the rim. The table was laden with good things to eat, everything on the never-never, but tasting all the better for that. There was a plate piled with scones, studded with cherries. Jam gleaming inside a small blue saucer. A bowl full of cream whipped into peaks like the snow on the Alps. Clementine had already stuck her finger into that and licked off the results.

There were small cakes topped with glistening icing.

'Fairy cakes, for my little fairies,' Dorothea had declared as she put them out.

Sandwiches cut into finger-sized lengths.

'Dainties for my little darlings.'

A bowl of summer berries, sprinkled with sugar.

'Precious jewels for my little gemstones.'

And oranges, peeled and segmented, laid out in a circle on a wide china plate.

From the middle landing of the tall, narrow house Clementine stood and watched as her mother dressed for the tumult of guests she was expecting. Dorothea moved to and fro, languid in the heat, naked except for a pair of faded knickers draped around her hips. Alfred stood behind the tall mirror watching his wife.

'I could get a passage to America,' Alfred was saying. 'There's plenty of work over there.'

Dorothea held up a dress covered in pink sprigs. 'How about this one?'

'The promised land, that's what they call it.' And Alfred laughed his infectious laugh.

'Or this?' Dorothea draped a length of tatty chiffon around her neck.

'There's a fortune to be made if you're prepared to risk it.'

'What do you think?' Dorothea plucked a pale-blue wrap from the bed and twisted it through her hair.

'You know we have to do something.'

Dorothea dropped the wrap to the floor and picked up a slip instead, all rippled and frayed around the edges. 'Can't you get another job?' she said.

'I've tried, but it's hard. Everything's difficult right now.'

Dorothea raised her slender arms and let the slip slither over her head, long strands of hair rising with the static. 'What about the children? We can't leave them behind.'

Alfred held open the cotton frock with the pink sprigs. As Dorothea stepped inside he pulled it up over her thighs and hips and the swell of her breasts. 'We may have to at the start,' he said, hooking the thin straps over her shoulders, then lowering his face to the hollow of Dorothea's breastbone. 'It wouldn't be for long.'

'How long?' Dorothea's fingers lingered on the curve of her stomach as she buttoned the dress all the way up the front.

'Three months, perhaps four.' Alfred touched Dorothea's stomach too.

'I couldn't leave my angels.'

'What about Clementine?'

'Clementine?'

Out on the landing Clementine held her breath.

Then Alfred said it. 'We could send for her later. She's a big girl now.'

Outside, the forbidden tree was covered in little green pods. It stood in the patch of wasteland at the far end of the garden, roots all tangled up with thorns.

'Never touch,' Alfred had said to Clementine when she was young. 'Never go near.'

A tree full of pods in the summer, all crunchy and plump.

'Never touch. Never lick. Never sniff. Never smell.'

Dripping with golden treasure for a few brief weeks in spring.

Clementine sucked on a last segment of orange as she hummed and picked and plucked. *Oh my darling*. Moving through the grass as silent as a moth, juice dribbled on her dress, small red welts rising on the surface of her skin from where thorns had scratched and plucked at her. Little seeds, little pods, little plates and little bowls. Sandwiches the size of a child's finger. A scone spread with jam the colour of blood. Also a fairy cake carved down the middle to make two.

The sun shone hot on the manicured lawn as the adults poured themselves another round of drinks. The table was a mass of crumbs and stains now, Dorothea's favourite china covered in smears. Two small children with golden hair hunched at the edge of the wilderness, their heads close together. *One. Two. Three. Four.* All the way to a thousand. Then they rose on dimpled legs and headed into the tall grass. 'Clemmie! Clemmie! Clemmie!' Whispering as they ran through tunnels cut into the undergrowth, towards a feast laid out beneath the magic tree.

Little cups of sorrel.

Little green pods.

Little plates of berries.

Little black seeds.

Once inside the den they were hidden forever. Two twins and their older sister. Invisible to anyone who might want to see.

That evening Clementine sat in her bedroom on the highest, furthest floor and waited as her parents searched. She was counting. *One. Two. Three. Four.* All the way to a thousand. Then some more. She waited for over an hour, tracking their movements in and out of the house. The pantry with its meat safe. The scullery with its copper. The coal-hole under the street.

Then she stood up on a chair and looked out over the back gardens full of onion rows and summer cabbages, currant bushes laden with fruit. She could see sheds covered in peeling paint and crumbling brick walls. She could see big sheets drooping in the heavy evening air.

She could see trees – and beneath them a thousand perfect picnic spots.

'Have you found them yet?' Alfred asked when Clementine finally came downstairs. He was checking the cupboard in the hall for the third time.

'Have you seen them?' Dorothea grabbed Clementine by the shoulders as she whirled from the front room to the back in the dress covered in pink sprigs.

'No,' Clementine whispered, but neither of her parents stopped to hear what she had to say. She stood for a moment by the back door staring out towards the end of the garden, a jungle of brambles and grass disappearing into twilight as the light fell away. Then she went upstairs to her bedroom again and waited some more.

It was Alfred who found them in the end. Tongues black, lips black, froth on their chins, sitting by the base of the laburnum tree, the remains of a wondrous feast spread all around. Little empty cups. Little empty plates. Little black seeds all sprinkled in their laps. As alike as two peas in a pod, ants already crawling inside their shoes.

Goodnight, Little Alfie.

Sleep tight, Little Dottie.

Two children dead before they'd even begun.

He appeared from out of the jungle as the night stole in, a dead twin on each arm, his skin scratched and scored from all the thrashing he had done to find what he had lost. Dorothea was standing in the centre of the manicured lawn when he emerged, straight and silver in the moonlight, her long shadow cutting across the grass. She screamed when she saw them, hands to her head. And from where she was watching on the highest, furthest floor, Clementine put her hands to her head too.

Alfred laid the small children down, one after the other, on the patch of tidy grass. Little Alfie and Little Dottie in their pristine summer clothes, feet in button-up slippers, faces like two wax dolls. Dorothea stopped screaming, a sudden plunge into silence. Then she fell too.

From the highest, furthest floor Clementine watched as two dead children and their mother spread out around Alfred like the petals of a flower. She frowned as from the very centre of Dorothea's crumpled frock a bud began to grow. Tiny at first, nothing but a spot in the darkness, then blooming and spreading, turning Dorothea from white to scarlet in the gloom. Then Clementine stepped down and knelt upon her bedroom floor to pray once more.

Dorothea was away for almost a week. When she came back she was no longer scarlet. Instead she was almost transparent. Her stomach concave. Glittering hair shorn. Clementine hid behind Alfred as they carried Dorothea up the stairs, head first, feet last. She breathed in her father's heavy scent of tweed and coal dust, underpinned now by the stink of whisky. The water of life. But not for Alfred. Not any more.

Alfred's fingers pressed into Clementine's skull as Dorothea passed, as though to hold her down. Then he removed his hand and headed upstairs too, behind his stricken wife. Didn't even look back as he was swallowed by the grey.

That evening Clementine watched once more from the landing as her father kept a vigil by Dorothea's bed. Her mother's breath rattled in the dim light. Dorothea's scalp was bald, prickled with stubble like a thousand miniature stars. On a table beside where she lay was a jewellery box lined with nappy velveteen and a hairbrush with a handle made of bone. And next to that, a photograph: black and white. To remind them of all that had gone. Two children pressed forever behind a cold rectangle of glass.

Three days later Alfred swung the axe – *chop, chop, chop, chop.* He danced while he did it, deep in the jungle at the end of the garden, like a whirligig. A turning dervish, wild and mad. Upstairs in her bedroom Clementine still knelt on the hard, dusty floor. Her knees were bare and covered in a pattern of purple bruises. 'Please, please, please, please,' she prayed. But she never did know what should come next.

They buried them in the cemetery, where a holly bush would blossom with a million red berries when winter came. Two small coffins stuffed with lace and linen, lowered into the mud. One, then the next. All the grown-ups crying as they filed out to watch.

'Poor little Alfie.'

'Poor little Dottie.'

But Clementine didn't say a thing.

Instead she stayed inside staring at the stained-glass window, all golden and emerald and red. The priest appeared, collecting hymn books once again. 'There, there, child,' he said, reaching out a hand.

But Clementine slid away along the pew of polished wood. 'Where have they gone?' she said, voice rising once more into the cool arc of the chapel. She didn't mean her parents.

'Why, child, the babies are in heaven.'

But Clementine didn't really need to ask. She knew already. *Suffer little children to come unto me*. The twins had gone to the promised land.

PART TWO

A Brazil Nut

SUMMARY REPORT OF POST-MORTEM

Date/Hour of Post-Mortem: *08/01/2011; 8:30 A.M.*
Pathologist: *Dr Edwina Atkinson c/o NHS Lothian*
Client Name: *MRS WALKER*
Case No.: *2011-88*
Date of Life Extinct: *02/01/2011 (DATE FOUND)*
Body Identified by: *Patrycja Nabialek, neighbour*

EXTERNAL EXAMINATION:

*The body is that of a white female measuring 5 ft 6 in.
and weighing 6 stone 1 oz. The deceased is wearing
a tweed skirt, a knitted cardigan, a blouse made of a
synthetic material, nylon tights, underwear and brown
leather shoes.*

*Age is undetermined, yet appears consistent with
somewhere between 75 and 85 years.*

*The body is cold and unembalmed. Lividity is fixed
in the distal portions of the limbs. The eyes are closed.
The hair is dyed red with white roots. Minor abrasions
(scratch marks) were observed on the deceased's cheeks
and scalp.*

*Upon removal of the victim's clothing a faint odour
of whisky was detected. Newspaper was discovered
wrapped around her middle. Minor abrasions (scratch
marks) were present on the lower half of both arms.
The fingernails are short, appearing ragged, and
fingernail beds are blue. There are no residual scars,
markings or tattoos.*

Cont./

2011

The Edinburgh City Mortuary was an unassuming sort of place. A low concrete building set back from a narrow chasm of a street. Margaret approached with caution. Death was a matter of the everyday here – best to take care.

She rang the bell at the public entrance and the door was answered by a neat man in highly polished shoes. 'Miss Penny?' he enquired. 'Janie said you might pop in.' Someone who knew Margaret was coming almost before she did herself.

The man's shirtsleeves were crisp, creases tight as origami folds. He ushered Margaret inside to a waiting area that constituted three empty chairs, a small table and a vase of plastic flowers. It was just like any other waiting area in any other public building. Except for that feeling of it being somehow outside of normal time and space.

'You're here to identify a client.' The mortuary manager waited beside Margaret, poised and neat, ready to deal instantly with anything that concerned the dead. The reason for her visit seemed to be a foregone conclusion as far as he was concerned.

'Well, not so much identification,' Margaret said. 'As information.'

'What's the person's name?'

'Mrs Walker.'

'Ah yes, Mrs Walker.'

The reputation of Margaret's client preceded her, despite being a mystery in every other way. Margaret pulled out her slim brown folder to address the facts, only to be interrupted by a sudden clamour – the sound of a vehicle pulling up outside. A black car come to head her off before she'd even begun, perhaps.

Two burly men, large and imposing, appeared out of nowhere to chap at the glass. The mortuary manager hurried to let them in. 'DCI Franklin,' he said, dipping his head as a woman entered first, elegant in a dark woollen coat.

'Hello, Donnie. Everything ready?'

English accent. Refined. Was there anyone in this city, Margaret wondered, who was actually born and bred?

'Yes, ma'am.'

'Good man.' DCI Franklin glanced at Margaret as she passed, then back to the mortuary manager. 'Straight from the scene of the crime, Donnie. Nice and fresh.' And the detective was gone as swiftly as she had arrived, in a sweep of tailored navy lined with a flash of silk. Not come for Margaret after all, it seemed, but to check up on another unfortunate just waiting to be seen to before being assigned to the grave.

The two police officers filled the space with their stab vests and their radios, their heavy belts loaded with a jumble of accessories. Outside it had started to snow again and on their shoulders small drifts of white melted away into the dark uniform weave. 'We'll go down, Donnie,' one of them said. 'Check everything's in order.'

'All right.' The mortuary manager lifted an arm as though to indicate the direction they should head in. But they were already away, down the corridor to another waiting room in the basement, where Margaret presumed all the corpses were kept. A shudder rippled through her as though someone had just walked over her grave. Black feet. Hair all stuck to the sofa. She pulled her red, stolen coat closer. It wasn't that she was afraid of dead bodies. It was just that she'd never had to meet one face to face before.

The mortuary manager turned to Margaret. 'You'll have to excuse me for a moment,' he said. 'There's been a murder.' A certain satisfaction shadowed his words.

'Of course.' Margaret understood now. Only the night before Barbara had instructed her as to the whys and wherefores of *Taggart*. 'Finished ages ago. Old-fashioned,' Barbara had gesticulated, the remote in one hand and a glass of rum in the other. 'All newfangled ways of killing now.'

In the empty waiting area, Margaret passed the time wondering exactly which of these newfangled ways of killing had led to today's delay. Knives in stomachs. Bodies washed up on a beach. Or some sort of invisible poison injected into the veins. She'd contemplated murder herself only recently, standing outside a family home in London wondering whether to ring the bell first, or just go ahead and do the deed. Stabbing with a steak knife or the sharpened edge of a spoon. Gouging, tearing, biting until an ashen-haired woman turned as red as the rug on which she lay. Or a rag, shiny with turpentine, pushed through the letter box. Followed by the flare of a match falling, falling, until the two met in a fiery embrace.

Margaret had been surprised at the satisfaction it could

give – the personal approach. After all, death in her family had always been something that happened off-screen. Grandparents, for example, lost forever in a car crash, or a suicide pact, twelve pills washed down with whisky. Or (more likely) fatty arteries and a weak heart.

'Do you have any pictures of them?' she'd asked Barbara once when she was young.

'Of who?'

'Your mum and dad.'

'No.'

'Why not?'

Barbara's answer wasn't so much a question as a line drawn in the sand. 'Do you have any pictures of me?'

It was true, Margaret acknowledged now, as she waited to be introduced to a dead body of her own. Despite all the years they had lived together (and all the years they had not), she never had seen any photographs of Barbara when she was younger. Nor of the two of them together when Margaret was younger too. Not outside that first tenement in Edinburgh, or gathered around the plastic Christmas tree Barbara insisted on putting up year after year. Not on that trip they once took to the seaside, three miserable days on a wet beach where Margaret stood in the Atlantic until her feet were blue and Barbara refused to remove her shoes. Not even from when it all began, Margaret as a baby wrapped in a blanket, perhaps, Barbara holding her up for all the world to see.

Except . . .

There had been one photograph, at least. Two dead, sleeping children pressed behind cold glass. 'Where is it?' she'd asked her mother only the night before, once the drama of her getting a job had subsided. But Barbara had just waved her hand as though to deny that such a thing ever existed and opened a fresh bottle of rum.

From somewhere down in the depths of the City Mortuary there was the rattle of a metal shutter rolling up. Margaret wondered if it meant the latest corpse was coming in or going out. She fiddled with the lucky coronation penny inside the pocket of her red, stolen coat. The signs in the corridor pointed downstairs to the 'Transfer Area' and upstairs to the 'PM Suites'. She brought out the penny and held it for a moment in the flat of her hand. The penny looked back, impassive, like the fixed eye of a dead bird lying in a gutter. Let the king decide.

So he did.

Upstairs, the Post-Mortem Suite was a melange of bright lamps and the slow swirl of constant movement. Several people were gazing intently through a glass partition into a space where technicians in white plastic aprons with blood smeared down the front were weighing and sawing and lifting and cutting on the other side. Long strip lights hung from the ceiling. Water ran constantly through a hose into a deep stainless-steel sink.

What remained of a man lay in the centre of the room, head elevated on a neck prop, chest held open by some sort of crank. His legs were mottled, marked with patches the colour of cooked lobster. His skin was glassy, as though he had been in the bath too long. Margaret stared at the man's arms. They reminded her of the missing limb from a grubby china cherub, severed long ago.

Arrayed along a shelf on the far side of the room were

what she imagined must be the victim's vital organs. Purple lungs embroidered with blue arteries. A yellow sack bulging with gut. On a set of scales, blood pooled around a liver dark as velvet. Next to it a technician cradled a brain in both hands. Somewhere a drill was being tested, a screeching, squealing sound.

Beneath her red coat, cold sweat crept across the surface of Margaret's skin. Just as she was thinking she ought to leave before anyone noticed, someone turned, looking over to where she stood pressed up against the wall. DCI Franklin in her smart woollen coat, frowning at the intrusion. Margaret held her brown folder up to her chest as though to demonstrate her credentials. Behind the glass partition a woman in green scrubs stopped talking, waiting for everyone's full attention to return to her. Margaret scrabbled for the door handle. Nobody turned to look as she exited. No one paid her any attention at all.

Down in the basement, the Transfer Area was cool and scented with disinfectant. Margaret drew in a deep lungful of its chilly, antiseptic air, relief flooding her ventricles. On a table in the corner a big ledger lay open. She glanced at some of the entries, wondering if she might find her client.

9 January. Suicide. Jumper, fully clothed.

11 January. Male. Discovered in water.

13 January. Decomposed, maggots.

Amongst other things.

'Welcome to the underworld.' The young woman wore white fisherman's boots along with her apron.

'Oh, I'm sorry. I was just . . .' Margaret's tights clung to the inside of her thighs.

'Aye, checking up on the inhabitants.'

'Well yes, I suppose so.'

'Couldn't face the upstairs, eh.' The technician laughed. It wasn't a question. She held out a hand covered in blue latex. 'You're Margaret, right? Margaret Penny.'

'Er . . .' Margaret held on to her brown folder, not wanting to offer her own hand in reply. She wasn't sure where the woman's blue glove might have been.

'Oh, sorry. Habit.' The technician pulled the glove off. Beneath it her fingers were rosy. 'You're here for Mrs Walker, right?' The technician's hand was surprisingly warm. Margaret's was freezing, as though she had been in the mortuary fridge herself.

'Donnie said he saw you upstairs.' The technician smiled and turned to the ledger. 'A bit green about the gills, that was how he put it.'

Green gills. Stomach contents probably green too. And the hollows of her cheeks. Margaret knew she had some-how managed to lose any polish she had left the moment she crossed the border. What was it about this city that always stripped her clean?

The technician smiled. A kind face, used to reassuring people in the face of their loved ones' untimely demise. 'Don't worry, it's normal in here. Now, let's see. Mrs Walker.' She ran her finger down through the entries. 'She's been here a couple of weeks now, I think.'

'Is that usual?' Margaret decided it was best at least to try to be professional, despite the continued churn of her insides.

'Not necessarily. Usually move them out in a few days. But it always stacks up at this time of year.' The technician grinned up at Margaret. 'Can be two or three months sometimes for the difficult ones.'

Margaret had a sudden vision of old people lying slumped in their hallways right across the city, no one but bluebottles their final companions as they waited for the mortuary ambulance to come and move them on. Bile burned in the back of her throat. That was probably green too.

'Here she is. Rack twenty-one.' The technician closed the ledger with a thump. 'Why don't you go to the viewing area. I'll bring her up for you to see.'

The viewing room was a relief after the rest of the mortuary – a still space, quiet, with muted lilac-coloured walls and air that smelled and tasted normal. Margaret sat on the small chair in the corner, her legs trembling just like her mother's fingers on that glass of rum. Where were those two dead twins, she thought. And to whom did they belong?

Along one wall there was another glass partition, this one covered by a Venetian blind, vertical slats folded shut. Margaret closed her eyes and waited. Her homecoming hadn't exactly been the holiday she had imagined. Not so far, at least.

'Cancer.' Suddenly there was a woman standing beside Margaret, her skin scrubbed bare just like the dead man upstairs. 'Dr Edwina Atkinson, pathologist,' she said, holding out her hand. 'And you're Margaret Penny.'

Margaret just took the hand that was offered and nodded.

Dr Atkinson was the same pathologist who ten minutes before had been upstairs dissecting and probing
and making all sorts of notes. Now she was instructing
Margaret. 'I was one of the doctors who did the Walker
post-mortem. We've got the report somewhere. Do you
have a copy?'

Margaret shook her head.

'Would you like a summary?' But the pathologist didn't
wait for Margaret to answer. She began to recite instead.
'Carcinoma. Tumours in lungs and bones. Heart disease.
Fatty arteries. Amongst other things.' It was rather like
Barbara's recital of her churchgoing activities, just without
the prospect of salvation at the end.

'Natural causes then?' Margaret was pretty sure this
was what the pathologist was telling her.

'Oh yes, diseases of all kind. No doubt one of them did
for her.'

'Any idea which exactly?'

'Not really.' The pathologist shook her head. 'Could
be any one of several. It can be hard to pin down with
someone who is old. Still . . . vital organs tell a story for
quite a long time after.'

'What do you mean?'

'Well, cardiac arrest, for example. You'll still see the
scarring on the wall of the heart for months. Maybe years.'

A heart that has been beaten, pummelled and cut into
tiny fragments, before being left to fester on a life-support
machine. Margaret knew all about that.

'Cigarettes, of course. Smokers' skin, all jaundiced.
Everything inside gone furry.'

Margaret had given up smoking when she turned forty, believing there was still time to create the life she'd always assumed would be hers – two silver-haired children grinning in crumpled Technicolor. Or something of that sort.

Dr Atkinson tapped absently at the front of her own chest, *tip-tap*, as though to indicate what might happen if Margaret allowed that sort of recklessness to re-enter her life. 'Or in this client's case, alcohol. Her liver was like paste. Bloated. Probably drank herself to death.'

Margaret saw again the forest of empty bottles lined up under her mother's kitchen sink and wondered if Barbara's liver might be going that way too. About the only thing she and her mother had managed to agree on in the last two weeks was whether to open another bottle once the one they had started was done.

'Had she been dead for a while?' she asked.

'Hard to say.' Dr Atkinson scratched at her nose with a well-trimmed fingernail. 'A couple of weeks, perhaps, probably more. There was decomp of course. Thankfully there weren't any maggots.' She pulled a face. 'I can't abide those.'

'Did she look . . . normal?' Margaret wanted to ask if Mrs Walker's hands and feet had turned black, a mummy in the making, but she wasn't sure of the correct terminology.

Dr Atkinson laughed. 'Not bad. The cold, you know. Kept her preserved. Got to be good for something.' The pathologist peered at the glass partition. 'Very thin though,' she added. 'If I remember right, hardly anything to her.'

'What age do you think she was?'

'That's your job, isn't it – date of birth?' Dr Atkinson turned to Margaret with a bleak sort of grin. 'But I'd say around mid seventies to mid eighties, judging by her skin and her hair. Hair can tell you a lot about a person. DNA. The keeper of our secrets.' Dr Atkinson touched her head for a moment. 'It's amazing, really, what you can learn from the dead.'

After Barbara had refused to acknowledge the existence of the dead twins it had been her turn to ask a question Margaret wasn't sure she knew the answer to. 'Why are you always trying to dig up the past, anyway?'

'It's my job now,' Margaret had laughed, raising a glass of red wine in a toast.

But Barbara wasn't playing. 'No,' she'd said, chest rattling. 'Isn't your job to lay the past to rest?'

Now, in the calm air of the viewing room, Margaret touched a hand to her own hair. She'd always wondered about her ancestors and here, perhaps, lay the key. Sheep stealer, maybe. Peddler of fake coins. Some sort of trouble-maker buried in her genes. A quick *snip* and who knew what might be revealed? Whereas Barbara had always insisted on being cremated. Wasn't that what she had tried to teach Margaret? *Leave no trace.*

'Did you take hair samples from Mrs Walker?' Margaret asked. She would have liked to have something physical of her client. At the moment Mrs Walker seemed all surface and not much else.

Dr Atkinson shoved her hands in the pockets of her uniform. 'No, no. We only do that if there is any ambiguity. There was nothing suspicious here – just an old lady who died of natural causes.' She glanced at her watch. 'It's nothing like the television, you know.'

Four murders an hour. An axe in the chest and head. A body giving up all its secrets just like that. Still, it didn't seem quite so unambiguous to Margaret. No one had been able to tell her Mrs Walker's first name yet.

'Look, I'm sorry.' The pathologist checked her watch again. 'I've got to go. Three more bodies to process. Get stacked up at this time of year. The famous Edinburgh backlog.' She held out her hand for another brisk shake. 'But make sure you get a copy of the report before you leave. Everything you need to know is in there.'

Margaret nodded. The nature and causes of a death typed out on two or three pages. Clues to a life retrieved from inside dead flesh and turned into prose. It all came down to paperwork in the end. Just like Janie had said.

Behind the glass there was the sudden sound of a door opening, the soft squeak of a trolley wheel. Dr Atkinson took a quick step back. 'Ah, just in time. The specimen.' The slats of the Venetian blind began to glide apart as Margaret stepped up too.

She found herself gazing into a small, oak-clad space. The light behind the glass was muted and dim. Three lily stems bowed gracefully in one corner. Just behind the partition the body was laid out, covered by a purple cloth with a golden braid. Margaret placed a finger on the glass wall between where she stood and her client lay. Here she was at last. Mrs Walker. Not alive. But not gone yet. Just waiting for the beginning of her end.

Except . . .

Dr Atkinson sucked in a small, sudden breath. 'For

God's sake!' (Though it was clear to Margaret that her client was long past God's help now.) 'That's not Mrs Walker. That's someone else.'

1937

Down in London the beginning of the end for the Walker family started with a coronation for a king who should never have been a king and ended with a phoney war. Nobody wanted the first and the second was only a warm-up for the cataclysm to come, but some people knew an opportunity when they saw one. And how to take it too.

'A memento of the big day.' The photographer went from door to door, working his way up through the streets from the great swathe of the river towards the Fulham Road. He came to Elm Row late in the afternoon, tired and despondent, to a series of tall, narrow houses separated by thin, damp passageways that ran through to the backs. The photographer twirled the buttons on his waistcoat. Surely someone here would want to celebrate the crowning of a new monarch with a family portrait, all present and correct.

Mrs Quinn.

Mrs Nolan.

Mrs Jones.

The Elm Row women all shut their doors in the photographer's face, one after the other, aprons stained with flour and chicken's blood, summer dresses all limp with the heat.

Mrs Fraser.

Mrs Yates.

Mrs Todd.

Even the woman with a fat baby on her hip. Mementos of one king's betrayal and another's sudden rise were obviously considered to be in poor taste in this street.

At last, the photographer came to number 14. Tall and narrow like the rest, five steps up to the front door. But here, instead of a grown woman wearing an apron, twelve-year-old Clementine Walker lounged outside. Her hair fell in pale tangles around her face. Her hem dragged in the dust. Her legs were bare. And her feet too, soles grey with dirt. But her eyes were still startling. First one thing then another, like small pieces of glass washed in from the sea.

'Take your photo, miss?' The photographer lifted his camera case with one hand and his cap with the other. 'To celebrate the coronation.'

Clementine twirled a rat's tail of hair between finger and thumb, then put it between her lips. 'It's not till next week.'

'Be prepared.' The photographer twirled one of his buttons in reply. 'Isn't that the motto?' He gazed at Clementine's legs, exposed from ankle to thigh by the shortness of her frock.

Clementine stared back, then removed the hair from her mouth, slick with saliva. 'I'll have to check with my mother,' she said, eyes sliding away from the photographer, then back again. 'You'd better come inside.'

In the parlour Dorothea looked confused. 'A photograph?' She turned towards the wall where two small children slept behind cold glass.

'For the coronation, madam.' The photographer stood in the doorway, cap neat in hand.

'What coronation?' Dorothea was languishing on a chaise longue that had seen better days, wearing a cotton nightgown that had seen better days too.

'Do you have a special outfit?' asked the photographer. 'You'll want to look your best.'

Upstairs on the highest, furthest floor, Clementine wriggled and jiggled, trying to get comfortable as she pulled on the best set of clothes she had. A white pleated skirt. A white knitted top to match. A band around the middle embroidered with blue and red crowns. Her special coronation outfit, donated (like everything else they owned now), all the rest of their nice clothes having disappeared piece by piece into a pawnshop on the King's Road.

In their place had come women each week, touching and smoothing their hair as they stood in the hallway. Mrs Quinn. Mrs Nolan. Mrs Jones. Trying to get as close to Alfred as they could, now that Dorothea was not the woman she had been.

'Just thought it might help . . .'

'A little thing I dug out . . .'

'More than we can possibly eat ourselves . . .'

They came holding bottles and pie dishes. Baskets full of old socks and cuts of leftover meat. Clementine watched from the landing as Alfred held on to the banister to keep himself upright, bathing the visitors in wafts of breath rinsed in whisky while they said their piece.

'Some apples from the garden.'

'A jug full of cream.'

Voices falling into whispers as they stretched to reach Alfred's ear.

'So sorry for your troubles.'

'So sorry for your loss.'

Except . . .

Dorothea wasn't dead yet. More like an angel floating in the night, drifting through the rooms on pale feet, nightdress trailing. *Say it, darling. Say it.* As Clementine, small and wraithlike in her turn, appeared by her side, clocks ticking down to midnight.

'Mummy?'

Taking Dorothea's hand in her own.

Emblazoned now in coronation white, Clementine pulled patched smocks over the heads of the twins. Little Ruby and little Barbara. One dark. One mousy. She pushed fat limbs through armholes and buttoned up the backs, then attempted to brush what little hair they had while Ruby stuffed hairpins into her mouth and Barbara sat mute. After that she took them downstairs to Dorothea's bedroom and let them play with the one-armed china cherub while she brushed and brushed her own hair.

On the ground floor in the parlour, the photographer fiddled with his equipment while Dorothea sat upright on the chaise longue, hair as white as a cockleshell now. Around her neck was a fox stole, head intact, eye glittering at the photographer every time he glanced up.

Clementine appeared at last, processing into the room with two toddlers staggering behind. Her hair rose around her head in a cloud of static, as though she had acquired a halo while the photographer had been tinkering with his lens.

'What's your name, miss?' he asked.

'Clementine,' she said.

'Clementine. That's pretty.'

'Yes,' she said tilting her head towards him. 'From the song.'

Oh my darling.

Though no one ever sang to Clementine any more.

The photographer did the duty shots first. One baby after the other sitting on their mother's knee – Ruby wriggling and squirming, Barbara all lumpen and frowns. When the photographer asked her to smile, Dorothea looked straight at the lens with a perplexed expression. 'What's my name?' she said.

'Madam?'

'Mama!' the baby on her lap called out and the woman dropped her head to the sound, hair tumbling over her face as the shutter clicked down.

After that they all went outside, the last rays of daylight shining through Clementine's hair as though to set her on fire. A young queen pouting on the doorstep, small white skirt raised to the top of her thigh. Two small acolytes sitting in the middle of the road stuffing gravel into their mouths. An old queen swaying on the top step draped in a fox fur, as though she was in charge of the proceedings. Crazy, thought the photographer as he pressed down the shutter over and over. They're all crazy. But still he went on.

Half an hour later, his own hair black with sweat, face as lined as the creases in his daughter's frock, Alfred Walker returned to 14 Elm Row as though on a matter of urgent importance. Which, of course, he was.

'Daddy! Daddy! Daddy!' A small clamour rose from the street as he appeared. But Alfred didn't respond. Instead he leapt up the front steps, passing his eldest in her coronation outfit as though she didn't even exist. As he went by, he adjusted the fox stole on his wife's shoulder, touching Dorothea's bare skin with the tip of one finger. Then he disappeared into the narrow hallway and took the bare boards of the stairs two at a time, a faint trail of whisky following in his wake.

The photographer adjusted his lens and wondered whether he should continue. Until Clementine's voice rose, thin but determined, into the silence. 'Shall we go on?'

So they did.

Clementine posing on the doorstep.

Clementine pouting in the doorway.

Clementine lounging on the green chaise longue.

Crazy, the photographer thought again as he pressed down the shutter. They were all crazy. But still he couldn't resist.

An hour on, and Alfred appeared again with a small bag in his hand. Dorothea was lying on the chaise longue once more, hair all across her shoulders. The children were upstairs getting changed into normal clothes. The photographer was packing up his case.

'They'll be ready in time for the ceremony next week,' he said to Alfred. 'Should be lovely.'

'Sorry?' Alfred seemed anxious. He kept looking at his watch.

'The coronation.'

'Oh yes,' said Alfred.

'You can pay me when I bring them round.'

'Right.' But Alfred wasn't really listening. Instead he went and stood outside on the front step looking towards the end of the street.

The photographer sidled past him, pulling on his cap. 'I'll be off then.'

But it was Alfred who left first. 'Just got to pop out,' he said. 'Can you mind them?' And down the steps he went, out into the middle of the road, three children upstairs and a wife in the parlour with a dead fox around her neck.

The photographer stared after him. 'What the . . .' And made to follow.

Then a woman came walking, passing Alfred at the point in the road where later a bomb would fall, leaving a crater that took years to be filled. She gave a quick nod as she went by and Alfred dipped his head in response, but neither of them paused to speak. No one but the photographer seemed to notice her arrival: brown-suited, no-nonsense lace-ups, small suitcase at her side.

'What are you doing?' she said by way of introduction.

The photographer was bemused. 'Sorry?'

'Off you go, now.' She spoke to him as though she owned the place.

'I beg your pardon?'

'We don't need your sort here.'

Then she turned to Dorothea who had emerged from the parlour, fox eyes gleaming, just in time to see her husband walk away. 'Good day, Mrs Walker. I think it is time we went in for our tea.'

*

She was a housekeeper. They had a house. Three narrow floors of London property and a coal-hole, all in dire need of supervision. Not to mention a madwoman and a set of baby twins. The midwife had come good at last.

'Call me Mrs Penny,' she said, as they gathered around her in the kitchen.

'Find a penny, pick it up, all day long you'll have good luck.' Dorothea laughed. The sort of laugh that made everyone stop and look at her, amazed.

'That's right, dear,' said Mrs Penny, cutting off the laugh and steering Dorothea towards a seat. 'Every penny counts.'

She wore an apron and gloves at the same time – for washing, for polishing, for making the fire. She could heave the coal while also rolling pastry. The family were bemused.

After she'd made tea in Dorothea's china pot, flowers still dancing round the rim, Mrs Penny took the girls upstairs.

'Let's start with a rule,' she said. 'This far – and no further.'

Clementine, Ruby and Barbara stared at Mrs Penny's finger as it sketched an invisible line on the floor. Mrs Penny was on one side of it, in the room that used to be their nursery, and they were on the landing in the cold. They gathered in the doorway while inside the room Mrs Penny laid her suitcase on the spare bed and snapped open the clasps. *Click-clack* and that's that. She unpacked with the three girls watching, as though to show them how easily she could make herself at home.

Brown skirt, tick.

Fawn blouse, tick.

Stockings, tick.

Brown cardigan, tick.

She got out a tortoiseshell comb, a powder compact with a matching puff and a glass bottle with a blue lid. Innoxa, Complexion Vitaliser (for even Mrs Penny wanted to look good). Then she took out a brown nut with something scratched on its shell. 'Have a look, girls.' She held it in her palm for them to see. 'But don't touch.' (Rule number 2.) 'It's the Ten Commandments.'

Thou shalt not bear false witness.

Thou shalt honour thy father and thy mother.

Thou shalt love thy neighbour as thyself.

Clementine gazed at the nut. She knew the Ten Commandments when she saw them. Just not scratched into the shell of a Brazil nut before. Little fingers twitched behind little backs, but it was Ruby's that crept forwards first.

'Now, now,' said Mrs Penny tapping with one finger at Ruby's grubby hand. 'What did I say?'

Later that evening, with the twins pinned down beneath a tightly tucked sheet, Clementine dared to ask the question to which there would never be a satisfactory answer. 'Where's Daddy?'

'Over the hills and far away.' Mrs Penny was working her way around all the kitchen surfaces with a bucket of soap and a cloth.

'Where's that?'

'Never you mind. Not your business.'

Though even then Clementine thought that perhaps it was. 'But when will he be back?'

'We'll see.' Mrs Penny always was a woman of few words. Though she made those few words count.

'Can I write to him?'

Mrs Penny slapped her cloth back into the bucket of suds, *flip-flap*. 'If he sends his address.'

'Don't you have it?'

'Now why would *I* have it – ' Mrs Penny pulled the cloth out again, wringing it between two large hands – 'with your mother just upstairs.'

Clementine left the kitchen and climbed the stairs to peer at her mother through a crack in the door. 'Mummy?' she whispered. But just as always, there was no reply.

Clementine climbed on to the highest, furthest floor then and sat on the edge of the twins' narrow cot instead. They were curled up like shrimps, one folded inside the other. 'He'll write,' Clementine whispered into the coral of a tiny ear. 'Just wait.'

But as far as Clementine knew, Alfred never did.

Two years later the Phoney War began with a list sent home from Clementine's school:

Plimsolls, tick.

Pillowcase, tick.

Vest, socks, knickers, tick.

Also a spare handkerchief and enough food for twenty-four hours. The essentials for evacuation. Just in case. For the first time in a long while Clementine was happy. 'Be prepared,' she said to the twins as they stood in her bedroom doorway each sucking on a segment of orange. 'You never know when they might arrive.'

'What, Clemmie?' A dribble of juice stained Ruby's chin.

Clementine threw up her arms. 'Bombs!'

Ruby shrieked and laughed. Barbara dropped her piece of orange onto the floor. She stared down at it, curled in the dust like a dead worm, all dirty.

Clementine darted back and forwards from her chest of drawers, piling everything she might need on a chair. Skirt, tick. Blouse, tick. Sanitary Towels (only recently acquired), tick. A small suitcase lay open on the bed, its insides clad in blue-and-white paper. She was nearly fourteen years old, the promised land suddenly within her grasp.

'Where are we going, Clemmie?' Ruby asked.

'To the countryside.'

'A farm?' Barbara clutched a small pink pig in her fist.

'Maybe.' Cardigan. Nightdress.

Ruby slid her fingers round the doorframe, leaving five sticky marks. 'With Daddy?'

'Perhaps.' Clementine stopped for a moment, frowning. Blazer, tick. Petticoat, tick. Hairbrush! She lifted a brush with a bone handle from the top of her chest of drawers and placed it next to the suitcase.

'What about Mummy?' Ruby poked at Barbara's segment of orange where it lay rolled in the dust, then picked it up and popped it into her mouth.

Clementine turned to her sisters. 'What about her?'

'Will she come too?'

*

Downstairs Mrs Penny ironed vigorously and muttered, 'It's all going to hell in a hand cart.' But she didn't mean the impending war. She meant Dorothea Walker, who hadn't got any better since Mrs Penny had arrived. Salts from the chemist. Daily doses of nettle tea. Crushed aspirin sprinkled on cold rice pudding. Despite Mrs Penny's best efforts, Dorothea still behaved as though she existed in a parallel universe.

Every morning Clementine stood by her mother's bed and whispered into her ear, 'Mummy?' Just in case. 'It's me.' But Dorothea lay, hair spread about her like a shroud, murmuring, 'My angels!' as two grubby three-year-olds rustled and giggled on the landing outside.

Cod Liver Oil. Oranges from the grocers. Rosehip syrup from the Violet Melchett baby clinic, one careful dose measured out each week on a silver teaspoon with a tiny apostle attached to the end. Mrs Penny had calculated the latest bill in her household notebook, rows of neat pencilled figures, each one scored through as it came and went. Whichever way she added them up, it wasn't looking good.

Clementine appeared now, standing by the kitchen dresser, small fists on small hips. 'Is my tunic ready yet?'

Mrs Penny thumped the heavy iron upright on the table, covered now by a sheet and a blanket with a torn satin trim she had found in the airing cupboard halfway up the stairs. 'Excuse me, madam, what's the magic word?'

'Bomb?' Barbara stood behind Clementine, clinging to her older sister as though she might be the last thing she would ever see in this world.

'Don't worry, Barbara.' Clementine removed her sister's

hand from her skirt. 'We'll be in the country soon. Then, when it's over, Daddy will come and get us.'

Mrs Penny snorted. 'Don't be so sure about that.' The housekeeper glanced towards an old tea caddy standing on top of the dresser.

Ruby ran into the kitchen shrieking, 'Bomb! Bomb! Bomb!' A trail of biscuit crumbs and coal dust scattering behind her.

'For goodness' sake, Clementine,' said Mrs Penny. 'Take your sisters upstairs and keep them out of my way while I get everything sorted.'

'For God's sake!' Clementine muttered, stomping back towards the door.

'I heard that, young lady,' Mrs Penny called after her. 'Just because a war's coming doesn't mean we can't keep our language clean.'

'Now's your chance, Mrs P. Get it all to yourself.' Tony, the other new arrival (though not so new now), tipped his chair back and chuckled as he watched the Walker pantomime unfold from his seat by the stove. 'Make a fortune in a war. All those soldiers.' He watched Clementine's bare legs as she made her way out into the hall. 'We could call it the Penny Family Business.'

'Don't be ridiculous, Tony.' Mrs Penny continued ironing Clementine's school tunic with a robustness its appearance didn't deserve. But she knew there was something in what he said.

Tony (louche and loud and full of winks and smells) had arrived the day they crowned the king who shouldn't really have been king. He'd appeared to find two babies sitting neat on upright chairs while Mrs Penny sang the national anthem, their mother upstairs in her bed singing too, but in a different key.

He'd come in the form of a whistle and a wheeze and a great big shout, 'Hey, Mrs Penny, heard you had a new position.' And she tried not to smile when she opened the back door. Mrs Penny had known Tony since her first-ever job. He had a way of conjuring the very thing Mrs Penny needed, even when she hadn't realized she needed it herself.

The first thing Tony did was to sit down by the stove and light up his pipe. 'You don't mind, do you . . .'

'No smoking indoors,' Mrs Penny frowned. But she didn't try to stop him, not that time, at least.

The next thing Tony did was dandle a baby on each of his knees. 'Upsy-daisy.' Barbara hiccupped. Ruby giggled. Tony liked children.

After dinner he said, 'I thought there was three of them.'

Mrs Penny rolled her eyes. 'The other one's in the coal cellar.'

'Why's that?'

The housekeeper wiped her hands down Dorothea's apron and took a packet of photographs from a drawer, delivered only that morning by a photographer with shiny buttons on his coat.

Clementine posing on the doorstep.

Clementine pouting in the doorway.

Clementine lounging on a green chaise longue.

'She wanted these and I said she couldn't.'

Tony looked at the photographs and laughed. A loud, booming laugh. 'Did you pay for them?'

Mrs Penny sniffed. 'I saw him off with the Ewbank.'

Tony laughed again, then put the photographs in his pocket. 'I'll deal with it, Mrs P.,' he said.

'What about these ones?' Mrs Penny held out two more photographs, one baby after the other sitting on Dorothea's lap amidst a tumble of white hair.

'You can keep those.'

So Mrs Penny reached for the tea caddy that stood on the top of the dresser and popped the photographs in next to a slip of paper with an address in America.

Clementine had been inside the coal-hole almost every day since Mrs Penny arrived the week before. Despite knowing the Ten Commandments off by heart, she didn't yet know how to honour and obey.

Tony shuffled along the passageway towards the coal-hole, hidden under the street. 'Aye, aye,' he said opening the door to a defiant girl, eyes flaring, face all black.

Clementine put down her two small fists. She hadn't been expecting a man.

Tony beckoned to her with a fat index finger. 'Come here, little thing,' he said. 'I've got something to show you.' Clementine shuffled forwards, hair greasy with coal dust. The man held something out towards her, glinting in the darkness. 'Would you like it?'

Clementine reached out, a small ghost in amongst the black.

Tony laughed and pulled the coronation penny away. 'But come here first and tell Tony all about it.'

So Clementine did.

*

Two years on, and the build-up to the Week of Crisis continued apace. Mrs Penny was in and out all day getting things that might be needed if the worst came to the worst. Tins of condensed milk, of thick syrupy fruit, a whole sack of flour. She fought in the grocer's over dried raisins and the very last jar of glacé cherries. Queued for darning wool and Cash's name tapes at the haberdashery, small white strips with their names embroidered in red.

Ruby Penny.

Barbara Penny.

Clementine Penny.

'But we're Walker,' said Clementine, standing with her unmarked school socks in her hand.

'Waste not, want not,' said Mrs Penny as she sewed the labels one by one into all of Ruby and Barbara's clothes.

She made them queue at the local church hall for gas masks, itching and fiddling in the line, complaining about the stink of rubber. She bought string so they could carry the boxes around their necks at all times. She purchased two pairs of little blue slippers with zips up the front to keep the twins' feet warm should they need to sit in a shelter outdoors. She bought a roll of heavy green fabric for the parlour windows and sticky tape to mark each pane of glass with an *X*. There were even luggage labels to tie to the buttons on their coats.

Label 1: Ruby Penny.

Label 2: Barbara Penny.

Label 3: Clementine Penny (scratched out).

'But we're Walker,' Clementine protested again.

Mrs Penny made her write the label once more.

'Wouldn't want you to get lost, now, would we?' Clementine pressed the pen nib into a fresh brown card, but the surname still came out as a blob.

Dorothea was building up to a crisis too. She languished in her bed, a constant keening rising and falling through every nook and cranny of the house. At night she kept them all awake with her wanderings. Up and down the stairs, creaking and swaying, calling out again and again as though searching for something she would never find. Tony slept with cotton wool in his ears. Mrs Penny with a scarf covered by a hairnet. The twins with small, sweaty palms pressed into each side of their heads. Only Clementine sat up in bed to listen, whispering her mother's name in reply.

The doctors came and went and came and went too, shaking their heads about where it would all end. Everything in the world was shifting. Alfred's whereabouts – unknown. Dorothea's status – mad. War or peace – uncertain. Mrs Penny's position – housekeeper, or perhaps something else . . .

It couldn't go on.

The Crisis Meeting was Tony's idea. 'Be prepared,' he declared. 'Should anyone ask. It's jurisdiction that matters.' Tony liked living in the tall, narrow house. He thought it had lots of potential for the cataclysm certain to come.

Two days later all the women from the street crowded into the parlour, the first time they had managed to get any further inside the house since Alfred had disappeared. Mrs Quinn. Mrs Nolan. Mrs Jones. Staring at a plateful of scones studded with glacé cherries, the centrepiece of a table set for tea. The women were impressed. A person who got hold of things that no one else could, was someone worth cultivating. Especially at times like these.

Mrs Penny poured tea from a pot with flowers all around the rim. Mrs Fraser. Mrs Yates. Mrs Todd. Offering them each a pretty white-and-gold teacup before pouring her own. A war might be coming, but there was no need to panic. Then they began.

The cost of wool.

The filth of the ragman (and his horse).

The difficulty of getting any decent help in current conditions.

'Really, it's impossible.' Mrs Jones touched a handkerchief to her lip. 'No offence intended, Mrs Penny.'

'None taken, Mrs Jones.'

Tony stayed in the kitchen to smoke and to belch. He had done his part just coming up with the suggestion. All he cared about now was his pipe with its black insides and constant access to a bottle of the sweet stuff. Rum, that was his tipple. He was very good at getting hold of things too.

In the parlour Mrs Penny waited until the women had eaten every scone.

'So light. So delicious.'

Spooned up the last of Dorothea's jam.

'You must let me have the recipe.'

And discussed each of their children in turn. Then she looked round the circle and said, 'I wonder if you might be able to help with "my" girls now . . .'

The women glanced at each other then looked away. They all knew this was why they had come.

'It's so hard for them, of course. Their father gone overseas, no idea when he might return. And now, what with a war coming . . .' The rim of Mrs Penny's china cup blinked in the light as she lifted it to her lips.

The women peered down into the dregs of their own tea, all washy and brown at the bottom of their cups. Everyone understood what a war would mean. U-boats and convoys. Husbands and brothers and sons sliding into the abyss. Why would a man return across one ocean now, only to be sent over another sea to fight to the death?

'And their poor mother . . .' Mrs Penny raised her eyebrows to the ceiling. 'Gone in another way altogether, I'm afraid.'

The women turned their eyes to the ceiling too, then to the door that led to the hall. They had never expected Dorothea to come to much and here was their proof. They all had their responsibilities. But none of them had madness snaking through their family. Not that they were prepared to admit to.

'Those poor girls. Nothing better than orphans.' Mrs Penny put down her cup. 'Might need someone to take them on. If the worst comes to the worst.'

The women all nodded in a slow and solemn manner. Everybody had been considering the worst for several weeks now. They flicked discrete crumbs from their laps to the floor. They were still wearing their hats. Some were still wearing their gloves. None of them wanted to take on any extra burden, would avoid it if they could.

Mrs Jones stared at a small pink thing wedged down the side of the chaise longue. It was a tin pig from a farm set very like the one her youngest son owned. She frowned.

Those girls. Nothing but thieves and wretches. Trouble from the day they were born. Shrieking and running, eating gravel right in the middle of the street. Still, everyone must do their duty. Mrs Jones cleared her throat.

'Of course, I could do it,' Mrs Penny said, placing a knife down on her empty scone plate. She rearranged the cosy on top of Dorothea's teapot. 'I have someone who could help with the paperwork. Nye & Sons, solicitors. But I might need your help too.' She folded her napkin and laid it by her plate. 'With the official side of things.'

Mrs Jones cleared her throat again and got in before anyone else could interrupt. 'How generous of you, Mrs Penny,' she said. 'An excellent idea. I'm sure we will all help in any way we can.' She looked around the circle of Elm Row ladies and invited them to disagree. For a moment there was silence. Then the circle of women began to murmur. 'Of course.' 'What a good idea.' 'How kind.' 'Just the thing.' A small rustle of assent running around the circle like a summer breeze. It came to rest on Mrs Penny as she lifted Dorothea's teapot once again. 'Well,' she said. 'Now that's sorted, would anyone like some more?'

When it was time to go, Mrs Penny helped them with their coats.

'How good of you to come.'

With their gloves, where necessary.

'Anything I can do, just ask.'

Saw them off down the steps.

Goodbye, Mrs Jones.

Goodbye, Mrs Nolan.

Goodbye, Mrs Quinn.

'Got to pull together,' she called out as she waved them all away. 'During these unpredictable times.' Then she shut the door behind them and wiped her hands together, *swish-swash*. All hers now. Well, almost. Just one last thing.

The worst came to the worst for Dorothea the following Friday night. Not bombs, but a whole other commotion. Men shouting. A woman shrieking. The phoney war over, the real war begun.

Barbara sat up in bed and howled, 'Ruby! Ruby! Ruby!'

Ruby sat up in bed and howled, 'Clemmie! Clemmie! Clemmie!'

Clementine stood on the top-floor landing and howled, 'Mummy! Mummy! Mummy!'

Until Mrs Penny came upstairs and said, 'Be quiet, all of you!'

Dorothea howled too as they carried her out, flat in their arms, nightdress dragging in the dust. 'Like a dog,' Mrs Penny said later. 'Like the wild animal that she was.'

'Shh,' said Tony from his seat by the stove. 'Little pitchers have big ears.'

'Little pitchers need water.' That was what Mrs Penny said. 'And somebody's got to pay.'

The next day the sisters gathered in the kitchen wearing their outdoor coats, as though they might be going somewhere too. 'Take off those ridiculous labels,' Mrs Penny said. 'You're not going anywhere. Too much work to do here.'

Clementine looked as though she might cry. 'But what about the evacuation?'

'I'll evacuate you, young lady, if you don't do as you're told.'

Ruby went upstairs chanting, 'Bomb! Bomb! Bomb!', a small handful of stolen peel sticky in her palm. Clementine went upstairs to frown at the pile of clothes neatly folded on the chair by her bed. Barbara went upstairs to play with her little tin pig. She'd been looking forward to a farm. Big cows. Smelly pigs. Girls with thick arms (as hers would one day turn out to be). But life, as she was to discover, didn't always go her way.

Later they all stood around the kitchen table where Mrs Penny had laid out a special tea – bread and butter sprinkled with hundreds and thousands, all the colours of the rainbow bleeding into the fat. At each of their places, alongside their teacups, was a little angel cake, vanilla sponge crowned with a butter-icing swirl. They all stared at the cakes. Then they stared at Mrs Penny. It was Clementine who spoke first.

'Where is Mummy?'

Tony cleared his throat and dug at the inside of his pipe. Mrs Penny wiped her hands on Dorothea's apron. 'Now sit down, girls, I've got something to tell you.' She pulled the teapot towards her. 'Your mother . . .' she declared, 'has departed.'

Goodbye, Alfred.

Goodbye, Dorothea.

'I will be your mother now.'

Hello, Mrs Penny. Came in as housekeeper. Went out as owner of it all.

Except . . .

A memory floating upwards in the night: an angel hovering in the doorway as Barbara watched from her bed, small eyes round like boot buttons in the darkness, gazing at the glint of metal in the angel's hand.

'Say my name,' the angel murmured as she bent to stroke Barbara's mousy tangle of hair.

'Barbara Penny,' said Barbara, hoping she had got the answer right, the cold touch of a blade against the warmth of her neck.

But the angel didn't reply, just drifted to the other side of the bed where Ruby lay still, hot breath panting, sharp silver blade slipped behind her ear too.

Then the angel was gone, a haze of light vanishing into the shadows, nothing but a dream. Until the next morning, when all three girls woke a little more light-headed, a little more lopsided, than they had been the day before.

2011

Maggots in the plugholes. Flies in the sink. Mouse droppings scattered over every surface. And a fridge full of rotting food. That was what Margaret had been expecting when she finally arrived at the scene of the crime. But that wasn't what she got. No police tape or fingerprint dust. No sign of forced entry. No need for a coverall suit to match her new, coverall life. Not even any latex gloves or those plastic things to stretch over her inappropriate shoes. Just a few scratches around the keyhole and a cold, empty flat on the outskirts of it all.

'Where should I go now?' she had asked, back at the Office for Lost People after the disaster of a missing corpse.

'You could try Mrs Walker's flat,' Janie said. 'Who knows what that might reveal?'

'Is there something in particular I should look for?' Margaret wasn't keen on going over a dead person's leftovers, particularly ones that had been hanging around for more than a month.

'Oh, the usual.' Janie waved a vague hand. 'Utility bill, NHS card. Anything that's relevant is good.'

'What's relevant?' But Margaret had known the answer to that already. Passbook, bank statement, cash. It all came back to money in the end.

'Correspondence is useful too,' Janie continued. 'Might help us track down a relative.'

'Haven't the police done that already?'

'Usually, within the city boundary, they do. They're brilliant in Edinburgh.' Janie smiled suddenly, sun rising in her face. (Married to a policeman, perhaps.) 'But Mrs Walker was right on the periphery. In a grey area, so to speak.'

Margaret nodded. She had quite a few grey areas in her own life right now. Only that morning her mother had asked how long she intended to stay. And Margaret had not been able to tell whether Barbara wanted to keep her, or to move her on.

From the depths of her office drawer, Janie dug out her latest offering. *Label 1 – Yale type.* The key to Flat Two, 47 Nilstrum Street. Mrs Walker's last-known abode before she checked out.

Janie handed the key over, continuing, 'The police aren't so good on the outskirts. Get sidetracked by other, more important things. Breaking and entering. That kind of stuff.'

'Oh,' said Margaret. For what could be more important than death? The End of Everything. Unless of course it wasn't suspicious, in which case it was just something that happened every day.

'They write up the sudden death report and leave someone else to do the legwork. Usually it goes straight to the crematorium via the Procurator Fiscal, but this one seems to have slipped through the net.'

By the time Margaret inserted Mrs Walker's key into the lock at Flat Two, 47 Nilstrum Street she felt as though she had slipped through the net too, out onto the periphery of it all, surfing the landscape of the dead. It had taken her two buses to get to her client's last dwelling place, slipping from one onto another in an attempt to lose the black car that appeared to be following, heart beating fast at the thought that what she had attempted in London might have finally caught up with her in the north. Only to end up in a street as bleak as Margaret might have expected for an old lady abandoned at the very end of her life. Dark tenements, dirty windows, a flurry of *To Let* signs and a row of small, decrepit shops – a baker, a Costcutter and an off-licence where you had to point to what you wanted through a wall of specially reinforced glass. It was just like the Edinburgh of Margaret's childhood. Unreformed.

She knew already that Flat Two was a rental – short term, all-inclusive, cash payment, no questions asked. Somehow Margaret already suspected that, just like her, Mrs Walker had appeared from somewhere else. The rent had been paid for three months only, although (as it turned out) Mrs Walker hadn't even needed that. Perhaps the Walker estate was due a refund. Enough for a wreath. Or a shiny coffin. But then again, there was the sanitation bill to consider. Somebody had to clean up after a corpse.

Unfortunately for Margaret, just as Dr Atkinson had pronounced, the corpse on the trolley in the Mortuary Viewing Area had not been Mrs Walker, but a man named Thomas Macleod. Nor had Margaret's client been waiting outside in the holding bay to be wheeled in next. She wasn't in either of the post-mortem suites, nor back in rack twenty-one of the fridge.

In fact, Mrs Walker hadn't been in *any* of the six fridges that loomed large at the back of the Transfer Area, where the technicians and the mortuary manager gathered in a tight huddle to confer. Margaret had waited as they pulled the cadavers from the shelves one by one, then slid them back one by one too – the bodies of Edinburgh stacked and racked, backed up already, even though it was still only the beginning of the year. Every single fridge shelf had been fully occupied; just not by the dead person Margaret was now responsible for.

After an hour of searching Margaret had phoned Janie from the mortuary office.

'Margaret. How's it going?' Janie sounded efficient. 'Found anything yet?'

'Er, no. In fact . . .' (How did one put it?) 'Mrs Walker seems to have escaped.'

It was Dr Atkinson who had given Margaret a consolation present, of sorts. Not a corpse, but paperwork. A copy of the post-mortem results, as promised. Natural causes, done for by age and disease, high levels of alcohol and tar. And stapled to that, a photocopy of the sheet of newspaper Mrs Walker had been wearing around her middle when she breathed her last.

The news-sheet was an account of Births, Marriages and Deaths some time in late November, five columns of neat prose detailing a series of lives once lived, now gone for good, in amongst others that had only just begun. Beneath the announcements was a small box bordered in black. ***This Morning***. Followed by a line of scripture in miniature text: *Suffer little children to come unto me . . .* The Episcopals, the Catholics, the Evangelicals or the Friends, spreading their wares in the face of the lost. The rest of the verse had been cut off by the mortuary photocopying machine. Margaret squinted at the tiny block of prose. 'Where's the original?'

'With the body, I'm afraid.' Dr Atkinson ushered Margaret and her paperwork towards the door. 'We like to keep everything together. They can't have gone far, though.' The pathologist seemed remarkably sanguine about the loss of Mrs Walker. 'She is dead, after all.'

In the hall of Mrs Walker's flat a single light bulb shrouded in dust hung above Margaret like a resident ghost. It was bone-chillingly cold. Cold enough for Mrs Walker to have frozen to death, cryogenically preserved within twenty-four hours of taking her final gasp.

Four doors, half open as though someone had just left, led off the hall to four rooms – kitchen, bathroom, bed-room and the living room where Mrs Walker had been found. Margaret knew the layout without needing a plan. It was exactly the kind of dingy Edinburgh rental accom-modation that she and her mother used to inhabit when Margaret was a girl. 'Dirty!' Barbara would declare when they first arrived at each new dwelling, standing in the middle of yet another empty hallway, brown suitcase in hand. But despite a million buckets of Flash, or the yellow squirt of Jif around yet another stained old bath, each flat still contained a thin layer of melancholy, coating everything they touched.

It had taken Margaret a long time to realize that the melancholy didn't come with the flat. It travelled with her. Clinging to her coat sleeves and secreting itself inside her own small bag (three pairs school socks, school skirt, grey jumper and a lucky coronation penny she had stolen from her mother's bedside drawer because . . . well . . . she turned out to be good at that). It was only when Margaret fled to London and never looked back that she discovered the melancholy didn't belong to her either. It belonged to her mother instead.

Mrs Walker's hall didn't contain a sense of melancholy so much as the absent air of the dead. Once here, now gone, nothing left behind but junk – a whole heap of it swept up into a rough pile behind the front door. Menus for Chinese takeaway, thick-crust pizza and a cascade from a local supermarket advertising festive deals on turkey, even though Mrs Walker had probably already been dead by the time Christmas came and went.

Margaret sifted through the pile, remembering Janie's instruction about correspondence and her mother's observation about the value of junk. There were a few envelopes in amongst the rest, one or two of them opened, others with heavy tread marks on the outside. Size eleven. Police issue. None of them was marked for a Mrs Walker. None of them was marked for a real person at all.

Margaret followed a trail of cold cigarette ash into the bathroom, where small sprays of ice were growing like ferns on the inside of the already frosted glass. The bath was an old cast-iron type, little green valleys carved into the enamel beneath the permanent *drip-drip* of the taps. It looked as though it hadn't been used for years, judging by the small collection of corpses gathered in its depths. Jenny-long-legs, some tiny flying creatures and a couple of spiders, their many limbs curled up.

Above the basin, propped on a grimy shelf, was a mirror all spotted and silvered, and next to that a lipstick worn to a small greasy stub. Margaret was surprised by the tiny scarlet indent left at the bottom of the tube. Barbara's lipstick had always been brown.

Beside the lipstick was a powder compact complete with old-fashioned puff. The powder was worn down to almost nothing. Margaret held it to her nose and a sudden memory of Barbara rose up, coat buttoned to her neck, bending to brush Margaret's cheek with her own powdered face as though she were an acquaintance rather than her own child. 'Be good when I'm at work.' Then the quiet snip of the front door as it fell to, and Margaret left behind with nothing but a list of rules.

Don't peek.

Don't pry.

Don't poke your nose in where you ought not.

Though that had never stopped Margaret digging into things which, even then, she knew she should not.

Mrs Walker's kitchen was bleak too, not bleach and wipe-clean roller blinds like at The Court, but the stale remains of a thousand cigarettes lurking in every corner. There was a table shoved into a recess and a built-in dresser lumpy with too many coats of gloss. The only source of heating appeared to be an ancient gas fire, burners all stained. Margaret tried the ignition switch, but as with the electricity, gas appeared to be something that was no longer included in the rent.

A single teaspoon with a spindle of a handle lay abandoned on one of the kitchen surfaces, stranded in a dried-up puddle of what must have once been tea. The spoon was silver, now tarnished, its surface a dark oily blue. Margaret rubbed a thumb across the tiny figure soldered to one end. St Jude, patron of lost causes. Or something like that. An apostle spoon, left behind to say its silent prayers for the dead. Margaret dropped the spoon back into the cutlery drawer along with all the other odd forks and knives. Tidying up was the least she could do now that Mrs Walker was no longer here to tidy for herself.

The only food Margaret could find was two tins of condensed milk in a cupboard and half a tin of peas in the fridge. It reminded her of Barbara's kitchen when she'd first arrived at New Year. Nothing but a cupboard lined with soup and an onion sprouting a green shoot. So, once the light had fallen away from the sky, Margaret had gone out and bought chips, hurrying home across icy pavements in her inappropriate shoes. It had been their first supper together in more years than Margaret had wanted to count, salt and the vinegary taste of sauce, eaten from their laps as though Margaret was still a child.

In the narrow scullery attached to Mrs Walker's kitchen another trail of cigarette ash dribbled across the floor to the window, where an old stub had been ground into the bare boards. Margaret stared down at the ghost of red on the filter. A fall of dust had settled along the window ledge like a first sift of grey snow. Margaret lifted the corner of the old net curtain and stood listening, uncertain. Voices, faint but distinct, rising from somewhere. The sound of children playing, high in the sharp frosty air.

In the living room a single armchair sat facing an empty grate. There was no sign of a fire any time in the last century, or anything on the mantelpiece but another small ridge of dust. The cover of the chair was greasy, pattern rubbed away at the top. Margaret tried to imagine a dead body resting within its confines. This was where Mrs Walker had breathed her last, after all, blood pooling in her wrists and ankles, a rattling in the back of her throat.

According to the police report there had been a glass tumbler on the floor beside the armchair, but Margaret couldn't see one now. She considered kneeling down on the filthy carpet to check. But she couldn't help thinking about her hands getting sticky with the long-accumulated debris of a human life – hair and cigarette ash, old skin and other bodily secretions which she didn't want to contemplate. Margaret had only been inside the flat for ten minutes and already she felt dusty all over, the cuffs of her mother's elongated cardigan picking up stray hairs and God knows what else where they stuck out from beneath her coat. Besides, Janie had been adamant. Margaret was here for paperwork, nothing more.

'Bibles,' Janie had elucidated. 'Perhaps medals.' That was what men left behind. Also leases and paybooks, bank statements and all sorts of other useful things. Women, on the other hand, left jewellery and that was pretty much that. 'If you find any,' she continued, 'we have to send it to UH in Glasgow.'

'UH?' There was a whole new jargon to the world of the (not quite) dead and buried that Margaret had never imagined she might become acquainted with.

'*Ultimus haeres*, the last heir,' Janie said. 'It's part of the Crown Office. If there are no relatives, they use the proceeds from the estate to pay for the funeral. It's all about ownerless goods.'

Ownerless goods. That was how Margaret had felt about herself as the life she worked so hard for in London vanished in a matter of months.

'And if there aren't any relatives . . .' Janie turned back to her computer as though that was a matter of no particular consequence. 'Then you will make the funeral arrangements yourself.'

Now that she was inside Mrs Walker's flat, Margaret knew that it might well come to that. For there was nothing of any particular interest that wasn't already in the police report. No birth certificate lurking unnoticed in a drawer, no proof of marriage folded beneath a pile of clothes. There were no bank statements, no letters or postcards. No photographs of children or any other human being. Not even of a dog.

The only heirloom Mrs Walker appeared to have left behind was an orange on a blue china plate, decaying now just like its owner, collapsed from the inside out. Margaret was surprised the police hadn't thrown it away when they first broke in. But then they hadn't thrown away the peas either. So perhaps tidying up was her responsibility after all, now that the body had been removed. One thing after another tossed into a black bin liner until all that remained was a slim brown folder full of paper. Nothing to smell or hold on to. No weft or weave. After all, Janie had made it clear that the police had other things to deal with – the stuff of life rather than the detritus of death.

In the bedroom, nineteen empty bottles were lined up around the wall. Whisky. The water of life. Though not for Mrs Walker, not any more. Just like her, the old lady had been a bedtime drinker. Not hot chocolate, but spirits, one glass after another until her liver had taken on the consistency of fish paste.

The underwear in the chest of drawers was as described – an old person's. Margaret took it out piece by piece, as though she could take Mrs Walker out piece by piece, then put her back together again more whole this time. Once she'd finished, she thrust her hands to the back of each drawer, just in case, only to find a couple of rusty safety pins and a scattering of nail trimmings. Also some sort of nut, dusty and grey, something indecipherable scratched on its shell. Margaret took the nut and popped it into her pocket. She was determined to come away with something, even if she had no idea what it meant.

In the wardrobe a coat hung, quiet and still in the darkness, just waiting to be filled. It was red, like Margaret's, but darker, the cuffs worn thin. Just like everything else in the flat, it had seen better days. Margaret dipped a hand into each of the pockets, hoping for treasure. But there was nothing except for two or three little pieces of orange peel, stiff and curled.

On the floor of the wardrobe was a plastic carrier bag, and inside that, a surprise. A simple shift dress, high neckline, no sleeves, elegantly cut. As Margaret lifted it from the bag the fabric slithered and shimmered as though drawn from the sea. A few tatty sequins winked along the hem like the flicker of fish eyes. It was a young woman's dress, something from a whole other era. Definitely not the kind of thing an old woman would fit into, with her thick joints and low-slung breasts. Then again, Barbara was old and her box-room wardrobe was stuffed full of clothes she couldn't possibly squeeze into any more either. So perhaps there was nothing unusual in that.

In fact, the more Margaret moved around Mrs Walker's flat, the more it reminded her of Barbara's box room. A space full of leftover items from leftover times. Only the other night Margaret had started to go through the wardrobe in the hope that she might find something more edifying to wear than a mid-length corduroy skirt and a blouse in a distressing shade of fawn. But so far all she'd found were trousers with elasticated waists and a blouse made of chiffon that Margaret knew would rip at the seams the moment she tried it on.

The blouse had been from another era too, small pleats circling its collar, tiny buttons running up the back. Pale stains of sweat from long ago had spread beneath each arm. It smelt of tobacco and loam, the slightest trace of linseed oil lingering in its folds. It was just the kind of thing Margaret would have loved to wear, if her arms had not got too fat with disappointment and age.

There was one thing in her mother's box room that had proved useful, however. A fox. Dead. Transformed into a stole. The fur was all fusty, the head eaten away by mange. But still, as Margaret draped the fox around her neck, for a moment she had been transformed too.

Now, in the absent surroundings of Mrs Walker's flat, Margaret adjusted the two tiny paws tucked in beneath her red, stolen coat. She hadn't bothered to ask Barbara where the fox had come from, or if she could take it for herself. If her mother didn't want to admit to any dead relatives, why would she bother about a dead animal? She had asked Barbara something else though, with which

Margaret was certain she would be able to help. *Suffer little children to come unto me . . .*

'Matthew 19, verses 14 to 16,' her mother had replied with a rapid blink of her papery eyelids.

'What's the rest of it?' Margaret asked.

Barbara had begun to cough then, a prolonged attack, frowning and waving Margaret away when she tried to help. 'The Ten Commandments,' she declared once she managed to regain her breath, chest heaving like she didn't have long for this world. 'Honour thy father and thy mother.' She rasped out the latter like some sort of injunction, even though they both knew Margaret had already failed at that. Margaret had stared down at the small block of prose on Mrs Walker's news-sheet, trying to remember the rest of the list. Murder and adultery. Loving thy neighbour as thyself. But Barbara wasn't finished yet. 'Thou shalt not,' she declared finally, breathing out her message as though it was the ultimate lesson by which one should live one's life.

In the gloom of Mrs Walker's bedroom, Margaret coiled the emerald dress back into its plastic bag. She was starting to understand why Janie emphasized paperwork. Whatever she thought of her client's few belongings, they weren't going to be any help in answering the important questions.

Name.

Date of birth.

Where Mrs Walker came from before she ended up here.

There was nothing in the flat but junk, just like the things Margaret had slept amongst for the past two weeks. Old suitcases. Heaters with broken dials. A wardrobe full of shoes too narrow for her feet. The stuff of life; it really was insignificant after all.

Except . . .

She found them on her way out – washed up against the skirting board amongst another drift of ash from a long-dead cigarette. Scraps of paper covered in pencil marks with the shaky demeanour of the elderly. Paperwork, at last.

Margaret gathered up the small torn pieces and carried them home in her pocket, triumphant. Two bus journeys later, no black car waiting for her at The Court, and she spread them out across Barbara's kitchen table, moving them around like a game of pairs until they made some sense.

Moyra.

Ann.

Rose.

And *Mary.*

A name for her client at last?

1953

'Ruby! Ruby!'

Down in the bowels of a narrow London house, seventeen-year-old Barbara called from the bottom of the stairs towards a room on the highest, furthest floor. It was morning. Eight thirty a.m., and a million spectators expected on the Mall. Another coronation, but for a queen this time.

'Ruby! Are you ready yet?'

Nothing to do but prepare. Scrub everything clean from the top to the bottom, then once more for luck. Barbara was ready, of course, and had been for weeks. Kitchen chairs all lined up in the hall, waiting to go out into the street. Plates and cups stacked up along the pantry shelf. Bottles of ale for the men. Tea for the women. Three kinds of cake. Sandwiches by the dozen on soft white bread. There were buns with raisins. Biscuits sprinkled with sugar. Crisps with their blue screws of salt. A feast in the making after all the years they had done without. Or enough supplies for an expedition to the slopes of Everest, where even now men with goggles and crampons were wedging themselves into the ice.

All over London the ragged remains of a long-drawn-out war were being swept away as the city began to live once more. Every day huge holes appeared on street corners in place of the rubble, iron skeletons growing out of the shattered ground to tower over grey streets. Every day men and machines churned the muddy surface of the earth where once there had been nothing but craters. Every day there was the *clack-clack-clack* of a million typewriter keys rising and falling. The scratch of pens on blueprints, of deals being made and lost.

All over London people were restless, moving here and there, taking themselves from one place to another. Men surging through rented bedsits. Women hauling babies (and all their other belongings) in deep, carnivorous prams. Small children crawled like flies over old bombsites, in and out of every crack and crevice. Young couples lingered on street corners pretending they had all the time in the world. The whispers and moues of love percolated from the underground, curling to the surface bathed in the smell of jazz.

London, it seemed, was rising, everything washed clean.

Amongst all that was new, the old remained too. Number 14 Elm Row, still standing tall and narrow in the middle of the street, all its secrets firmly intact. Outside, the house was in need of a clean coat of paint and a set of replacement railings, its grimy windows and walls requiring a good scrub-down. Inside there were cracks as thick as a man's thumb between skirting and floorboards, chunks of glass wedged in to capture any movement before it was all too late. In the bedrooms, sheets were cut in two and turned outside-edge to outside-edge before being sewn up the middle. The smell of cheap boiling-meat rose through all the rooms. Despite Mrs Penny's continued good efforts, everything was just a bit worn down.

But still, there were signs of change here, too.

In the garden a tomato plant grew out of the gravel. In the scullery there was a machine in which to wash clothes.

In the kitchen there was a shiny metal cupboard where food could be stored – powdered custard and boxes of suet. Eggs, all fresh, six at a time. On the dresser, next to an old tea caddy, there was a jar of lemon sherbets for Mrs Penny to suck while she did the ironing and a bread bin containing Paris buns from the baker's van. And in the corner of the kitchen by the large earthenware sink, a Potterton boiler – Mrs Penny's pride and joy.

But it was in the parlour where the most change had come. Still with its heavy green curtains. Still with its fat cherub, preening and armless in the middle of the mantelpiece. But now the photograph of two sleeping children had vanished. The heavy furniture had been pushed back and covered by white sheets. The dark walls washed down with distemper. A rope had been slung across one corner of the room and draped with a bedspread to provide an alcove in which a person could undress. The sideboard had been cleared of everything but a series of enamel bowls: blue rims, white insides, towels stacked next to them in two piles. The worn cover of the chaise longue was shrouded in plastic sheeting ready for a woman in trouble to lie down on. And by the door, hidden away so no one might see, there was a discreet metal bucket with a fitted lid, contents waiting to be sloshed out in the scullery sluice when the time came. It was the second Penny Family Business, in full swing now the war was long gone. No longer catering to soldiers – blackmail and cigarette lighters, a girl whose hair twirled all about her face – but for those who had fallen in another sort of way. Tony's latest suggestion as to how they could all help make ends meet.

'Ruby! Ruby!'

Barbara called again as she climbed steadily to the highest, furthest floor. Barbara never had visited a farm, but her arms were as thick as a milkmaid's now, fresh from squeezing the teat. She was the working type, always had been. Whereas it was typical of Ruby to lie long in bed.

On the top landing two closed doors faced each other, one belonging to Barbara, one to the sister who no longer was. Clementine. Girl of hair that twirled. Lover of oranges, of promises not kept. Clementine. Over the hills and far away. Or somewhere much further than that. Gone for nearly ten years now, nothing left behind except a charred ID card stamped with the word, *DECEASED*.

And Ruby, of course, sleeping in Clementine's abandoned bed. Lying in state now amongst Clementine's rumpled sheets, hair thrown out in a tousle as dark as Clementine's was once fair. Underwear and kirby grips scattered on the floor where once Clementine's stockings had lain in small pools. Amongst face powder in pancake form and lipstick worn to a stub. Small palettes of mascara smoothed down with spit. Before she knocked on her remaining sister's door, Barbara ran two hot palms across the back of her newly pressed frock, all flared skirt and nice printed pattern, ready for the celebrations to come. It was damp outside, a soft rain falling, but Barbara could already feel sweat gathering beneath her breasts. She had sewn the dress herself, as taught by Mrs Penny, but still the bodice felt just a little bit too tight. The front of the dress was covered by an apron, which she smoothed down too before she lifted her hand to knock. *Be prepared.* That was the motto. For behind the door Ruby was surely still sleeping. And Barbara was certain her sister wouldn't be wearing any clothes.

Out amongst the scaffolding of post-war London, fully dressed for some time since, Ruby Penny hurried through the streets. A jewel of a thing, seventeen and counting. Tony's little gemstone. A little gemstone of her own inside now.

'I can do you a special rate,' the woman had said on the phone. 'Seeing as how we're in the same business. But it will have to be first thing. I don't want to be the only person in town to miss the main event.'

The queen of course, the queen. Everybody's darling on this particular day.

'You'll need to bring your own change of underwear and a spare towel, just in case. But of course you know all that. Shall we say nine?'

Silk and velvet. Canadian ermine. Embroidered satin gown, Ruby recited as she ran, pushing her way through the coronation crowds, trying to memorize the details of the ceremony to come, should anyone ask later where she had been.

From west to east, from north to south, people were heading towards the centre of the town. Just like her they wore their Sunday best, good shoes polished, hats firmly in place. They carried small flags, all red, white and blue, their arms laden with blankets, baskets full of sandwiches and flasks. Children of all shapes and sizes milled and called, laughing and pushing, getting in the way.

Ruby twisted and turned into any gap she could find. 'Excuse me. So sorry.'

She wished she had Clementine's little suitcase with her right now, the one her sister used to keep on top of the wardrobe in the hope of somewhere other than this. If she had, Ruby could have held it out in front of her, parting all comers, pressing forward like a mermaid at the prow of a ship.

'So sorry. Excuse me.'

Inside, a set of new linen, a set of silk slips, a set of pristine knickers all enclosed by blue-and-white-checked paper, a new beginning just waiting to bloom.

Instead it was raining and the suitcase had vanished many years before, just like her sister; gone forever to the promised land, never to return. Shoved into a basket were Ruby's towel and her spare underwear, grey from endless washing in that cold earthenware sink. Her change of clothes was hidden in the bottom, covered by a tatty blanket with a torn satin trim, as though she too was carrying sandwiches and a flask instead of one pair of knickers, a skirt and a blouse made out of chiffon, with small pleats looping around the neck.

She'd risen early, six thirty a.m; plenty of time to splash cold water on her face in the scullery sink before anyone else came down. She'd put on her smartest skirt and jumper and over that a jacket with three big buttons on the front. Already she was beginning to sweat. Despite the rain, the weather was warm and muggy beneath the smirr, moisture gathering under Ruby's armpits as she shoved her way through the crowd. Her hair clung to her scalp, not washed for a few days now, in the knowledge that it would need to be washed and washed and washed again once the whole thing was done. Having a child was one thing. Getting rid of a child was something that might take time to rinse away.

At last the Underground came within Ruby's reach. She pushed her way down into the dark stuffy tunnel, reciting the names as she waited on the platform for the train to come. *Cunningham, Tovey, Noah, Tedder.* All the queen's horses. *Eisenhower, Tipperary, McCreery, Snow White.* Ruby had memorized the entire coronation service, just in case. Including the queen's own outfit and the eight greys that would pull her coach.

Back in Elm Row all the silver cutlery was laid out on the kitchen table in front of Mrs Penny, ready for the feast. Twelve forks. Twelve knives. Twelve dessert spoons. Twelve silver teaspoons with little apostles soldered to the ends.

Except . . .

However often Mrs Penny counted, two of the spoons were gone.

'There should be twelve.' Mrs Penny touched each apostle spoon where it nestled inside its cocoon of purple silk, scowling and then counting again as though it might make a difference. 'My mother gave me this set. She'd be very disappointed they're not all here.'

Barbara frowned from the other side of the table where she stood polishing cutlery with a tea towel. Even now she could not imagine Mrs Penny with a mother. Someone who rocked you in their lap. Someone who sang as they laid you down to sleep. Then again, she thought, as she put down one fork and picked up another, nothing in this house was ever as it ought to be. She had never known a mother who did those things either. And as far as Barbara knew, there should be eleven apostle spoons left, not ten.

Only half an hour to go before the princess arrived at the Abbey, and they had all given up on Ruby. 'Where is that girl?' Mrs Penny muttered, moving to the stove now so that she could clatter her kettle and her pans. She'd been asking the same thing over and over for years and never got a satisfactory answer. Neither she nor Barbara (nor even Tony) expected an answer now.

Barbara gave one anyway. It was what she did. 'Perhaps she's gone to get the milk?'

'Don't be ridiculous.' Mrs Penny flicked her apron at the hotplate. 'The milk van was hours ago.'

'Maybe she's gone to watch the parade with a friend.' Tony was sitting by the stove, chair tipped back on its hind legs. He sucked on the stem of his pipe with his thick, wet lips, then tipped his head back too and dribbled rum down his wide-open throat. Tony had started early that morning, knowing nobody would dare to complain this day of all days.

Mrs Penny humphed and flicked her towel at the wide target of Tony's belly until he closed his mouth again. Rule number 57 – no fraternizing (particularly with the opposite sex). But Mrs Penny suspected, just like everyone else in the house, that Ruby had broken that rule many times before.

Barbara tweaked the cutlery lying before her on the table in its neat formations. Then she went to the pantry to hang up her apron, her forehead a little clammy, her hands a little damp, heart going all pitter-patter where it was squeezed too tight by the bodice of her dress. Just once, she thought, just once it would have been nice for the two of them to have done something together. A procession of eight thousand. Three million spectators. Six and a half yards of train. Everybody else had managed the logistics. A space in front of a television set. A new outfit. A party out on the street. Everyone except Ruby, who always had preferred to keep herself to herself.

Ruby's bedroom had been empty when Barbara had gone in, of course, blue faded cover pushed back, eiderdown rumpled, a few discarded hairpins scattered on the floor. Nothing left behind but a shape pressed into the mattress and a lucky coronation penny hidden beneath a chair. Not even a note. Barbara had realized then that she should be used to it by now. Ruby never had been reliable. Here one moment, vanished the next. The only predictable thing about her was that she was unpredictable in every possible way.

Swathed in her sensible apron, Barbara had sat instead on the edge of Ruby's deserted bed and stared at the wall, from where a panoply of people stared back. Women with red spotted kerchiefs and sharp hips drinking cola out of bottles. Men in sunglasses trailing half-smoked cigarettes. A thousand glossy magazine pages (or thereabouts), ripped from their seams, all from the US of A. Land of the Free. Provider of the Brave. A place where all sorts of promises were made and kept.

That small hole inside Barbara which would never be filled had opened up all of a sudden then, as empty as the spaces in Mrs Penny's apostle spoon set. Barbara preferred pictures of the royal family, of horses and kitchen gadgets that could be purchased in the smart shops of the West End. The twins always had been two sides of the same coin. Ne'er the twain shall meet.

She'd wondered, just for a minute, if America was where Ruby had gone to now. Only the week before her sister had declared her intention of travelling there, as though if she wished such a thing it could only come true.

'But how will you afford it?' Barbara was nothing if not practical. Every penny counted out and every penny counted back in.

Ruby lifted a tiny mascara brush laden with black to her eyelashes. 'I'm saving up,' she said.

'Saving up with what?' Ruby had never had any sort of job as far as Barbara could see.

'None of your business.'

Barbara had been sitting on the floor fiddling with her sister's lucky coronation penny. 'She's not there, Ruby,' she said, spinning the coin to a blur on the floorboards. Heads to America. Tails to stay at home.

'How do you know?' Ruby blinked twice in rapid succession, tiny black filaments falling to rest on her powdered cheeks.

'Because . . .' Barbara felt a familiar heat then, running all through her. 'Clementine's dead. Just like Mother.'

Ruby pouted at herself in the mirror. 'No, she's not.'

Barbara watched the coin falter – 'Yes, she is, Ruby. Mrs Penny said so,' – then fall. Tails, just like always.

'You shouldn't believe everything Mrs Penny says,' Ruby had replied, licking her lips to a shine. And that had been the end of that.

'Barbara! Barbara! Hurry up. It's about to start.'

From deep in the pantry, next to enough supplies for an army should an army be required, Barbara rubbed at her eyes now with the edge of her apron as she heard Mrs Penny calling to summon the troops. Then she took the apron off and smoothed down the pleats on her new dress. The sandwiches were sandwiched. The buns were baked. Everything was ready. What more could she ask?

'Tony! Tony! It's about to begin.'

As Mrs Penny called again, Barbara took Ruby's lucky coronation penny from the pocket of her apron and tucked it into the pocket of her dress instead. *Leave no trace.* Wasn't that the Walker family motto?

Now, without Ruby, it would be the three of them once again, gathered around the television set for this momentous occasion. Mrs Penny with her rules.

'No feet on the chairs, Barbara, I've told you!'

Fat Tony sucking on his rum.

'Anyone fancy another?'

And Barbara, of course, the last of the Walkers. Nothing left behind but her. Always second best. Sitting quietly in the corner considering the whereabouts of two lost sisters and a twelfth apostle spoon.

Far away in another part of London, in a small, square room, in a small, narrow bed, Ruby listened to the beginnings of Psalm 122 as it filtered through the wall.

I was glad when they said unto me,
Let us go into the house of the Lord.
Our feet shall stand within thy gates . . .
For there are set thrones . . .

Children's voices soared up into the arches of the

Abbey and Ruby soared with them, reciting the names as she went. *Lady Moyra. Lady Anne. Lady Jane.* All the new queen's attendants. *Lady Rosemary. Lady Mary. Lady Jane* again. *Attend on me.*

Mrs Withers had already attended on Ruby. No fuss. No mess. Just warm water and soap and a red rubber tube, amongst other things. A sip of cheap, fiery liquid to help it all go down. Now all Ruby had to do was wait, while next door a princess became a queen.

Through the wall Ruby could hear Mrs Withers shifting about, trying to get the best picture on her little grey television screen. Lying in her iron-framed bed, she stared up at where damp spread across the ceiling. The bed was just like the one she and Barbara used to share before Tony agreed that she could have Clementine's instead. In a room scented with lipstick and oranges, a thousand cigarette ends floating in the gutter outside the window like a shoal of tiny fish. Here, though, there was even plastic sheeting laid out beneath the linen, just like there had been when she and Barbara shared. Ruby shifted now and felt its crinkle. A real home from home.

Tudor Rose.

Scots Thistle.

Welsh Leek.

Ruby counted the embroidered motifs for the new queen's gown as earlier Mrs Withers had counted the cash. Fat fingers, just like Tony's, each one licked with a flick of her tongue. Ruby had stood, sweaty and damp in her best jumper, waiting for Mrs Withers to tell her she was not too late. Finally the older woman had folded the notes in half and said, 'All there, dear, as we agreed.'

Mrs Withers was a large woman with a two-string pearl necklace clasped tight around her throat. She wore her hair in rollers and had a floral housecoat wrapped over her best dress in preparation for the ceremony to come. She had placed Ruby's cash in a wooden box, locking it with a miniature key that appeared by magic from her clothes and disappeared the same way. 'A very important day for all concerned,' she said, holding out a slip of paper to Ruby. A receipt for cash, paid in advance. Everything prepared.

Sirs, I here present unto you Queen Elizabeth, your undoubted Queen.

God save the Queen . . .

God Save the Queen . . .

God Save the Queen . . .

God Save the Queen.

Through the wall, now, Ruby listened as Mrs Withers saved the queen along with all the rest, two fingers of whisky to burn the back of her throat. Ruby shivered, skin pale as a creature dredged up from the deep. She would have loved a whisky right now. She was clad in nothing but a gown too, a petticoat turned grey with too much washing, cold trickles of sweat running between her thighs. Her clothes were behind an old folding screen in the corner of the room, just like the bedspread draped across the corner of the parlour at 14 Elm Row. A family business Ruby understood from both sides now.

Jewellery and cloak.

White linen gown.

Perfumed oil.

A canopy of silk.

Mrs Withers had hidden Ruby beneath a canopy while it was done too – silk for a queen, an old sheet for her. The queen had been anointed with a special potion. But Mrs Withers had anointed Ruby with a basin of grey water and a cold, rubber tube. She'd kept her eyes closed throughout.

She lay now, reciting: *orb, sceptre, rod of mercy, royal ring.* She would have liked to have a ring of her own to wear. But all she had was a little silver teaspoon hidden in the bottom of her basket and a Brazil nut tight in her hand.

Thou shalt do no murder.

Thou shalt not commit adultery.

Thou shalt not steal.

Ruby knew the Ten Commandments off by heart. She was only seventeen years old and she had already broken them all.

A few hours later and Ruby woke to find Mrs Withers sitting beside the bed, money laid out on the table beside them. Big banknotes, painfully acquired. 'So, my dear, have you thought about what I said earlier?' Mrs Withers pressed a surprisingly delicate finger down onto the stack of paper notes, pinning them to the surface beneath. 'We can call it your first month's wages, board and lodging thrown in.'

Ruby stared at Mrs Withers' finger with its small polished nail. It had never occurred to her when she arrived that morning that the ending of one life might lead to the beginning of a new one too.

'No need to even go home, if you don't want to.' Mrs

Withers was holding something else now. A small glass with a slick of golden liquid swilling in the base. 'Just start next week when you are well enough.'

Ruby blinked and stared at the grey pearls embedded in the fat of Mrs Withers' neck. Inside her belly an ache was beginning to spread, down through her pelvis, up into the cavity of her chest, unfurling into all her vital organs – liver, kidneys, heart. She tried to pull herself higher in the bed, hair in dark streaks stuck to her neck.

'But I haven't brought anything with me.'

Seeing Barbara all of a sudden, back in another tall house on the other side of town. Washing up in the scullery, perhaps. Dragging chairs in from the street.

'There, there dear, not to worry.' Mrs Withers put a hand towards Ruby as though to help her. Or perhaps to hold her down. 'We can start everything anew.'

A gold coach.

Eight horses.

A thousand acorns sent out into the world to grow into enormous trees.

Ruby subsided into her damp pillow. She knew it wasn't normal. But then again, none of this was normal. One day amongst millions that would never be the same again. Not for the new queen. Not for Barbara. Not for Ruby either. She struggled to lift herself up once more, felt the glass pressed cold against her lip. A hand on the back of her neck where once there had been the touch of a silver blade. Then a piece of dirty paper pressed into her palm. A receipt for cash in lieu of services rendered, no harm done.

*

Nine forty p.m., and inside Clementine's old room, sheet neatly folded, blue cover pulled tight, Barbara sat on the edge of the bed turning and turning a penny in her hand. Britannia on one side. The king who should have never been a king on the reverse. All dead now, of course, just like most of the people Barbara had ever known.

She tried to imagine what the new queen was doing, hair unpinned perhaps, just like Barbara's, feet resting on a padded velvet footstool while she ate a slice of her very own cake. Barbara turned the penny in her hand once again. Heads to America. Tails to somewhere else. All her life Barbara had been unlucky. Perhaps things would change now.

Nine forty-two p.m., and in the damp London evening fireworks flew from the Embankment. A thousand children clambered onto buses, laughing and chattering from all the excitement. And Mrs Withers opened the back door of a tall, narrow house in the east of the city and made her way outside.

Nine forty-five p.m., and Barbara spun a coin on the floor as the new queen flicked a switch. Fountains ran like liquid silver. A girl with startling eyes shivered in a bed with a narrow iron frame. And one small foetus (lumpy and unformed) was flushed away into the city's sewers.

London was rising. Washing itself clean.

2011

The very next morning, up early with the rise, and Margaret Penny returned to the territory of the dead. Not Flat Two, 47 Nilstrum Street this time, but the row of small, decrepit shops nearby. One baker, one grocer, one candlestick maker (or something of that sort). Research, that was what Margaret called it. Or one more chance to get under Mrs Walker's skin.

When she arrived, icy slurry still ran thick in the gutters, the tenement walls were still black. But this time the sky was as pale as a bird's egg, all washed clean by a fresh fall of snow in the night.

It had been her mother who pointed it out. Not the names on the scraps of paper gathered from Mrs Walker's skirting board –

Moyra,

Jane,

Rose,

And *Mary,*

– but the shopping list on the reverse.

Margaret had been studying the scraps when Barbara shuffled into the kitchen the night before. 'Where are these from?' Barbara had said, gesturing towards them. Rum slopped dangerously from the edge of her glass.

'It's nothing. Just work.' Margaret went to sweep the pieces of paper away. She didn't want her mother contaminating the only evidence she'd managed to acquire so far.

'But what's written on them?' Barbara picked up one of the scraps before Margaret could stop her.

'Names, I think,' said Margaret, brushing the rest of her treasure out from beneath her mother's grasp. 'Moyra, Jane, Rose and Mary.' She was still trying to work out which came first.

Barbara seemed startled for a moment, turning the scrap of paper in her hand over and back again as though she might somehow be able to break a hidden code. Then she held the scrap out towards Margaret. 'Are you sure?' she said, frowning. 'This says something different.'

Together they peered down at yet another shaky message from the dead. There was no doubting that Barbara was right. Margaret had missed it. Too concerned with solving a more elevated type of mystery to concentrate on the prosaic. *Peas*. That was what was written. It was easy to piece together the rest after that.

Eggs £1.

Paris Bun.

Tetley Tea Blue Bag 80.

Gold Blend.

It was a shopping list. Nothing more, nothing less. The last meal of the deceased. Margaret wondered then if she should have asked Dr Atkinson about stomach contents, while Barbara sat down on one of the kitchen chairs and lifted her rum glass to her mouth with both hands as though taking communion at the church. Thank you, Jesus. Thank you, Allah. Thank you, God.

Back in the land of the deceased, and Margaret began with the grocer. Who Dares Wins and all that. In Costcutter the two men behind the counter turned their eyes up to the ceiling when Margaret approached with a packet of chocolate fingers.

The older one said, 'We've told it to the police already.'

'Told what?'

'About the thieving.'

'The thieving?'

'They'll not have given you the report then,' the younger one said.

What was it with this town, Margaret thought, that everyone believed she already knew something when she hadn't even worked out yet what to ask.

'Used to come in all wrapped up in that coat of hers,' the elder of the two said. 'Just a tin of peas at the counter. Butter wouldn't melt. You know the type.'

Margaret thought of her mother. 'Yes,' she said.

'Took us a while to realize it was her. Old ladies, not your prime candidate.'

'What did she steal?' Somehow it didn't surprise Margaret to discover that her client was a thief.

'Cigarettes. Super Size.'

Margaret looked at the cigarette rack positioned well behind the till.

The younger man cut in, to explain. 'Only came when there was one of us on,' he said. 'Then she'd ask for something off the top shelf. Couldn't refuse. Just an old lady.' Perhaps it was he who had been on duty when Mrs Walker pulled her scam.

Margaret looked around at the shelves stacked high with breakfast cereal and washing powder, rolls of toilet paper and gallons of bleach. Mrs Walker might have been old, but she seemed to know all the tricks in the book.

'We never worked it out until we caught her with the oranges.'

'The oranges?'

'Aye. Lovely sweet ones displayed out front. Clementines, six for a pound. Bargain. She bought the peas like usual then left. Five minutes later we realized two punnets had vanished.'

'How did you know it was her?'

'We followed the peel.'

'The peel?'

'Aye.' And the older man laughed now. 'She'd left a trail. All along the gutter. Couldn't wait. Tucking into one of our oranges right there in the street.'

Beneath her red, stolen coat, heat prickled across Margaret's skin as she remembered a box room black as midnight, misshapen orange held to her lips. 'Did you report it?' she asked.

'No.' The man gave a shrug. 'Just took them off her. Left her a couple though. It was Christmas, after all.'

A Christmas clementine, collapsed and decaying just as Mrs Walker had collapsed and decayed too. 'So how did you find out about the cigarettes?' Margaret queried.

'We checked the CCTV after that, caught her in the act. In black and white, like.' The man laughed again, taking Margaret's money and dropping it into his till. 'What a chancer.'

'Why didn't you prosecute?' If they'd prosecuted there might have been some paperwork.

The man leaned his elbows on the counter and scratched at his beard. 'Never saw her after that. Must have been around the time that she died. Have you tried next door?'

Next door was the baker's, a window full of heart attacks just waiting to happen. And the reflection of a black car trundling slowly down the icy road towards where Margaret stood. Beneath her red, stolen coat, Margaret's heart set up a little pitter-patter. She bent her head further towards the bakery window, pretending an inordinate interest in hot Scotch pies. Hot macaroni pies. Hot sausage rolls. Margaret hadn't eaten a hot sausage roll for years. Now was her chance.

She opened the door of the baker's with a swift ding and a clatter, to a blast of hot air and warm, fatty pastry. Salvation. Of a sort. The black car outside continued on its way as though it had nothing to report, pulling over on the opposite side of the road to collect a girl waiting on the corner. Margaret ran a hand through her hair as though everything was normal. She knew it was probably time to put paranoia to one side and get on with the rest of her life. Why else had she come north?

'Oh aye,' said the girl behind the counter when Margaret enquired. 'She's dead, isn't she?'

'Did you know her?' Margaret fiddled with a small purse she had found tucked inside a handbag in the box-room wardrobe, so old now it was practically back in fashion, with its triangular sides and chunky gilt lip. The purse was empty except for one pound fifty-three pence in small change borrowed from her mother's pension, and a tiny tin pig, all battered and scratched. Margaret wondered how many sausage rolls she could get for a pound.

'Aye,' said the girl. 'Came in two or three times.' The girl was young, well under twenty. Two or three times probably seemed like all her life.

Margaret studied a row of Empire biscuits with jelly sweets on top. She wondered how many she could get for fifty pence.

'Kind o' creepy though, isn't it? Lyin' there all that time and no one knowin'.' The girl shivered and rubbed her hands up and down her own youthful flesh.

'What kind of things did she buy?' Margaret was certain her client had to be more than tinned peas and a single orange all gone to rot.

'Mornin' rolls.'

'That's all?'

'Aye. Never anythin' else.'

'Not Paris buns?'

'P: is what?'

'Never mind.' Margaret was disappointed. Nothing more than plain white bread. Mrs Walker remained elusive.

'But it's not me you'll be needing to speak to.' The girl wrapped a single sausage roll inside a greasy paper bag and held it out to Margaret. 'It's Pati.'

'Pati?'

'Yes?'

And there, behind Margaret, was a woman curved in all sorts of places, hair peeping out from beneath a woollen tammy, tips dyed a vibrant auburn shade. 'You'll have come about Mrs Walker,' she said, two shopping bags hanging from each of her hands as though she were some sort of modern-day milkmaid. 'I've been waiting for you to arrive.'

*

In the sharp cold of an Edinburgh morning Margaret Penny discovered that Flat One, 47 Nilstrum Street was as different from Flat Two as it was possible to be. No ice on the inside of the windows. No dust rolling up against the skirting boards. No naked light bulbs dangling from the centre of every room.

Instead it was muted lampshades, soft furnishings and rugs on all of the floors. There were candles on the mantelpiece, each decorated with the imprint of a flamboyant, beseeching saint. On a coffee table was an ashtray with *Welcome to Bratislava* written around the rim. There were several collections of Russian matryoshka dolls clustered on the sideboard in small family groups. And flocks and flocks of tiny wooden animals, all polished and smooth.

On the dining table in the alcove a bowl of oranges studded with cloves jostled up against another full of incense. Jasmine and frankincense. Sandalwood and musk. It was like falling down a rabbit hole and ending up in a whole new continent, the entire flat smelling of cumin and paprika, the heady scent of cardamom seeds and garlic, chopped, sliced and fried with onion, or perhaps just eaten whole. It couldn't have been more different from Mrs Walker's flat across the cold stone close. Or the maisonette at The Court, all scented with Fairy Liquid. In fact, it was rather like the place Margaret had always imagined she might live before she ended up in a rented London apartment with hard tiles on the kitchen floor and walls like fields of virgin snow.

From the far end of the sofa, feet stretched out before a set of rotating coals, Mrs Walker's next-door neighbour gestured with an expansive arm. 'Welcome,' she said, 'to my home.'

She was wearing some sort of uniform, dark blue with a pale stripe across the bottom of each short sleeve. She looked a bit like a cleaner, though Margaret suspected she probably had a PhD in astrophysics. Biochemistry, at the very least. On her feet were a pair of mauve slippers and for a moment Margaret was envious. She hadn't found slippers in the box-room wardrobe yet, not even a fawn-coloured pair.

Pati grinned at Margaret now, a great flash of white. 'My name is Patrycja. Patrycja Nabialek. But you can call me Pati if you like.'

So names were where Margaret began. First name. Surname. Other names that Mrs Walker might once have claimed. 'Does Moyra mean anything. Or Mary? What about Ann?'

'Oh no.' Pati shook her head. 'The police asked me too, but I don't know. She was just Mrs Walker. Anyway . . .' She ran a hand across her auburn crown. 'Names don't mean anything, do they? So easy to change.'

Margaret knew this was true. You called something one thing and five minutes later it got to be known as something else. A good investment, for example, secured by champagne in the bath, only for him to turn out to be someone else's husband.

For a moment in the warmth of Pati's living room Margaret wondered if perhaps it might be better for her to return south and start over after all, build her own room full of spices and matryoshka dolls, one where her head and her feet didn't touch the walls at quite the same time. Her mother wasn't exactly begging her to stay.

'You'll be leaving soon, no doubt.' Barbara's current mantra.

Nor was she forthcoming about the past they shared.

'Nothing worth telling.'

Or about the possibilities of a united future.

'No chance of grandchildren now, I suppose.'

(Although for a moment then, Margaret had been tempted to get out a photograph of her own. Two silver-haired children in crumpled Technicolor. How easy it would be to deceive.)

But Margaret knew that one thing would only lead to another and she wasn't sure she had the strength any more to keep up such a pretence. Besides, if she stayed much longer in the cold north she felt certain she would have to tell the truth eventually. About everything she had ever lost. And what it was she had been hoping to find.

Alongside the candles decorated with saints, Pati's mantelpiece was covered in all sorts of photographs. Snapshots and portraits, family groupings in frames. Coloured ones and black-and-white ones, high gloss and sepia-tinted. A hundred faces from some other world watching Margaret's every move. Unlike her, Pati seemed to be surrounded by a million relatives. So that was what Margaret tried next.

But Pati shook her head again when Margaret enquired. 'I have no idea. I just helped with her shopping once or twice.' She leaned forward to pick up one of the chocolate fingers. 'I asked, of course. But . . .' Pati bit the finger clean in half. 'Do you have a family?' she said.

'Yes,' Margaret lied and took out the crumpled Technicolor photo.

'Lovely,' said Pati returning it after only a cursory glance. For a moment Margaret was offended on behalf of the ashen-haired woman. But then Pati offered her gift in return. 'She reminded me of my grandmother,' she said. 'Mrs Walker. Trouble, you know. Stubborn. Kept herself to herself.' Pati talked with her mouth full. Something Barbara would never have allowed. She gestured towards the mantelpiece. 'Of course, my grandmother is dead now too.'

Margaret looked over again at all the people staring at her from above the fireplace and wondered which of them was Pati's troublesome grandmother. 'Did Mrs Walker ever show you any photos, or invite you into her flat?' she asked, more in hope than any sort of expectation.

Pati licked chocolate from the side of her mouth. 'Oh no. Not even when I brought up the shopping.'

'But you were the one who raised the alarm?'

'Yes,' Pati said. 'I'd gone home for Christmas. I came back for New Year. I knocked on her door, but there was no answer.' Pati shrugged. 'I thought she was just, you know, a bit the worse for wear. Is that how you say it?'

Margaret nodded. Nineteen empty bottles came to mind. New Year in Scotland. Something else that hadn't changed much since she had been away.

Pati sighed and wiped her hand on her dark navy trousers. 'I waited a couple of days, knocked again. But it was too late . . .' She shrugged once more, a mute, regretful gesture, as though if only she'd tried harder everything might have been different.

'Where is home?' It wasn't Margaret's job to make the next-door neighbour feel responsible for a troublesome old lady who'd gone and drunk herself into the grave.

'Poland. Well, I suppose it is Edinburgh now, too.' Pati leaned back into the sofa, curling her feet up beneath her, slippers and all. Something else Barbara would never have countenanced. 'I came a few years ago. I work for Nightingales Care Service.' She laughed. 'Old people are so funny, don't you think? All those stories. It's hard not to get involved.'

So here was Barbara's bum-wiper. A member of an Edinburgh Margaret had never known. Cosmopolitan, multilingual, prepared to work hard for a whole new existence and a handful of cash. 'Do you know why Mrs Walker was in Edinburgh?' she asked.

Pati shrugged. 'This city's like that, isn't it? Attracts all sorts.' And she laughed and pointed at herself. 'I was a student back in Poland. But here I'm something different.'

Me too, thought Margaret. Receptionist. Personal Assistant. Manager of Administration. Now a refugee from the south. Nothing left but a job finding families for people who were already dead. It was one way to start over. Though Margaret was beginning to think that perhaps it might prove more useful as a quick exit if only she could get the case closed. 'Was Mrs Walker expecting you to call round when you got back?' she asked.

'I don't know. Though I said I could do her hair if she wanted.'

'Her hair?'

'She dyed it. Red, like mine. Well, more like orange.' Pati ran a hand along a thick strand of her own bright hair, lustrous and glowing in the gauzy light of the rotating coals. 'She had a recipe. At least that was what she told me. Involving coffee granules.' Pati held up her cup. 'I bought her some specially, but of course it was too late. You're drinking them now.'

Margaret coughed, swallowing hard. 'I didn't know she had red hair.'

'Have you not seen her?

'Sorry?'

'At the mortuary. I thought you would have visited.'

Dead flesh all white and frozen. A corpse vanished from a fridge. There was a story there, but Margaret wasn't sure Janie would approve of her telling it.

Pati looked sad for a moment. 'They appear then they disappear. That's life, isn't it? I see it at work often.' She glanced at Margaret across the top of her coffee cup. 'We all get lost somewhere along the way, don't you think?'

The soft whirr of the electric heater filled the room, the scent of cloves intermingling with a brief trace of melancholy that Margaret recognized before it drifted off. Pati got up to touch a photograph on the mantelpiece. A family grouping – mother, father, two daughters and a son smiling as the shutter was pressed down. 'These are some of mine, but I never even met them.' Pati gave a small wave of her hand. 'All gone, just like that.'

Margaret shifted. She didn't want to ask how that had happened. Anybody could disappear from their lives if they really wanted to. But she had the feeling that disappearances in Pati's family were likely to be eradication of a whole different kind.

Pati smiled again. 'I don't know where Mrs Walker

came from and I don't know where she went. But she did give me something.'

Margaret sat up straighter. Here it was. A birth certificate, perhaps. Some sort of letter.

'They often do that, old people, when they get near the end.' Pati was searching for something on the mantelpiece. 'Start to distribute all their possessions.'

Margaret nodded, though she couldn't say that she knew what Pati meant. The only old person she had ever known for more than a passing acquaintance was her mother. And Barbara Penny wasn't the sort of person to give away anything when she could hold on to it for herself.

'Little ornaments and things.' Pati picked up a photo in a frame and put it down again. 'How do you say it. Knick-knacks.'

A Gift from Bratislava. A whole flock of camels polished to a shine.

'We have to be careful at work though. Don't want to be accused of stealing.'

A photograph of two silver-haired children safe inside the pocket of Margaret's coat.

'Old people. A species all to themselves.' Pati picked up a photograph in a black frame and handed it to Margaret. 'Here's my grandmother.'

And Margaret found herself staring into the eyes of a woman gazing back through a thick spiral of cigarette smoke, languid yet defiant, her lips coloured dark. For a moment, Margaret wanted more than anything to see a photograph of her own grandmother – real or adopted. She missed her, all of a sudden, even though they had never even met. She handed the picture back to Pati. 'What was it Mrs Walker gave you?'

'Oh, yes.' Pati replaced her grandmother on the mantelpiece along with all the rest and drifted over to the table. 'Though it's all gone now.'

'Gone?'

What was it with this search; it gave with one hand and took away with the other.

'I had to eat it.' Pati reached towards the clove-studded oranges. 'Otherwise it would have gone off.'

Two Christmas clementines. The remains of Mrs Walker's festive theft.

Pati returned to the sofa and helped herself to another chocolate finger. 'It came wrapped in this, though.' She stretched out a hand to Margaret.

Crumpled and curled at the corners, stained with age and scented with cloves, it was another piece of paper folded into four. Margaret took the little note from Pati's fingers, before folding it out. The top of the paper was marked with an imprint – *Rose & Sons, jewellers of distinction* – while on the bottom was a name scrawled in pen. Next to that was a phone number. London calling. Margaret knew at once what this was. More of Mrs Walker's paperwork. And her ticket back to the south.

1944

Down in the depths of London at 14 Elm Row there was a war on. The one outside. And the one indoors too. Neither was pretty, but the one indoors was the most lethal for all concerned.

Two little girls, their hair tied up with fraying bows, one dumpy like a pig, the other startling, hid in the scullery away from all the rules.

'Ruby! Ruby! Where are you?'

Along the passageway in the kitchen, Mrs Penny called, while in the scullery, eight-year-old Ruby watched as her sister Barbara tried over and over to force a heavy sheet through the mangle. Down there, through the back, it was all dark stone floors and unwashed clothes, surfaces scrubbed bare. Nothing to look at but a huge, empty copper. Still, despite the cold, Ruby liked the scullery. It was the one place she could escape from Mrs Penny's cries.

Ruby watched as Barbara struggled against the weight of saturated cotton, the sheet slithering back into the sink. Barbara wiped at her forehead, then put an arm down into the grey suds and started again, face pink with effort. Ruby sat on the damp shelf opposite and swung her legs, not doing anything to help. After all, she woke every morning in their shared bed into the cold embrace of urine. Mrs Penny's rule number 109 – whoever makes the mess cleans the mess. Along with all the rest.

No cheek.

No answering back.

No swearing.

Mrs Penny always looked at Tony when she said that, sitting by the stove in the kitchen with his feet up. 'Bloody . . .' Tony choking on his rum, face flooding, while Ruby and Barbara stood silent by the kitchen dresser. Rule number 43 – don't speak unless you've got something important to say.

Five years on from Alfred's disappearance and Dorothea's sudden demise, and the house was the same, the furniture was the same, the rooms were the same. But everything else was different.

In the garden an Anderson shelter huddled in a muddy dip, dug into what used to be a perfect patch of manicured lawn. A tangle of scrawny spinach grew over the top, but not much else. Dig for Victory. Or in Mrs Penny's case, dig for nothing much at all.

In the kitchen, a tea caddy sat on top of the dresser filled with stiff little photographs of a woman holding a baby and a few old letters from America, read once before being put away for good. Also, all the relevant paperwork Mrs Penny had required to set everything straight – adoption certificates, an admissions form, the deeds to a house. All the little Walkers turned to little Pennys now.

In the pantry, a few precious eggs soaked in a bucket of preservative. Next to them a box of shrivelled potatoes sprouted with abandon, each one covered in a rash of purple eyes. Along the shelf were packets of dried milk and a bottle of cod liver oil for dosing on a Sunday with a small silver spoon. In the cupboard with the wire-mesh front lay tiny cubes of pale cheese, a sliver of butter in its

white china dish and a couple of rashers of bacon laid out
like two pieces of flesh sliced from the thigh of a child.

Upstairs in the bedroom, where once Dorothea had
brushed her hair, Mrs Penny's bottle of Innoxa sat on
one end of the mantelpiece, while at the other a Brazil nut
with the Ten Commandments scratched into its shell still
cast its spell. In the wardrobe her fawn blouse hung ready
for a special occasion, while in the darkness her suitcase
waited, should a swift exit be required.

In the spare room where the children used to play,
Tony muttered and wheezed of an evening, while under
his bed, in a box all locked and bolted, a small pile of
treasure grew. The proceeds from the first Penny Family
Business, going full throttle now.

On the landing, in a cupboard, lay a photograph of two
dead children wrapped in a torn scrap of sheet, while on
the very top floor two sisters shared a bed with a narrow
iron frame, rolling together in the night, poking each other
with sharp little knees and hot little palms. And across
from them, where once she had prayed on knees all dirty
and bruised, eighteen-year-old Clementine guarded her
lair.

Where was that girl now? Hair falling in twirls. Eyes
you couldn't look away from. Five foot eight and slender
with it. Everybody's darling. Then some more.

'I told her to be home by nine.' Mrs Penny stood at the
kitchen table thumping pastry.

'She'll be here.' Tony packed a cherished ration of
tobacco into his black-rimmed pipe.

'I hope you're not going to smoke that in my kitchen.'

'As though I'd dare,' Tony muttered, and winked at

Barbara who was staring at him from her corner by the dresser, having done the best she could with the sodden sheet, which was not much good at all.

Ruby stood by his knee. 'Tony . . .' she said, her startling eyes first one thing then another.

'Call me Father,' he said, pipe clamped between his teeth.

'Father Tony . . .'

And Tony laughed, big cheeks wobbling. 'Good one, little girl.'

Mrs Penny tutted and wiped flour from her hands onto Dorothea's apron. 'Ruby, haven't you got chores to do? And Barbara, don't stand there like a dullard. Come here at once and help arrange the tins.'

Ruby slid herself half onto the arm of Tony's chair. 'What would you do if Clemmie never came home, Tony?'

Tony patted down his jacket with one hand, searching for his matches. 'I don't think we have to worry about that, do you?'

Ruby slid further onto the chair and held out two small fists. 'Left or right?' she said.

'Eh? Right.' Tony tapped at one of Ruby's hands.

She uncurled four small fingers and a thumb to display a book of matches stolen from Tony's waistcoat pocket only a moment before. Tony grunted and picked it up, fat fingers brushing for a moment against Ruby's palm. 'Clemmie's a good girl,' he said staring now at the place between Ruby's legs where at any moment a neat little triangle of cotton might be revealed. 'She knows which side her bread is buttered.'

'Who's she out with tonight, Tony?'

'Never you mind.' Mrs Penny's voice snapped across the room from where both she and Barbara stood at the table, one with eyes glaring, the other with her jaw hung down. 'It's not your business.' Mrs Penny frowned at Tony and gave a quick jerk of her head. 'And you'll smoke that outside if you know what's good for you.'

Tony heaved himself up from his chair, dislodging Ruby from where she was perched. 'Time for a puff,' he said, lurching towards the back door. Ruby made to follow.

'Time for bed,' said Mrs Penny, standing in her way.

Upstairs, an hour later, light falling away from the sky, Ruby hung her eight-year-old body from the window in the highest, furthest room. Frightened to let go, Barbara held on to Ruby's ankles as she'd been instructed. 'What can you see, Ruby?' she asked.

The swifts. The dark clouds sliced with blue. Silhouettes walking through the streets. Ruby could see everything. All of life spread out across London, breathing and sighing in the twilight. She wished she was out in it too.

Barbara crouched behind her sister. All she could see was the dingy wall, half green, half distemper. And her sister's neat backside. 'Ruby . . .'

'Shut up, Barbara, or they'll hear.'

'*I* want to look.'

'You're too scaredy.'

It was true.

'Tell me what they're saying then.'

'I can't hear if you don't shut up like I said.'

Down, down at the far end of the street, tall and slender, Clementine Walker leaned in towards a man. Her eyes were still startling. Her breath was still sweet. But she was all grown up now.

'Well, you're a peach,' the man murmured into Clementine's ear, voice thick with several glasses of cheap gin. He moved his head in towards the perfume of her neck. 'A real soft one.'

'Mmmm,' she said, fingers travelling along the folds and seams of the man's overcoat, exploring every tunnel and twist.

The man brought up his own heavy hands over the back of Clementine's smart little jacket. 'A real doll,' he drawled.

'Yes,' Clementine agreed, sliding her palms beneath the heavy wool of his uniform and up towards his armpits, feeling for cigarettes in one pocket, perhaps one of those chrome lighters in the other, a hard little rectangle pressed against his chest.

'Like to tease, do you?' The soldier flexed his thumbs over the wings of Clementine's shoulder blades where they rippled beneath a blouse with pearl buttons down the front.

'Maybe.' Clementine arched her body away from him, a delicate curve, then stood back and held out a cigarette for him to light, slid from behind his own ear. The man stepped back too, a slight stagger, patting at his chest and pulling a lighter from the pocket on his uniform. It glinted in the twilight.

'Did you get it?' Clementine said, holding up the cigarette, fingertips painted a dark gloss.

The man flicked the lighter. 'What do you think?'

Clementine bent her face to the small flame, light flaring on her brow. 'I think you did,' she said.

The man laughed then, a sour exhalation, and snapped the lighter closed. He fumbled at his coat for a moment, reaching for an inside pocket. 'I think you're right,' he replied.

Back at 14 Elm Row, down in the depths of the kitchen, discussions were flowing. Love words and sex words and words about legs and breasts. The Penny Family Business in full swing.

Tony sloshed rum, dark and viscous, into his glass. 'Something big's coming,' he said. 'I can feel it.'

Tony was having a great war. Too old to fight. Too fat to wield a fire hose. Too contrary to wear a Home Guard helmet. He was an entrepreneur through and through. Girls and Booze and Cigarettes and Rum. Mrs Penny disliked him intensely at times. But what could she do? It was Tony who made the wheels turn.

'What did you have in mind?' She stood over the kitchen table as though it was the Allies' last defensive line, pressing a hot iron down onto Clementine's smartest blouse.

'She's got someone on the go now. Something serious.'

'How do you know?' Mrs Penny edged the nose of the heavy iron up into the pleats around the collar.

Tony sucked up some rum between his two front teeth. 'I can't breathe for the perfume she leaves behind in the hall.'

'Doesn't mean it will come to anything.' Mrs Penny

lifted the iron away from the blouse with a heft and placed it back on the hotplate. She didn't want to burn the chiffon. Never knew what treasure it might reap.

Tony made a gesture in the air, two hands in parallel curving out, then in, then out again. 'With her attributes that won't be a problem.' He laughed, wheezing and coughing up a hack of phlegm which he spat towards the fender, where it sizzled against the grate.

'Don't be disgusting, Tony.' Mrs Penny licked her finger and touched it to the heavy base of her iron, where it spat and sizzled too. 'She'll want her cut,' she added.

'Of course,' said Tony. 'Got to look after the prize.'

Upstairs Ruby sat on the bed she shared with Barbara, leaning in towards Clementine who'd slipped in through the front door like a whisper, nothing but the faintest hint of oranges lingering in the hall to let anyone know she had returned. Barbara sat cross-legged on the floor, shivering in her nightgown. She wished she could sit on the bed too, but there wasn't enough room for three. One way or another, Ruby always made sure that she got to the right place first.

'What's his name, Clemmie?' Ruby gazed up at her older sister, hair all curled and smooth.

'None of your business,' said Clementine. She put a hand to Ruby's head and touched one of those fraying ribbons. Her cheeks were still coloured from the night air outside. A faint smell of cigarette smoke lifted from her clothes.

'Is he the one?' Ruby's face was eager.

Clementine laughed at that. 'Not likely,' she said. 'He's just work. Tony wanted me to take him on.'

'Do you always take on the ones Tony wants?'

'Usually,' said Clementine. 'If they're good for business.'

'What business, Clemmie?'

Clementine looked at Ruby. 'Never you mind,' she said, lifting a fingertip to her forehead and running it along the curve of her eyebrow. 'Not something you need to know about.' Then she dropped her hand and smoothed her skirt instead, before twisting on the bed to reach for her bag. 'Shall we look then?' she said.

And two heads, one dark, one mousy, nodded in unison. 'Yes, please.'

Downstairs in the kitchen Tony dribbled more rum onto his tongue and looked thoughtful. 'Maybe we should invite this one to the house. Do the whole number.'

Mrs Penny was waiting for her iron to heat again. 'Do you think he's worth it?'

Tony shrugged. 'Could be. She's got good taste. Can smell money at a thousand paces.'

Mrs Penny pressed her fists into her waist. 'I could get a chicken.'

'Could you?' It was a long time since Tony had tasted chicken.

'Might take a while though. Two weeks, perhaps. Maybe more.'

Tony giggled then, a strange sound. 'Just enough time for her to hot him up.'

A photographic agency, that's what Tony had called it

in the beginning. Little cardboard images of a girl, all twirling hair and startling eyes, posing on a chaise longue, for any gentleman who cared to pay. He sold them in the pubs where women never went, Clementine in her short frock, hair all ablaze, socks frilled around her ankles above a pair of button-up shoes. It was a good living for a while, before she got too old.

Then the war came. And with it the first Penny Family Business. Soldiers, soldiers, soldiers all the way, lined up to take whatever they could. Clementine taking whatever she could in return. Hair curled with hot papers, lipstick begged or stolen, lines drawn up the back of her calves 'But what does she do with them?' Mrs Penny asked, though she wasn't certain she really wanted to know.

'She has some fun,' Tony insisted, though he never said how exactly.

Mrs Penny would watch as they set off every evening down Elm Row – a fat man with tobacco-stained teeth and a slender, startling girl, out to do some hunting in the middle of a blacked-out night. Mr Quinn. Mr Nolan. Mr Jones. Or other men just like them, waiting in the shadows for Clementine to walk past. She was only fourteen when it started. Mrs Penny often wondered how long Tony allowed the fun to go on before he intervened.

'Blackmail,' Tony would announce when the two of them came home, torches held low in the darkness. 'Works every time.' Then he'd laugh and pour himself a large rum to celebrate, tucking the proceeds into the pocket of his waistcoat, while Clementine disappeared upstairs with her share. Foreign cigarettes and packets of hairpins. Razor blades and soap wrapped in paper printed with flowers. Once a single square of silk.

'But what will we do when the war is over?' Mrs Penny said to Tony, standing with her own cut – a tiny bottle of eau de cologne – ready to barter with the butcher's wife for extra rations.

'God knows.' Tony sucked at the end of his empty pipe. 'Get drunk like everyone else.'

'But what if she doesn't want to continue?' Mrs Penny loved bacon. But she loved eau de cologne more.

Tony looked up towards the ceiling. 'There's always the next generation to come.'

Upstairs, two little girls and one grown one flicked through page after page of a foreign magazine. Reupholstered bras. Shining kitchen gadgets. Cars as huge as boats. Glossy pictures smuggled from the promised land where petticoats were made of real netting and lipstick came in every imaginable shade.

'I'd like to drive a car some time,' said Clementine, staring at a vehicle as sleek as the polish on a church pew.

Barbara was gazing at a picture of an electric mixer. 'I'd make cakes every week.'

'I'd eat until I was sick,' Ruby said, pausing at an advert for chocolate.

The other two nodded. They all agreed with that.

The United States of America. Land of the Free. Provider of the Brave. Supplier of soldiers for the Penny Family Business, then some more. 'One day I shall go there.' Clementine ran her fingers across an image of a man, a woman and two children sitting at a table laden with dishes. 'They look shiny, don't they?' Sitting in a kitchen with a very reflective floor.

'But how will you get there, Clemmie?' Barbara said. 'Won't it take a long time?' A land with all of those things couldn't possibly be anywhere nearby.

'By boat.' Clementine touched her finger to the picture of the mother.

'But what about the torpedoes?'

'Don't be silly,' said Ruby, pushing an elbow into Barbara's side. 'The war will be over by then.'

'How do you know?'

'It just will be.'

'When will you go, Clemmie?' Barbara sounded anxious.

'Soon,' said Clementine, her voice distant, as though she had already left.

'You'll take us with you.' Ruby's voice was piercing in the gathering dusk. It wasn't a question.

Clementine flicked the pages of the magazine closed and laughed. 'Of course,' she said. 'I'd never leave you.' Then she reached for her bag again and said, 'Look what else I got.'

Two small oranges glowing like two small suns in the gloom.

They hid the leftover orange peel the next day, scattering it inside a small brown suitcase that Clementine kept on top of the wardrobe in her room. Ruby stood on a chair to get it down, scrabbling with her fingers to try to get a grip. Barbara held on to Ruby's ankles once again, fingertips pressed tight against the bone.

'Don't squeeze so hard!' Ruby jerked her leg away from Barbara's grasp as she tried to ease the suitcase forward. The wardrobe wobbled.

'But what if someone finds us?' Barbara's fingers were slippery now.

'They won't, if you would just keep quiet.'

'I'm scared.'

'Just count, Barbara, like Clemmie showed us. *One elephant, two elephant,* all the way to a thousand.'

Barbara closed her eyes and began. *One elephant, two elephant,* all the way to . . . But she couldn't help it. Her hand just squeezed all the tighter at the thought of what Mrs Penny would say.

Ruby squeaked and kicked out. 'What are you doing? Let go!'

But it was too late. The wardrobe wobbled again. The chair tipped. Barbara just had time to panic before the suitcase came tumbling down, sliding over the edge as though from a precipice, thumping off the very top of her head. 'Ow,' she cried, eyes all swimmy. She knew she ought not to cry. But it hurt.

Ruby picked herself up from where she had tumbled to the floor too, along with the chair and the suitcase. She brushed dust from the front of her skirt and went to stand at the door for a moment to check if anyone else in the house had heard. 'It's all clear,' she whispered at last, as though they were on a mission in occupied France rather than in their older sister's bedroom. Then she came back over and lifted Clementine's suitcase onto the bed.

It was a battered little thing, all scuffed and dented, rather like Barbara's head. Barbara fingered her scalp where a bruise the size of a precious rationed egg was just starting to bloom. Ruby stretched out two small hands to the suitcase's metal clasps and pressed down. *Click-clack*, open up. The promised land within her grasp at last. Then she lifted the lid.

The suitcase was empty. Ruby stared down into its bare insides – an empty rectangle lined with blue-and-white-checked paper. She frowned, a small crinkle on her brow, then ran her hands all around the bare paper surfaces.

'What are you doing?' Barbara asked.

'Just checking.' Ruby seemed disappointed.

'Checking for what?' Barbara was whispering now, as though at any moment Clementine might come and catch them digging where she knew they ought not.

'Secrets.'

'What secrets?'

But Barbara knew already what Ruby meant. Clementine had a lover that Tony and Mrs Penny didn't know anything about. 'He's called Stanley.' That was what Ruby had said the night before as they lay in bed, knees pressed to knees, fronts pressed to backs, nibbling at their illicit oranges, licking juice from their chins. 'He gives her things.'

'What things?' Barbara had asked.

'Little cards and stuff. Jewellery.'

'How do you know?'

'Because I stole some.'

Barbara knew that was true, too. Ruby liked to steal things just because she could. Pennies from Tony's pockets. Mrs Penny's talcum-powder puffs. 'Never tell, Barbara. You've got to promise.' Holding out her hand, small palm anointed with spit. *Tell no one.* That was their motto. Though there was always something in Barbara that just wanted to confess.

Barbara stole too, of course. A lifetime's habit. She had a hidey-hole out back beyond the stump of the laburnum tree. In it there was a silver teaspoon that was part of a set and a pink pig made of tin that she had liberated from a neighbour's child.

In fact, everyone stole in their house, one way or another. The last biscuit from the tin. Scraps of coal for a cold bedroom grate. Tony smoked in the pantry when he thought no one was looking. Clementine had a drawerful of cigarette lighters slipped from the pockets of men who wouldn't dare complain. And hadn't Mrs Penny stolen them? At least, that was what Clementine said.

'Does Clemmie love Stanley?' Barbara liked to understand the order of things.

Ruby turned in the bed, forcing Barbara to turn too. 'Don't be silly.'

'Doesn't she want to get married?'

'Not married, stupid. She wants a ticket.'

'Where to?'

'To the promised land, of course.'

Now, in Clementine's bedroom, all scattered with stockings and hairgrips, Ruby lifted the suitcase and turned it over, inspecting the bottom. But there was nothing to find there either. Disappointed, Ruby turned it back and dug into the pocket of her skirt instead, pulling out a few pieces of orange peel and scattering them inside the empty case. 'Go on,' she said to Barbara. 'You too.'

Barbara looked at the small orange furls lying on the blue-and-white-checked paper. 'What for?'

'To remind her not to leave without us.'

'She wouldn't, would she?'

'Just in case.'

So Barbara dropped one little piece of peel after another into the open suitcase, scattering them like confetti at a wedding. Or petals dropped on top of a coffin as it was lowered into a grave. 'But what if it's too expensive for three of us to go?' Barbara always worried about money. Mrs Penny had taught her that.

'Stanley will pay.'

'But what if Stanley is killed?'

'Then she'll find someone else.' Ruby pushed Barbara aside and shut the case, snapping the clasps into place. *Clack-click.* She stood up on the chair once more, lifting the little case high above her head and edging it back to where it had come from. When she stepped down, her hands were all grimy. She used the bottom of her skirt to wipe them. 'Clementine,' she said, 'will never leave us.'

Barbara stared at Ruby. 'Father left us.'

Ruby pulled the chair back to where it normally stood by Clementine's bed. 'That's different.'

'And Mother left us too.'

Ruby shook her head. 'No, she didn't.'

'Where is she then?'

But Ruby was gone, slipping out onto the landing and down the stairs without any sort of reply.

*

A month later the bombs flew in like rain. Cascade after cascade, just like the soldiers who had flooded out of London into the heart of Europe only the week before.

'Bloody hell,' said Tony. 'It's the bleedin' Apocalypse.'

This time even Mrs Penny didn't tell him to mind his tongue.

The bombs whistled as they fell, just to make sure everyone knew they were coming, but without giving enough time to run away. Tony called it a sick joke. Mrs Penny called it the crime of the century – Hitler's secret weapon, sent to destroy them all at the last.

In the shelter earth fell too, showering Ruby where she sat opposite Tony and Mrs Penny, fretting about earwigs and worms and small, crawling creatures getting under her clothes. Ruby hated the shelter. It stank of damp and the stuff they used to preserve the eggs, painted onto the walls in an attempt to prevent condensation. Mrs Penny made Ruby sweep it out when she had been naughty. It was always freezing, however warm the night outside.

'Why can't we stay indoors, under the table?' Ruby complained.

'Because,' Mrs Penny said.

'Because what?'

'Because I said so.'

Rule number 20. The answer to everything. Or so it always seemed.

Ruby knew she could die in the shelter. Suffocating in wet earth and mangled spinach plants, corrugated iron pressing down against her chest. She'd rather die in the open air, night sky soaring, the sound of swifts in her ears, everything around her blazing.

'Perhaps we should sing a song.' Tony was nervous. He kept jiggling his empty pipe against his front teeth.

'Don't be ridiculous, Tony.' Even Mrs Penny seemed rattled. The bombs had been going on for a while now, night and day.

'Where's Clementine?' asked Ruby.

Mrs Penny and Tony glanced at each other then looked away. Mrs Penny brushed at the front of her dress, sweeping trickles of earth out of her lap.

'She'll be here later.' Tony fiddled with his empty pipe. 'Probably sheltering somewhere else.' He knew it was strictly no smoking in the shelter. He hadn't even bothered to ask.

'I hope the chicken's all right.' It had taken Mrs Penny a lot of bartering to organize the centrepiece of their special meal. Razor blades and soap wrapped in paper, the odd pair of stockings distributed up and down the road. She'd handed over six packets of cigarettes and even some of Tony's rum before the bird had been secured (though she hadn't told Tony that yet). Even then it was a scrawny thing, ill-fed, hardly any meat on it. Still, Mrs Penny had high hopes. Who knew what might follow once its legs and breast were offered up?

'I'm sure the chicken will be fine,' said Tony. 'After all, it's dead already.' And he squeezed out an asthmatic laugh.

Mrs Penny rolled her eyes up to the rippled, corrugated roof. 'God help us,' she muttered. And she didn't mean from the bombing.

Ruby thought about the chicken with its golden skin, roasted now and sitting to cool by the kitchen window. She couldn't remember the last time she had eaten chicken.

Then she remembered something else they had all forgotten.

'Where's Barbara?' she said.

'Ruby! Ruby! Get back here this instant.'

Ruby ran. She ran under black skies. She ran under cascades. She ran across what was left of the lawn and back towards the house. She ran to the scullery with its huge empty copper. She ran through the pantry with its packets and its tins. She ran into the kitchen with a chicken cooling on a blue plate. She ran to the parlour with its fat cherub perched on the mantelpiece, still missing an arm. She ran upstairs to Mrs Penny's room with its hairnets and its Brazil nut. To Tony's door, locked as always, box of treasure hidden beneath the bed. She ran to the highest floor of all, to the room where two little girls shared one little bed. Fat Barbara. Dumpy Barbara. Little pig Barbara. Not anywhere to be seen. Then she ran into Clementine's lair.

Outside five minutes later, and the bombs were falling like rain while Ruby stood in the street at the front of the house looking up and down the road. She heard it coming before she saw it.

WHEEEEEEEEEEEE.

And they said if that happened . . .

Run!

So Ruby did. Right towards where the rocket was about to land.

There was a whistling, then silence when it finally arrived – that moment of quiet which meant it was going to drop right on Ruby's head. Ruby stopped running then and just had time to think, *This could be it!* before down the cascade fell. Bricks and dust showering her head. Splinters of wood, of metal and of glass. Somewhere a voice calling, 'Help me!' Far away like some sort of distant echo. 'Help me!' Wondering for a moment if it was Barbara crying out for assistance, waiting for Ruby to come. Then she heard it again, right by her ear as she lay somehow in amongst the gravel. 'Help me.' Her own voice, calling over and over.

Until . . .

'Ruby? Whatever are you doing?'

Ruby woke to find herself sitting in the middle of the road, her skirt all rucked up around her waist, one shoe still on her foot, the other disappeared. Behind her, number 14 was intact. In front of her, the neighbours' house had vanished into dust. And the neighbours too. Then there was Barbara, standing in front of her, not a scratch on her fat little face.

'Ruby,' she was saying. 'What are you doing? You know we're not allowed outside when the Warning goes.'

Mrs Penny cried. Neither Ruby nor Barbara (nor Tony, for that matter) had ever seen Mrs Penny cry before. Real tears making small silvery tracks down her cheeks, all gone to ash like everything else. Their clothes. Their hair. And all the things in Mrs Penny's kitchen. Every piece of china broken or smashed.

'There, there,' said Tony, his fingers patting out a hesitant rhythm on Mrs Penny's arm, small puffs of dust rising from her sleeve. 'We'll get another chicken.'

For the chicken was ruined too. Splintered with glass blown in from the kitchen window. There was no way to salvage even one little bit. Not a leg or a neck, not a thigh or a breast. Not even a wishbone.

'Bloody bombs. Bloody Germans.'

Neither Ruby nor Barbara had ever heard Mrs Penny swear. They stared at her from where they stood by the corner of the kitchen dresser, shrouded in plaster dust like a pair of ghosts. Everything was all topsy-turvy. These really were extraordinary times.

It was bread for supper, the butter speckled with grit of some description. But they didn't complain. Ruby was still hearing everything as though it was very far away. Tony was brushing up glass and swearing under his breath. Mrs Penny just sat in a chair and didn't do anything.

They spent that night hunkered down in the parlour, protected by its curtains, thick and green. Mrs Penny snored and Tony wheezed and Barbara lay silent as though she were already in a grave. She hadn't said a word since she had appeared like magic and told Ruby off. Through the gloom Ruby watched the way her sister's eyelashes made small, mousy curves upon her plump cheeks. Barbara could sleep through anything; or so Ruby thought.

Ruby didn't sleep at all. At least, that was how it seemed. All night in her mind she ran and ran through the tall, narrow house again, in and out of the coal-hole, the scullery and all the other rooms, looking for something she'd missed but couldn't quite recall. It was only when dawn crept into the room under the thick green serge that she remembered. Clementine's suitcase. Gone from the top of the wardrobe, just as Clementine was gone too. And the house opposite. A gap into which the sun shone and the rain fell and the wind blew for many years to come.

PART THREE

An Emerald Dress

ADMISSIONS RECORD

DOROTHEA WALKER née STIRLING

Patient Admission No: *641*

Date of Admission: *24 August 1939*

Any previous Admissions: *None*

Occupation: *None*

Date of Birth: *18 July 1900*

Place of Former Abode: *14 Elm Row, London*

Bodily Condition & Mental Disorder:
*Physical health poor. Somewhat emaciated.
Hair very long. Tendency to bite if feels
threatened. Often refuses food. Hallucinations.
Uncertain of surroundings. Constant wandering.
May require restraint.*

Cause of Insanity: *Death of twins.*

Signed (Director): *Dr Gilbert Sanday*

Witness: *Mr William Nye, solicitor*

2011

London by train was an unexpected delight, luxury Margaret had almost forgotten existed (even of the second-class kind). Only a few short weeks since the Beginning of the End, and already she had raised herself from the indignity of the overnight bus and got herself a seat on an early train to the south. As they rushed towards the great metropolis, Margaret ate smoky bacon crisps from the trolley and wondered if perhaps the life she had led for thirty years was not yet over. Paperwork had its uses, just as Janie had declared. London had called Margaret and here she came.

The trip was unauthorized. But then Margaret understood that her whole job was unauthorized in some way. Off the proper books. A woman whose life was discarded over landfill, chasing a dead person with no discernible past. Other than a piece of paper wrapped around an orange, something which suggested that, however she might have ended up, Mrs Walker once had the wherewithal to pay.

One emerald necklace.

Two earrings to match.

A brooch in the shape of a star.

Margaret had phoned in advance, of course. She was expecting a shop assistant, or a manager perhaps: Rose & Sons, jewellers of distinction, but got something different instead.

'William Nye & Sons, solicitors.' The voice down the wire was low and circumspect. And somehow Margaret wasn't surprised that her search for paperwork had conjured a lawyer at last.

'I'm calling regarding a Mrs Walker,' she said.

'Mrs Walker?'

'From Edinburgh.'

The voice hesitated for a moment, then moved on smoothly. 'May I ask who's calling?'

'Margaret Penny.'

The hesitation this time was more pronounced, the woman's tone when she spoke again burnished with caution. 'To whom do you wish to speak?'

Margaret frowned. 'To whom do you think I should speak?'

'I'll put you through to Mr Nye, shall I?'

'Yes,' said Margaret and was placed on hold.

'No, dear. No.' Mr William Nye's voice when it came on the line ebbed and flowed like a distant sea. Margaret strained to hear. 'Never had a client from that place.'

'Oh,' Margaret said. 'That's disappointing.' Mr Nye was rather old, she could tell. 'Perhaps one of your colleagues . . .'

'One of my colleagues, yes, yes. But no, they don't either.'

'Oh.'

'Sorry not to be more helpful. Got to go now. Call by if you're ever down this way.'

Mr Nye's voice drifted off and the receiver was replaced. But before Margaret could put down the phone at her end there was a click on the line and she heard those caramel tones once more. 'Ms Penny. I'll look forward to meeting when you come down. I've made an appointment.'

The pause stretched out between them, two women breathing alongside the hollow echo of something left unsaid. It was Margaret who broke first. 'I'll look forward to it as well.'

She paid for the ticket with a previously engineered sleight of hand – an expenses form liberated from Janie's desk, the younger woman too busy rummaging in her drawer for a Yale-type key to notice anything untoward. Before she left that first time, Margaret had weaselled out the finance department in the basement just like a woman who used to be Administration Manager for a financial services firm. There was no hiding place where free money was concerned, not for Margaret Penny, anyway, not any more.

She handed the form in herself. 'Not regular procedure,' said the Finance Officer, plucking at a spot on the underside of his jaw. But Margaret just pointed to where she had forged the signature in the relevant box. 'Oh, Mrs Maclure,' the young man nodded, stamping the form and reaching for his cash box. 'She used to work for this department.' It was the Edinburgh Way, working in Margaret's favour once again.

Four and a half comfortable hours later (no drunks, no sticky seats, no paper bags to be sick in), and Margaret stepped from the train in her stolen coat, straight into the pulse of London. People and noise and bustle and fuss. An explosion of everything she had missed. She took a breath, filling her lungs with grit and fumes, sweat and effluence, the dirty, slushy air of a city always on the move. Then she breathed out, pushing away that grey place in the north, frozen forever beneath its frigid dome of ice. As she gripped her small blue holdall ready for action (four pairs knickers, spare bra, toothbrush and a bottle of something called Innoxa borrowed from the back of her mother's bathroom cabinet), someone barged past her, not even bothering to turn and make amends. But Margaret didn't mind. Unlike Edinburgh, where not much seemed to shift from one day to the next, in London everything changed every hour, every minute, every second almost, everybody moving from one thing to the other without giving the past a second glance. Margaret knew what it meant. She could be whoever she wanted to be in London. And if she didn't like that, she could be something different instead.

Nye & Sons solicitors was tucked into a tiny backstreet on the fringes of the City. Just off Ironmonger Lane; Dickensian but real. Its entrance was marked by a narrow black door with a brass plaque polished almost to oblivion. Far above Margaret, glass towers loomed, windows glittering with pale January sun. But down at street level the plaque shone with a dull light, *William Nye & Sons*, worn down to a shadow of its former self. One more of a dying breed, Margaret thought, running her finger over the soft dimpled surface. Then she pressed the bell.

The man who opened the door was old. Really old. Beyond decrepitude. Practically a cadaver. Margaret stood on the doorstep, the waft of decay drifting towards her, and wondered how it was exactly he still stood. This solicitor must be nudging ninety years old, overdue for the pit or the furnace a long time since.

'Mr Nye?' she said.

The old man frowned as though this had once been his name but he couldn't recall if it still was.

'Mr William Nye?'

Before dipping his head in agreement, hand tight on the doorknob as though to hold himself up: 'Senior,' he said, his voice quivering.

Mr William Nye Senior, solicitor of a very ancient kind, was wearing full undertakers' garb: black jacket, black trousers, black waistcoat with six black buttons. He was tiny inside them, all skeleton and not much else. Margaret wondered if he wore old-fashioned braces under his waistcoat to hold everything in place. The old man's trousers ended well above his shoes. And his jacket was fastened out of sequence, one side hanging lower than the other. Margaret was sure that he would mind if he knew.

'Margaret Penny,' she said holding out her hand. The old man blinked, his eyelashes almost bald. He swallowed once, Adam's apple bulging against the tight buttoning of his shirt. A little rime of saliva had gathered at the corners of his mouth like a small tide of salt. Margaret tried not to stare. The old man didn't offer his hand in response, so she dropped hers. 'You said to call by. If I was in the neighbourhood.'

Mr Nye's fingers twitched on the doorknob. 'Margaret Penny,' he murmured. 'In the neighbourhood.'

'May I come in?'

'Come in?' Beneath his tight collar Mr Nye's skin flushed the faintest hint of turkey red before returning to its almost translucent state. 'Yes, yes. Of course.' He shuffled back to let her enter, both he and his sombre outfit merging to one against the dark interior wall.

Margaret ducked as she stepped through the door into a narrow passageway, squeezing past the old man to a hint of raw onions and boiled meat. The floor was a crazy maze of tiles, all chipped and broken. Paint peeling from the walls. But beneath the decrepitude there was a cold elegance that told Margaret everything she needed to know. There was money here, or had been once. But more importantly, there was paperwork. Dictated, notated, marked, boxed and filed – little pieces of paper guarding the secrets of those who wished to flannel and obscure. Margaret knew that she was getting close to something at last.

The passage gave way to a tiny room, low plaster ceiling bowed at its centre as though filled with the accumulated secrets of two hundred years. Just like the passageway, the whole room was made of shadow. In one corner a standard lamp threw out an ineffective cowl of light. There were books, lots and lots of them, looming from ceiling to floor. On the mantelpiece there was a stoat, stuffed, with a tiny hole in its skull. The stoat regarded Margaret through two black eyes, one winking, the other dull. From beneath the lapels of her stolen coat a fox winked back.

The biggest item in the room was a huge mahogany desk, nothing on it but a blotting pad and three telephones with large circular dials. There was no sign of the woman with the circumspect tones. The prehistoric Mr Nye edged past Margaret to stand behind the huge desk himself, knuckles pressed deep into the blotting paper, hands trembling with the effort of keeping himself up. 'I wasn't expecting a visit so soon,' he said, his voice a remote echo of what it must once have been.

'Just passing,' Margaret lied.

'Do you live in London?' Mr Nye peered at her, pupils glimmering like tiny bits of grit.

'No,' Margaret said. 'Well, yes . . .' The stoat eyed her too. 'Well, sometimes.' She tailed off.

'Sometimes,' repeated Mr Nye, as though this slippery answer was all he might expect from a woman like her. The tip of his tongue protruded for a moment from his almost non-existent lips. 'Well . . .' he said. 'I suppose you'd better follow me.' He scrabbled with one of his cadaver hands towards an edition of British Bankruptcy Law volume 9, grasping and pulling at a section of bookshelf that revealed itself as a door. Open sesame, thought Margaret, to all the paperwork Janic could ever desire.

Mr Nye's inner sanctum seemed even smaller than the room outside. Another bulge in the ceiling. Another leering lamp. But what really filled the space was what hung on the walls. Paintings. Hundreds of them (or thereabouts). All shapes and all sizes, from skirting board to cornice. A thousand naked women staring at Margaret.

Behind her there was a movement in the air, a faint expulsion. Mr Nye appeared to be laughing. Not a joyful sound. 'My collection,' the old man said, shutting the disguised door with the faintest of clicks. 'All my girls.'

At least that was what Margaret thought she heard him say.

Mr Nye shuffled himself behind another huge desk. 'I would offer tea . . .' He pressed a finger to his temple, where a squiggle of blue beat out a continuous thrum.

'Don't worry.' Margaret thought it unlikely that William Nye knew where the kettle was kept, let alone the teabags. What mattered here was business, not the niceties of cake.

Mr Nye's finger pressed a small dent into his skin. 'Mrs Plymmet usually does that kind of thing.'

'Mrs Plymmet?'

'My assistant.'

The woman with the caramel tones.

Mr Nye Senior gestured to a chair on the opposite side of the desk. 'Please sit down.'

The chair was very upright. An improving, Sunday sort. Margaret eyed it for a moment then did as she was told. 'Is she working today? Mrs Plymmet, I mean.' She held her ancient handbag tight in her lap as though to protect herself against some sort of unspecified threat.

'Today . . .' Mr Nye pushed his finger along what used to be his hairline but was now just an extension of the naked dome of his head. 'Yes, yes. But I think she's out.'

'And your colleagues?'

'My colleagues . . .'

He seemed confused. Margaret understood at once. There were no colleagues, not of any sort. She changed tack. 'Do you come into the office every day?' Mr Nye couldn't deny that he was well beyond working age.

'Not every day.' Mr Nye glanced around the room before letting his gaze return to Margaret once more. It was surprisingly steady for a man with tremors everywhere else. 'But I like to come and sit with them once in a while.' He gestured with a shaky hand to the naked women on his walls, breasts and ankles and hipbones (amongst other things) all thrusting themselves towards where Margaret sat.

'Is one of them your wife?' Two could play the kind of game Mr Nye seemed to enjoy.

The old man gave a sort of cough, licked at the crust of white around his mouth. 'No, no. They're . . .'

Margaret eyed the walls again. 'Yes, they're very . . .'

Dirty. In more ways than one.

Mr Nye's thin lips stretched back over what remained of his teeth. Margaret couldn't be sure, but he seemed to be smiling. 'Do you still collect?' she said. No reason not to be polite.

'Occasionally.' Mr Nye flicked his eyes towards a small empty space on the wall to his left. 'Now and then.'

Margaret looked at the space too. 'My mother has one that would fit perfectly there.'

Small and brown, propped up against the box-room wall.

'Your mother.' The old man slid his eyes back towards her. 'Does she live in London too?'

But Margaret hadn't come all the way south to discuss the contents of her mother's box room. 'How about your son?' she asked. 'Does he collect?'

'My son?' The old man's eyes gleamed for a moment, needle points in the gloom.

'Nye & Sons. I thought . . .'

Nye Senior blinked twice. 'There are no sons.'

Margaret knew when a line of conversation had been cut. She decided to get on with the reason she had come. What difference did a son lost or found make to her? 'My client,' she said, reaching for the slim brown folder. 'Mrs Walker.'

She waited for the polite denial of such a person's existence. But it never came. Instead Mr Nye crouched forward in his chair, hands trembling, tongue tracing the line of his faint top lip. 'Yes. Mrs Walker,' he said. 'Why don't you tell me everything you know?'

On the train south Margaret had done a résumé for Mrs Walker in the hope that it might prove more elucidating than she knew it really was.

Shopped at Costcutter, always wore a red coat, dyed her hair red too, smoked Supersize, enjoyed whisky, paid in cash. Thief. Was anywhere between seventy-five and eighty-five years of age (or thereabouts). White skin, blue lips, liver like paste. Wore a skirt, a knitted cardigan, nylon tights, and owned a green dress with sequins along the hem. Left behind an orange on a plate, half a tin of peas, and some sort of nut with something indecipherable scratched in its shell. No paperwork to speak of other than a sheet of newsprint detailing Births, Marriages and Deaths, and a jewellery receipt.

As they passed the Angel of the North standing broad and proud on its hilltop, Margaret had wondered what would be left of her should the worst come to the worst – a catastrophic derailment, carriages crashed and mangled, everybody inside crisped to a stick. There'd be nothing to identify her but the remains of a red, stolen coat and a photograph of two silver-haired children who should have been hers, but weren't.

She hadn't even said goodbye to her mother, just slipped out of the front door onto tarmac glistening with frost and headed to the train station before anyone else was awake. No black car waiting in the car park to see Margaret go – nothing pursuing from her past. And she didn't bother to leave a note. How long would it take to raise someone from the dead? A day? Two days? Or a lifetime, perhaps. There was a certain thrill to it. Running. Reminding Margaret of the person she had once been. And could be again, perhaps. For as she'd hurried up the hill away from her mother's blue-and-yellow lilo, Margaret had known that this could be the new beginning she was after. Besides, what was it Barbara always said? *Leave no trace.*

Through the wall in the small outer office of Nye & Sons solicitors, one of three large phones began to ring. Margaret stopped reading through her list of objects lost and found, thieving habits and a jewellery receipt scrawled with the solicitor's phone number many years before, and waited for someone to speak. A hundred women (or thereabouts) looked down on where she sat.

'William Nye & Sons, solicitors.' Liquid vowels seeping through the wall.

'Ah, Mrs Plymmet.' Mr Nye pushed his thin lips once more into what constituted his smile and waited in silence until they both heard the receiver being replaced. Then he pressed a button (also disguised) on the underside of his desk. In the antechamber a bell sounded and a voice echoed through.

'Yes?'

Mr Nye's voice echoed back. 'Mrs Plymmet, will you come in, please.'

Mrs Plymmet entered from behind Margaret's chair. 'Oh, I'm sorry. I didn't realize you had a client.'

'Not a client, Mrs Plymmet.' Mr Nye indicated Margaret. 'But a visitor from the north.' He made a small sound that could have been amusement, or perhaps something else.

Margaret turned in her chair. 'Hello,' she said.

Mrs Plymmet coloured, just the faintest of blushes under her orange skin. She was old too, but not as old as Mr Nye. More sixtyish than ninety, rings rattling on her fingers where the knucklebones stood out.

'Mrs Penny is enquiring about a Mrs Walker,' said Mr Nye. 'I was about to assure her we have never had any clients of that name. Can you confirm?'

'Yes, Mr Nye,' said Mrs Plymmet, and bent her head in accord.

'Thank you, Mrs Plymmet. That will be all.' The old man dismissed his assistant as though he still came to work every day and told her what to do, rather than the other way around.

Then he leaned forward across his desk and studied Margaret in a manner that made her feel as though he could see right through her red, stolen coat. 'I think that's everything too, don't you?' He pointed to a piece of headed notepaper that had suddenly appeared on the desk in front of them. 'But if you'll write your address here. Just in case. I wouldn't want you to miss out if something should arise.'

Margaret had one last go as they stood on the doorstep,

the old man holding her hand for a brief moment with a surprisingly tight grip. 'Why do you think your phone number is written on the jewellery receipt?' she asked.

But Mr Nye Senior was already retreating, disappearing back into the dark.

Margaret's real appointment happened in a place not twenty minutes' walk from Ironmonger Lane, in the dark corner of a monumental gallery, in front of a painting covered in a savage sweep of oil.

'Very valuable,' the warder said as he led Margaret further and further along a marble corridor towards the designated meeting point. 'Out of fashion for a while. But worth a lot now.'

The girl in the portrait was impossibly young, laid back on a green chaise longue, skin flaring like the centre of a jet of gas. She was naked apart from a pair of green shoes, legs laid out all this way and that. Her eyes followed Margaret wherever she stood.

Margaret waited beneath the strange apparition for ten minutes until the real reason for her visit to London appeared – the details of the appointment written out on the back of a Nye & Sons business card and slipped into her hand as she left. Brisk and resolute, clattering down the marble corridor without a backward glance. A Londoner through and through, hands clasped tight around a bag, hair a helmet of dazzling bronze. She wore a coat that belted in the middle and ended just above two bony knees. The lines around her mouth were set as rigid as her hair, the result of a thirty-a-day habit since she was barely out of her teens. Jessica Plymmet, come to keep her word.

As she approached, Margaret put out a hand for a welcome shake. But just like Mr Nye, Jessica Plymmet kept hers to herself. So Margaret dropped her hand once more and got on with business. She was in London, after all. Who had time for the pleasantries of life? 'Thank you for meeting me,' she said, forgetting for a moment that it was Mrs Plymmet who had arranged to meet her.

Mrs Plymmet dipped her head in a gesture that suggested it was nothing. 'Your mother was kind to me once,' she said.

'My mother?' That was not the introduction Margaret had been expecting.

'I wrote just before Christmas with all the news – an old friend looking to be in touch.' The older woman adjusted the collar of her coat. 'You meet all sorts of people in the law.'

Solicitors and Associates. Clerks and Partners. Complainants and Complainers. Secretaries toiling away through the back. Barbara had told Margaret often, as she was growing up, how tiring it was to drudge away for fifty years in the service of the courts. But she had never mentioned an acquaintance down in London.

'I didn't know you knew my mother.' There was an opportunity here if Margaret wanted to take it. The first person in thirty years who might reveal something about her past.

But that wasn't why Mrs Plymmet had come. 'The phone number . . . on the receipt,' she said. 'May I see it?'

'Of course.' Margaret opened her slim brown folder and took out the receipt from Rose & Sons, jewellers of distinction.

Mrs Plymmet took the ancient piece of paper, all crumpled and curled, and studied it carefully. 'It's our number,' she conceded, as though Margaret needed this confirmed.

'Do you recognize the handwriting?' Margaret asked.

'No.' Mrs Plymmet looked away.

'But why do you think your number was written there?'

'Just in case.' The older woman stared at Margaret for a moment as though daring her to ask more. 'And look what happened.'

She was right, of course.

Margaret took out her photocopied sheet of Births, Marriages and Deaths, unfolding it carefully to reveal a dusty nut and a flutter of paper scraps detailing a series of girls' names. 'Do these mean anything to you?'

Mrs Plymmet frowned down at the nut. 'No,' she said.

And this time, Margaret believed her. More or less. She folded up the photocopied news-sheet, all its treasures inside, then closed the slim brown folder. For a moment the two women stood in silence, Mrs Plymmet staring at the painting on the wall beside them, Margaret staring at her.

Then the older woman said, 'I have something you might be interested in.'

'Oh yes?'

'It's not much.'

'But there is something.'

Mrs Plymmet dipped her head in acknowledgement and slid a hand beneath her coat. She paused for a moment before pulling out a faded cardboard wallet, tied with a ribbon that must once have been a deep shade of pink.

'What is it?'

'The Walker file.'

And Margaret felt it at once. That tingle that began in her fingers and travelled like mercury straight to the centre of her heart. 'Where does it come from?' she asked.

'From the filing cabinet, of course.'

'Mr Nye denied having a client called Walker.'

Mrs Plymmet made another gesture, unmistakable in its dismissal. 'He's a very old man now. Not what he used to be.' For a moment her eyes glowed, the colour of a tiger's hide, before she turned them back towards the folder in her hand.

Then Margaret understood. Here was a woman just like her. Receptionist. Administrator. Personal Assistant in more ways than one. A dish on the side that never quite became the proper meal. Margaret gazed at the large diamond that adorned the third finger on the older woman's right hand. At least Jessica Plymmet had got something useful out of her arrangement. Not just a single, working lady trapped by the follies of her youth.

'It may not be relevant.' Mrs Plymmet held the file out towards Margaret. 'But I thought you ought to have it.'

Margaret reached to take what was being offered. Mrs Walker within her grasp once more.

But the other woman hesitated, just for a moment, before releasing the Walker file into Margaret's care. 'It's important, don't you think?' she said, glancing at the painting once again. 'To honour one's debts where one can.'

1961

Ruby with her eyes so bright, a stone more precious when cut, steeped in blood much thinner than water (buckets of the stuff), wandered around the gallery as though she owned it. Which, in a way, she did. For tonight it was her looking down from all the walls. Legs all this way and that.

She shimmered as she walked, slithering through the crowd in an emerald dress cut high at the neck, landing just above the knee. She was only twenty-five, but she sashayed through the throng as though she knew all there was to know of life. Then some more.

Mr William Nye Senior thought he knew all there was to know of life too. A vibrant man with vibrant hair and a thirst for the unusual in amongst the orthodox. Also a scar on his back where shrapnel had once pierced his insides. 'Lucky,' declared the doctor in the army hospital as he dug at the wound. But William Nye Senior knew even then that it had more to do with being in just the right place at just the right time. The mess left behind by the man standing next to him taught him that. Afterwards it was simply a matter of grasping life when it came.

He watched now as Ruby slid through the crowd towards where he stood – a young woman in need of nothing but a jewel or two to offset the gleam of her hair. Mr Nye delighted in young women and he delighted in art. Here, the two merged. From high on the wall a naked Ruby gazed down at him, dashed onto the canvas with thick sweeps of oil. In the portrait Ruby wore nothing but the same pair of shoes she had on now.

'Her azure veins. Her alabaster skin. Her coral lips. Her snow-white dimpled chin.'

Rape of Lucrece. How apt. Though it was the girl's eyes that really made the point.

Another young woman standing next to him turned with a frown. He hadn't meant to speak out loud, but it seemed he had. The young woman was shorter than the model on display, with a rounder face and hips, pink spots already visible on her cheeks. Her hair was set in a perm, though she couldn't have been much more than twenty-five herself. 'Sorry, did you say something?'

'Shakespeare,' Mr Nye said, giving a slight dip of his head.

The young woman blushed, then blinked. 'I don't . . .'

'Never did it at school, eh?'

The young woman was about to reply, but Mr Nye Senior had already turned to look the other way.

School had been dull. School had been regimented. School had been a place to bear, day after day, like home now, until she could work out how to get away. Barbara, also dressed in her best but unremarked upon and dull, gazed for a moment at this vibrant man with his vibrant hair and then, like him, at her twin.

'Come to the opening,' Ruby had said when they met on their usual bench, in the usual rain. 'It will be fun.'

'I don't know, Mrs Penny might not like it.' Barbara had sat with her coat all buttoned and her handbag clipped shut.

'Who cares what Mrs Penny thinks!' Ruby wore a mackintosh with a belt, a black jumper rolled high up her neck. Even in the drizzle she still managed to dazzle, her slender fingers parsing an orange as though they were one and the same. 'You've got to have some fun, Barbara. I've said so a thousand times. Come and work for Mrs Withers. I'm sure she won't mind.'

Barbara watched the long curl of orange peel as it fell, unregarded, to the wet ground. Out, out, she thought, into the light, into the world, where one can eat an orange whenever and however one likes. 'I can't,' she said. 'Mrs Penny doesn't have anyone else.'

'She has Tony.'

'Tony won't last forever.'

'Neither will you.'

Barbara blinked as a raindrop caught her eyelash, the world suddenly blurred. She could imagine what Mrs Penny might say if she went to join the opposition. 'Good riddance to bad rubbish!' Just as she had done all those years before when they discovered Ruby had gone east, preferring to carry buckets at Mrs Withers' behest rather than their own.

Even then, Barbara had wondered if Mrs Penny meant her too.

'What's she ever done for you, anyway?' Ruby was sucking at a segment of orange as though it was a lollipop.

Barbara stared at the fruit between Ruby's lips. Mrs Penny had never left, that's what she had done for Barbara. Three storeys and a coal-hole, all still intact. The only person who actually needed Barbara, whereas Ruby had never needed anyone but herself.

Still, where had it actually got Barbara now that she was grown? A job opening the door to stricken women, taking their coats and carrying out buckets of their leftovers that they couldn't face themselves. For a moment, sitting in the rain with a piece of orange sticky in her hand, Barbara felt all hot and clumsy. Ruby was right. What was she, after all, but the recipient of a lucky coronation penny that only ever fell to tails.

'All right then,' she said to her sister. 'I will.'

When the night came Barbara sat in her room on the highest, furthest floor and unscrewed the lid of a shiny bottle of nail polish as though it was the most precious thing of all. Barbara didn't normally wear nail polish. It always rubbed off with the wash. But this time she painted her fingertips one by one, three careful strokes in a fashionable shade – Pink Goddess – to match the pink of her cheeks. When she was finished she sat on the edge of the narrow bed waving her hands to dry the nails off, before going downstairs to iron the best dress that she had.

'Where do you think you're going?' Mrs Penny sat by the kitchen table sorting buttons into one box and spools of cotton into the next. She still expected to know everything about anything happening in the house in Elm Row, even though there were hardly any of the original Walker family left.

'Out,' said Barbara pressing the iron down onto more self-sewn pleats.

'Who with?'

'A friend.'

Mrs Penny paused in her sorting and leaned forward

in the chair to rub at her legs. 'It's not a boy, is it?' She had varicose veins now, dark threads stitched through her skin.

Barbara lifted the heavy iron and stood it on end. 'A boy?' she said.

'A young man then. You know fine what I mean.'

Barbara flushed, an ugly shade, curling her freshly glossed nails in towards her palms. 'No,' she said.

But Mrs Penny sat back, satisfied that she had understood. 'As long as you're here for the morning appointments. Don't want to have to answer the door myself.'

Mrs Penny might be running a house for desperate women. But she didn't want anyone to think she was desperate herself.

Barbara lifted the dress from the ironing board and shook it out carefully. They both regarded the handmade garment: pinched waist, flared skirt, modest neckline. Not that much different from the one she'd made for the coronation all those years before. Both of them noticed that the hem was not as regular as it might have been.

'You'll need a cardigan.' Mrs Penny always wore a cardigan. Brown, two pockets dangling by her hips. 'Freeze to death otherwise.'

Barbara folded the dress over her arm, taking care not to crease the skirt. 'I won't. I'll be fine.'

'Don't say I didn't warn you.' Mrs Penny still liked to have the last word. 'And don't be late back, or the door'll be locked.'

When she left the house at 14 Elm Row that night, Barbara took a cardigan after all. Best to be prepared. She hurried to the bus stop, gloves on, coat buttoned to the neck. In her hand she clutched a purse. On her mouth she had applied her lipstick with care. Barbara had never been to an art opening before, or anything of that nature. She wasn't sure what to expect. Either way, when she finally arrived, she had never imagined what she would see. A thousand naked Rubys staring down from every wall.

'I'm sorry.' The man next to her turned now to where she stood, a brief touch of his fingers on her arm. 'I didn't mean to offend.' His lips glistened for a moment in the sparkle of the gallery spotlights as though he had been licking them clean.

Heat prickled up and down Barbara's arm where his fingers met her sleeve. She wished she hadn't worn a cardigan after all. 'No,' she said, the small spots on her round cheeks colouring up. 'It's just . . .' She waved a hand in Ruby's direction. 'My sister.'

'Oh.' The man was surprised.

'Yes.' Barbara took a sip from the wine glass clutched in her hand. It tasted sour. All men were surprised, one way or the other.

'And you are?' The man had removed his hand from Barbara's arm now.

'Barbara,' she murmured into her glass. 'Barbara Penny.'

'And she is?' The man gestured to the paintings on the wall.

Barbara angled her head towards her naked sister, then back to where a young woman in a green dress shone bright in the centre of the room. 'Ruby,' she replied.

Mr Nye Senior blinked, raised a hand to his vibrant

hair to smooth down its vibrant curl. Then he began to smile. Not a matter of luck, but the right place at the right time. Such was the way of Mr Nye's life. For he had met these girls before, in another time, at another place, their faces like small moons staring down at him from the highest, furthest floor of a tall, narrow house. And another child too, screaming, 'Mummy! Mummy! Mummy!' as his father (the original Nye Senior) shouted instructions in his turn. 'Not like that. Like this. Like this!' The woman's bare feet twisting in his hands.

The girls' mother had been screaming too as they carried her out, nightgown dragging in the dust. She almost bit his father on the wrist. 'God damn it!' As she called out over and over, 'No! No! No!' until they got her into the car.

He had been a young man then, barely eighteen, not yet pierced by searing metal and the knowledge that one must grasp life when it came. He had just been following his father's orders as he helped manoeuvre the woman into the back seat.

But he did remember this. How her nightgown had concertinaed up. The revelation of her long, pale limbs. The shock of the cleft at the top, hair all curled and coarse, and that slice of flesh all glistening and pink, exposed between the crevice of her legs. William Nye had never seen beneath a woman's clothes before then, and certainly not like that.

As instructed, he had tried to hold the woman still against the car's leather seats as she writhed and twisted. Blood had raced through every part of his body as he gripped on tight, pressing a crescent of small, white tattoos into her flesh. She flailed and kicked like a wild thing, hair all this way and that. He hadn't been able to contain her, thought she must get loose, until someone at the open car door gave a slap, *smack-crack*, and then the woman had flopped like a dead thing, her head all crooked, her limbs all slack.

The car door had slammed shut and they'd driven through the darkness, him sitting with the woman's feet limp in his lap. He hadn't tried to pull down her night-gown, or smooth her hair. Or cover up the crevice of her flesh. Instead he rode with her as she was. Exposed.

Ruby made it through the crowd to them at last – an older man with a gleam in his face and her twin sister standing awkward in a home-made frock. She bent towards Barbara and kissed her on the cheek. Barbara started, almost pulled away. Since when did they do that? Then Ruby stood back up and waited to be introduced. 'Barbara,' she said. 'How nice of you to come.' As though she hadn't been the one who invited her sister in the first place. 'And this is . . . ?' She let the sentence trickle away. All along the bottom of her frock a row of sequins winked and blinked like a thousand tiny eyes to match the startle of Ruby's own. She smelled of oranges. And beneath that, the linger-ing scent of linseed oil.

Barbara turned to introduce the man in return, but he had failed to tell her his name. 'I'm sorry . . .'

'Mr William Nye,' he interrupted now. 'Solicitor.' And he held out an elegant hand.

'Charmed.' Ruby slid her own small hand into his palm, letting it rest there for a moment like an injured bird.

Mr Nye raised Ruby's hand to his lips and said, 'The pleasure's all mine.'

Then Ruby slipped her hand away and turned to her sister once more. 'Come outside, Barbara,' she said. 'I want to smoke.'

'You can smoke in here.' Mr Nye was already holding out a packet, the white tip of two cigarettes pulled clear. One for him. One for Ruby. None for Barbara with her crooked hem.

Ruby frowned, then linked her arm through Barbara's as though they did it every day. 'No thanks,' she said. 'My sister and I prefer to be alone.'

Outside, away from the gallery's bright glare, down a side alley that felt much more like home, Barbara pulled out a packet of Craven A from her bag and lit two cigarettes at once. She sucked hard at the pale filters, then handed one to Ruby where she was lounging against a rough wall. 'I didn't know you smoked, Ruby.' Barbara pulled the cardigan closer around her shoulders and glanced at her sister's fingernails, where a neat neutral slick shone in the dark compared to the garish gloss of her own.

'Everyone smokes.' Ruby held the cigarette to her mouth for a small sup, before letting it hang loose at her side. 'Besides, you never asked.'

Barbara pulled at her own cigarette, eager for the rush. Ruby was right. Smoking was everywhere. Even Mrs Penny enjoyed an occasional Kensitas now and then when she thought there was no one to see.

The two sisters stood side by side in the darkness, Ruby trickling smoke from her nostrils. 'What do you think of the show?' she said.

Barbara flicked some ash onto the dirty ground. 'It's all right.'

'All right?'

'There's a lot of you on display.'

Ruby laughed. Rule number 23 – modesty in all things. 'Does Mrs Penny know you're here?' she asked.

Barbara ignored the question. 'Does the artist pay you?'

Ruby's cigarette gave a gentle crackle as she inhaled. 'That's one way of putting it.'

Barbara frowned and inhaled too. Rule number 5 – always make sure one is paid the going rate.

'He said I could have one of his new paintings, though.' Ruby tapped ash away to her right, a small shower of grey.

'What are they like?'

'Small. And brown.'

This time they both laughed. No one who had ever met Ruby could possibly describe her in such a way.

'Are they valuable?' Barbara couldn't imagine art being anything but the province of the rich.

'I shouldn't think so. He's devastatingly poor.'

'Why do you do it then?'

'Because he asked me.'

Barbara shivered inside her cardigan. This was forever the difference between them. She would always say 'No'; Ruby would always say 'Yes'.

'Besides, he might be useful in the future.' Ruby blew a small cloud of smoke up into the night air. 'Anyway, enough about him. What do you think of Mr Nye?'

'Mr Nye?' Barbara shrugged. But she could still feel the

tingle of his fingers where they had pressed through wool to her skin.

'I've met him before, you know.' Ruby rubbed at the sprinkle of ash on the ground with the tip of her green shoe.

Barbara drew smoke hard into her lungs. 'He didn't say.'

'He probably doesn't remember.'

'Where was it then?'

'At Mrs Withers', of course.'

Eight years since the young queen was crowned, and still Mrs Withers preferred to answer the door herself. 'Just in case,' she would say. 'Should I wish to refuse.'

Ruby's job had always been to wait through the back, down the corridor in the dark, a shadow person holding coats one moment, scrubbing out stained enamel bowls the next. She would wait as the bell rang, watching Mrs Withers hurry to survey her guests as though she hadn't expected them to call. 'Mr and Mrs Smith,' they would murmur as they entered.

The difference with him had been the voice. Those elegant vowels, loud and precise. And the fact that he wasn't afraid to announce himself as himself.

'Mr Nye,' he said.

'Of course.' Mrs Withers had even given a slight dip of her head as she stood aside to let him pass.

Ruby knew at once what it meant. This man was money, from his thick hair to the polished tips of his shoes. Here was a man who paid – for inconvenience, for things best left unsaid. What mattered to him would not be the cost, but that he got what he wanted first.

From where she stood in the dark Ruby could practically taste it, the banknotes passing from one hand to the next in the front room, followed by the ritual of whisky poured into cut glass. She had seen it through the keyhole many times, though she had never yet been invited inside. Eight years, and still Mrs Withers did not trust her with those grubby pieces of paper. Though she encouraged Ruby's liking for spirits every single night.

Just inside the front door on the cold tiles of the hall, the girl who had arrived with Mr Nye faltered as though afraid to progress. She was dressed as if she might be going to church, in pale-yellow gloves and a matching hat. Ruby emerged from her place in the shadows trying not to laugh. She couldn't remember the last time she had worn a hat, if ever. It was more the kind of thing her sister Barbara might own.

Ruby touched the girl on the arm. 'Hello,' she said. 'I'm Ruby.' The girl was trembling all over. She seemed even younger than Ruby had been when she first came to stay in Mrs Withers' house, nothing to her name but a Brazil nut and a towel turned grey by the wash. Ruby held out her hand. 'Shall I take your gloves?' she said.

The girl looked at her hands, startled, as though she hadn't even realized she had put the gloves on. Her face was bleached, nothing but shadows and shapes. She pressed a bag to her stomach as though to protect it. Too late, thought Ruby, too late. 'Perhaps your hat?' she said.

The girl gave a quick shake of her head as though if

Ruby took her gloves or hat she might take something else more precious too. Then she began to weep.

'She was only sixteen.' Ruby plucked a tiny strand of tobacco from her lip. 'At least, that's what Mrs Withers said. I thought she might have been even younger.'

Barbara drew a thick slug of smoke into her lungs. 'Mrs Penny wouldn't allow it.' Rule number 42 – married ladies only. Even those who had managed to get themselves pregnant in ways they wished they had not. Barbara had a sudden urge for a glass of rum to sweeten the filth as it all washed down.

Ruby laughed. 'I bet there's not much money in that now Tony's getting on. No one to charm them onto the chaise, either before or after.'

Barbara shrugged. Ruby was right. Women didn't come flocking to Elm Row in quite the way they once had. Tony was huge now. His fingers were stained. He drank too much. But he still threw winks at Barbara from his place by the stove – the only man who ever had.

'You should ask him for a job, Barbara.' Ruby took a last pull at her dwindling cigarette.

'Who, Tony?'

'Mr Nye, of course.'

'Why would I do that?'

'He's a solicitor.'

Barbara frowned. 'What use would a solicitor have for me?'

'You're a drudge, aren't you? Might as well drudge for him as for Mrs Penny. At least you'd get a desk.'

'Why don't you ask him?'

Ruby tossed the remains of her cigarette into the gutter. 'Maybe I will, but it won't be about a job in his office.'

Barbara dropped her cigarette as well, two bright little stubs rolling together in the dark. 'What do you mean?'

Ruby stretched out her elegant shoe, crushing out both little flares. 'You'll see. He's worth much more than that to me.'

Back inside the gallery, hot now and filled with a fug of alcohol and smoke, Mr William Nye Senior stood in front of a painting. Ruby with her arms all this way and that. Ruby with her legs thrown down. Ruby with her startling eyes staring right back. The kind of girl one could fall in love with, if one didn't take care.

The artist, a man with a half-grown beard and old-fashioned shoes, stood by Mr Nye's side. He was only young, but he liked to pretend that he knew much more than he did.

'This one, I think.' Mr Nye pointed.

'A good choice.' The artist nodded.

Between them the two men considered the savage strokes of paint.

Mr Nye leaned towards the small label attached to the wall. 'What's it called?'

'*Bucket Girl Number 3.*'

'Bucket girl?'

The artist laughed, biting for a moment at one of his fingernails where it was ingrained with dark paint. 'It's what she does. Spends her days carrying buckets of blood. Like a butcher.' Then he laughed again.

Mr Nye Senior saw the thin stain of red around the top of Mrs Withers' bowls before she carried them out. 'Do you paint her often?'

'Yes. She's my current inspiration.' He turned to Mr Nye. 'Would you like to see more?'

'I can come to your studio perhaps?'

'Yes, that would suit.'

The two men shook hands. Both of them understood. Everything was for sale, if the price was good enough.

'Buying another painting, Father?'

'Ah, the prodigal.' Mr Nye turned with a small smirk of distaste to a tall gangle of a young man standing behind him, glass of water in his hand. 'Where have you been?'

'At the office.'

'You work too hard, boy. Got to get out, grasp life while you can.' Nye Senior gazed at his son for a moment, then past him to where Ruby was weaving her way towards them again. The men all turned at her approach.

'Who's this?' Ruby said as she arrived. Barbara trailed in Ruby's wake.

Mr Nye Senior gave an inconsequential wave of his arm. 'My son, William Junior.'

'How charming.' Ruby didn't even wait for the young man to put out his hand, just reached in and kissed him on both cheeks.

William Junior's colour rose to beetroot before Ruby had even pulled away. 'Pleased to meet you,' he said because, well, that was what one did.

Ruby laughed. 'The pleasure's all mine.'

Mr Nye Senior glared. The artist snorted wine into his glass. Barbara stood behind her sister and frowned.

'Oh,' said Ruby waving her arm in an inconsequential way too. 'This is my sister, Barbara.'

The young man, hardly even twenty-one, turned to Barbara and put out a hand. 'Pleased to meet you. I'm Will.'

Barbara put out her hand too. 'Yes,' she said.

Both their palms were damp.

As they shook, the rest of the group somehow glided away and they were left to fend for themselves – little pig Barbara, all grown up now, and the graceless Junior Nye, nothing between them but a thousand naked Rubys gazing down from every wall. The younger Mr Nye, awkward and angled, watched Ruby traversing the room with his father by her side. He unravelled a large handkerchief from his pocket and gave his temples a wipe. Why was it exhibition openings were always so claustrophobic? Even his feet felt hot. Ruby's little row of sequins winked at him from across the distant floor. 'Does everyone know your sister?' he asked Barbara.

'No one knows my sister,' said Barbara. 'Not even me.'

Three weeks, and in the artist's studio Ruby laid herself out on the chaise longue, the cover rough beneath her naked flesh. A tiny emerald hung loose on a thin gold chain around her neck, spooling between her breasts. She closed her eyes as Mr Nye Senior leaned forwards to arrange her limbs – her legs, her arms, her hips laid out just so. His breathing was heavy as he hauled himself on top, trailing a finger from her collarbone to the pale ring of her nipple, then down across her stomach to her hips. These he fitted under his own with a confident hand.

Beneath his own hot limbs, Mr Nye Senior felt the sharp edge of Ruby's hipbones rising in a desultory fashion to meet his own. She smelled of death, that was what he thought. Of the soap which Mrs Withers used to wash all her girls. He thrust once, then twice, as beneath his chest a small emerald pressed sharp into his skin. Thrusting again, head bent, he saw once more the pearls embedded in Mrs Withers' neck. The thick mounds of her arms. Mr Nye Senior liked flesh. A wad of it. Easy to grasp. But Ruby's flesh was almost impossible to hold, all splayed and white, slithering beneath him like some sort of fish. He thought of the woman in the motorcar, her feet all limp, and grunted as he came, a generous spurt. Once, twice, three times, pulling out at the end. His sperm trickled down Ruby's leg to stain the cover of the chaise. Her startling eyes regarded him as he rolled away, first one colour, then the next. Beneath her skin he could feel already the azure that ran cold in her veins.

Three weeks, and Barbara and her longing and her solicitor's son (forever Junior, however old he got) were engaged in a damp embrace in a seaside boarding house. There was nowhere to wash but a small sink in the corner. The bed was hardly wider than the one she had slept in as a child, two sisters embracing, knees tucked in behind knees, breath hot on the back of the other one's neck.

Barbara kept her eyes open the whole time they did it, watching the ceiling, the walls, the light bulb and the curtains with their small blue flowers as they danced and tipped. It was Nye Junior's first time. And hers too. He fumbled with where to go. Got it wrong more times than not. Pushed and pinched at Barbara's soft flesh as he plunged and bucked about. His body was taut and bony, all skinny and flat, while hers was plump and florid, like a girl brought up on a farm.

As Nye Junior hung over her like a crab, bumping against the frame of the bed, Barbara knew that he was thinking of it too. Ruby, head back. Ruby, legs spread. Ruby waiting for it all. Not of a hand-sewn dress with a crooked hem and carefully ironed pleats, but a twist of orange peel and the scent of a warm neck pulsing for a moment next to his own. Still, as Nye Junior finally pushed his way in, once, twice, three times, before he gasped and it was done, Barbara thought of all the good that might come from their awkward embrace.

A father sitting by a fireside.

A mother sewing buttons on a shirt.

While upstairs, on the highest, furthest floor, a child would be smiling as it turned over in its sleep. Not a trap, as her sister, Ruby, might call it. But a family, all of Barbara's making. One that she could keep for herself.

2011

The building on the outskirts of London was as grey and austere as the residents trapped inside. A train ride away from the centre of it all (on the periphery once again), and Margaret came to her next destination – an old people's home stuffed full of ancient, incapacitated humans left by their relatives to die. It would not be an edifying end to finish in a place like this, nothing between her and her Maker but slop spooned from a plastic bowl. But then, as Margaret was discovering, most ends were not edifying, however it was they came.

The Walker file had not proved edifying, either. Or not as much as she had hoped. A thin cardboard wallet with nothing in it but a copy of an old admissions form.

'Where's the rest?' Margaret had asked Mrs Plymmet, turning the cardboard wallet this way and that. No birth certificates. No marriage certificates. Not the sort of paperwork Janie had hoped for at all.

The woman had just shrugged, tightening the belt on her coat as though she really ought to be getting away. 'Destroyed,' she said. 'Or perhaps there was never anything else.'

'But you're certain this is the same Mrs Walker as my client?'

'Well, it's the only Mrs Walker that we have on our books.'

The form had been as stained and yellow as Mr Nye Senior's teeth. It dated back to just before the war. Seventy years, give or take, ancient history as far as Margaret was concerned. There was certainly nothing in it that referred to a Mrs Walker of around her client's age.

But there was an address. A home for the elderly out on the fringes of London, a last outpost for its residents before the certainty of death. Also a name. Dorothea Walker. Someone new raising her head to gaze at Margaret from the shadow of the past.

The manageress of the old people's home met Margaret at the door. 'Pleased to meet you,' she said. 'Mrs Fielding. But call me Susan. Do come in.' She was wearing a smart tailored suit of jacket and matching skirt and, as she led the way indoors, she gave off the faintest hiss of nylon rubbing against nylon. An echo of Barbara, pursuing Margaret from the north.

The entrance hall was a strange combination of the institutional and the grand, a floor clad in vinyl and a ceiling as high as a house. The smell of industrial detergent lingered in the air, punctuated by a whiff of something floral sprayed from a can. Nurses and staff from all continents criss-crossed the wide floor, some wheeling trolleys, one pushing a cart covered in plates, more wielding bedpans and trays full of pills. They appeared from one passageway and disappeared down the next, bustling in soft-soled shoes, while somewhere, out from the very fabric of the building, Margaret was sure she could hear voices calling, high and plaintive, rather like the sounds of children playing outside Mrs Walker's flat.

'Welcome to my Home!' Susan Fielding smiled as though she owned all that she surveyed, urging Margaret through to a small office partitioned off a section of the hall. It was a space not unlike Margaret's box room up north, but crammed with paperwork this time rather than wall-to-wall with junk.

Susan Fielding sat down behind a utilitarian desk, rearranging her suit to make sure it didn't get creased, and said, 'So you've got an indigent, have you?'

'Yes,' Margaret replied. 'Maybe. That's what I'm trying to find out.'

'A Mrs Walker. About eighty or so?'

'As far as I can tell.'

'Well . . .' Susan Fielding tapped at a blue plastic ring binder on the table before her. 'I've checked my records and no one of that name or age appears to have stayed here.' She frowned as Margaret raised a hand. 'Or a Dorothea, if that was what you were about to ask.'

'Oh. That's a pity.' Margaret was disappointed. She'd only been in the home for a few minutes and already her one lead had dropped to nought.

'Yes, it's a shame,' Mrs Fielding agreed. 'I like to help out if I can. Especially with those left all on their own.'

'Do you get a lot of them?' Margaret hadn't imagined an indigent rota being required in a place as imposing as this.

'Oh, yes.' Susan Fielding leaned back in her chair for a moment. 'I've been to more funerals than I can count where it's just me and the crematorium officer to see the person out.'

'But what about their relatives? Don't they attend?'

'Often there aren't any. Or they're impossible to trace. Or our clients have simply outlived them. It happens more than people think.' Susan Fielding gave a little shake of her head. 'They say we all die alone, don't they? But these people do so more than most.'

'These people?'

'London attracts them.'

'Who?'

'The neglected. The abused. The abandoned. The lost.' Susan Fielding ticked the categories off on her fingers as though they were a register of museum exhibits rather than the collected remains of the human race. 'They have to end up somewhere and this is where they come. We try to look after them as best as we can.' She paused for a moment, plucking something from the lapel of her jacket. Then she looked at Margaret. 'And you, Ms Penny, do you live in London?'

And for the first time since she returned south, Margaret wondered if London was the advantage she had once thought.

Margaret had been six years old (or thereabouts) when she and Barbara landed in the northern city that became the only home she'd ever properly known. Thumbnails bitten to the raw, still wetting the bed at night more often than not. 'Don't worry, runs in the family,' Barbara always used to mutter, but it was still Margaret who was made to strip yet another rented bed of yet another urine-stained sheet.

'Why do we have to move again, Mummy?' she had asked as they sat in another launderette watching the sheet circle inside an industrial-sized washing machine. She already missed the dirty heat of London summers. The rumble of Underground trains like monsters growling beneath the streets. And once a man who tickled her, while upstairs all the babies cried.

'Because – ' Barbara swiped her headscarf at Margaret's thumb where it was stuck in her mouth – 'we just do.' Whatever else Barbara had once been, she was Mrs Penny now.

They came with a battered suitcase and they never left. Over the hills and far away. The latest in a series of anonymous, rented rooms strung out from south to north, nothing but barely furnished bedrooms and knickers left to drip-dry into the sink. Carpet sweepers and tinned soup. Buckets of Flash and ten pence pocket money for the corner shop. Parma Violets in see-through wrappers and the soggy cardboard of a Sherbet Dip.

'Will we stay this time?' Margaret asked as they packed up the suitcase once again and made their way to the last bus north.

'Perhaps,' said her mother. Which, Margaret discovered later, was about as good as it was ever going to get.

They arrived in a cold and huddled Edinburgh to a flat that was all high windows and gaping ceilings stained with damp. Except in the narrow bathroom, where the ceiling was low slung and clad in an orange kind of pine that turned out to encourage mould. At night the Edinburgh wind rattled through the ancient window frames, keeping Margaret awake. The floors were covered by a cheap kind of carpet that created electricity when she rubbed at it with her socks. The furniture came from second-hand junk shops, so battered Margaret could have scratched, stabbed, burned or gouged out filthy messages on the underside had she not feared that Barbara would find out at once. She

slept between yellow nylon sheets from the nearest Wool-
worths and an eiderdown that her mother seemed to have
owned for a hundred years, hoping beyond any realistic
proposition that she would not pee again in the night.

The flat was on the third floor of a tall, black tenement
that wept water when it rained. High above a bookie's
and a pub, six flights of dark, narrow stairs. It was noisy
day and night with constant buses, the shouts of gamblers
and drunk people advertising their lack of anything better
to do. The neighbour who shared the landing with them
took in men for a living. The woman on the floor below
never answered the door. For food there was a chip shop.
For pleasure there was a pub. Also a sauna that Barbara
insisted Margaret run past when she made her way to
school.

The children on the street congregated around the
door of the close when they discovered a newcomer had
appeared: bare legs, dirty skirts, trousers too short at the
ankles. 'Where are you from?' they said, picking at their
noses and wiping their fingers on their grey school
V-necks in a way that would have horrified Barbara if she
could see.

But Margaret never did know the answer to that.

Now, at the residential home for the abandoned down
south, Susan Fielding offered coffee. 'It helps with the
workings of the mind, don't you think?' she said, going to
a cupboard and taking out two mugs and a bowl of sugar
lumps. Though Margaret preferred red wine for that.

Just as in Pati's wonderland of a flat, a small coterie of
objects lined Susan Fielding's desk. A miniature china dog.

A stone painted and varnished with a picture of edelweiss. There was even a pair of silver sugar tongs that belonged in an Edwardian tea party rather than on an office desk. Keepsakes. Mementoes. Reminders of the dead. Or a horde of useless objects left behind by those with no one else to take them on. Margaret ran her thumb over the smooth surface of a tiny matryoshka doll secreted in the pocket of her coat. Did Mrs Fielding inherit all these treasures, she wondered. Or was acquisition just a perk of the job?

Susan Fielding reached for the tongs, plopping one lump of sugar into each of the steaming mugs as though they were small pets that needed to be fed. 'Hot and sweet, Ms Penny. Hot and sweet.' The tongs glinted under the bright office lights as Susan Fielding's teeth glinted too. The manager turned one of the cups towards Margaret, before taking a small, satisfied sip from her own. When she put the mug down the trace of her lips was marked out on the thick china rim in a sort of orange kiss. 'Now,' she said, moving a pile of paper from one side of her desk to the other. 'Shall we get on?'

Margaret put down her mug. 'But I thought Mrs Walker wasn't in your records.'

'Oh, I don't mean her. I mean Dorothea.'

'But you said she wasn't in there either.'

Mrs Fielding gave a shake of her head. 'Oh, you won't find Dorothea amongst these records.' She tapped at the blue folder with one determined finger, then turned towards another pile of files. 'Dorothea was one of the dispossessed.'

*

Awkward. Recalcitrant. Unwholesome. Mad. Before it became a residential palace for the elderly, the Home had been something else instead. An asylum with long corridors and tall, echoing rooms; beds stretching out from wall to wall. ECT and insulin treatment. Lobotomies and drugs. One thousand patients wandering the wards with no one to mark their passing but nurses dressed in starch.

'All gone now, of course.' Susan Fielding waved a hand in the air as though she had swept away the crazy people herself.

'What happened to them?' Margaret was intrigued. Lost to the earth, to the sea, to the four winds north, south, east and west? Or an armchair, perhaps, in an empty Edinburgh flat.

'Dispersed,' Susan Fielding declared. 'Or buried in the grounds.' Her voice dropped lower. 'Or cremated and disposed of somewhere else.'

Disposed of. That was one way of describing what happened once the blue jets of gas did their job.

'And Dorothea Walker?' Margaret was still hopeful that this, her only lead, would result in some solid revelation.

'Mad as a hatter,' Susan Fielding declared. 'Died before they could throw her out.'

'Throw her out?'

'Classic care in the community. All the rage in the Eighties – help them to help themselves.' Susan Fielding shifted in her chair; another slither of nylon beneath her skirt. 'It's much better now, of course.'

A waft of bleach sifted through the thin partition wall, mixed with a bass note of stewing steak burnt to the bottom of a pan. 'When did Dorothea Walker die then?' Margaret asked, wondering if it really was true that things had improved so much.

'1980.'

A small silence hung in the air between them. 1980? 1980 was the year Margaret had fled from that silent, unforgiving city in the north to this big, sprawling city in the south. Seventeen, with nothing but a pair of black boots and a canvas satchel slung across her hip. It seemed impossible that she should ever have been alive when Dorothea Walker was too. 'But the admissions form is from 1939,' she said.

Susan Fielding paused for a moment as though counting each of those years too. 'Yes,' she frowned. 'Dorothea Walker lived here for more than forty years.' Then she hurried on. 'Alas, nothing remains of her now.'

Lost to the wind, to the sea, to the air.

'Except . . .' The manageress flicked her eyes to the stack of files piled up on one shelf.

'What do you mean?' said Margaret.

'The thing is, I really ought to see proof.'

'Proof?'

'Of your relationship to the deceased.'

'But I don't have a relationship with the deceased.'

'Then your letter of permission – from a personal representative of the dead.'

A personal representative of the dead? But it wasn't a message from beyond the grave that Susan Fielding wanted. It was paperwork, of course.

Margaret rummaged in her bag and brought out the slim brown folder. Out of that she produced a copy of a letter with bubbles over the *is* that provided her with all the authorization she might need.

'Yes,' said Susan Fielding after a brief perusal. 'That will do.' Then she stood and went to the door. 'Maricel,' she called to a passing nurse. 'Can you ask Beverley to come to my office straight away, please.' She turned back to Margaret. 'Maricel comes from the Philippines,' she said with a smile. 'One of our best.'

Beverley didn't come from the Philippines, or anywhere else. She came from Neasden. 'Lived there all my life,' she said as she led Margaret past fire doors and cleaning cupboards, small staffrooms and emergency exits of all kinds. 'Never fancied anywhere else.'

Margaret pursued Beverley down the long corridors, pursued herself by the faintest trail of biscuits gone stale and disinfectant bought in bulk.

'Have you come for me?' an old lady wearing a sagging nylon dress whispered to Margaret as they crossed through one of several lounges, shuffling and sidling close enough to hook one knobbled finger onto Margaret's red, stolen coat. The old lady wore a thin cloak of melancholy that Margaret recognized at once.

'Now, now Mrs Storey,' Beverley said, turning back. 'No prisoners today, love.' She unhooked the old woman's finger and held the door for Margaret as they went out. 'Thinks you're her daughter come to take her home,' she said as they moved on past cold ceramic tiles that curved their way up the walls.

'Does her daughter visit much?' Margaret looked back

over her shoulder to where Mrs Storey was now staring at her through a panel of reinforced glass.

'She hasn't got a daughter.'

They continued down more corridors, past rooms with doors firmly closed and others ajar, Margaret catching glimpses of men and women bent low in their chairs, rocking and murmuring, or standing still and silent in the middle of a room as though uncertain which way to go now they had come to the end of their lives. This could be Barbara before too long, she thought, obese and incapacitated, hair diminishing rapidly, stuck forever in a bed. Either that, or with some kind of disease eating away at her lungs, stranded in a hospital ward as she wheezed down to her last. Then again, in not so many more years, it could be Margaret too, nothing to her name but a pair of elasticated trousers and a ragged fox fur around her neck. After all, not everyone would have someone like Beverley to see them out. Neasden. That promised land. It made Margaret wonder if perhaps her retreat from the north had been a little too hasty.

'And where are you from?' Beverley stopped all of a sudden at a locked door, turning to look round at Margaret as though she had read every one of her thoughts.

'Edinburgh,' Margaret replied. The alternative seemed too difficult to explain.

'Lovely city,' Beverley said, turning back. 'If a little cold.'

Dorothea Walker's file had been cold too, a case long dead (rather like the patient herself), ready for the shredding machine several years since. It contained a record of the last forty years before she died – her admissions number, her medical condition and several different diagnoses of the status of her mind. All of these seemed to have changed over the years, requiring a range of treatments as the fashions in therapy changed too. Shocks. Baths. Drugs. Basketmaking. And finally the talking cure (but the latter only once it was all too late). Eventually they seemed to have left Dorothea alone to wander the corridors at will, a guinea pig rotting slowly at the bottom of its cage. Then, when the next innovation was in the air (turn them out to fend for themselves), Dorothea did the sensible thing and died.

There was no hint of a previous life, of any family member left behind to grieve. As with Margaret's client, Dorothea's past was nothing but a land enclosed by mist. Once here, now gone, nothing much in between that anyone had seen fit to record. There was paperwork, just as Janie had specified, but none of it was of any use.

Still, even though it was over thirty years since Dorothea had turned to dust, it didn't feel sufficient to hand back the file and leave by the front door. This dead woman was the only link Margaret had to a more recent corpse up north.

'Did anyone know what Dorothea was like?' she asked as she closed the madwoman's file, more from desperation than anything else.

'Oh, yes.' Susan Fielding picked up a glass paperweight from her desk as though to study its heft. And the care assistant from Neasden came into her own.

Beverley had met Dorothea Walker.

Margaret was surprised. 'You don't seem old enough.'

'Oh, bless you, love, but I am. Started here in '79 when I was just a young thing. Nearly sixty now!' Beverley was clad in a uniform of daffodil yellow with dark-green piping down the legs. It clung to her generous fifty-something curves in a way that was flattering rather than not.

'Beverley is one of our longest-standing employees.' Susan Fielding gave an ambiguous smile. 'She remembers them all.'

'I try my best.' Beverley leaned up against the side of Susan Fielding's desk, making herself comfortable amongst all the memorabilia of the lost.

'What was she like? Can you remember?' Margaret was interested now.

Beverley raised her eyes to the strip light suspended from the ceiling. 'Oh, she was sad. Sad. Always brushing and brushing at her hair.'

'We like to keep their hair short now, if possible,' Susan Fielding interrupted, a hand to her own well-calibrated cut.

Beverley continued as though Mrs Fielding hadn't spoken. 'Silver, it was. All about her like a cloud.'

'Did she talk much?'

'Oh, yes, dear, but not so as you'd understand. Same thing over and over. "My angels, my angels."' Beverley raised her hands to the ceiling as though she too was calling down the heavenly host.

'My angels?'

'That was what she called them. Her little twins what died.'

'Was that why she was here?'

'Who knows, dear?' Beverley gave a shake of her head. 'Could be anything in those days.' Susan Fielding cleared her throat as though to indicate the time for questions was over, but Beverley wasn't finished yet. 'Used to sing too. "Oh my darling." Do you know it?'

And for a moment Margaret thought the care assistant from Neasden might break into song. Ruby lips and forty-niners. Kisses for little sisters.

Susan Fielding obviously thought so too, for she stood up all of a sudden and pushed back her chair. 'I think . . .'

'Did anyone visit her?' Margaret pressed on. She didn't want to lose what could be her last chance.

'Not that I remember, dear.' Beverley shook her head. 'But then I wasn't on shift all the time.'

'But what about when she died? Did she leave anything behind?'

'Oh no, dear.' Beverley stood up now and smoothed the trousers of her uniform. 'She never had a thing other than what the hospital provided. Her solicitor dealt with it all at the end.'

William Nye of Nye & Sons solicitors. Slowly rotting in his cage now, too.

Susan Fielding went over to the door. 'Thank you, Beverley. You've been a great help.' And she held it open to show her longest-serving care assistant out.

'Then again,' Beverley said, propping herself back against Susan Fielding's desk, 'there are the boxes.'

'The boxes?'

'Everything the patient brought with them when they first arrived.'

Down, down they went, deep into the bowels of the residential home, the smell of damp intensifying the further into the basement they got. They passed through a series of square spaces, each darker than the next, full of old chairs and tables with only three legs, wardrobes with doors missing and empty yawning insides. Eventually they came to a wooden door with a lock all painted in black. Beverley took a large key from the pocket of her uniform. Two hands. Two turns. And it moved at last. 'Open sesame!' she said.

They had arrived in a small and dusty room stacked from floor to ceiling and back again with junk. A replica of Barbara Penny's box room up north. No emergency exits. No windows out into the light.

'It's stuff from the old hospital.' Beverley touched her hand to a switch at the side of the door and a dim light glowed yellow in the darkened space. 'Some of it was on display for a while on the balcony over the dining hall. But then *she* arrived . . .' Beverley pointed to the ceiling. 'After that it was all packed up.'

Earthenware plant pots. Porcelain soap dishes. Giant thermometers. Whistles on strings. Heavy woollen uniforms. Ceramic bedpans. Ledgers of all sorts.

And these.

'Admission boxes,' Beverley said. 'I found them one day when I was down here rooting around.'

Margaret peered at the pile of solid wooden boxes. 'What's in them?'

'Oh, all sorts. Clothes. Jewellery. Purses and combs. Things that the patients brought with them when they first arrived.'

And there it was again, that prickle through every one

of Margaret's bones. This wasn't paperwork. It was something much more precious than that.

It took Beverley three goes before she got the right pile, dust smeared all down the front of her uniform, though somehow Margaret felt certain that the care assistant from Neasden wouldn't mind a bit.

'Thank God she was one of the last,' Beverley said when she finally hauled out a wooden box all battered and scratched, handing it down to where Margaret was waiting to receive. They both craned in to look as Margaret opened the lid, kneeling at the altar of a woman long dead in the hope that she would illuminate an old lady more recently deceased.

A nightgown with pink ribbon threaded through the neck.

A hairbrush with a handle made of bone.

Two US dollar bills, soft as rags.

And an envelope, unsealed.

Margaret picked up the envelope. It was light as air. A single-page will, perhaps. A birth certificate. A letter with an instruction from the dead. In fact, inside was this:

Three locks of hair, faded now. Blonde. Mousy. Dark. Each tied with a piece of ribbon that had once been pink, too.

Margaret and the care assistant from Neasden gazed at the little cuttings of hair in silence, as though trying to decipher some message sent back from the past. Then Margaret said, 'Why three?'

'What do you mean?'

'You said twins.'

'Oh, yes.' Beverley took the envelope from Margaret

and peered closer inside as though the answer might be there (which it was). 'She used to say there was another, coming to take her away. Never did, of course. We thought she'd just made her up.' Beverley gazed into the dark vault of the basement ceiling. 'Now what was the name?' she said.

An orange decaying on a plate. A jewellery receipt wrapped around a Christmas gift. Margaret stared down at the three little locks of hair.

Oh my darling.

'It wasn't Clementine, was it?'

'Yes.' Beverley's face opened up. 'That's it. Clementine. How did you guess?'

1944

Clementine Walker, lithe as a deer and just as fast, ran through the dark with her torch held low. Just off the train, she was late again, but didn't care one bit. She would not be going back to 14 Elm Row tonight. Nor ever again, if her plan worked out. Far to the east bombs fell, a *woof woof woof* as they hit, followed by the *yap yap yap* of the guns in reply. The streets were deserted; people fled to the comfort that was underground, knee to knee inside their corrugated huts or huddled on platforms deep below the road.

But Clementine showed no fear as she ran, no inclination to dodge from porch to porch or any other street-level shelter she could find. She preferred the open air to the enclosed. The clouds. The stars. The trees as they loomed up out of the night. Fires on distant rooftops. Sirens wailing. The constant drone of planes. Clementine liked the thought that one moment she might be here, and the next she might be gone. Besides, she had an important appointment to make.

Out of a side alley a warden appeared, holding on to his tin hat. 'Get to cover, Miss!'

But on she ran. Eighteen and fully grown. Hair tamed and curled. Eyes that saw it all. Running along the pavements in her silent shoes towards the heart of a city she no longer called home.

The soldiers who had swarmed through the streets only the month before were all gone now, vanished into battle across that short stretch of sea between two warring coasts. Out beyond the narrow channel they had marched their way to glory or been left to roll and lurch in the surf; wading through water, seaweed clinging to their boots, shooting their way across the dunes, or ending their lives face down on a cold French beach.

As Clementine ran through the dark she thought of them all. The patina from their fingertips on her neck. The rough press of their uniforms up against her chest. She'd been busy for weeks anointing each one with whatever he needed before moving on: their chins resting in the cup of her collarbone, faces buried for a moment in amongst the lustre of her hair. She'd loved each of them in those moments. Now she couldn't remember any of their names.

Except . . .

In the nook of a pub, hidden away in the lounge, they had sat knee to knee as he spoke about what was to come. 'They won't tell us, but we all know. It'll be France. The big one.'

Stanley Shaw. Face like a pale harvest moon, glimmering with sweat and something else too. Belief in the Almighty. And his plan.

'The bombs'll start after we leave. A week perhaps. A few days. Who knows?'

Soldiers on beaches, wet sand in their mouths. The whistle of bullets piercing a thousand chests. Men sunk in shallow water, rifles clogged with salt.

Clementine pressed her knee close against Stanley's as though to ward off the worst. But Stanley shifted slightly, the two of them still touching but not quite as tight.

Unlike every other man Clementine had ever met, Stanley Shaw had never put a hand to her in a way that he ought not.

'What should we do when it happens?' said Clementine, moving her knee close again.

Stanley's fingers were loose on his pint glass. 'Be prepared,' he said.

And Clementine knew at once what he meant.

Where was that photographer now, the one who twirled his buttons as he pressed the shutter down? Lost already, perhaps, beneath battlefield mud. Or fallen through the cold night air to land in an unlikely, foreign place. Sunk to the bottom of an ocean, lying covered by a pall of silt. Or waiting in a pub just like this one for the announcement they all knew would come. *All infantry. All pilots. All sailors. All men. Rise up and head for France.*

All around Clementine smoke drifted and coiled in the air. From a corner someone barked a laugh, too loud, suddenly cut off. In the saloon a song had started, running ragged through the throng, rising and falling, petering out for a moment until someone picked it up again with a shout. Tight in her hand Clementine clasped the small tumbler of gin that would have to last her all night. It was warm, the liquid thick in her throat. She placed her other hand on Stanley's arm and said, 'Tell me again about home.'

In the nook of a pub, hidden in the lounge, Stanley Shaw spoke. Of plains as wide as the sky. Of wind sweeping through corn. Of horses, sleek and brown, galloping along endless wooden rails. For all of Clementine's life everything had been narrow and dark, cluttered with people's secrets and their promises that never worked out. A house full of rooms that started as one thing and ended up as something worse. A mantelpiece scattered with berries. A head shorn and prickled. A coal-hole that dirtied her hem. Also a penny circling in the darkness. Heads to the future. Tails to somewhere else.

Stanley Shaw spoke on. Of beans lying in a colander. Of tomatoes as big as his hand. Of two boys sitting at a table and, behind them, a man and his wife. And looking down on everything from its place on the wall, a small stitched sign in a frame: *God Loves Us All.*

The gin trickled and burned its path down Clementine's throat as she listened to everything Stanley had to say. She knew what she was being offered. The promised land, within her grasp at last.

Down, down in the shelter, in a hole dug deep into the dirt, eight-year-old Ruby sat listening to the bombs, while far away in the centre of the city her sister Clementine ran on into the night. Eyes bright, a jewel of a thing just waiting to be cut, Ruby knew that the big American would not be coming tonight. There was the precious chicken all roasted now and cooling on a blue china plate. A pot of potatoes peeled and ready to boil on the stove. There was a pile of cutlery just waiting to be laid out. Six knives, six forks, six spoons. But there had not been the sign Clementine promised for when the time came.

Outside, somewhere far off, rockets fell. One hundred an hour, coming down with a whistle and a buzz. If she concentrated Ruby could hear the faint *WHEEEEEEE* as they flew in, the clap and crump as they hit. Inside the shelter, earth trickled from the corrugated roof. Just like her sister, Ruby would have preferred to be outside. With the swifts. The dark clouds sliced with blue. Standing defiant in the middle of the road as the rockets flew over her head. At least there she could watch for Clementine to come home too.

In her palm, all hot and damp, Ruby turned and turned something, just in case. Heads to the north. Tails to the south. A lucky coronation penny waiting to come good.

'What's that you've got?' Even in the dark Mrs Penny never missed a trick.

Ruby curled her fingers hard around the coin, pushing her small fists deep into the folds of her skirt. 'Nothing.'

'Nothing, my eye.' But Mrs Penny didn't persist. Ruby had always been sly. A liar and a thief. Forever being instructed to go and sit in the coal-hole under the street. But tonight Mrs Penny would not insist. Down here with the stink of London mud gathering in like a grave, rules shifted and morphed into different shapes. Everyone needed something to believe in, particularly during times as wicked as these. Besides, Mrs Penny was holding a talisman of her own. A Brazil nut carved with the Ten Commandments.

Thou shalt not.

In a dark moment, in a dark corner of the house, as Clementine had returned from her nook in the pub a few weeks before, Tony had blocked her way. Rum shone wet on his lips. 'What's happening with the American?' he said, one hand flat on the dirty plaster wall, the other gripping the wooden banister so that Clementine could not escape. 'Your mother's arranging a chicken. Don't want it to go to waste.'

Clementine turned her startling eyes away from the man who had once saved her from a coal-hole, but who stank now of sweat and the black remains of a pipe. 'She's not my mother.'

Tony leered at Clementine. 'Might as well be.' A cake with a butter-icing swirl. A name on a label, scratched out.

'Get out of my way, Tony.' Clementine put her hand to the wainscot, as though to propel herself up and out of his grip.

'Not until you tell me.' Tony leaned in towards her, air wheezing through his chest.

'Tell you what?' Clementine shifted, her back against the wall now, staring at the big-bellied man in front of her, her eyes radiating disgust.

'I've heard all sorts of things.'

'What things?'

'That soon they'll be shipping out.'

Clementine touched a finger to her hair where it lay across her forehead. 'Well, you seem to know more than I do.'

Tony laughed then, phlegm rattling in his throat. 'I can tell when you're lying, Clemmie.'

'Why would I be lying?'

'All that treasure for yourself.'

Razor blades and cigarette lighters. Magazines with cars as big as boats.

Clementine took her hand away from the wall and ran it down the front of her skirt as though to brush off all sorts of filth. 'All you ever think about is money, Tony. Don't you realize there's more to life than that?'

'Like what, Clementine?'

Beans in colanders. Horses galloping along endless rails.

'Well, if you don't know that by now, I can't help you.' Clementine moved forwards, ready to push her way past.

Tony shifted closer, only an inch between them, his breath rank with milk always on the turn and the sweet stench of rum bought on the cheap. 'I've only ever been good to you, haven't I?' he said, trapping Clementine with the bulk of his body as though trapping a sheep against the rails of a pen. 'Thought there might be something in return.'

Clementine laughed then, a hollow sound echoing up the narrow stair of the house. 'You've had plenty, don't you think?'

Tony put his mouth close against Clementine's ear. 'Always room for more,' he breathed, leaning his body forwards just a little until it touched the place where Clementine's legs criss-crossed beneath the smooth fabric of her skirt.

Clementine's eyes flashed all of a sudden, flat and glassy in the gloom. 'I don't do that any more,' she said.

Tony's breath was damp on her neck, staining her skin where all those soldiers had queued to lay their heads. 'I'll give you something in return,' he murmured.

Clementine twisted her head away. 'I don't want any of your money, Tony.'

Tony's fingertips pressed into the bone running above Clementine's breasts. 'Not money.'

'What then?' She breathed in shallow sips of air so as not to inhale his stink.

'I'll tell you a secret.'

Clementine stilled for a moment. 'What sort of secret?' Secrets were the currency that flowed through her veins.

'One you'll want to hear. About your mother.'

'I told you, she's not my mother.'

'Not Mrs P. Your real mother,' he said.

For a moment there was silence between them, the whole house waiting to hear what might be revealed. Then Clementine shifted her body, brushing for a moment against his. 'All right then,' she said, dipping her hair towards him.

At last Tony leaned back. 'Good.'

Clementine moved fast then, quick as a deer disappearing into a wood, up one stair, then the next. 'But not me,' she said before he could reach out and grasp her. 'I'll give you Ruby. Isn't it little girls that you like best?'

Two days later, and Clementine had taken her sisters for a trip. A treat, she said, just for them and no one else. A journey into the heart of the city to visit a cathedral that would never fall.

Up, up and up some more they had gone, climbing a secret, spiral stairway inside the tower towards where a dome would loom above them like the sky. Up, up past small windows covered in grime. Past black ironwork and tiny wooden doors set flush to the wall. Up, up past a maze of hidden corridors, glimpsing men in tin hats turning to wink or to grin, the murmur of their voices seeping through the stone. Clementine always had known how to get into places others could not. 'Tell no one,' she had said when they first set out. 'And I'll show you something special, just for us.'

How could they not follow her after that?

It was Ruby who came out first, through a narrow door into a huge open space – a walkway set high in the roof, nothing but an iron railing between her and oblivion on the black-and-white tiles far below. She headed straight for the edge, rising on tiptoe to peer over, heart beating with the thrill of the height.

Barbara came next, breathing hard, eyes wide with fright, heart pitter-pattering at the thought of her body falling, falling. She pressed herself hard to the wall, hot palms flat against cold stone, as far from the railing as she could get.

Clementine came last, laughter rising like a lark into the high arc of the dome. 'Don't worry, Barbara,' she said. 'It's quite safe. Nothing can knock this church down.' Not its pinnacles or its turrets. Its statues stapled with iron. Nor its great winged angels. St Paul's was a monument to survival amongst a wasteland of rubble and brick.

Ruby pointed to where the walkway carved a path around the dirty wall and back to where they stood. 'What's it for?' she said.

Clementine laughed again. 'Secrets. It's the Whispering Gallery. You stand here and whisper your secrets and they come out on the other side.' She pointed across the great expanse of nothing. 'Shall we try it?'

'Yes,' said Ruby, clapping her hands, the echo bouncing back as though she was somehow applauding herself. Secrets were something she was good at.

'There's just one thing, though.' Clementine stood with a hand on the edge of the precipice. 'They have to be real secrets or it won't work.'

Clementine sent Barbara to the other side first, a small pig pressed in towards the wall, shuffling along with one tiny step after another as though it might somehow save her if the worst came to the worst. She was only halfway round when Clementine put her mouth next to Ruby's ear. 'Do you want to know a real secret?' she said.

Ruby was excited. 'Have we started?'

'Not yet. This is just for you and no one else.'

Ruby looked over to where Barbara was still making her way to the far side. 'What is it?' she breathed.

'I'm going to visit Mummy.'

'Mummy's dead.'

'No, she's not.'

From each side of a wide open space, two girls, one startling, the other ordinary in every way, whispered secrets to each other in the hope that they would learn something new. Round and round for ten minutes, Ruby setting one secret off, Barbara stranded alone on the far side trying to gather it in. 'I can't hear anything,' Barbara kept calling, her tiny, plaintive voice drifting over the cavernous space.

'You're not listening hard enough,' Ruby called back.

'You're not whispering loud enough,' Barbara replied.

'Don't be silly. You can't shout a whisper.'

But even then Ruby had known the truth. It wasn't the volume that was to blame. It was the nature of the secret that mattered the most.

They tried for five minutes more with no success. Then

Ruby said, 'Let's swap.' And turned to Clementine to see if she agreed.

But Clementine had vanished. Slipped away through the narrow wooden door and back down the winding staircase like a whisper all of her own. Ruby leaned over the rail and looked down to the black-and-white tiles on the floor far below, to a man standing in the shadow of a pillar. She knew at once what it meant. For the real secret was Stanley. And next to him, her sister Clementine, small hand inside the buttons of her lover's coat. Ruby stared down into the abyss, feeling the prick of another secret pressed into her palm. Small and star-shaped with a red stone at its heart, a tiny brooch offered to her by Clementine in return for a promise made but not yet kept.

'If I give this to you . . .' Clementine had said, as little pig Barbara continued her slow shuffle towards the other side of the dome, 'you must keep it somewhere safe. Otherwise they'll think you stole it.'

Pennies from Tony's pocket. Powder puffs from Mrs Penny's drawer. Ruby knew that Clementine was right. Everyone stole in their house. Even Barbara had a hidey-hole out in the wilderness of the back garden, nothing in it but a little pink pig made of tin and a blue slipper freckled with mould. Also something Ruby hadn't expected – one of Mrs Penny's silver teaspoons, miniature apostle attached to the end. The moment Ruby had seen it she'd wanted one for herself. So the next time Barbara was in the scullery washing out a sheet and Mrs Penny was at the butchers queuing for meat, Ruby took one, scooping the silver spoon from its purple velvet cocoon: no longer twelve apostles, but ten.

Ruby gazed at the small, sparkling thing lying in her older sister's hand. 'Is it precious?' she said.

Clementine had laughed, then. 'Of course, Stanley gave it to me. But I think it will suit you best.' Ruby put out her hand to take the little brooch, but Clementine closed her fist. 'You can have it,' she said. 'But there is something I want you to do for me first.'

Ruby watched now as far below the two lovers whispered their own secrets to each other – Stanley bending towards her sister, Clementine standing on tiptoe, small incisors gleaming in the dark. She held her breath as Stanley put his hand into the pocket of his overcoat and held something up. Two slips of paper, like two tickets for a boat. And in the other an orange full of sweet juice and hard little pips. Ruby felt it then, the rush inside her chest. For she knew that the promise she had given to Clementine would be made good soon.

A month later as Ruby huddled in the shelter and the bombs flew in like rain, Clementine took a train from the centre of London to a place where grey asylum walls rose up from landscaped grounds. When she arrived, she knew at once that she was in the right place.

She stood in the huge entrance hall, decrepit in its fading splendour, staring up at the cavern of the roof. The ceiling had been painted grey, like everything else in Clementine's life. But not for much longer, she hoped.

'Can I help?' A woman in a uniform addressed her from behind a bundle of files.

'I'm looking for Ward Three,' Clementine said, bringing her gaze back down.

'Oh yes. It's that way.' The woman pointed towards a long, empty corridor behind closed doors. 'But you'll need an escort. All the rest of the place has been given over to the wounded. I'll take you if you want.'

Down corridors, along passageways, through rooms that stank of iodine and blood. The heels of Clementine's best shoes tapped out an urgent rhythm on the hard floor coverings as they walked, echoing against the ceramic tiles that curved up all the walls. They passed doors locked tight and others that opened to reveal a million injured soldiers (or thereabouts) splayed out on the beds. Legs and arms shot off. Skulls with missing pieces replaced by small tin plates. Here they were, all the men who had marched to glory with rifles held high above their heads. Splashing out of the surf. Running across a sodden beach. Scrambling for the safety of a dune that crumbled constantly beneath their boots. Men who had crawled past gun emplacements and tangles of barbed wire, past German soldiers, only nineteen, with their sudden haunted faces and their calls of 'Nein! Nein! Nein!' Men who had marched onto the fields and plains behind the cliffs, past the bodies of the dead, slumped over, face down in the road, or lying bloated in the rain. Here they were, sleeping now in a ward with a hundred others, saved to go on with life. Salvation. That was what Clementine wanted too. And for Stanley to take her home.

Just one more thing first.

Far, far away, down a corridor that led nowhere but here, Clementine and her guide came to another set of locked doors. 'It's not ideal,' the woman in uniform said. 'But they had to go somewhere once the war began.'

Through the glass pane Clementine could see a small nurses' station portioned off from the rest of the space. Behind that, row upon row of beds stretching out like graves. 'There are so many of them,' she murmured.

'Oh, yes.'

'Do they ever get out?'

'Oh, no.' Her escort was certain about that. She tapped on the door to attract the attention of someone inside. 'Couldn't risk them wandering about now that the soldiers are here.'

Inside, the smell was terrible. A foetid cloak of disinfectant and stale urine, the sweet stench of perspiration left unwashed. Clementine put a hand to her nose and tried for a moment to breathe through her mouth. To her left was a nurse, fat and pink-faced, lolling on a chair. Next to her a matron in a grey dress. The woman in uniform who had escorted Clementine was talking to the matron and gesturing back at her as she spoke. The matron nodded, then pointed towards someone at the end of the ward.

Sitting on a bed, far away at the furthest possible point, was a woman dressed in a regulation asylum gown. At first to Clementine she seemed identical to all the rest. Emaciated. Feet bare. Body angled and gaunt. The woman swayed back and forwards where she sat, just as the others swayed too, some of them standing between the beds, or wandering up and down the central aisle. They all seemed to be talking to themselves, muttering words, occasionally raising their hands or shaking their heads. But where the other patients' scalps were shorn, all around this woman's head was a cloud of silver hair.

Clementine started towards the end of the ward, walking fast before either the matron or the fat nurse could tell her to stop.

'Ten minutes!' the matron called out. 'No more.'

Another patient appeared by Clementine's side, walking with her for a step or two like a ghost. 'Have you come for me? Have you come for me?' she whispered.

'No,' said Clementine.

'Sorry.' The woman bobbed her head. 'So sorry.'

'Ivy!' the nurse with the florid cheeks shouted. 'I've warned you before. Don't touch.'

Ivy rolled her eyes back. 'So sorry. So sorry.' A sudden white glaze before her normal stare returned.

Clementine kept her own startling eyes to the floor until she came to the final bed, no one left to encounter but the woman with the halo of hair. She glanced at the woman's toenails where they rested on the linoleum floor, thin and curled like the talons of a bird. Then the woman raised her head.

Clementine stared for a moment, just as the strange, pale woman stared back. It was Clementine who spoke first. 'Hello, Mummy,' she said.

They sat side by side on a bed covered with a thin blanket of cloth – a mother and a daughter, together again at last. Dorothea swayed back and forth, back and forth, her hand gripping Clementine's wrist. 'My angels,' she repeated over and over. 'My angels.'

'No, Mummy. It's Clementine.'

But Dorothea just swayed and swooped some more, the springs of the mattress groaning and singing beneath them as though to match the music in her head.

It was Clementine who broke the impasse, reaching for the small brown suitcase she had brought with her. Nylons and knickers. An underslip thin as a ghost. A nightgown. A bottle of toilet water. And a hairbrush with a handle made of bone. 'Shall I brush your hair, Mummy?' she said.

At once Dorothea stopped swaying. 'They took it,' she said. 'They took it.'

'Or would you like to brush it yourself?'

Clementine laid the brush down on the bed between where they sat. Dorothea stared at it, transfixed, then lifted her hand to her own hair as though she had only just noticed the cloud of gossamer all around her head.

Ten minutes, and Clementine sat brushing and brushing Dorothea's hair from the crown right down to the tips. Over and over Clementine brushed, singing as she did, until the hair almost sang too. 'Oh my darling . . .' Until a ragged chorus rippled round the ward in response.

Oh my darling, oh my darling,
Oh my darling Clementine . . .

Stroke after stroke, silver strands floating from Dorothea's head, attaching themselves to the sleeves of Clementine's coat. Ten minutes to make up for what they had both lost.

It was never going to be enough.

When the time was nearly gone, Clementine glanced over her shoulder to check that the fat nurse wasn't near, then reached into her bag and withdrew a little compact and a manicure set with a pair of silver scissors that glinted in the light. She opened up the compact and placed it in Dorothea's hands, pointing to the mirror so that Dorothea might see her reflection – a lady worn thin, but still here, surrounded by a shimmering cloud of light.

Dorothea gazed, entranced, at herself, as Clementine leaned forwards and caught up a pinch of her mother's hair at the very tip. She made a cut, *snip-clip*, and at once Dorothea dropped the compact into her lap. 'I cut it,' she said. 'I cut it.' Gripping on to Clementine's wrist.

An angel in the night. A cold blade against the warmth of a young girl's neck.

'Yes, Mummy,' said Clementine, touching Dorothea on the arm. 'I know.' And she folded the little sprig of silver back inside her manicure set.

'Time to go now,' the matron called out. 'The rockets will catch you if you're not careful.'

'All right,' Clementine replied, picking up the compact. She closed the handbag, then the case, held the hairbrush for a moment before placing it in Dorothea's lap. 'Goodbye, Mummy,' she said bending and putting her lips for a moment to her mother's cheek. Then, as she rose to go, she folded something else into her mother's fist. Two dollar bills of a not inconsiderable denomination. And a slip of paper imprinted with the name of a ship.

A ticket to the promised land. Just in case.

2011

Three years on from the Crash, and Margaret could practically smell the money shored up in the houses all around, embedded in the clean red bricks, in the white-pillared porticoes and the neat little hedges cut into squares. It was trapped behind the portcullis security shutters and sunk into the window boxes already planted and blooming even though it was only the beginning of the year. Unlike the cold austerity of Edinburgh, it was as though financial winter had never happened here. No boarded-up shops. No slurry in the gutter. No faded *To Let* signs or black cars spraying slush all over her coat. Just clean, empty pavements and vehicles as big as tractors, no mud on their wheels.

In her slim brown folder (not quite so slim now) Margaret had the beginnings of a life and death report:

A receipt for an emerald necklace.

An admissions form for a lunatic.

And now a copy of a death certificate for a Dorothea Walker, provided by Susan Fielding in return for a small fee. For where there was death, so too was there life. Or birth, at least.

So here Margaret was, back in the heart of it all, London's quiet, moneyed lands. A Borough, not a District. Royal, not Municipal. A haven for those who could afford several homes and a boat at the same time. The streets of Kensington and Chelsea, where no one could imagine that anything had ever gone wrong.

The Chelsea Old Town Hall and Register Office was like all municipal buildings built over one hundred years before – solid, with a pediment over the door, exuding benevolence and grace. It was nothing like the buildings constructed out of today's wealth, all glass and security turnstiles, nowhere for children to roam, or even scratch their names. Even so, the section Margaret required was still hidden away – down the side, through a small door into an annexe carpeted in municipal brown. Births, Marriages and Deaths. Nothing but the ordinary every-day.

The man behind the enquiry desk was small too. He took off his glasses and polished them on a corner of his blue-striped shirt as Margaret made her request. 'Have you tried the Internet?' he said. 'You can find all sorts there.'

'Oh, yes,' Margaret lied. 'But I thought I'd come in person to get the benefit of your expertise. Besides, I'm in rather a hurry. It's a matter of life and death.'

Margaret had come in person because the Internet required a debit or a credit card – that small rectangle of plastic which confirmed one had money, or the promise of it, at least. The personal approach allowed her to pay in cash. Here one moment, gone the next, a nice clean transaction, no questions asked. There always had been something about Margaret that sought to leave no trace.

The man slipped his specs back on. 'Well, I suppose I could help, if it doesn't take too long.' Flattery. Worked every time. 'What you can do is a general search of the indexes if you like, then I'll do the verifications.'

'Verifications?'

'Where I go and check in the archive, then tell you if we have the documents that you need.'

Margaret wanted to ask why she couldn't just check the documents herself. But then again, these were people's lives she was dealing with, not just inconsequential pieces of paper covered in black and red type.

'Eighteen pounds . . .' said the man, rubbing at his glasses once again. 'You get up to six hours' search time and eight verifications, then a fast track on the actual documents. *Here to help*,' he said, quoting his Royal Borough's slogan, or something like it.

Paperwork, Margaret thought. Within her reach at last.

The indexes were on microfiche, ordered by year. Line after line of people's surnames for each annual quarter, followed by their first name, their dates and the volume and page number the clerk would need to track the actual documents to their final resting place. Margaret searched under 'Stirling', Dorothea's maiden name as per her admissions record and the certificate that marked her death. Straight away it produced a result, hovering in front of Margaret on the small grey screen:

Births Quarter 3: Stirling, Dorothea, 18 July 1900.

Margaret felt a small thrill in her chest as she made a careful note of the accompanying index number. One certificate down. Who knew what might be revealed next? She flexed her fingers, hoping that Dorothea's marriage had taken place in the same part of town in which she was born, and set out once more on her search.

An hour later, and the lucky coronation penny proved

its worth again. *Marriages Quarter 2: Stirling, Dorothea, m. Walker, Alfred, 6 April 1922.* A new dress, best Sunday shoes, a small hat perhaps, confetti or rice thrown over the bride and groom's heads before a wedding breakfast of ham, toast and eggs. Margaret sat back in her chair and stared at the line of text crammed in with all the others on the microfiched screen. Dorothea Walker née Stirling, all of twenty-two. Owner of a bone-handled hairbrush and a nightgown threaded with pink. Sweetheart. Wife. Madwoman. Corpse. Mother of two young twins (deceased) and a daughter named Clementine, aka Mrs Walker, dead now too. Lover of oranges, whisky and red coats just like her own. Margaret was pleased that she had something in common with her dead client. One way or another they had both been stripped bare, and now Margaret was finding them some new clothes.

She began searching for her third certificate in 1922, the year Dorothea and Alfred were married, assuming that their daughter was the legitimate kind. Unlike 'Stirling', there were lots and lots of 'Walkers', many of them with the initial 'C'. By the time Margaret got from the last quarter of 1924 into the first quarter of 1925 she understood why someone might need six hours. Her eyes itched and wavered as she ran her finger down yet another hazy screen, tracking the many Walker births in quarter two:

Walker, Charles
Walker, Clarinda
Walker, Crispin
Walker, David
Gone too far.
She stopped and slid her finger up the list again in

reverse. Doing something backwards sometimes had a way of revealing what had previously been missed. Walker, Elizabeth. Walker, David. Walker, Crispin. Then there it was. The culmination of a trail of orange peel dropped in a gutter.

Births Quarter 2: Walker, Clementine, 12 June 1925.

No longer dead, but alive and well once more.

Margaret had checked Births, Marriages and Deaths before, of course, the moment she got to London thirty years since. In through the hallowed halls of Somerset House, just seventeen, nothing to her but a pair of black boots and a canvas satchel slung across her coat. 'Margaret Penny,' she had whispered when they asked for her name. '19th July 1963.'

They had come back almost before she'd had time to sit. Penny, M., born to Penny, B., Wingfield's Maternity Hospital (all demolished now). 'It doesn't say adopted, does it?' she asked, more in hope than in expectation. But the woman who had called up the relevant certificate just shook her head. Here was final confirmation of what Margaret had known but never believed. Her mother was her mother. That was the end of that.

The first confirmation had come when she was thirteen years old, doing her homework in the living room of their latest Edinburgh flat.

'Where do babies come from?' she had said, digging at the underside of the table with her pencil because she knew now that no one would check.

'Where do you think!' Barbara had replied, running her new Hoover up and down the carpet, making the nylon crackle and spark. Barbara had instructed Margaret in the biological facts of life from the moment Margaret could walk. 'Never get caught.' That was her mantra. 'You don't know where it might lead.'

Margaret sighed and lifted her feet as the Hoover roared along beneath. 'I mean, where was I born?' she said.

Barbara released the catch on the Hoover and folded the handle almost flat. 'Down south, of course. I've told you. London.' Barbara was very taken with the Hoover and its amazing powers of suction, as though she had spent an entire lifetime up to that point just sweeping dust around from one dirty place to the next.

'But where in London?' Margaret persisted. A trait that came straight from her mother, as far as she could tell.

'In a nursing home. All gone now.' At least that was what Margaret thought she heard her mother say.

'What about my father, where's he?'

Barbara pushed the Hoover as far under the sofa as it could go. 'Over the hills and far away.'

'Where's that?'

'Who knows?' Barbara's voice sounded far away too as she bent double, just like the Hoover, to make sure she had picked up every speck of dirt. 'Let sleeping dogs lie, that's what I say.' She straightened then, put a hand to her hair. 'Besides, none of his business. Or yours for that matter.'

Though, even at thirteen years old, Margaret had thought that perhaps it was.

Still, she didn't ask again. Barbara's womb was due to be cut out the next day, which was why Margaret was pondering the miracle of birth while her mother was determined to make the flat nice. 'Women are cursed,' Barbara had said when she found out the news. Hormones and bodily changes. Cancer of the breast. 'Still, it's best to get rid of what is no use.' And she'd glared so hard at Margaret when she said it that Margaret had thought she must mean her rather than some vital (but redundant) organ instead.

But that evening, as though to make amends, Barbara had gone out into the gritty chill of an Edinburgh night and got them chips for tea, in paper soft and damp. Salt and the hot scent of vinegary sauce, plates laid out on a tray. Two forks. Two Tunnock's Tea Cakes for a treat. Eaten in front of a tiny black-and-white television set. It had been a rare moment of peace between them, in amongst all the rest.

The very next morning, with every surface scrubbed, Barbara placed a patterned headscarf over her hair, freshly permed for her encounter with the operating suite. Then she buttoned her navy mackintosh all the way up her neck and said, 'I've asked Mrs Hamill to look in on you,' as Margaret stood waiting for the obligatory brush of her mother's brown lips against her cheek. For the first time in a long while, Barbara's grip on her daughter's shoulder was fierce. It was Margaret who pulled away first.

Barbara adjusted her coat at the hem and smoothed a hand down the front. She looked as though she was going shopping for sliced white bread and a tin of peas, rather than taking the bus to the Royal where she would go under the knife. 'Don't bother to visit,' she said. 'Wait until Thursday when I'll be up and about.' Then she was gone.

Margaret came home from school that night to an empty flat and waited as she had been told. Homework complete. Teacups ready. A whole packet of sticky Soreen's Fruit Loaf sliced and buttered. She sat on the edge of the Dralon sofa until it was quite dark, waiting for Mrs Hamill to come and keep her straight. It was only after three hours that she thought perhaps the worst had happened ('Dead, I'm afraid, a slip of the scalpel, just a mistake') and went and tapped on the neighbour's door herself.

'Gone out,' Mr Hamill said. 'Up to see her sister. Be back tomorrow, or the day after that.' He stank of smoke from a pipe that Margaret knew his wife did not allow.

'Oh,' said Margaret. 'It's just . . .'

'Everything all right, hen?' Mr Hamill's dentures shone in the gloom of the close, the gleaming veneers at odds with the decrepitude of his face. He shuffled slightly in the doorway, his camel-coloured cardigan sagging at the waist. 'You can come in if you like.' He gestured with the wet end of his pipe, saliva glistening on the stem.

Margaret blushed to her toes, and back. 'No,' she whispered. 'I mean, yes. Everything's fine. Goodnight.' Then she went back upstairs and ate nine slices of Soreen's fruit loaf all in one go, just because she could.

The next day, with nothing in the cupboard but the usual tins of peas and soup, Margaret took the pound note left by her mother on the kitchen table ('Emergencies only!') and went for chips instead. Down, down the dirty

stairwell. Down, down the filthy close. Out into the cold
Edinburgh night. She discovered then that Edinburgh in
the dark was very different from during the day. More
rackety. Full of curses and shouts. Men standing in groups
on the corner. A sauna with a beckoning light. The pub
with its flare of chatter and smoke. Margaret scurried past
it all, knowing then that if she ever got the chance, this was
the world that she wanted to explore.

Back at home she ate the chips straight from the paper,
licking grease and salt from her fingertips before wiping
them on the bottom of her skirt. She washed the chips
down with a can of sparkling juice and a Tunnock's Snow-
ball, shredded coconut falling all across her lap. When she
was finished she got up and coconut dropped to the floor
like a first scattering of winter snow. She didn't bother to
clean up.

Instead she went digging, just because she could,
moving around her mother's bedroom in stops and starts
as though marking out a crime scene, wary in case she
missed anything. On her mother's bedside table she found
an empty glass, the rim all sticky, and a paperback book
with the corners turned down throughout as though Barbara could only manage a page or two at a time before she
fell asleep each night. In the drawer she found a comb
made of tortoiseshell, all mottled and yellow, and a packet
of cigarettes with only two left. Also a dirty teaspoon with
a miniature figure attached to the handle. Margaret was
tempted by the teaspoon. But she knew her mother would
know who to blame if the spoon disappeared, just like the
womb Barbara once owned but now did not.

In a drawer on the other side of her mother's bed she found a slim, square box made of red plastic. And inside that a rubber disc dusted with Boots Best from the tin that lived in the cupboard above the bathroom sink. The rubber disc rose in a small dome, rather like Margaret imagined Barbara's stomach must have risen up to meet the first cut of the surgeon's knife. She pressed her greasy fingertip to the rubber and it dipped down then popped back in a small cloud of powdery dust. Margaret stared at the perfect print she'd left behind, then shut the lid of the box, *snip-snap*, and slid it back into the drawer. Maybe her mother wouldn't notice. Whatever the rubber thing was, it didn't look as though it ever got much use.

In the bottom of her mother's big chest of drawers she found an apron folded into a square and a broken china cherub wrapped in a blanket with a torn satin trim. Underneath that was a painting, all dirty and brown, smelling of linseed oil and covered in a thick layer of newspaper and dust. And at the very bottom of the drawer, as though Barbara intended to keep it hidden not just from Margaret, but from herself too, a photograph of two children sleeping, in black and white.

In the gathering dark of an Edinburgh night Margaret looked closely at the photograph. The children were pale, lips frozen in two small pouts. Their hands, where they rested on their laps, lay still as the grave. Hair a tumble of curls. Cheeks the colour of porcelain, just like the china cherub. Margaret touched a finger to the cold glass. She had always wanted a family. And here it was at last.

Mrs Hamill came round on the third day. 'Oh, my

dear,' she said, her face all flushed beneath her mohair hat. 'You won't tell your mother, will you?'

'No,' said Margaret, fiddling with a large brown penny she had discovered tucked away next to the photograph. Something so commonplace she had decided it wouldn't be missed.

'It'll be our secret.'

'Yes,' said Margaret. *Tell no one.* She was already good at keeping secrets. Like mother like daughter, she stored them all up.

On the Thursday, as instructed, she went to the hospital and found Barbara sitting up in her bed as stern and unbending as before she went in. There was no sign that she'd just had an operation, let alone one that ended the possibility of new life. Their conversation lasted about three minutes before they ran out of things to say.

'Are you behaving yourself?' Her mother was wearing a dressing gown in a shade more suited to a baby than a middle-aged woman who'd just had her womb cut out.

'Yes,' said Margaret, wondering when it would be best to enquire about the two sleeping children. A brother and a sister, perhaps. Some cousin from the past.

'Are you doing whatever Mrs Hamill says?' Barbara's voice had an edge to it, as though she knew Margaret must already have disobeyed (which, of course, she had).

'Yes,' said Margaret, hoping there was no sign that she hadn't eaten anything but chips for the last four days. 'Does it hurt?' she ventured, because what else was there to ask, other than a question that might open up the past?

Barbara's eyes were like two piss holes in a pile of grey snow. 'A little,' she said, shifting her body as though it too was made out of the same china as the grubby cherub. 'But it'll be better soon.'

Margaret handed over a bar of Fruit and Nut that she had bought with the remains of the pound note. 'Would you like some?'

'Thank you, dear.' Barbara broke off a square before handing it back. 'You have the rest.'

Together they ate their small pieces of chocolate while contemplating the gauzy yellow curtain that surrounded the bed. Margaret swallowed hers and wondered if it would be OK to have another piece. 'Will you be home soon?'

'Soon enough.' Barbara seemed wistful for a moment, as though five days in a hospital bed was the only holiday she had ever had. 'Then it will be a new beginning.'

Margaret wasn't sure what that meant. She held up a crumpled paper bag containing another treat bought with her pocket money from the little Pakistani grocer that was new to the street. 'Would you like an orange?'

'No, thank you, dear.' Her mother grimaced then, skin carved out about her mouth. 'Too difficult to peel.'

When they showed Margaret her birth certificate several years later in the foyer of Somerset House, there was a great blank in the space where the father's name should be. So it had been the immaculate conception after all. *Our father who art in heaven.* Or over the hills and far away, just as her mother had said. Though by then Margaret knew that whatever had gone on, it had definitely been far removed from God.

'What does it mean if his name's not on it?' she asked, just to be sure.

'Oh, all sorts, dear. It's very common.' The woman had smiled at her in a way that suggested she had heard this question many times and knew what was at stake. 'The man might have died, perhaps. Or maybe he and your mother were never married. Have you asked her?'

Barbara, womb still intact, pulling the Hoover out, pressing her foot to the red button, starting up the vacuum's roar once more. 'Good riddance to bad rubbish.' The only other piece of information about her father Margaret ever got.

'No,' she said.

'Or he might have been married already,' the woman smiled. 'To someone else instead.'

So Margaret asked them to look up Barbara's marriage certificate too, just in case. But that didn't exist either. 'So sorry,' said the woman, a pussycat bow made out of rayon drooping from her neck. 'Sometimes that's just the way it is.'

'It's fine,' said Margaret. And in some ways it was. She'd never had a father, so what was there to miss? Besides, she'd been brought up in Edinburgh. In that city, 'Mrs' was as much a statement of intent as a matter of fact.

Margaret left Somerset House with nothing but her black boots and a borrowed satchel swinging across her hip, walking out into a wave of London traffic, a city full of chatter and smoke. She knew then that just like the excising of her mother's womb a few years before, this was the end of something. But also a beginning, perhaps. She looked about, to her left and her right, then took a large brown penny from her pocket and prepared to toss. Heads to the east. Tails to the west. Either way, she was seventeen now. Time to start life afresh.

Back down in London thirty years hence, and Margaret continued her pursuit of the dead. Moyra. Anne. Rose. Or Mary. A daughter for Clementine Walker, perhaps. Someone out there who had no idea that the woman who gave birth to her was now lying dead in the north.

As she searched, Margaret wondered if she ought to ring Barbara, let her know that she was safe. Then she remembered her mother's expression when Mr Wingrove had called from West Leith about the indigent funeral rota. Outraged. As though to answer the phone would be to invite the Apocalypse into her life – a troublesome daughter, perhaps, returned from the south, neither of them able to admit to the mistakes of the past. Besides, Margaret knew that Barbara had always been ex-directory, in more ways than one. So what difference would this time make? Also, Margaret understood something else now that she had never understood before. Children were easily acquired. And just as easily sloughed off. Two silver-haired strangers in crumpled Technicolor had taught her that.

As though to prove her right, there was no sign of a child for Clementine Walker in the steady microfiche haze of the Chelsea Register Office computer log. Nor on any of Margaret's searches that combined Mrs Walker's name and date of birth. Just like Margaret's own clouded past, the real substance of her client's life was lost to the world in all its width and breadth. No husband or offspring. Not even a dog. Just two dead siblings, a father who vanished from the records, and a mother who went mad.

The clerk just shrugged when she asked. 'It was common, then,' he said. 'War, you know. Lots of people moved around. Records got destroyed. She might have been bombed out. She might have got married and changed her name. She might have gone abroad. Plenty of them did that.'

Out of curiosity Margaret looked up the lost Walker twins too. They weren't strictly relevant, of course, but there was something about those little deaths that she wanted to mark in some way. She found them in the third quarter of 1933, July–September. Two Walkers, initials A. and D. Lost one summer's evening, never to return. Margaret stared at them for a moment, two little deaths recorded on a long list. Once here, now gone, the centre of a family scattered into a void.

Then she turned the microfiche off with a blink.

The Walker family – born, married, died – all complete now. A birth certificate for a Dorothea Stirling, dated 1900. A record of Dorothea and Alfred's wedding in 1922. Two pieces of paper from 1933 registering the demise of two little twins. An admissions form consigning Dorothea to the madhouse and another to mark her death. And from 1925, a certificate marking the birth of a Clementine Amelia Walker. Margaret's dead client, risen again.

It was enough paperwork for Margaret to close the case for good. At least, that was what she thought. Just one more thing to do before she could claim her invoice for services rendered and begin her new life in the south.

1963

She arrived on the doorstep with a basket and a rug. Not much more than when she'd left over ten years before, except that now she was no longer slim enough to fit into any of Clementine's clothes. Barbara opened the door expecting a hawker trying his luck. But in his place she found Ruby, trying her luck too.

'What are you doing here, Ruby?' she said. It wasn't really a question.

Ruby lounged in the shadows, a step or two below. 'Well, that's a nice welcome for your long-lost sister returned at last.'

Barbara pulled the door behind her until it was nearly closed, nothing but a needle of light thrown out onto the step. 'You know you can't stay here. My landlady won't allow visitors.'

'What's she got to do with it?' Ruby shifted her basket from one arm to the other. 'You pay your rent, don't you?' Ruby always had liked to argue. Nothing changed there.

'What do you want, anyway?' Barbara glanced up at the dark windows rising three floors to the top. She couldn't see them, but she knew they were there. All the other single girls, their faces pressed to the glass.

Ruby put a hand to her back as though it had begun to ache. 'I need some help,' she said, coat falling open. 'I came to you first.'

*

Ruby had fled to the artist first, a few streets away from Mrs Withers' house, down a dirty alleyway and up a narrow stair. She had stood panting at the top, palm against plaster that crumbled at her touch, waiting for a man with paint embedded in his fingernails to answer her knock. She heard him before she saw him, crossing bare floorboards on his paint-covered feet, a jangle of music trickling out from beneath the door, the scent of linseed oil trailing in his wake.

'My bucket girl!' The artist had laughed when he opened the door. 'What brings you here?' His beard had grown out. His hair was longer. A cigarette hung from his paint-stained fingers, burned almost to a stub.

Ruby smoothed a rat's tail of her own hair between finger and thumb. 'I was wondering if you needed me to do some work.'

The painter flicked ash towards where she stood, glancing at the swelling beneath Ruby's dress. 'I'm sorry, darling. I don't do work like that any more.'

Ruby's cheeks flushed. 'Well, perhaps I could stay for a while. Until you are ready to work again.'

The artist shrugged. 'But where would you sleep?'

'On the chaise longue.'

'The chaise longue is occupied at present.' And the artist laughed again, the way he used to laugh over her.

From inside the studio Ruby smelled turpentine and paint now. And underneath that something like jasmine wafting along the floor. The music tumbled towards them in a soft, continuous flow. She put her hand up against the doorframe. 'What's her name?'

The painter stepped out and closed the door behind

him so that Ruby could not see in, and the person inside could not see out. 'Now you know I don't do names,' he said.

'Could you lend me something then? Just enough for a couple of months.' The curve of Ruby's belly bulged between them, hard as a bell.

The painter spread his fingers as though to show how money ran through them like water through a sieve. 'You know me.'

'I'll give you back the painting.' Ruby began to rummage in her basket. 'You could sell it.'

'That brown thing.' The artist laughed again, flicked more ash to the floor in a small grey drift. 'Not my best work.'

Ruby stopped rummaging and stared at this man who had seen her with her legs all this way, then that. It was the artist who looked away first. 'You should try your benefactor,' he said, closing the door behind him. 'He bought everything of yours that he could.'

Mrs Withers had thrown Ruby out when she began to show. At least that was the story Ruby liked to tell. 'The clients wouldn't like it,' Mrs Withers had said, pouring a large whisky and drinking it down in one toss.

Ruby stood by the cold parlour fire and stared at the empty glass in Mrs Withers' hand. She would have liked a large whisky – that tail of flame chasing down her throat.

'When were you going to tell me?' Mrs Withers dug for the string of pearls buried in the flesh around her throat. She had got much fatter over the years, ever since Ruby had arrived to carry all the buckets to and fro.

Ruby shrugged and stared at where, beneath her floral wrap, Mrs Withers' stomach spread out like dough. Under her own skirt Ruby's skin stretched tight.

Mrs Withers poured another slug of whisky and tossed that down in one go too. 'I'm not a charity, you know.' She wiped at her wet lips with the back of one hand. 'If you'd told me sooner there might have been something we could do.'

Mrs Withers probed at her neck with a delicate fingertip as though searching for something to hold on to against the bad luck coming her way. Somewhere inside Ruby something scrabbled for a moment: a small, blind creature exploring its new home.

'Then again . . .' Mrs Withers stopped digging, two fat fingers caressing a small pearl at last. 'It might still be possible.' She peered at Ruby, eyes glimmering in the evening light. 'Even at your stage it can always be arranged.'

Ruby departed the same night. Out of the front door, nothing left behind. She took with her the basket she had brought when she first arrived, a painting that was dirty in more ways than one and a tarnished silver teaspoon with an apostle attached to the end. Also a Brazil nut with the Ten Commandments etched into its shell. She arrived at her sister's doorstep a few hours later, darkness pressing in on all sides.

Barbara's bedsit was tiny compared to the house where Mrs Penny and Tony still held sway. But unlike 14 Elm Row, it was all Barbara's own. Smelling of bacon rind fried over gas rings, of cheap coffee and even cheaper scent, it was a haven of subdivided rooms and shallow baths twice a week. Every night, mice ran across every ceiling. Every morning the landlady began her assault on another bottle of brandy. Every evening young men in narrow trousers came to call. It wasn't special, but it was Barbara's own promised land, at last.

Barbara's wage as a drudge in a solicitor's office was enough for one room and an alcove. What more could she need? In the alcove, behind a curtain, lay the bed with its damp and lumpen mattress. Above the fireplace, on the mantelpiece, there were two teacups stacked up alongside a bowl and a plate. Above them was a mirror, foxed and spotted, hanging from a chain. On the opposite side of the room, a double-ring hotplate and a sink for washing both dishes and clothes. The walls were papered with something that had once been patterned with roses, indiscernible now beneath a sheen of grease. The single gable window was surrounded by cracked and peeling paint, but the glass was bright and clear, polished with vinegar and newspaper by Barbara once a month. It was hung with a pair of net curtains, a startling white against the grey of everything else. From outside, far below, there was the constant sound of children echoing up from where they played in the street.

Ruby and Barbara, twins but not a bit alike, stood in the doorway – one young woman with thick arms, the other with a small creature fluttering inside. Ruby looked at Barbara's room and saw what she could get. Barbara looked at Ruby and saw what she had lost. Two sisters on the threshold of a new life. Barbara had neglected a chance

to help her sister once before when Ruby had asked. She
didn't need to be asked twice.

Three months, give or take, to wash everything clean. Sing
the songs their mother should have sung them. Cook the
meals their mother should have cooked. Three months
for them to lie together of a night once again, Barbara
with her back pressed to the alcove wall, Ruby with her
back pressed to her twin. Three months to build a new life
together out of the old.

It never was going to be enough time.

One month in, and it was Barbara who went to work
every day with her hat and her gloves, returning each evening with packages of food wrapped in greaseproof paper.
Cream crackers and bottles of milk. A loaf of bread. Three
tomatoes and some slices of ham. In return, Ruby spent all
day lazing in the alcove or wandering in and out of all the
other subdivided rooms, bringing home her own little
gifts. Soap wrapped in paper. Perfume in a bottle with a
glass stopper. A piece of patterned fabric for a tablecloth.
Once even two oranges, peeled and segmented, laid out on
a plate.

One month, and Barbara hunched by the gas fire
sewing at something that was meant to turn into a baby's
smock. 'Will it be a boy or a girl, do you think?' she said.
Above her, on the mantelpiece, a small brown painting
looked down at where she sat – the only thing Ruby had
brought with her that she had not taken from someone
else first.

'It will be a girl,' said Ruby, standing at the window,
hand pressed to spine, gazing down at a circle of children

skipping in the street. Beside her the table was strewn with breadcrumbs and puddles of tea, a magazine with a glossy cover, the corners all folded and ripped. Dirty cutlery clogged the sink. Toothbrushes stained with white stood in one of their only two mugs. The bed lay rumpled, pillows flung all about, a chiffon blouse in a crumple on the floor. Ruby was supposed to tidy the room each morning, but it only ever seemed to get more cluttered.

'How do you know it will be a girl?' Barbara wrestled with her needle. The fabric was stiff. Totally unsuited to anything a small child might need.

Ruby ran a finger along the grimy windowsill, then rubbed the black spot of dirt onto the fabric of her skirt. 'I just do.'

'If it is a girl . . .' Barbara was still a person who liked to be precise, 'what will you call her?'

'Clementine, of course.'

'Clementine?' Barbara looked up for a moment, frowning, came eye to eye with the small brown painting and looked quickly away. 'Clementine Penny?' Even to her this sounded odd.

'Clementine Walker, of course,' said Ruby. 'We must reclaim our roots.'

Barbara kept her head down. She poked hard with her needle through the stiff fabric, piercing her thumb. They didn't have any roots except Mrs Penny, as far as she was concerned.

Two months, and Ruby stood by the small gas ring burning some kind of soup when Barbara came in from work. 'What is that smell?' Barbara said, gloved hand to mouth, hair in disarray, that sick feeling she'd had for some weeks now in her stomach.

'It's French,' said Ruby, frowning at the black specks rising to the top of the pan amongst a shimmer of hot fat. 'Everyone's making it.'

'Where did you get the ingredients?' A pot stuffed with onions and beef stock that made Barbara want to retch. It reminded her of someone crying in a distant room, no one coming to answer her call.

Ruby waved a wooden spoon in the air, a small shower of brown droplets speckling everything they met. 'Oh, here and there. I got a tin of Ambrosia for afters.'

Barbara hated rice pudding. Mrs Penny always made them eat it cold when they were young. She peeled her gloves away from her sweaty hands and peered into the small cupboard that doubled as their food safe. It was empty, apart from a tin of peas she had bought some weeks before. There had been two oranges there only that morning. And half a loaf of bread.

She stood up again, pressing a hand in towards her waist. 'You know we can't afford anything fancy,' she said. Food was a source of anxiety for Barbara (along with everything else).

'What's life if it isn't fancy?' Ruby dipped a small, tarnished teaspoon into the pot. She blew across the surface of the thin liquid.

'Where's the bread?' Barbara removed a pair of stockings from the back of a chair so that she could sit down.

'I've cut it already.'

'But we need it for breakfast.' Barbara looked around

for somewhere to put the stockings, but everywhere was covered, so she folded them into her lap.

'No, Barbara.' Ruby pointed with her wooden spoon at the pot of soup, a mass of soggy bread covering the surface. 'It floats on top. Like this.'

Two and a half months, and they ran out of money for the gas, those little hissing jets faltering and falling low one night before disappearing with a pop. Barbara tried to light them again, over and over, the matches burning down to black each time. 'Christ!' She knelt back to survey the charred little corpses scattered on the hearth, her forehead hot and cold at the same time. 'We'll have to borrow a shilling for the meter.'

'I already owe them,' said Ruby, lounging like a seal on the crumpled eiderdown. She was wearing nothing but a pair of pants and a vest.

Dark shadows cut into Barbara's cheeks. 'Owe them what?'

'Shillings,' said Ruby. 'For the meter. Lots and lots.' She ran her hands over the bulge of her stomach where it protruded from the vest. 'You've no idea how cold it gets here sometimes, even when it's sunny outside.'

After that it was coffee. Then toothpaste. Then soap. Then the electricity meter, the dial spinning down, neither of them with a penny to slide into the slot.

'I had a penny once,' said Ruby, sitting at the small table rubbing at her swollen feet. 'But it disappeared.'

Barbara shaved the thinnest slice she could from their last piece of tongue and kept silent.

Then there was the rent. 'It's double now.' The landlady stood in the hall when Barbara came home one evening after a long day of taking down someone else's notes. The landlady's arms were folded, blouse buttoned all the way to the dip at the bottom of her throat. A wave of cheap brandy washed out of her as she spoke.

'What do you mean?' Barbara said, lifting a gloved hand to cover her nose.

'There's two of you, isn't there. Soon be three.' The landlady tapped her fingers three times on her forearm as though to emphasize the point. 'Maybe even more.' And she looked Barbara up and down then as though she knew something Barbara did not.

'But it's still one room.'

'Can't have room shares if there's only one bed.'

Barbara lifted her handbag and flipped open the gilt clip. 'I'm not sure I have the extra right now. Can you wait until the end of the month?'

The landlady unfolded her arms and placed them on her hips instead. 'Is she married?'

'What do you mean?' Barbara looked up from her purse.

'Rent or no rent, you can't stay if she's not married. It's not that kind of house.'

'But you just said . . .'

'Well, I've changed my mind.'

The two women stared at each other for a moment. 'But where shall we go then?' Barbara said.

'That's your business. I'll give you a week.' The landlady leaned forward then and gripped Barbara on the arm as though she was doing her a favour. 'By the way, you do know she steals things?'

'What?'

'Just ask the other girls.'

Upstairs, Ruby was standing before the mirror apply-ing lipstick from a brand-new tube. 'What does she mean, Ruby?' Barbara demanded. She hadn't even taken off her gloves.

'I have no idea.' Ruby pouted at herself. 'She's just an old witch.'

'But we need money,' Barbara insisted. 'What about the baby's father? Can't you try him?'

'No.' Ruby gave up colouring her lips and took out a pencil instead to draw lines around her eyes.

'Why not?'

'Because.'

And Barbara knew there was no reply to that. Besides, the baby's father could have been anyone, as far as Barbara was concerned.

'Anyway . . .' Ruby smudged the pencil line with the tip of her index finger. 'Isn't there someone else we could ask?'

'Like who?'

'Your Mr Nye, for example.' Ruby waved the pencil in the air in a nonchalant gesture as though it was nothing to her that in only seven days they would be left out on the street.

Barbara looked away. 'He's not my Mr Nye,' she said. If there was one thing she was not prepared to share with Ruby, Nye Junior was it.

Ruby turned back to the mirror. 'But you'd like it if he was.'

*

Mr Nye Senior had been eating dinner with his wife and son when Ruby arrived barely three months before. She'd watched them through a crack in the door, all three frozen in place with their cutlery suspended somewhere between plate and mouth, as the housekeeper announced her arrival. It was Nye Senior who'd put down his knife and fork first. 'A client,' he said, pushing back his chair and exiting into the hall where Ruby was waiting with her basket on her hip. She had come straight to Nye Senior after the artist had shown her the door.

In the elegant vestibule they regarded each other – the older man with a scar on his back, the younger woman with two beating hearts inside. Then Mr Nye Senior gave a sort of semi-bow and held out his arm. 'Miss Ruby Penny,' he said. 'Charmed, I'm sure.'

The study was like the man. Meticulous, but with a certain flair. Books with gold spines. A rug woven with damask. A desk with a deep walnut sheen. Mr Nye Senior took the chair behind the desk as though it were a matter of course.

'How long?' Nye Senior was a lawyer. He liked to get to the point.

'Too long.'

Mr Nye picked up a silver letter opener from his desk and ran one finger along the engraved blade. 'There are things which can be done.'

Ruby shook her head. 'It's too late.'

'Surely Mrs Withers . . .'

But Ruby just shrugged her shoulders. She could still feel that cold rubber tube inside her. This time she would keep what she could.

Mr Nye Senior bent his head in acknowledgement that his usual way of doing things would not be accepted here. 'Then I'm not sure what you think I can do, my dear.' He lifted his hands and held them out as though to indicate the uselessness of a room full of books.

Ruby put a hand upon her hip. 'I need somewhere to stay.'

'Well, you cannot stay here.' Mr Nye Senior inclined his head towards the dining room from which he had just come. 'Family is family, after all.'

'I don't have anyone else to ask.'

'Have you tried our mutual friend?' An artist with paint embedded in his toes.

Ruby looked away, colour rising up her neck. 'He's not inclined.'

'Well, my dear.' Mr Nye Senior stared at Ruby's stomach. 'Then I can't say I'm inclined either.'

'But you have more money.'

Mr Nye Senior smiled and pushed a hand through a curl of vibrant hair that had fallen over his forehead. 'I think you'll find I've been more than generous in that regard.'

Ruby looked away, thinking of a necklace and two earrings to match stitched into the hem of an emerald gown. 'How about your son?' she said. 'Perhaps he might help.'

For a moment Mr Nye Senior's eyes blinked at her just like those of the stoat on his office mantelpiece. 'My son? What's he got to do with it?' Ruby stared back, hand running across her stomach where it protruded from her coat. Nye Senior coloured then, a deep stain right at the centre of each cheek. When he spoke again his voice was ice. 'Perhaps you should try your mother – Mrs Penny, isn't it? I'm sure she could help.'

Ruby flushed herself, a raw kind of red. 'Mrs Penny isn't my mother.'

'Or your sister then.' Mr Nye moved out from behind his desk. 'She, in particular, might be interested to hear what you have to say.' He spread out an arm to show Ruby the door. 'After all, that's what family is for, isn't it? Times like these.'

Two and three-quarter months together, and Ruby and Barbara walked back towards 14 Elm Row. Undemolished. Undivided. Three storeys and a semi-basement stretching up to a gable window in the roof. It wouldn't be for good, Barbara was certain about that, just for whatever they could get. She went straight to the front door to ring the bell. Ruby went for the back.

Through the kitchen window, Ruby watched Mrs Penny beating pastry as though it might be the last thing she ever did in life. Tony was still sitting by the stove poking away at the insides of his latest pipe. But he looked old now, grizzled, his face a thick map of veins. In the crook of his elbow a toddler was balanced, small frilled skirt riding up around her waist. Inside Ruby's swollen belly she suddenly felt her own creature pressing down.

'Ruby!' Barbara's face appeared from the narrow passageway at the side of the house. 'What are you doing?'

'Just looking.' Ruby didn't even bother to lower her voice.

'Well, stop looking,' Barbara hissed. 'And come back round the front.'

The front door was opened by a young woman with a short skirt and a baby on her arm too. She glanced down at Ruby's bulging stomach. 'Come to join the throng?'

'Not likely,' said Ruby, pushing past and heading towards the stairs.

'So sorry,' said Barbara as she stepped inside too. She was still wearing her gloves.

The hall had been repainted, brown to the level of the dado rail, dirty cream above. The floorboards were covered with a long roll of red lino, easy to scrub. At the bottom of the stairs, stacks of folded cotton nappies were waiting for someone to carry them up. From the floors above came the distant sound of young women talking, the occasional slamming of doors. Water ran constantly through the pipes, accompanied by the plaintive wails of a hundred babies (or thereabouts). The latest Penny Family Business. Fallen women still; just those who kept their babies this time, at least for a short while.

Downstairs, Barbara sat in the kitchen drinking tea poured from Dorothea's pot. Tony sat opposite, one eye leering in a continuous kind of wink. At the table Mrs Penny still kneaded her pastry with a vigour that belied her age. 'Well,' she said. 'What did you expect?'

It wasn't a question and Barbara knew not to bother with a reply. How was it, she thought (not for the first time) that Mrs Penny had it all, while she and Ruby had nothing but themselves?

'Wilful, that's the word. Nothing but trouble.' Mrs

Penny began to gather up her pastry scraps. 'I warned you once before. Runs in the family.'

On the other side of the stove Tony poured himself a shaky tumbler of rum. Barbara pressed her arm towards her stomach to quell a sudden twist in her gut. She would have liked a taste of rum herself right now. Ever since she'd stepped back into this house, her insides had begun to cramp.

'I suppose you've got no money.' Mrs Penny squashed her pastry into a grey lump with the heel of her hand.

'Who told you that?'

'One has one's sources.' Above Mrs Penny a neon strip light crackled and sparked. 'You could come back here, I suppose,' she said. 'I can always do with another pair of hands. Though I don't imagine madam would agree.'

Barbara held an arm up against her forehead for a moment, cold sweat suddenly gathered along the line of her hair. 'No, I suppose not.'

Mrs Penny wiped her hands on a tea cloth and came to stand in front of Barbara. 'You know she'll take what she can get and leave you with nothing.'

'She won't.' Barbara dropped her arm and held tight to her teacup instead, trying to still the tremor in her hand.

'She's done it before. Went to work for Mrs Withers, didn't she? Never gave you a second thought.'

Good riddance to bad rubbish. Wasn't that what Mrs Penny had said?

'But she's my sister.' Barbara's cup chattered in its saucer despite her grip.

'What's that got to do with anything?' Mrs Penny

looked down at Barbara, shaking her head as though she'd seen how it would work out years ago and had just been proved right. 'Neither of your sisters has turned out very reliable. Where are they when you need them the most?' Mrs Penny bent suddenly and removed the rattling teacup from Barbara, putting it down on the table with a clatter of her own. 'I tried my best,' she said. 'With you, in particular. But all that time together and you never learned a thing.'

Barbara stared up at the only mother she had ever known, alert now for something she must have missed. 'What are you talking about?' she said, face creased with confusion and the cramping of her gut.

Mrs Penny stood before Barbara, two flour-dipped hands on her hips. 'Can't you see what's right in front of you?' She shook her head again. 'Your sister, of course. Not satisfied with the father, had to have the son too.'

Outside, Ruby was waiting for Barbara on the corner where once Clementine had stood, leaning against the wall in a nonchalant manner. Barbara came walking towards her, hurried and shaky, handbag gripped before her like a shield. Ruby, big now but still with a certain grace, levered herself off the wall. At her feet was an old suitcase, insides stuffed full.

'Where have you been?' Ruby started to complain as soon as Barbara got near. 'I've been waiting for ages.' She gestured to the suitcase. 'It's too heavy for me to carry on my own.'

Barbara stood directly in front of her sister, her face grey, like the remains of Mrs Penny's pastry. 'What did

Mrs Penny mean?' she said. 'Not satisfied with the father, had to have the son too?'

Ruby flinched and turned her startling eyes away from her twin. 'We should go now, Barbara, before she tries to stop us.'

'Is she talking about Mr Nye? My Mr Nye?'

'I have no idea.' Ruby fell back against the wall where once Clementine had fallen back too.

'What did she mean, Ruby?' Barbara didn't raise her voice often, but this time all the young women watching from the gable windows could hear.

Ruby turned her gaze back to her sister's pig-like face. 'Don't shout, Barbara, it doesn't suit you.'

'Just tell me the truth, Ruby, for once in your life, or I'll have to take Mrs Penny's word for it.'

Ruby laughed then. A horrible, abandoned sound. 'You'd believe Mrs Penny over me. The woman who stole everything we ever had. I told you, but you never listened. She's a thief, nothing but a parasite. Why shouldn't I take what I want, when she took everything from me?'

A terrible, heavy, coldness spread through Barbara then. Pennies from Tony's pockets. Mrs Penny's powder puff. Soap with a patterned wrapper. Or perfume with a glass stopper for a lid. Mrs Penny had been right. There was nothing Ruby wouldn't take if she wanted it for herself. A silver apostle spoon because Barbara took one first. A dead sister's bedroom because Ruby always had loved Clementine the most. And now, just because she could, a tall man in a narrow seaside bunk. Someone who dreamed of oranges while Barbara dreamed of something else.

A father reading by a fireside.

A mother sewing buttons on a coat.

A baby smiling as it turned in its crib.

Barbara clutched her side all of a sudden as a hot pain stabbed right in the centre of her gut. Not cramps this time, but everything that had always been in front of her, but which she had never allowed herself to see.

'It's not Mrs Penny who's the thief, Ruby,' she said then. 'It's you.'

Night drew in like a cloak as Barbara ran through the streets of London, nothing but a handbag held tight in her arms. Down main roads, down side roads, down cul de sacs and back. On, on, towards the familiar stink of the river and of tidal London mud.

She ran until she could run no more, straight to where the water flowed far below her, thick and glinting in the dark. Then she stood swaying on the edge, cold seeping up through the soles of her shoes, imagining her body falling, falling, disappearing just as Clementine's had disappeared. Nothing left behind but Ruby to do as she liked.

Blood rushed through Barbara's arteries and into her brain, sounding like a great ocean inside the middle of her head. What was it Mrs Penny had told her once? It runs in the family. Fat Barbara. Pig Barbara. Always second best. And she needed it then, just for a moment. Salvation. Or something like it. The pull of the water dragging her under, running through her hair like a cold-fingered nurse, racing to fill up her ears and her mouth. For all Barbara had ever wanted was Ruby. While all Ruby had ever wanted was whatever she could have for herself.

Then she stepped away. Bent double. Vomited. Hot bile spattering to the concrete pavement, onto the hem of her second-best coat.

Three hours later, darkness wrapping around everything it touched, Barbara limped back to the bedsit to find all the windows ablaze. She fumbled in her handbag to get at her key, only to discover that the door was already open, a small whirlwind waiting for her in the hall.

'I told you,' the landlady was shrieking. 'I said. No girls like that in my house.' The little woman clenched her fingers tight around the top of Barbara's arm.

'What?' said Barbara. 'Let go.'

'I told you.' The woman jerked Barbara towards her, spit freckling Barbara's cheek. 'I said. I won't have it.'

'Leave me alone,' Barbara cried. She twisted her arm away and stumbled for the stairs, tripping as she made her way up.

On the top step another girl stood waiting, nightgown falling to her knees. 'We called an ambulance,' she said as Barbara blundered past. 'There was an awful lot of blood.'

At the door to her room, Barbara stared across at the alcove where a stain, bright as a pillar box, had soaked through from the eiderdown to the mattress. On the floor a chair had been knocked over, a bloody handprint on its seat. On the table Mrs Penny's suitcase lay open, all its contents spread about. A jewellery box lined with nappy velveteen. A fox fur eaten away by mange. A china cherub, chipped and dirty, its rosy mouth rubbed pale. There was a bottle of Mrs Penny's Innoxa. A photograph of two children sleeping behind cracked glass. And next to that, two spoons, once silver, now tarnished, two tiny apostles attached to their ends.

Barbara stared at the spoons, the bowl of one nesting inside the other, as thick clots of blood began to seep from between her own legs now. One last chance, gone forever. Then she raised her hands, still wearing her gloves, and swept everything to the floor.

PART FOUR

A Photograph

CERTIFIED COPY OF AN ENTRY OF BIRTH

LOCAL REGISTER OFFICE

Application No. B 056112

REGISTRATION DISTRICT: *Kensington*

BIRTH IN THE SUBDISTRICT OF: *Chelsea*

When & Where Born:
  12 June 1925, 14 Elm Row, London

Name, if any: *Clementine Amelia Walker*

Sex: *Girl*

Name & Surname of Father: *Alfred Walker*

Name, Surname & Maiden Name of Mother:
  Dorothea Walker née Stirling

Occupation of Father: *Works Manager*

Signature, Description & Residence of Informant:
  A. Walker, Father, 14 Elm Row, London

When Registered: *18 June 1925*

Signature of Registrar: *M. G. Ellison*

CERTIFIED to be a true copy of an entry in the certified copy of a Register of Births in the District above mentioned.

2011

The funeral parlour belonged to Scotmid, the same organization that ran the supermarket where Barbara stocked up on her rum. Cheap. Family oriented. *A member of your community from cradle to grave.* No wonder Margaret's search for a missing corpse had ended up here. This must be where they brought all the lost souls.

She had phoned from London to give Janie the good news. A story to tell, at last. 'Excellent,' Janie had replied. 'I'll see you tomorrow then, with the paperwork.'

Except . . .

London was unauthorized. Margaret was still supposed to be in the north. She pressed the last of her pound coins into a slot in the phone box outside the Chelsea Old Town Hall. 'What time do you want me?' she said hoping for afternoon at least.

'Ten a.m.,' said Janie. 'And bring Mrs Walker's possessions.'

'Her possessions?'

'You'll find them with the body. We've got her back, it seems.'

Margaret came home on the last train north, sliding from one day into the next as it heaved and wheezed its way up the east coast. Most people slept throughout, squeezed into narrow bunks, but the remains of Margaret's expenses wouldn't stretch to that. Instead she rode north in a carriage that was empty except for herself and a brown folder laid out on a table, less slim now than it had been just a few days before.

The sleeper was expensive, but Margaret knew now that sometimes that was how life's little wrinkles worked themselves out. Besides, they opened the buffet car after Newcastle and she feasted on smoky bacon crisps once again. Life had a funny kind of circular motion to it that Margaret was just beginning to enjoy.

'We collected her three days ago.' The director of the funeral parlour was a mild man who wore a dark suit and an expression more akin to a helper at a children's party than a person who buried the dead. 'Didn't realize anything was wrong until we consulted the paperwork. Not complete, you know. No date of birth.'

'Yes,' said Margaret. But not for long, she thought.

'Instant dismissal if we hold a funeral for the wrong person.' The funeral director held out a business card that declared he was also a community relations officer. 'Used to work in finance,' he said. 'Got out long ago.'

Margaret wished then that she had got out long ago too. Well before the disaster of a man with hair the colour of slate in the rain. Or two children in crumpled Technicolor that should have been hers but weren't. Before bailiffs and solicitors' letters. Before a rag soaked in turpentine dropped through a letter box, followed by a match. Not to mention twelve dusty pills on a cold kitchen floor and a bottle of cheap wine gone sour.

At the very least she might have had a better outfit. The director cum community officer wore his well – black but with the faintest stripe of charcoal, a tie dip-dyed claret.

Though Margaret thought she could go one better. For she had a dead fox hidden beneath her coat.

Mrs Walker was in the basement being rinsed clean. Down a narrow stairway, past several empty coffins propped up against a wall. In the middle of the room was a long table covered by a cloth. Beneath the cloth was a body.

Mrs Clementine Walker at last.

Margaret's client turned out to be as slight as a wren, all tiny bones and not much else, just as Dr Atkinson had said. It was as though somewhere along the line of her life she had drunk all the medicine and shrunk, nothing left but a shadow of herself. No wonder she had been so easy to miss.

'I'll leave you alone then.' The funeral director was already heading back up the stairs. 'Michaela will look after you. She's our expert when it comes to being prepared.'

Michaela was young. In her twenties perhaps, maybe thirty. 'Call me Micky,' she said to Margaret. 'Everyone does.' Smothered from head to foot in a gigantic apron, hands sheathed in a pair of latex gloves. 'I'm glad someone's come to help. I was beginning to wonder if anyone was going to claim her.' Micky adjusted some silvered tubing where it emerged from beneath Mrs Walker's sheet, liquid running like mercury through the dead woman's vital organs, blood siphoned off, all the rest flushed clean.

Margaret was unnerved, as though her client might be washed away again before she'd had a chance to close the case for good. She held up her brown folder. 'I'm just here to collect her possessions.' Though even Margaret knew by then there was more to it than that.

'It's always good to get some advice, though.' Micky picked up a large make-up brush.

'I can try, I suppose.' Margaret had never considered a career as an embalmer, even though up until this moment her own life had been about as embalmed as one could get without actually being deceased.

'I need to know what she might like,' Micky said. 'Hair and make-up, that sort of thing. Wouldn't want to send her off painted the wrong colour.'

Mrs Walker's hair was dyed, just as Pati had said. White at the roots and a sort of self-concocted fiery orange at the tips. Margaret could see that it was in dire need of retouching and she was sorry, all of a sudden, that her client hadn't been able to hold on long enough for that. 'Can you do something about her hair?' she said.

Micky had combed Mrs Walker's hair straight back from the forehead, and despite her slightness (or perhaps because of it), the new hairstyle suited Margaret's client. It made her seem rather like a graceful reposing queen, nothing but the faintest hint of violet on her eyelids and a small mouth rubbed pale until it almost wasn't there. It was rather like looking at the china cherub, just without the shorn-off limb.

'Do you mean dye it?' Micky asked.

'I suppose so.'

'We wouldn't normally.' Micky put a hand to Mrs Walker's brow and stroked the dead woman's hair back from the crown of her head to the tips. 'But perhaps we could for her.'

Mrs Walker's skin was like the cherub's too, a translucent quality that Margaret now realized was common in the dead. She reached into her bag and pulled out an old-fashioned powder compact worn down to its last few crumbs. 'I think she'd like this for her face.' Mrs Walker might be pickled inside, but Margaret knew what she would prefer on her cheeks. 'And lipstick too,' she said.

Micky produced a folder and wrote on the outside, *Mrs Walker, deceased.* 'Colour?' she said.

'Scarlet,' Margaret replied.

Micky started to make notes in flowing, curling script. 'And what do you think she might like to wear?' she said. 'We've got the clothes she was found in.' She pointed with her pen to the only belongings Mrs Walker seemed to have left: a skirt made of tweed; a patterned synthetic blouse; tights all wrinkled around the knees and ankles; and, perched on top, a pair of scuffed brown lace-ups, size five like a schoolgirl's, as though Mrs Walker had never quite grown up.

Both women looked at the pile of raggedy clothes, then at the fragile corpse. Just like Margaret, Mrs Walker appeared to have dressed herself out of somebody else's wardrobe. A kind of bag lady, perhaps, rummaging through other people's stuff to make a living, pushing a shopping trolley of jumble-sale finds around expensive streets. That would explain the lack of any useful sort of stuff. Pension books and bank statements, rent receipts or letters from a cousin or a niece. Margaret's heart gave a small leap. Was this how she would end too if she decided to head back to the south? Drifting from borough to borough with nothing but a small blue holdall and a pair of inappropriate (now ruined) shoes?

Micky frowned at where Mrs Walker lay becalmed

beneath her cloth. 'We could put her in a shroud, of course.'

Scrubbed clean, white as the freshly fallen snow out-side.

'But perhaps you know of something better?'

And Margaret knew at once that she did.

Micky touched the sheet about where Mrs Walker's ankle might be. 'I also encourage people to put something into the coffin with the deceased. A memento of sorts.'

A dusty nut, perhaps. An orange on a plate. Or maybe just some scraps of paper scattered over the corpse. Moyra Walker. Mary Walker. Ann. All the children Mrs Walker longed for, perhaps, but never had.

'Mobile phones are a favourite.'

'Mobile phones?' Margaret couldn't imagine why any-one would want to be buried with their mobile phone. Wasn't the point of death that you finally left all that behind?

Micky laughed. 'The relatives want it. Sometimes the deceased. In case they aren't really dead.'

'Wouldn't it be too late by then?' Margaret said.

'Yes, but death isn't rational, is it? We get all sorts in here.'

'Yes,' said Margaret, 'I'm sure.'

'Do you know where she came from?' Micky was tick-ing off boxes on her form.

'London originally. Who knows, after that?'

'London,' beamed Micky. 'Now there's a place.' Which was one way of putting it. She tweaked the silver tubes again, the last of Mrs Walker dripping through into a great plastic vessel beneath. 'Do you come from London?'

'Yes,' said Margaret. 'Well, sort of. How about you?'

'Me? No.' Micky looked up and smiled. 'Ireland,' she said. 'Celtic Tiger before it lost its roar. Can't you tell?'

And then, of course, Margaret could.

'I might try my luck in London,' Micky said. 'I'm sort of filling in time here, if you know what I mean. Waiting for the client who appears with money strapped beneath their clothes along with a note saying, "For the embalmer".' She laughed then, a lark surfing an Irish breeze.

'Do you get that often?'

'Money? Occasionally. But never the note.' Micky laughed again. 'It's usually jewellery stitched into hems.'

Bibles and paybooks for the husbands. Jewellery for the wives. Margaret glanced over at the neat pile of Mrs Walker's clothes. Perhaps there was a fortune sewn into the waistband of her client's jumble-sale skirt. One thousand fifty-pound notes folded concertina-style and secured forever by a needle and thread. Or failing that, a brooch.

Micky laughed again, as though she knew exactly what Margaret was thinking (which, of course, she did). 'There's none. I've checked. But you can look if you like. Wouldn't want to burn up someone's inheritance before they'd even had a chance to read the will.'

Margaret went over to the pile of clothes and lifted them one by one, just to be sure, a fumble at the hems and the cuffs, all her fingers deep in Mrs Walker's weft and weave. But Micky was right. There was nothing there that should not be, other than the absence of anything significant at all.

Micky put down her file, all the boxes ticked now.

'We'll wait for you to sort out the details with Janie before
we get her prepared. Is there anything else I can help you
with?'

'This,' said Margaret, picking up a piece of newsprint
from beneath Mrs Walker's pile of clothes. Her client's one
remaining possession, such as it was. 'May I take it?'

'Of course,' said Janie. 'What's hers is yours now.'

At the Office for Lost People (deceased), Margaret began
with a brown folder full of paper and ended with a story
about children (long dead), mothers (mad) and a woman
who was born, then lost, then born again beneath an
embalmer's sheet in Leith. She laid out all the treasure
she had accumulated across Janie's desk in the hope that
an invoice for services rendered would be issued in swift
response.

A jeweller's receipt.

An admissions form.

A certificate for death.

A certificate for marriage.

And another one for birth.

'The crematorium will be pleased,' said Janie, tapping
at those neat teeth with her biro as she surveyed everything that Margaret had brought. 'It's about time Mrs
Walker was moved off their pending list.'

'Dorothea and Alfred,' said Margaret. 'Two dead
twins.'

Janie shuffled some papers on her desk. 'Clementine,
you say?'

'Yes. Clementine Amelia Walker, born 1925. I have her
birth certificate here.'

'Excellent.' Janie looked into her computer screen and pressed a few buttons on her keyboard. 'It's paperwork that matters, in the end.' She started flicking through the forms, all the *i*s dotted, all the *t*s crossed, barely glancing at the other odd objects Margaret had brought along.

A twist of orange peel.

Some paper scraps.

An envelope with three small clippings of hair.

Forms were Janie's *métier*. The rest was just rumour and speculation, nothing but anonymous stuff to hold in the hand. When she came to the certificates from Chelsea she frowned at them for a moment while Margaret held her breath. 'Everything seems to have arrived very quickly. Normally it takes a week or so for official documents to get here, unless you go in person, of course.'

'Oh.' Heat flashed up beneath Margaret's coat. She could feel her face shining like a beacon pointing directly towards an unauthorized trip to London undertaken with some defrauded expenses cash.

'You must have special powers of persuasion for them to have sent the certificates so soon.'

Margaret swallowed. 'I told them it was an emergency. High death count in Edinburgh needing to be cleared.'

'Yes,' said Janie. 'Right.' And she flushed too, a delicate shade to match her jumper.

Margaret's heart lay down again after that. Her lie hadn't been a lie at all, just a rearrangement of the truth.

'She was known as "Mrs", wasn't she?' Janie was staring at her computer monitor again, adding words to a form. 'But you're saying she never married.'

'Yes,' said Margaret. 'No. I mean, not as far as I can tell.'

'Well . . .' Janie added the title 'Miss', before the word 'Clementine'. 'All sorts of women pretend to be married. Even in this day and age.'

Margaret nodded. It was the Edinburgh Way.

'1925 makes her a bit older than we might have thought. Perhaps the cold preserved her.'

Black lungs. Liver like paste. Not to speak of the holes in Mrs Walker's bones and her brain. Margaret wasn't sure it was the cold so much as the whisky that had kept her client pickled for so long.

Either way, Janie tapped the precious d.o.b. into her computer screen. 'You're certain it's her, not some mix-up.' Janie obviously liked to double-check, in case somebody double-checked her.

'Well, there is the jeweller's receipt.'

Janie rummaged in the folder for the crumpled piece of paper still giving off the faintest scent of cloves. 'How does that fit with the subsequent identification?'

'Clementine Walker was their client.'

Rose & Sons, jewellers of distinction, visited before a foray into a long-abandoned admission box. A shop door that opened with the ding of an old-fashioned bell. A smart young woman who appeared from somewhere down in the depths. A firm that was still in the same family even after fifty years. Magic, Margaret had thought then. Happens more often than you think.

'Yes,' the young woman had said when Margaret enquired. 'We do keep records. Even some from as long ago as this. If you'll just give me a minute.'

And a minute was all that it had taken before the confirmation came back. 'Walker, Miss. Initial C.,' and the same phone number that had already summoned Margaret on the flying visit south. Her client was her client. No doubt left.

'There's this too, of course,' Margaret said to Janie, indicating the piece of newsprint once wrapped beneath Mrs Walker's clothes.

'What's this?' said Janie, with a slight wrinkle of her neat little nose.

Not Births, Marriages and Deaths, but a Bible verse. Margaret pointed to the box all bordered with black. '*Suffer little children* . . . Matthew 19, verses 14 to 16,' she said.

'And?' Janie poked at the news-sheet. She didn't seem quite as convinced as Margaret that its everyday exhortation to do good provided the final proof that Clementine Walker was indeed the corpse reposing down in Leith.

'The Ten Commandments,' Margaret said. 'That's what the rest of the verse is. Murder and adultery. Loving thy neighbour as thyself. Not to mention stealing, of course.'

'But what's that got to do with Mrs Walker?' There was the tiniest hint of irritation in Janie's voice now.

'It's written on the Brazil nut.'

'The Brazil nut?'

And the dusty nut retrieved from the back of a drawer came into its own.

'Can you see?' The smart young woman at Rose & Sons, jewellers of distinction, had beckoned to Margaret when she'd asked. 'It's the Ten Commandments.' And she had laughed, eyeglass held up to her face. 'Thou shalt not.'

Margaret had been amazed at how the indecipherable scratches suddenly took on their proper life when she peered through the eyeglass too. *Thou shalt do no murder. Thou shalt not commit adultery. Thou shalt not steal. Thou shalt not bear false witness. Honour thy father and thy mother. Love thy neighbour as thyself.* Barbara Penny's Ten Commandments, etched into Mrs Walker's nut.

'Well, I suppose that gives us some sort of connection,' Janie said. 'Religion, at least. Shall we say Church of England? She came from London, didn't she? Like you.'

'Yes,' said Margaret, though she didn't remember telling Janie that she was from that great metropolis down south.

'And have you any idea why she was in Edinburgh?'

'No,' said Margaret. For a moment a dead fox's small paws dug into an area just above her breast. She had pondered that question several times herself on the train ride north and come up with a blank. Mrs Walker was nothing but a refugee in a cold land, just like her, waiting for the next move to somewhere else.

Janie sighed. 'I'll need to add the nut to the official file, I suppose, just to keep things clear. Have you brought it with you?'

'Yes,' said Margaret and fished for it in the pocket of her coat.

But just like Mrs Walker before it, the dusty Brazil nut was gone.

'Sorry,' said Margaret, pulling out orange peel and a small tin pig in amongst a spray of sausage roll crumbs. 'It seems to have escaped.' Followed by a lucky coronation penny. Not so lucky now.

Janie was annoyed. 'Well, what happened to the brooch, then?' she said. 'That at least would prove the connection beyond any doubt.'

Small and star-shaped, with a red stone at its heart. Margaret had asked about the brooch herself before she left Rose & Sons for good, along with all the other jewellery listed on the receipt. A shiny coffin. Or a larger hearse. Perhaps even some flowers. Margaret knew it was money that mattered. Emerald necklaces with earrings to match could buy a very good funeral should there be any of the treasure left.

'Sorry,' the young woman had said. 'Sold long ago, according to these records. Anonymous buyer. Handled by a solicitor's firm. Nye & Sons?' And she raised her eyebrows. 'All except the brooch, of course. That just disappeared.'

Margaret had wondered then where the brooch had gone. She would have liked to hold something in her hand that her client had actually owned – passed down through the family from mother to daughter, perhaps. Jewellery. Wasn't that what women left behind, more often than not?

'It wasn't in the flat, was it?' Janie sounded hopeful for a moment.

'I don't think so,' said Margaret, shifting the fox fur so that its paws hung less dangerously beneath her coat. She could tell already that her invoice for services rendered might not be quite so swiftly forthcoming as she had hoped. It seemed Mrs Walker's story wasn't over yet.

'Well.' Janie pushed away her forms for a moment. 'Perhaps you'd better go and find out for sure. We can't close the case without it.' She rapped at her teeth once

again with her biro, *tip-tap and that's that*. 'Besides . . .'
She lowered her pen now and pinioned Margaret with
the pale glitter of her eyes. 'Everyone leaves something
behind, if you only know where to look.'

1980

The call had come on an ordinary September day, wind tossing dirty leaves all about the Edinburgh streets.

'I have to go to a funeral,' Barbara had said, standing by the sideboard in their latest living room holding the telephone receiver as though for the first time ever it had delivered good news.

Seventeen-year-old Margaret could hear the dialling tone from where she was sitting at the table, hair hanging across her face, turquoise painted onto her toes. 'Whose funeral?'

'An old friend. In London.'

'What old friend?' As far as Margaret was concerned, her mother didn't have any friends. Not in Edinburgh and not in the south either.

'None of your business.' As usual, Barbara hadn't been interested in illumination, only in what might happen next. 'I'm going tomorrow,' she said.

'Can I come?' For the first time in several months Margaret saw a future opening up before her in a flare of chatter and smoke.

'No.' Barbara seemed particularly firm on that. 'You've got to get a job.'

'Why?'

'Because.'

And as Margaret knew already, there never was going to be an answer to that.

Down, down in the big city in the south, the original

Mrs Penny lay dead on a slab. An old lady eaten away by cancer, from the inside out, finally succumbing to the fact that no one (not even her) could go on forever, however hard they tried. It was serendipity really, Barbara thought, when she arrived at the undertakers' all belted up inside her latest coat. Mrs Penny always had said there was a cancer at the heart of the Walker family. Now it had eaten her too.

Barbara watched as fluids ran in one tube and Mrs Penny seeped out of the next. Trust the only mother she had ever known to select embalming. Preserved for as long as possible, even in the grave.

The funeral director was pleased to meet Barbara at last. 'They're burying her in the Old Church plot.' He dipped his head in acknowledgement of their arrangement. 'I thought you'd want to know.'

'Thank you,' Barbara replied, all her discreet enquiries finally adding up. Barbara was nothing if not efficient; Mrs Penny had taught her that.

'Nye & Sons are organizing it,' the funeral director went on. 'No next of kin left, they said.'

'Really.' Barbara put a finger to the patterned scarf firmly knotted at her throat. She would see about that.

The office just off Ironmonger Lane had not changed one bit. The stoat still winked from the mantelpiece. The books still ran from ceiling to floor and back. That girl still sat behind a huge desk, older now and with more rings on her fingers, hair still gleaming like a helmet of bronze. Barbara Penny was ushered in to sit before Mr Nye Senior's desk once again, hands clasped on her handbag, legs firmly crossed. What was it about life, she thought then, that it had this circular motion she could never quite escape?

Mr Nye Senior was older now too, hair just starting to recede, a smooth blue vein lying beneath the skin of his forehead. He didn't come out from behind his desk this time, just coughed for a moment before he started, leaning back in his chair until it creaked. Then he read Barbara Penny the relevant bit from Mrs Penny's will.

When he was finished both of them sat looking at a slim box of silver apostle spoons that lay before them on the desk. Barbara Penny's inheritance, such as it was.

'Who did Mrs Penny leave the house to?' Barbara knew there was treasure to be had in London. Bricks. And mortar. And slate. Why else would she have bothered to come south?

Mr Nye Senior flicked his eyes away from Barbara for a moment. 'It will be sold.'

'And the proceeds?'

'To the Children's Society. In memory of her work.' Mr Nye Senior curled his fingers around the silver blade of a paperknife. 'A very worthy cause.' He lifted the knife, let it gleam for a moment in the low office light. 'Not that there will be many proceeds, I shouldn't think. The house is very run down.'

Over the other side of the desk, in the upright chair, Barbara uncrossed her legs, then crossed them again. Middle-aged now, Rainmate secure in her bag. Her arms were thick, with flesh just starting to go loose. 'Perhaps it might be possible for me to make a claim,' she said. 'As her daughter.'

'Her adopted daughter,' corrected Mr Nye Senior, putting the blade down again as though he was on more secure ground now.

'Yes, but . . .'

'Only if the adoption was official. Approved by a court, I mean.'

'Was it not?'

Mr Nye Senior gave a wave of his hand. 'Not as far as I know. I don't have any certificates, I'm afraid. War and all that. Unofficial adoption. Happened a lot at that time.'

Barbara leaned forwards. 'Perhaps you might be able to help me prove it. Given your expertise in sorting things out.'

Mr Nye Senior just smiled, a smile of ever-diminishing returns. 'I'm not sure about that,' he said, looking around the walls of his office at all the naked women. 'A conflict of interest, perhaps.'

'A conflict of interest?' Barbara frowned.

'There was the matter of the painting.'

'The painting?'

Mr Nye Senior nudged at the blade of the paperknife with the tip of his index finger. 'I seem to remember asking you about it once.'

Twenty minutes later, in a dark corner of a gallery on a busy London street, Barbara Penny stood in front of a painting covered in a savage sweep of oil. The girl in the portrait was impossibly young, laid back on a green chaise longue, nothing to wear but a pair of shoes to match.

A gallery warder stood beside Barbara, hands in gloves just like the ones Barbara used to wear. 'Our most recent acquisition,' he said. 'Not popular. But important, in the British tradition. It's rather alluring, don't you think?'

Skin flaring like the centre of a jet of gas. Eyes that followed Barbara wherever she stood.

The warder indicated the label down on the right. '*Bucket Girl Number 1*. The artist did a whole sequence.'

Including a small brown painting, dirty in more ways than one, living in the bottom of Barbara's chest of drawers, reminding her not to forget.

'He's dead now. Tragic, really.'

Tweed suit. Bare feet ingrained with paint.

'Drank himself to death. Quite common really. Amongst the artist types.'

'Where are the rest of them?' Barbara held a slim box of silver spoons beneath her arm. Ten out of twelve. It was something, at least.

The warder shrugged. 'Who knows? Around and about. They pop up from time to time.'

In a vault. In a crate. In some collector's house. In a container shipped overseas for someone else's delight.

'Rarely out of storage now, not fashionable yet.'

Disappeared into a void, into a lacuna of time and space. Yet still Ruby always managed to be handled with gloves.

'Thank you,' Barbara said to the warder as another woman came clicking down the hard gallery floors towards where they stood. 'I'll remember where it is now, should I ever come again.' Then she turned to where Jessica

Plymmet had arrived beside them. 'Hello,' she said. 'You have something for me, I think.'

Two women, two sides of the same coin (almost, but not quite) sat together in the gallery tea room, both still wearing their coats.

'Thank you for coming,' said Jessica Plymmet, cup of tea by her elbow, forgetting that it was Barbara Penny who had made the arrangement rather than herself.

'That's all right,' said Barbara. 'Anything I can do to help.'

'It was lucky, I suppose. That you phoned when you did.'

'Yes,' said Barbara. Though even then she didn't really think ten silver spoons was quite as much luck as she deserved. Barbara wondered for a moment what had happened to that coronation penny, disappeared years ago from some dingy Edinburgh flat. She could have done with some luck now that she was back in the south.

'I wrote to you,' Mrs Plymmet said, lifting her teacup and regarding Barbara over the rim. 'Several times.'

'Really,' said Barbara. 'You must have got the wrong address.'

Mrs Plymmet blinked as though that was an unlikely scenario. 'And where do you live now?' she asked.

'Oh, here and there.' Barbara looked away. 'You must come to visit sometime.'

But she never did give Jessica Plymmet the address.

Together the two women, both survivors of a sort, put down their cups and lifted forkfuls of Victoria sponge to their mouths instead. Icing sugar fell to their plates like a first sprinkle of snow, jam running through the middle of each slice like a thin seam of blood. It was Jessica Plymmet who made the first move.

'How is your daughter?' she asked.

Up, up amongst dark buildings in the Athens of the North, seventeen-year-old Margaret packed a bag. Four pairs knickers, two pairs tights, a jumper all sloppy across the shoulders and a pair of jeans impossibly tight. She laced black boots at the ankles, slung a canvas satchel across her chest (borrowed from a friend and never given back), and tucked a lucky coronation penny into a pocket pressed close against her hip. It wasn't a lot, but it was enough for a new beginning. A life full of chatter and smoke.

For Margaret was leaving. Margaret was on her way out. Over the hills and far away. Heads to the south. Tails to somewhere else. Away from tall grey buildings. Away from tenements that wept in the rain. Away from a city where all anyone talked about was the weather, even when they meant something else.

'Get a job,' her mother had said. 'If you want to make something of yourself.'

So Margaret had. Three months' work experience in a local solicitor's office, courtesy of a phone call to one of her mother's associates. The only advice Barbara gave her when she found out was this: 'You'll need to wear a skirt.'

Margaret had arrived on that first day with her hair freshly combed and her legs clad in nylon that dug in at her crotch. 'Ah, the new girl.' The senior partner had rubbed his hands together when Margaret was brought in to make his acquaintance. Just seventeen, a faint hint of brown on her lips, pancake applied with care to her cheeks. Margaret stood on the heavy woollen carpet in the partner's office and watched as he rubbed one hand across the other, over and over, as though he never could get them clean. Despite his seniority (or because of it, perhaps), the senior partner did not invite Margaret to sit. He leaned back in his chair instead and said, 'Great future ahead, if you know the meaning of hard work. Look at everything your mother has achieved.'

Barbara Penny, a 'Mrs' with no husband, a mother with no womb, a woman who worked her fingers to the bone every week but never seemed to enjoy anything in life. If I end up like my mother, Margaret thought then, I'll kill myself. But she had no intention of that.

Margaret managed one month and three days before it was done. 'No stamina, young people,' the senior partner murmured down the phone to Barbara when she enquired as to what had gone wrong. 'Don't know how to help themselves.'

'What did you do?' Barbara demanded, standing in a kitchen scrubbed until it almost wasn't there.

'Nothing,' Margaret insisted, lounging by the counter eating a slice of toast without even using a plate. Crumbs fell to the kitchen lino that Barbara had polished only the night before. 'It wasn't like I thought it would be,' Margaret said through a mouthful of jam. As though that explained everything.

'Well, what did you expect?' Barbara got down in an awkward kneel on the floor, work skirt pulled tight against the back of her thighs. She brushed the crumbs into a dustpan with a vigorous flick of her wrist. 'Life's not all picnics and roses.'

Not that Margaret had ever thought it was.

'Sometimes it gives with one hand,' Barbara said, rising and tossing the crumbs into the pedal bin, 'and takes away with the next.'

Margaret swallowed the last bit of her toast and went to put on some more beneath the eye-level grill. She knew that her mother was right. For she had taken exactly what she wanted. And given something away too.

Barbara left for work ten minutes later (floor all swept, door closed with a solid thud) and Margaret locked herself into the damp, scanty bathroom, twisting in front of the mirror to catch a glimpse of the bruises just starting to blossom on her hips. The fingerprints were clear to see, a crescent in brown and yellow pressed into her flesh. Margaret touched her finger to the place where the skin was still tender. He had been rougher than was necessary. Quite unpleasant, given what she had been offering. Still, Margaret had got what she needed from the exchange. Pound notes in large denominations, lifted from the senior partner's desk while he went to wash himself in the sink. Enough for a quick exit. When the time came.

Margaret picked up her mother's lucky coronation penny from where she'd laid it on the edge of the bath – weighed it in her hand. Heads to the south. Tails to somewhere else. Margaret spun the coin on the cold tiles of the floor as bathwater ran fast and hot. Let the king decide, she thought.

So he did.

*

In the cafe at a gallery down south, a small package was passed from one woman to the next. 'Your sister asked me to give this to you,' Jessica Plymmet said. 'Should I ever come across you in the flesh.'

Barbara Penny's hand twitched slightly as she picked up the envelope, her name written across the front in Ruby's looping, childlike script. 'What is it?' she asked, as though opening the envelope might lead somewhere she did not want to go.

'I'm not sure.' Jessica Plymmet understood why Barbara Penny might be wary. After everything she had read in the Walker file, she couldn't be certain where it might lead, either.

Barbara picked up her empty cup for a moment as though to read the tea leaves peppering its insides, then set it down again when they turned out to be no use. She put a finger to the knot of her scarf, tight now like a noose hanging above a trap. Then she lifted the small envelope and began.

It was a papery thing, small and thin. But Barbara was not deceived by that. A love token, perhaps. The seal on a pact. Or something to remind Barbara of everything she had ever done wrong. And everything she had tried to do right. The reverse was stamped with the name of a psychiatric unit somewhere on the outskirts of town. Tall and grey. Looming out of its grounds as it had done for over forty years. Barbara paused for a moment as she ran her thumb over the insignia.

Then she lifted the flap.

Inside the envelope was a page from a magazine, folded so many times the picture was almost rubbed out. Still,

Barbara knew exactly what it would show before she flattened it out. A man, a woman and two children, sitting at a table in a kitchen with a very shiny floor. She unfolded the picture carefully so as not to rip the paper. Then she stared down at what was inside.

It was Barbara who spoke first this time. 'Where is she?' she said. Beneath her pancake, colour had vanished from her face.

'I don't know.' Jessica Plymmet dipped her eyes to the table. She'd been wondering that herself, for some time now. 'She went abroad, I think.'

'Abroad?' But it wasn't really a question. Barbara knew what it meant. Lost to the sea, to the winds, to the earth. Lost to the north and the south and the east. But not the west, perhaps. A country with a billion souls (or thereabouts), the perfect place in which to follow a trail. Or to start as one person and end up as somebody else. Ruby had gone to the promised land, just as she had always said.

'Have you heard from her recently?' Barbara asked, not certain which answer she wanted the most.

For a moment Jessica Plymmet seemed lost, bereaved almost, as though something important had been excised from her life. 'No,' she said, picking up her teacup to cover her confusion. 'Not for a long time. Ten years.'

'But you do know where she is now?'

'I don't, I'm afraid.' Mrs Plymmet put her cup down. 'I've tried to find out, but your sister is as difficult to track down as you are.'

Barbara shifted in her seat. At least one part of her plan had worked. 'Is Mr Nye involved?' she asked.

'Younger or older?'

'Older.' Though even after all these years Barbara's heart went all pitter-patter at the thought that the younger Mr Nye might be revealed again too.

'No.' Jessica Plymmet was particularly firm on that. 'Mr Nye Senior's gone to a funeral,' she added.

'A funeral?' Barbara was surprised. Two in as many days.

'Yes,' said Jessica Plymmet, touching with a napkin at a crumb of icing sugar caught on her lip. 'For a client. At a nursing home, on the outskirts.'

'And the younger?' Barbara wasn't sure she wanted to know, but it was probably best to find out.

'The younger went abroad too. He . . .' Jessica Plymmet cleared her throat for a second, as though she had something difficult to impart (which she did). 'He died. In a car crash. Some time since.'

A man all skinny and flat, bucking in a damp seaside bed. Barbara sighed and lifted her own teacup to cover the small flash of disappointment that even after all these years still rushed across her face. What was it about all her chances that they only ever led to nought?

Across the table Jessica Plymmet straightened her fork on her plate. 'I'm sorry,' she said.

Barbara put down her cup. 'I'm sorry too.'

Both of them knew what the other woman meant.

Barbara touched the corner of the magazine cutting. 'And this,' she said, pointing to the tuft of hair that lay within its folds. Silver, as though cut from the tresses of an angel. 'Who does it belong to?'

'It's your mother's,' Jessica Plymmet replied.

'Mrs Penny's?'

'No. Your real mother's,' she said.

At number 14 Elm Row, just returned from scattering Dorothea Walker to the winds at last, Mr Nye Senior laid a fire in the front-room grate. Once a parlour with curtains thick and green, the room was empty now, all dirty walls and floor stripped bare. But Nye Senior knew already that it would be perfect for his study. A place where secrets could be made and kept.

Despite years of skimping and neglect, 14 Elm Row still stood, in amongst the general decrepitude all around. Miners' strikes. Bin strikes. The three-day week. Postal workers and gravediggers refusing to deliver and dig. The house had seen it all and survived. Gutters choked with lilac. Lintels leaking into brick. A money pit, some people called it. An opportunity, was what Mr Nye Senior saw. And Mr Nye Senior always had known how to secure things that were not really his to keep.

In the cold glory of the Walkers' former parlour, he crouched now at the grate with an anonymous file of paperwork in one hand and a battered old tea caddy in the other. Inside were the leftovers from another era – a record of everything he had ever done wrong. And everything he had ever done right. Birth certificates for two children christened in linen and lace. Death certificates for the same. Official adoption certificates stamped by an accommodating judge, transforming two little girls from Walker to Penny overnight. An admissions form with his father's signature on it, securing medical detention for as long as might be required. An ID card stamped *DECEASED*. And

the sale deeds for a house. Also a last will and testament
naming the remaining daughter, read out only that morning, in part at least.

Mr Nye Senior crumpled Mrs Penny's will and placed
it in the grate along with all the other Walker paperwork.
Good riddance to bad rubbish. Wasn't that what she
always used to say? He tipped the contents of the battered
old tea caddy on top. Some stiff little photographs showing a woman sitting on a chaise longue with a lumpen
baby in her lap. And a whole series of letters from America asking for someone to please write back. It only took
a moment for everything to go up.

The flames rushed through Mr Nye's secrets as though
through fresh air, burning and sparking with a blue-and-
orange light. As the fire spread, he threw on the final
contents from the very bottom of the tea caddy – two tiny
snippets of hair, as golden in their first moments as they
were now in their last. All that remained of a pair of twins,
long shrivelled in their graves. The hair shrivelled too as
Mr Nye Senior watched it disappear to nothing. Then he
levered himself up and went to the sideboard to fetch
himself a drink.

There was only one thing Mr Nye Senior did not
submit to the flames. An admissions form for a Dorothea
Walker, a memento of sorts for a woman whose feet had
lain limp in his lap. Mr Nye's fingers trembled for a
moment on his glass as he remembered the slice of flesh
between the crevice of her legs. Despite all the women in
his life he wondered now if it had ever got better than that.
If his son had survived, perhaps? Delivered him grandchildren who would laugh as they ran from the front door

to the back? Mr Nye brushed at the shoulders of his suit where ash from the paperwork of all Dorothea Walker's descendants had floated up.

Still, life was what you made of it. And hadn't he made this? Three storeys and a coal cellar, all intact. In a part of town that would only ever go up. Also a new maid who would clean any mess tomorrow, down on her knees like the good girl that she was – just arrived from the Philippines in search of a new life. The maid knew an opportunity when she saw one. And Mr Nye would reward her, just as he had rewarded all his young women in the past.

But before that, there was one final reward Mr Nye Senior wished to acquire for himself, just because he could. A painting, small and brown, the perfect size to fill a gap on his office wall. Barbara Penny's visit might have been unexpected; trouble, perhaps, had he not taken care to destroy everything that was left. But it also meant opportunity – the chance to get back what was rightly his. And opportunity was what kept a man such as Mr Nye Senior standing, despite all the years that might pass.

Leaving his fire still burning, Mr Nye went out into the hallway to the large, old-fashioned phone. Mrs Plymmet was not what she had once been, but she was still reliable, at least. Able to track down any address he might ask for, however obscured by all the time that had passed. The receiver hung heavy in Nye Senior's hand as he waited for those liquid vowels to speak.

'William Nye & Sons solicitors.'

'Mrs Plymmet. I need you to find an address for me. And take some dictation. A letter.'

'Of course, Mr Nye. Proceed.'

'Dear Miss Penny . . .'

There was a pause at the other end of the line, as though Jessica Plymmet was deciding (which, of course, she was). Then William Nye Senior heard a sound he was not used to. A click as the receiver was replaced.

Barbara Penny rode home to the north with nothing but a case of silver apostle spoons tucked into her bag and a small tuft of Dorothea's hair tucked into her purse. The last relics of the Walker Penny family, not including herself, of course, or the sister she had lost to the west.

But Barbara wasn't expecting to hear from Ruby any time soon. After all, she had vanished into a country of a billion souls, if what Jessica Plymmet had said was correct. Chasing after the ghost of a person Barbara knew for certain had been dead for almost forty years. Still, as they passed the bridges of Berwick, crossing the border from the south, Barbara felt again the echo of that emptiness she'd carried inside her whole life. Trust Ruby to have been right about one thing. Their mother had been alive, until last week, at least.

She arrived in Edinburgh as dark crept down from the sky, stepping from the train into the sedate bustle of Waverley ready to tell her tale at last. Of children born and died. Of madwomen dragged out into the street. Of sisters lost and abandoned. Of a mother who had tried in her own way to keep her daughter safe.

On her way back to the flat she bought chips, a treat for her and Margaret to eat together before they settled to everything else. Warm and damp in their paper, smelling of salt and hot vinegary sauce. She arrived at their door with her coat unbuttoned and her patterned scarf all loose. For what was there to do now that both her mothers were dead? Set up a wail about how everyone had always left her? Or go home to do what any real mother did best. Cleave to her child, however inadequate the attempt.

'Margaret!'

Barbara's voice had an urgency to it as she came up the stairs of the close, calling out as she opened up the door to the flat they shared together, a mother and a daughter with nothing between them but people who Barbara was certain now would never be coming back. She called again as she pulled off her coat to hang on the rack, hurried with their chips into the kitchen.

'Margaret!'

But there was only silence in reply.

For there it was again, that hole in the air that Barbara had experienced once before. Nothing in the kitchen but a note on the table held down by a single tin of peas:

Eggs
Bread
Milk, 2 pints
Jam

Barbara Penny's own list of instructions, left behind the day before for a daughter who had left her behind too.

Margaret Penny crossed with her mother at the border. One to the north. The other to the south. Ne'er the twain shall meet. One clutching a box of silver spoons. The other a coronation penny pressed up against her hip.

When the moment for a quick exit came Margaret had taken it, as she'd always known she would. Climbed on the first bus south that she could find and settled in at the back. Down, down long motorways, past service stations and cafes where the windows shone long into the night. On, on into the early hours of the morning, orange velour seats scratching at the underside of her knees. Men drinking one can of Special after another until they fell comatose onto the back of the seat in front. Down, down to the dirty, bustling streets of London where nobody knew her name or where she had come from. Nor where she might go next.

She took the coronation penny with her, just in case. *Find a penny, pick it up, all day long you'll have good luck.* Because luck was what Margaret knew she needed now, more than anything else. She hadn't bothered to leave behind a note. For Margaret Penny had learned at least one thing from her mother.

Leave no trace.

2011

A lilac hat. A turquoise suit. A coat the colour of wet sand. And a Rainmate, just in case. The scene of the second crime was not as cold as the first, but it had the disadvantage of containing so many belongings it was hard for Margaret to know where to start.

Back at The Court, taxi waiting outside to take her to Mrs Walker's flat so that she could complete her task, Margaret rummaged through her mother's personal belongings in a manner that she knew would never have been allowed if Barbara had been there to watch.

Capacious underwear. A whole drawerful of thermal vests. Bedsocks and reading glasses. A tumbler with something sticky around the rim. Some things had changed over the last thirty years, but less than Margaret might have imagined. Still, however hard she searched there was no sign of what she had come looking for. A Brazil nut with the Ten Commandments etched into its shell. Nor of the woman who must have stolen it, vanished all of a sudden just like Mrs Walker's corpse.

For the first time since Margaret had returned from a lifetime in London, Barbara was nowhere to be seen, disappeared like the final piece of Janie's jigsaw. Hadn't even bothered to leave a note. When Margaret first stepped into the empty flat, she'd not been certain whether to be pleased or worried at this new development. Then, when she called out and got no reply, she decided to be neither. After all, Barbara's business was her own and nobody else's – she had always made that quite clear. And Margaret knew an opportunity when it presented itself.

She went through each room in a systematic manner, digging up all sorts. Greasy brown lipstick in the bathroom. A half-bottle of rum hidden behind the empties under the kitchen sink. That plastic tree her mother had always insisted on putting up every Christmas when Margaret was young, rolled beneath the cabinet in the living room as though its silver limbs had not been folded out this year. There were even the contents of an ancient suitcase, falling around Margaret to pepper the bedroom carpet like shrapnel as she pulled the case from the top of her mother's wardrobe, lid yawning wide. A jewellery box of nappy velveteen. An apron unfolding as gracefully as a bird. A bottle with a glass stopper that bounced off the bed. Margaret knew that somewhere in amongst all this stuff there was a story. But it wasn't the story she needed the answer to now.

Even so, it was strange going through her mother's belongings in the absence of their owner, as though the worst had happened while Margaret had been occupied elsewhere. Perhaps Barbara had gone out to pray at one of her many churches and ended up under a number 24 bus instead. Nothing left for Margaret to do but sort out what should be kept and what should be donated. The stuff of Barbara's life ladled into bin bags for distribution across the charity shops of Edinburgh. Recycling, it was the new religion. Just as Mrs Walker had recycled a sheet of newspaper into a makeshift layer of clothes.

After all, it was only that morning Margaret had found Barbara praying for salvation. Seven a.m. and just off the sleeper, blown in on the cusp of a snowstorm ready to close her case for good. Only to find her mother down on her knees in front of the television, forehead pressed to the carpet, quilted dressing gown stretched tight across the great expanse of her rump. *Help me, Jesus. Help me, Allah. Help me, God.* Though Margaret never had been certain what exactly Barbara needed to be saved from.

'What are you doing?' Margaret had gazed at the strange apparition of her mother seeking some sort of benediction.

Barbara jerked at the sudden interruption, twitching and banging her head on the television set as she tried to get up. 'Christ!' As though she'd been caught in the middle of a particularly excoriating confession (which, perhaps, she had). 'I dropped the remote,' she mumbled, rolling back onto her haunches, followed by a long and painful wheeze of her chest.

But the remote was where it always lay, on the arm of Barbara's chair, hidden beneath the TV guide.

Margaret moved forwards then. 'Here, let me help you.' For there was something odd about seeing her mother prostrated – as though she was making some kind of cry for help.

But Barbara just flinched, lumbering into a kneeling position, her face a startling puce. 'Don't fuss.' Breath whistling and wailing as though she was an express train running towards a station with no plans to stop.

'Have you lost something?' Margaret prepared to prostrate herself in her mother's place. 'I'll find it if you like.'

'No,' Barbara insisted, clutching the pockets of her dressing gown as though to hold everything in place. 'I can do it myself. Not useless yet.' Then she reached for her grey NHS stick and began to lever herself up.

Margaret had seen the sticky liquid shining on her mother's lips. Communion already over for the day, not even eight o'clock.

Once Barbara got back in the armchair, thighs spreading to fill the whole space, the two women stared at each other over the great expanse of beige.

'Back so soon,' Barbara said. It didn't appear to be a question.

'I was going to ring you.'

But both mother and daughter knew this was not the truth. Still, Margaret ploughed on. Who Dares Wins (and all that). 'I've come to close the case,' she said. 'Get out from under your feet.'

'Well, that's that then.'

And there it was again. That look. Fear. Or something like it. Scuttling across her mother's face.

Margaret had stared at Barbara then, her hair all scrawn and scruff, white tufts sticking out in odd directions. It had grown so sparse Margaret realized all of a sudden she could see right through it to her mother's scalp. 'You helped me solve it, actually,' she said, a child again just wanting her mother to be pleased. 'Matthew 19, verses 14 to 16.' And she took the Brazil nut from her coat pocket so that Barbara could see.

'What?' Barbara's whole body twitched, hands aflutter, as though she'd been given some sort of electrical shock.

'The Ten Commandments. Can you believe it?'

Though by the look on Barbara's face, it had seemed that she could. Just for a moment she flashed all puce once more, from beneath the collar of her dressing gown right up to the crown of her head. A distress flare lighting up a dull morning, before the colour dropped away again to nought. Then Barbara's chest set up a great heaving and a moaning, as though she might be about to expire in her armchair, right there, right then. Nothing between her and Mrs Walker but a roller blind and a kitchen that smelt of bleach rather than ash.

'Mum!' Margaret rushed to her mother's side, dropping the Brazil nut in her fright. It bounced once on the carpet before rolling away.

Barbara gasped and wheezed, struggling for breath, waving Margaret off with a sweep of her arm like the last desperate gesture of a drowning woman, catching her daughter on the cheekbone, *thwack,* with the remote control gripped like a weapon in her hand. 'Nothing but tourist tat. One in a million.' At least that was what Margaret thought her mother said, before she backed away.

The television blinked on, sound booming, as Barbara's rough breath subsided to a series of small, marshy pants. 'Just leave me alone,' she said in a strangled kind of voice, eyes resolutely to the front.

'But . . .'

'You get on with your life. And I'll get on with mine.'

Back to the box-room dungeon. Back to an invoice for services rendered just waiting to be cashed. And after that, what next? A wave of familiar melancholia had rolled over Margaret then as she stood in the living-room doorway staring at the back of her mother's head. What was it about her life, that the only person who really needed Margaret was a dead person lying on a slab in some anonymous embalmer's suite?

'By the way, that girl called.' From her armchair, Barbara heaved and puffed as she tried to get the words out over the noise of the television set. 'Said to tell you she's in Leith.'

Margaret was confused for a moment. 'In Leith. Janie?'

'Said you'd find her down there.' Barbara twisted round in her chair.

'Find who?'

'Your client.'

'Mrs Walker?'

It was only afterwards that Margaret realized her mother looked then as though some sort of ghost had waltzed right over her grave.

Margaret found what she was looking for quite by chance. Kneeling on the lino in her mother's kitchenette, wondering where to search next. Quilted and threadbare, in a colour that had once been pink, her mother's dressing gown shoved into the washing machine as though awaiting its annual bath. If the Brazil nut was going to be anywhere, surely this would be the place.

Margaret pulled the dressing gown from the drum, still dry, and tried to shake out all its creases and folds. Then she spread it across her mother's kitchen table as though she were laying out a corpse. There was something forlorn about seeing the garment without her mother inside it. As though without it Barbara must be lying comatose somewhere out by the bypass, no daughter to help her as one last prayer died on her lips. Or perhaps she had just gone for a drink with Mrs Maclure to discuss the iniquities of children long absent suddenly returned. Even now, Margaret could never be sure which way her mother might fall.

The dressing gown was just as Margaret had last seen it, dried strands of mini Shredded Wheat still clinging to the front. Margaret picked them off one by one, brushing down the frills as she did so to keep everything neat. Then she dipped her fingers into each of the dressing-gown pockets to find fluff, threads and a single loose button covered in pink stretchy fabric. Then something else. Not a Brazil nut with the Ten Commandments scratched into its shell, but an empty envelope with a postmark dated sometime before Christmas. And on its flap, the imprint of a solicitor's firm. Nye & Sons of London. Jessica Plymmet writing to an old friend with all the news.

Three weeks of cat and mouse amongst the snow and ice of Edinburgh and the black car caught Margaret the moment she stepped outside. Her only escape route was back to a box room with no emergency exits. Margaret knew that this time she was captured. Nowhere left to run.

The car made a graceful U-turn, snow crunching slowly beneath its heavy wheels, a window gliding down as it pulled up alongside. The driver leaned over to speak. 'Margaret Penny.'

It wasn't a question.

'Want to go for a drink?'

A drink for Margaret meant red wine. A drink for DCI Franklin meant coffee. Being an officer of the law, the DCI prevailed. There wasn't much preamble. In fact, the DCI didn't even take off her coat, just squeezed herself into a seat opposite Margaret in one of the local coffee shops and began to interrogate. 'You were at the mortuary.'

'Yes.' Margaret blushed slightly as though she had done something wrong.

'I thought so.' DCI Franklin folded the foam on top of her cappuccino, then licked the spoon clean. 'I checked,' she said, lifting the cup and swallowing what seemed like half of the contents in one. 'Janie gave me the details. I like to know who's nosing around on my patch.'

Margaret dribbled milk from a small plastic container into her black coffee, watched it swirl then sink. 'I'm looking into Mrs Walker.'

'Mrs Walker?'

'The old lady from Nilstrum Street. Died alone in her flat. I'm on my way there now.'

'Oh, yes. One of those.' The detective spoke as though it was a commonplace occurrence. She wiped at her mouth with a paper napkin. 'I'd have got my officers to do a bit more digging, but cuts, you know.' She shrugged.

Margaret nodded. Austerity Britain.

'We had to reallocate resources,' said the DCI. 'There's been a murder.'

But Margaret wasn't complaining. The combination of cuts and a suspicious death had got her the job.

'Wouldn't normally involve a civilian.' DCI Franklin took another mouthful of her coffee (the whole cup almost gone now) and stared at Margaret as though expecting her to reply.

'No.' Margaret shifted a little in her seat, suddenly

sweaty. The cafe was muggy, condensation dripping down the windows. Just like her mother, she had kept her coat buttoned to the neck. Despite her success with dead people, she wasn't sure a dead fox was quite the right impression to give to the police.

The detective leaned forward and tapped the brown folder that lay between them. 'So,' she said. 'Did you sort it?'

Mrs Walker (Clementine). Shopped at Costcutter. Always wore a red coat. Enjoyed whisky. Paid in cash. Ate morning rolls and tinned peas until she died of numerous diseases aged eighty-five. Thief.

'Really?' DCI Franklin looked interested at last. She put down her empty cup. 'Maybe she's got a record.'

Margaret put her cup down too, though it was still half full. 'That's been checked already. Births, Marriages and Deaths. The certificates came today.'

DCI Franklin laughed and swivelled her legs out from beneath the table, showing a quick flash of sunshine lining her navy coat. 'Not those records. Criminal.'

'Oh, yes.' Margaret flushed again. 'But won't your officers have looked at that?'

'Yes, probably. They're a good unit in Edinburgh, the Enquiry Team. Suicide, drugs, accidents with cars.' DCI Franklin waved her hand. 'They see it all.'

Somehow Margaret got the impression DCI Franklin had seen it all too. 'Are they your team?'

'God no. Not for me. Death out of nowhere, no one to blame.' DCI Franklin pulled a face. 'I'm strictly suspicious. Murder, you know. DNA.'

Sheep stealer. Peddler of fake coins. How easy it was to

be the one who caused trouble. You just had to be born to it, it seemed. 'Is Mrs Walker likely to have a criminal record?' Margaret asked. 'She was only an old lady, after all.'

'Even criminals get old, you know. At least, some-times.' The DCI laughed. 'But some people have a way of avoiding the system. It's easy to disappear if you really want to. People do it all the time.'

'Yes.' Margaret considered her whole life strewn across London landfill and knew that this was the truth.

DCI Franklin stood and began to pull on her gloves. 'Shall we go then?'

'What?' Margaret looked up from the muddy remains of her coffee, palms suddenly damp. Her antics in London come to rest at her feet at last. 'I thought there'd been a murder . . .'

The detective smiled. 'Yes.' A tired smile, as though a not-insignificant part of her wished she would never see another dead person ever again. 'But you've got a body to dispose of that's clogging our system. And a scene of crime to search first. I thought I'd help you do it thoroughly this time.'

The scene of the first crime was as cold and gloomy as it had been when Margaret visited only a few days before. The light bulb in the hall still dredged in dust. The shadows of long-vanished pictures still lingering on the walls. In the bathroom tiny corpses still huddled in the deep end of the bath. Shadows were advancing from every corner. The gloaming hour, wasn't that what Barbara called it, when the spirits came to the fore.

'Christ,' said the DCI as they stepped into the hall, wrapping her dark woollen coat around her legs as though for protection. 'No wonder she's dead. It's like a freezer in here.' She blew on her fingers and turned to Margaret. 'Now where do you want to start?'

'In the bedroom.' Margaret was certain about that. 'There's something I need to collect.'

'Right. Well, you look there and I'll try the rest.' DCI Franklin was nothing if not efficient with her resources. 'One way or another we'll close the case today.'

From the bottom of Mrs Walker's wardrobe, Margaret retrieved what she had really come for. A party dress fit for one last celebration. The perfect alternative to a shroud. She pulled the emerald dress from its plastic bag, holding it up towards the diminishing light as it slithered to its full length, the few remaining sequins dancing once again. The dress wasn't in great shape: a few holes here and there, patches eaten away by moth. Micky might have to add 'seamstress' to her list of accomplishments just to get it looking neat. Margaret laid the dress across Mrs Walker's bed and peered at the hem. It wasn't hard to see what she had come for. A single sequin hanging from a thread. Even in the gathering gloom of Mrs Walker's bedroom Margaret could see that it was different from the rest. Not green like the sea, or the eyes of a witch. But red, like a single trail of blood.

Fabric slippery beneath her fingers, heart setting up a little pitter-patter beat, Margaret lifted the thread and began to follow it round the hem. It zigzagged in a haphazard line as though it had been sewn in a hurry. Or by someone who didn't care for needlework and the time that it took. Margaret followed the thread almost all the way round and back to the start before she found what she had been certain must be there. Knobbled and lumpy, hidden away in a fold of emerald cloth. A brooch, perhaps, small and shiny, five starry points.

Except . . .

It was something much more ordinary than that.

Margaret sat back on the bed and stared down at what she had found. An orange pip, all desiccated and skeletal, just like Mrs Walker lying naked now beneath the sheet in Leith. She sighed, disappointment rattling for a moment inside her chest. What was it with Mrs Walker, that nothing about her life ever seemed to come to an end?

DCI Franklin appeared in the doorway. 'Found anything?' she said.

'Nothing,' said Margaret. 'An orange pip. Sewn into the hem.'

DCI Franklin came over to look, two women staring down at the tiny white eye. 'That's not an orange pip,' the DCI said. 'It's a clue.'

Under curling lino. Beneath all the pillows. In between the sheets. Margaret and the DCI searched until they had a handful of orange pips, but not much else. Inside kitchen cupboards. Between mismatched bowls. In amongst the forks and teaspoons. Down beneath the bath.

There was even a solitary seed stranded forever in one of Mrs Walker's empty whisky bottles. The DCI was intrigued. 'What did you say she died of, again?'

'Everything,' said Margaret. 'Take your pick.'

They tried the living room last, the DCI running one finger along the edge of the mantelpiece until it came away almost black. The fireplace beneath was black too, dark and empty where once a fire would have been lit. Margaret bent to look and saw two orange pips sucked dry wedged between the irons of the grate.

'Look at this,' said the DCI, pointing at something on the mantelpiece, a trickle of dust drifting down to settle on the top of Margaret's head.

'What is it?' Margaret stood up again, brushing at her hair. She couldn't see anything unusual in amongst the grime. No photographs or candles imprinted with beseeching saints. No flocks of wooden animals polished to a shine. But then, as the DCI continued to point, Margaret understood. Not an orange pip this time, but a ridge of dust, thin but distinct, as though something had been propped up behind it not that long ago. The two women stared at the small line of dust for a moment. Then they turned and looked beyond it, straight into the arms of the chair in which Mrs Walker had breathed her last.

'Did you search it before?' the DCI said.

Margaret shook her head. 'That's police work, isn't it?'

The DCI laughed then, before handing over a pair of blue latex gloves retrieved from the pocket of her coat. 'You're the detective now.'

Down, down, down, down. Margaret searched the armchair with a rigour she had not employed before. Attack. Best form of defence. Wasn't that what Barbara always said? Pushing her hands between the armchair's cushions and its ancient frame. Past fabric stained with the remains of the dead. Black hands. Black feet. Trying not to think about putrefaction as she shoved her fingers past strands of hair and tiny mangled feathers. Past bits of orange peel gone brittle and stiff. Past greasy cloth and old furniture foam that disintegrated at her touch. Past a hairpin bent out of shape and crumbs from a stale morning roll. Past nail parings and dust, dust, dust, arms almost up to the elbows in a dead person's leftovers before she touched what she had been looking for all along.

Proof beyond reasonable doubt.

Not a brooch, but a photograph. Black-and-white and stippled with age. An imprint on the reverse. *W. H. SYMMONS & Co. Est. London 1933.* On the front was a picture of a woman sitting in a chair, wearing some kind of gown that didn't quite cover her legs. She looked perplexed, as though just off camera there was something she ought to know about but couldn't quite understand. And pinned up against the woman's breastbone – a tiny, star-shaped brooch.

Magic, thought Margaret. Happens all the time.

She held up the photograph to show DCI Franklin. But DCI Franklin was occupied with something else. Phone pressed to ear, frowning and staring at Margaret.

'It's your mother,' she said.

1970

Ruby with her eyes so bright, once a jewel of a thing, now cut all this way and that, emerged from the last of several incarcerations and opened up her admission box to find this:

A dusty Brazil nut.

A tarnished spoon.

A star-shaped brooch with a red stone at its heart.

And a ticket to America. The promised land at last.

She hummed as she lifted everything out, 'Oh my darling,' to accompany the hum that resided permanently now beneath the bony layer of her skull. They handed her the clothes she had been wearing when she arrived too – a jumper all worn at the elbows and a skirt with a pin to hold it together at the waist. Also a green dress with sequins dancing along the hem. Ruby laughed when she saw the dress. It reminded her of something she had lost, but was determined to get back.

'Now, Miss Penny . . .'

'Walker.'

'Yes.' The Head of the In-Patient Unit looked away as though she'd had this argument many times before (which, of course, she had). 'I'm afraid we haven't managed to get in touch with your sister. Barbara, is it?'

'Yes.'

'Or any other relative.'

'What about the child?' Ruby fixed the Head of the Unit with that disconcerting stare. They were sitting in a small office partitioned from a great cavernous hall, the grey walls of the asylum looming all around.

'Yes.' The Head of the Unit closed the fat file in front of her and placed her hand on top. 'I'm sorry. But you know as well as I do, Miss Penny, the child did not survive.'

'She did.' Ruby gazed at the Head of the Unit with those startling eyes.

The Head of the Unit turned her own gaze away. 'But how do you know, Miss Penny?' Ruby was still difficult to resist, despite everything that had passed.

'Because.' Ruby was insistent.

The Head sighed, a small despairing sound. They had worked with Ruby Penny on and off for several years now, but it never did seem to do any good. If anything it just made the patient more adamant about things that had never been. 'Well,' the Head said, trying to move the conversation on. 'It would be good to get a sense of what you plan to do next.'

Ruby blinked and jingled the few coins she'd been given to help her on her way. 'I'll get the bus, I suppose.'

'Yes, but where to?'

'Why do you need to know?'

The Head of the Unit had completed a course in how to assist a patient out into the world. But none of her training could assist her with this. 'Have you considered the halfway house I mentioned?' she said, as though that might make a difference.

Ruby didn't even bother shaking her head. She wasn't being deliberately recalcitrant. She was just being herself. 'I shall travel into London,' she said.

'Are you sure that's a good idea? You know what happened last time you were allowed out on day release.'

Last time Mr Nye Senior called the police. The time
before that the artist had called the police too.

'I promise I won't go near them again.' Ruby said
this with her fingers crossed behind her back as though
she were five years old again, not a grown woman of over
thirty now.

'You know it would be better if you tried to keep out
of trouble.'

Ruby laughed. Wasn't that what Mrs Penny had always
said? Nothing but trouble, right from the start.

The Head of the Unit pressed a finger against the side
of her skull where an insistent throbbing was just beginning to take hold. She coughed. 'There is your medication,
of course,' she said, holding out a prescription already
filled in with a scrawl. Medication was an important thing,
the lever they were encouraged to wield if all else failed.

Ruby stopped stuffing the contents of her admission
box into her old basket and looked up. 'I don't need pills
any more.'

'They're there to help you.'

'I thought I was better.'

'Well, yes . . .'

'So why would I need to take pills.'

Ruby wasn't asking a question. And besides, the Head
of the Unit didn't have a reply. Instead she began to fiddle
with a long rope of wooden beads that hung down the
front of her polyester blouse, like a rosary. Counting her
patients in and counting them out again once they were
cured. 'Well, if there's anything we can do,' and she laid

the prescription on the table well within reach. She was amazed when Ruby replied, 'Yes. There is one thing.'

'Oh?' Despite everything, the Head of the Unit was always willing to help.

'I need to make a phone call.'

'A phone call?'

'To my solicitor, of course.'

People who fry their brains. People who slash their wrists. People who hear voices inside their heads. People who wear nightdresses out into the street. Ruby Walker had seen it all, and then some, in the six-and-a-half years she had been incarcerated at someone else's behest. At times, she had been one of the worst.

In and out of a series of asylums, chasing something she couldn't quite see but knew that she had lost, Ruby had discovered the hard way what happened to women who would not comply. In police cells. In hospital wards. In rooms where the walls were covered in padding and cloth. Not to mention all sorts of treatments. Paddles to shock the brain. The boom in little blue pills. The drip of a syringe as a needle point pressed in towards a vein. Also what happened at night behind tall grey walls when women were harnessed to their beds and all the lights were off.

Still, Ruby found a way to prosper when all around her seemed lost. Razor blades and cigarettes. Small tablets of all descriptions secreted beneath the tongue. Treasures hidden away behind toilet cisterns and inside bars of soap, or stitched into hems to keep them safe. Though it wasn't how she'd imagined her life might turn out, Ruby had been right at home amongst the madwomen once it became clear that those on the outside did not wish to facilitate her release. In some ways she hadn't even minded. Ruby always had been one of the abandoned. Or simply one of those who refused to desist.

But now that she had found what she wanted, it was time to move on.

Sitting at a desk with the phone to her ear while the Head of the Unit hovered outside, Ruby recognized the voice on the other end at once. Pale-yellow gloves and a matching hat, holding a handbag to her stomach as though to ward off the worst. A girl whose whole body had trembled as she'd waited for the butchery to start. Over ten years had passed since Ruby first met Jessica Plymmet. But she'd known even then that the girl would never forget.

'Nye & Sons solicitors.' Those liquid, caramel tones.

'It's Ruby Walker.'

'Ruby Walker?' Suspicion curled around the young woman's every vowel.

'We met before. I would like to meet again.'

Ruby listened to the pause on the other end. She'd got used to knowing when to be silent and when was the right moment to speak.

In the end, it was the woman on the other end of the line who spoke first, in a manner that suggested she did not want someone through the wall to hear. 'All right.' And Ruby was delighted to discover that despite the years that had passed, Jessica Plymmet still aimed to please.

They arranged to meet at a jeweller's shop on Tidbury Street. Rose & Sons, jewellers of distinction, just a few streets away from the office with the stuffed stoat. Ruby arrived first, wearing a smart coat liberated from a hook on the back of the Head of the Unit's office door, carried to the bus stop inside a basket in which nobody thought to look. It was amazing what people left in Ruby Walker's way, when really they should not.

When Ruby rang the discreet buzzer to the right of the jeweller's front door, she was wearing an odd assortment of clothes. A green dress with its hem hanging down. Sandshoes borrowed from a nurse. A pair of tights taken from a patient who would only use them to hang herself if she could. Still, Ruby knew the people inside the jeweller's shop would not be overly concerned. Despite outward appearances, it was often the crazy ones who turned out to be worth the most.

Ruby was welcomed into the jeweller's by a small man who bowed as she came through the door, giving her the kind of look that certain psychiatrists used to give her when they first met. When Ruby showed the old man why she had come, he took her straight through to his office. She knew that he could smell it already. A profit to be made.

There in the dark of the jeweller's back room, Ruby spread out everything she had managed to gain and everything else she had managed to keep.

One emerald necklace.

Two earrings to match.

A brooch with a single red stone at its heart.

And several other things, more precious than not.

The jeweller squeezed his eye into a tiny magnifying glass and examined the treasure, piece by piece. Across the table Ruby watched him and understood that the news would be good. The man's cheek twitched every time he picked up a new item. 'Excellent condition,' he murmured, holding an earring close. 'Well chosen. Nice setting. Where did it come from?'

'A gift.'

'And this one?' The broker held up a string of grey pearls, small moons liberated from the thick flesh of a neck.

'Oh, here and there.' Ruby looked away for a moment. She always had been good at acquiring things which were not strictly hers to keep.

The only aberration was the star-shaped brooch with its little red heart. The jeweller's cheek didn't move at all as he lifted that to his eye. 'Best keep it,' he said, dropping the magnifying glass back on the desk. 'Not worth a thing, I'm afraid. Paste, dear. Nothing but a fake.' The jeweller held the brooch out towards Ruby. 'They made a lot of them during the war. Love tokens. Keepsakes. That kind of thing. But pretty.' He smiled at Ruby, cracking open his teeth for the first time. 'You should wear it yourself.'

Outside on the shop floor, Jessica Plymmet was waiting when Ruby and the jeweller came back through into the light. Twenty-six now, or thereabouts, still with those bony knees she never could disguise, Jessica Plymmet didn't seem so very different to when Ruby had first met her in Mrs Withers' hall. She was still clasping a handbag to her midriff as though ready for an assault. But her hair was more of a helmet now, her face a kind of mask.

Ruby knew she too had changed since they last met. No longer a young woman ready for life, standing in the shadows waiting to be handed a coat. There were creases around her mouth now that seemed to be fixed. Wrists no bigger than the thin branches of a tree. Her hair was run through with tiny rivers of white. And she suspected that if the wind blew too hard, it might blow her off. Up, up and into the sky. Over the hills and far away. Into a gutter, or a rich man's bed, or the oblivion of a bar still open at four a.m. Or across an ocean, perhaps. Still, Ruby Walker had been kind to Jessica Plymmet once when no one else had cared. That was what had counted then. And that, Ruby knew, was what would count now.

There wasn't any small talk. Ruby got straight to the point. 'I want you to keep these for me.' She placed a velvet bag on the jeweller's glass counter. A tiny star-shaped brooch pinned to her lapel winked at Jessica Plymmet across the shop floor and Ruby saw the way that Jessica Plymmet blinked back.

'What is it?' Jessica Plymmet approached, but she knew not to touch.

Ruby pulled at the drawstring of the bag, the lightest of tugs, opening up a glimmering pool for Jessica Plymmet to see. 'I want you to look after them for me. Then, if I ever need money, I'll get in touch.'

Ruby watched as Jessica Plymmet twisted the ring she now wore on her right hand – a not insubstantial chip, more glittery than glass. Ruby was glad to see that something of what the young woman was owed by Mr Nye Senior was going her way at last.

Jessica Plymmet stared down at the small heap of treasure inside its velvet bag. 'Why don't you sell them yourself?' she asked.

Shoplifters. Drug addicts. Kleptomaniacs. Thieves.

Ruby had spent what felt like a lifetime protecting the few things she had from mad people of all sorts. 'It's better if someone else keeps them safe,' she said. 'I'm not exactly sure where I'll be staying next.' She didn't want all her treasure to fall into the wrong hands if she ended up back in a cell once again.

'Are you going somewhere?' Jessica Plymmet liked to understand the detail. Just so that she could keep everything straight.

Ruby glanced away for a moment. 'There's somebody I'd like to find,' she said.

'Abroad?'

'Perhaps.'

Jessica Plymmet nodded. The younger Mr Nye was abroad. Had been for some time.

Ruby drew the strings of the small velvet bag tight. 'You'll be my last resort,' she said to Jessica Plymmet. 'Just in case.'

'In case of what?'

'Disaster. Or other emergencies.'

'Well, I suppose . . .' the younger woman faltered. 'If you trust me.' No one had ever asked Jessica Plymmet to be their last resort before. Nor their salvation should disaster strike.

Ruby nudged the bag across the counter. 'The jeweller has a note of what they're worth now. Don't take any less. When I need some money I'll phone and you can sell some, then send me the cash.'

'But why not just take the cash now?'

'Money can be unreliable,' replied Ruby. 'One minute you have it. The next it's disappeared.'

Into the pockets of orderlies. The aprons of matrons. The hands of other patients when their advances proved too difficult to resist. Hard cash, earned the hard way, just like in Ruby's youth. Money for a walk in the yard. For an extra portion of dessert. Or for razor blades, ready and waiting, for when it all became too much. One slash to the wrist, then the splash and trickle of blood. Ruby had tried it, several times.

Except . . .

They always found her before it was too late. Locked her up afterwards with the other women for whom it had been too late long since, standing between the beds or wandering up and down the aisles as though they couldn't remember how they had got there or where they were going next. Whispering into the walls to find out each other's secrets, just as she and Barbara should have whispered into the walls of St Paul's if they had really wanted to hear each other speak.

Still, that was where Ruby had found what she had been looking for ever since she was eight.

'Mama?'

Just as Clementine had said. Sitting on the end of a bed, at the end of a long ward, singing, 'Oh my darling', just as Clementine had told Ruby she would. If only Barbara could see, thought Ruby, then she'd know what I told her was right. Their mother, their real mother, swaying and rocking as she brushed and brushed her hair, nothing to her but a hospital gown and toenails curled in towards the soles of her feet.

Before they dragged her away, Ruby sat with Dorothea and sang too, holding one of her mother's hands in her own, while with the other she checked through Dorothea's bedside drawer. A hairbrush with a handle made of bone. Two dollar bills of a not-inconsiderable amount. And an ancient ticket to America. The promised land, at last.

Ruby was nothing if not practical. She knew what it all meant. Her mother might be alive. But she was also mad. Whereas Clementine was overseas, just waiting for her little sister to search her out.

Jessica Plymmet nodded now as Ruby handed over her treasure – a bag full of gemstones, hard earned. 'I could get you a job if you wanted,' she said. 'And a bank account.' Ruby Walker might need help, she thought, to heal whatever was broken inside. Perhaps Jessica Plymmet could deliver it herself.

But Ruby shook her head. She knew the other woman didn't really understand. What use did Ruby have for a bank account when she'd lived her entire life on the wrong side of the tracks? So she made Jessica Plymmet swear, instead.

Tell no one.

And asked her to write out a receipt. On the nearest headed paper they had to hand: *Rose & Sons, jewellers of distinction.* Just in case.

'Can you put your phone number here, so I don't forget?' Ruby indicated the bottom of the piece of paper.

'Of course.' And with a quick stroke across the page, Jessica Plymmet wrote down the number for Nye & Sons solicitors. 'But how will I know that it's you?' she said. 'When you call, I mean.' Jessica Plymmet was nothing if not thorough. Ruby was pleased about that.

'We'll have a code word.'

'A code word?'

'Yes.' Ruby smiled. 'It'll be our secret.'

Jessica Plymmet blushed. A fetching shade. She had only ever had one secret before and that had involved Ruby Walker too. 'What word do you want to use?' she asked.

Ruby folded the receipt for the jewellery and put it into the pocket of her stolen coat. 'Clementine,' she said.

Jessica Plymmet hesitated for a moment, then gripped her handbag tighter. 'All right. I'll do it.' She was familiar with the contents of the Walker file kept under lock and key in Mr Nye Senior's desk. As she was with all Nye Senior's secrets, whether he knew it or not.

Ruby smiled. 'And you won't tell Mr Nye.'

Jessica Plymmet didn't hesitate. 'No,' she said. 'No need for that.'

It was just before they left, with a brief goodbye on the pavement outside, that Ruby asked for one more thing. Well, two to be exact. 'It's about my sisters. Can you give these to them, when the time seems right.'

Two envelopes, each embossed with the stamp of a psychiatric unit somewhere to the south. One already sealed, addressed to a Barbara Walker, flat and papery with some piece of paper folded up inside. The other with *Clementine* written across the front.

'Isn't your older sister . . .' Jessica Plymmet wasn't certain how to put it. 'Dead' seemed so final, especially when Ruby had only just been released.

'No,' said Ruby. And she unpinned the star-shaped brooch from her lapel and popped it into the envelope, sealing the lumpy package with a flick of her tongue.

'Do you have their addresses?' Jessica Plymmet asked.

'Oh no.' Ruby shook her head. 'But perhaps you can help with that too. My sister Barbara, in particular. I'd like to know where she lives.'

Jessica Plymmet twisted the ring on her finger for a moment, turning the chip of diamond in towards her palm. 'Yes,' she said. 'Why not.' She was a woman of ways and means, after all. Official letters were what she did best. *Dear Miss Penny . . .* Perhaps it would hit its mark.

The letter arrived at Barbara's bedsit a few weeks later.

Dear Miss Penny . . .

Not quite a 'Mrs' yet.

She opened it at her breakfast table, no warning that it was anything other than the unassuming papery thing it first seemed. Barbara scanned what it said before putting it down amongst the crumbs. The news that she had been waiting for, found her out at last.

The letter had caught up with Barbara when she was living in a one-roomed flat in a different part of town, no forwarding address. Yet there it was, left on a table in the hall amongst all the other mail, no suggestion that it might explode at her touch. She had a new job now, though it didn't pay as much as the last, and she still shared a bathroom down the end of a corridor, cold tiles against her bare feet. But just like all her sisters, dead, abandoned or lost, Barbara Penny was determined that she would do things the way that she wanted. Or not do them at all.

The letter didn't say the same thing as the ones she used to get years before. *Dear Miss Penny . . .* From hospitals or police cells, or other kinds of places where they kept mad people safe . . . *Your sister needs your help.* Crossed out, redirected, passed on from bedsit to bedsit until they found her once again. Then kept in her handbag for weeks until she tore them into tiny pieces and scattered them outside to the wind. Barbara never could understand how Ruby got them to do it, when their job was to lock her sister up. People who fry their brains. People who slash their wrists. People who hear voices inside their heads. Barbara knew that madness ran through her family – wasn't that what Mrs Penny always said? Still, she clung to the idea that it was through Ruby's veins that madness ran the most.

The other envelopes had always been scribbled over with, 'please forward to . . .' or 'not known here . . .', until they found their mark. And then Barbara had known that she was safe, at least for a time. But this letter slid through her door with an envelope like virgin snow, single postmark only, signed at the bottom by a Jessica Plymmet on paper marked with the Nye & Sons stamp. Long thighs. Bony knees. And a hand on a silver blade. This letter threatened all sorts of things that Barbara understood at once. Jessica Plymmet. A young woman already steeled against the disappointments of her age, much like Barbara herself. There was only one other person Barbara could go to, in circumstances such as these.

That night at Mrs Penny's Home for Troublesome Girls there were babies wailing as though they would never stop. All over the house, from the kitchen to the highest, furthest floor, infants of all sizes and dispositions shrieking and bawling fit to burst. Barbara sat with another cup and saucer in her hand thanking God, or whoever, that she had managed to escape. Opposite her, in his usual place, Tony sat with a child on his knee. Six-and-a-half years old, or thereabouts, skirt rucked above her small knees. Tony held the girl round her waist and ran his fingers up and into her armpits so the girl giggled and shrieked too.

'Well, what do you want me to do about it?' Mrs Penny was lining up bottles of milk in sterilizing pans for all the little bastards upstairs. 'I don't want to see her, either. Stole everything I had.'

A fox with a mangy head. A photograph of two dead children. A blanket with a torn satin trim. Barbara sipped at her cup of tea. Our things, she thought. Some of them, at least.

Across on the other side of the stove Tony coughed and winked at the child, who had slid off his knee now to play with an old tea caddy, all battered and scratched.

'How about Mr Nye?' Barbara said. 'Maybe there's something he could do?'

Mrs Penny lifted her heavy kettle and began to pour boiling water into the pans to heat the milk. She let out little huffs of breath as she did it. Her chest wasn't sounding much good these days. Perhaps something bad ran through her veins too. 'Mr Nye did his bit all those years ago, don't you think,' she said.

Both women stared at the little girl as she wriggled and squirmed against Tony's knee.

'But you, on the other hand . . .' A thin dribble of milk slid from Mrs Penny's wrist as she tested its heat. 'I can always do with someone who knows the meaning of hard work.'

Barbara glanced at Tony, who dipped his head and leered at her in response. She looked back at the rows of bottles on the kitchen table. The stack of nappy buckets waiting by the scullery to be swilled. Then she stood up, laid her cup and saucer back on the kitchen table and beckoned to the child to follow.

'No thanks,' she said.

Working in an office had spoiled Barbara. There was no way she would ever carry buckets for a living now. Besides, she saw the way that Tony gobbled at the little girl's fingers when they took their leave.

Run, she thought then. Run.

So that was what Barbara did.

North, north, to dark skies and sad men in three-piece suits. From one solicitor's recommendation to the next. North, north, to Juniors sitting in her kitchen and Associates lying in her bed. North, north, to Partners who would take her out for lunch at obscure hotels rather than visit the kind of places she could afford to call home, bucking and braying just like the first time, though it never did come to the conclusion that she hoped. For Barbara was scarred inside, that was what she always thought. Something rotten in her belly right from the start, just like Mrs Penny had said.

It was one of Barbara's solicitor friends who suggested her last move, as letters continued to pursue from the south. 'Scotland,' he said, pulling his underpants up two skinny legs. 'Going on holiday next week. Whole other country. They do things differently there.'

Barbara didn't take much when she crossed from England into the cold world of the north. A cherub with a broken arm. A photograph of two dead children pressed behind cold glass. And a small brown painting, dirty in more ways than one. The only roots Barbara had left.

She crossed the border at midnight, small girl sleeping heavy against her knee. She smiled as they disappeared into the darkness. This would be Barbara's newfound land – somewhere nobody would see her coming, unless she saw them first.

2011

The hospital lay on the outskirts of town. Another periphery, well away from the centre of it all, not bakers and candlestick makers this time, but car parks and a main road that led directly to the south. Just as with the mortuary, Margaret approached with caution. This was a place where life and death huddled constantly together. She couldn't be certain what she might find.

Her mother was huddled too: not dead yet, but lying comatose in a bed at the far end of a ward. On one side of her was the grey NHS stick, propped up by the bedside cabinet. On the other was Mrs Maclure.

Mrs Maclure was as bowed and unassuming as she had been when Margaret last saw her standing outside the chapel after the funeral of a person neither of them had known in life. Except this time she was sitting on an orange plastic chair next to an unconscious Barbara and a small machine that blinked on and off with a heart sign to show there was still hope. Margaret pulled up a chair of her own and sat on the other side of Barbara's bed, uncertain whom she should address. Her mother was incapacitated. And only recently Margaret had used Mrs Maclure's name to perpetrate a fraud. *Thou shalt not steal. Thou shalt not bear false witness.* But in the end it was Mrs Maclure who showed her the way.

'Did you have a fruitful trip to London?' she enquired with the smallest dip of her head. It wasn't the first thing Margaret had expected to be asked.

'Yes, thank you.' It was out before she could conjure a suitable lie.

'Oh good,' Mrs Maclure nodded. 'Such an interesting place, London. Full of all sorts. Of course you know that, having lived there for . . .'

'Thirty years.'

'Really, that long? The way your mother talked it seemed like only yesterday that you went to the south.'

Margaret tugged the corners of her coat up into her lap as though she were a child seeking protection. She didn't have any kind of answer to that.

Mrs Maclure bobbed for a moment in her chair. 'And was it a good trip?'

'Yes,' Margaret said. 'Very useful, thank you.'

'I heard that.'

Certificates in black and red. Births, Marriages and Deaths. Not to mention an unauthorized expenses form. Was there anything that Mrs Maclure did not know before Margaret had announced it first? She decided to change the subject – get back to the urgent matter lying in front of them now. 'Do you know where they found her?'

'Oh, out and about.' Mrs Maclure waved a vague hand. 'Down in Leith, I think, at some funeral parlour.'

'A funeral parlour?'

A corpse laid out beneath a sheet.

'Or perhaps a church.' Mrs Maclure bowed towards Barbara for a moment as though making a small prayer herself.

Margaret shifted a little in her chair. Either scenario sounded plausible. Ever since she'd turned up on Barbara's doorstep wearing a stolen coat and clutching a bottle of

rum, her mother had seemed obsessed with the prospect of death knocking at her door. Or the possibility of
securing eternal life. 'Has the doctor been round yet?' she
asked.

'Oh yes, dear.' Mrs Maclure smiled, revealing those
two long canines. A wolf in sheep's clothing. Or perhaps
someone who really did know where all the bodies were
buried, just as Barbara had said. 'But I told her to come
back when you were here.'

'Thank you.' Margaret felt suddenly tired, her long
night on a slow train catching up with her at last. Also
there was something discomfiting about Mrs Maclure, as
though she knew more about Margaret than she understood herself.

Mrs Maclure got up suddenly and began to button her
coat. 'Are you going now?' Margaret asked. Her heart set
up a little pitter-patter at the prospect of being left with
sole responsibility for her mother.

Mrs Maclure bobbed again. 'Oh yes, dear.' She picked
up her handbag and tucked it into her side. 'It's you she
will want to see when she wakes up. Don't you think?'

DCI Franklin had said the same thing when she drove
Margaret to the hospital, signalling, checking mirrors, and
pulling out onto the snow-covered roads with unnerving
accuracy and speed. 'She'll need to see a familiar face when
she comes round.'

'Yes,' said Margaret, remembering the last look that
had passed between her and Barbara. Fear, or something
like it. 'Did they say what was wrong?'

'No,' said the detective, gripping the steering wheel

with efficient leather gloves. 'But she's still breathing. That's what counts.'

As they sped through two sets of traffic lights on the cusp of amber to red, Margaret said, 'How did they know you'd be with me?'

DCI Franklin didn't even bother to look round. 'This is Edinburgh,' she said. And even Margaret understood then what she meant.

Two roundabouts and a zebra crossing taken at speed, and the DCI's next question didn't take Margaret by surprise either. 'You're from London, aren't you?' Janie had obviously done her work. 'What brings you here?'

'Oh, just because . . . My mother. She's older now.' One never knew when one might need a family to provide the perfect excuse.

The detective glanced in the rear-view mirror. 'London,' she said. As though she knew there was a story Margaret could tell about that. 'Very interesting place.'

Margaret held the lapels of her coat closed over the paws of a fox and hoped that DCI Franklin wasn't warming her up for some sort of confession about the real reason she had fled north. 'Thank you,' she said. 'For giving me a lift. I know you're very busy.'

'You're welcome.' DCI Franklin revved through another amber light. 'Anything else, just ask.'

'There is one thing.' Who Dares Wins (and all that). Margaret glanced at the detective, who was frowning now as though one favour was just a favour, whereas two was a suspicious act. 'Have you been following me? In your car, I mean.'

DCI Franklin laughed then, astonished. 'Following you?' she said, turning to look at Margaret. 'Why on earth would I do that?'

'Stroke,' declared the consultant when she came to see what could be done. A woman around Margaret's age, wearing a pair of smart black shoes with flat heels – appropriate in every sort of way. Margaret slid her own feet beneath the orange chair as the consultant looked at her notes first, then at Barbara and finally at Margaret. 'Seems she had some kind of shock. Though at her age, with her condition, it could have happened any time.'

'Her condition?'

Short of breath. Struggling to get in and out of a chair. A stick to help her walk. (Not to mention an obsession with religion.) It turned out that it wasn't idleness or contrariness or drinking too much rum that Barbara suffered from. It was a heart condition, after all.

'She'll need a lot of looking after, if . . .' The consultant suddenly jiggled the stethoscope round her neck. 'I mean, when she comes round.'

'Right.' Margaret stared at her mother's face, sunk into the pillow as though into the satin lining of a coffin just waiting for the lid to be nailed down. Was this it then? The beginning of the end. Not shuffling and dribbling around the corridor of some old people's home, but chopped down like a diseased tree, no questions asked.

The consultant wrote something on her clipboard. 'She won't wake up for a while.'

'How long?' Margaret wanted certainty. But she knew

that, unlike with her dead client, there would be none of that here.

'Hard to say.' The consultant frowned. 'But you can talk to her if you like. Tell her a story. Then she might wake up and tell you one back.'

The story began down in London when Margaret decided to return a coat. Out on the steps of the Chelsea Old Town Hall and Register Office with a clutch of certificates in her hand. Births, Marriages, Deaths. Even then Margaret had wondered if this was what her mother had experienced. That Damascene moment, like a flare in the chest, propelling Barbara towards whatever church she could find. Episcopal. Catholic. Evangelical. Friends. The belief that anything could happen – and probably would.

The suburban road had been much as it was when she'd last come to visit on that cold New Year's night. Quiet and full of cars parked end to end, everything slick with late-January rain. The house was as solid and intact as it had been three weeks before, too. No boarded-up windows. No soot to stain the brick. Instead it was just new glass bristling in the living-room window and those stained panels above the door – gold, green and red.

Margaret hadn't bothered to ring the bell. Why compound the offence? Instead she left the coat in a bundle on the doorstep, a parcel of red. She had almost escaped along the path, up, up and away, back towards the north, when the shout came, a rectangle of beckoning light thrown out as though someone inside had been waiting for just this chance. 'Hello!' A woman with ashen hair.

'I hoped you would come.' Calling for Margaret to return to the scene of everything she'd done wrong. And everything she was now trying to put right.

They stood opposite each other on the narrow garden path, one woman lit up by the glow of a family house, the other standing in the shadow of the past. Two women, two sides of the same coin, ne'er the twain shall meet. Except, of course, they had. A life laid out on a small, stained table in Margaret's local coffee shop. What was it, she had thought then, that always made her second best?

The woman's silk blouse rippled in the low light spilling from the front door. 'Will you come in?' she asked. And for a moment Margaret had been tempted. That rug the colour of blood. Those walls painted the colour of the sun. But then she shook her head. 'I'm sorry,' she said. And she was.

For alarms going off all at once. For the screaming of baby monitors and the howling of dogs. For the wail of smoke detectors. For the shouting, 'Bloody hell!' as the flames ran out, crawling over the carpet, leaping up the stairs, consuming everything that lay in their path – a man with hair dark as slate in the rain and two silver-haired children crouching in their beds.

Except . . .

When it came to it, even that had not turned out quite the way Margaret thought it might.

A family house all silent and dark – empty, she hoped. A rag soaked in turpentine taken from her pocket, then shoved deep inside the front door. A match struck hard against the side of a box and dropped through the letter box too. The pop as one ignited the other, a plume of blue flame rising up. Margaret had stood back then, waiting for it all to take hold, happy that he would lose everything he owned, just as she had lost all she owned too. Arson. Criminal damage. The intention to harm. It wasn't nothing. But it was, perhaps, what he deserved.

Then she'd glanced up.

The two faces gazed down at her like small satellites from behind black glass. They stared at each other for a moment – two silver-haired children, and a woman who should have been their mother, but never was. Sheep stealer. Peddler of fake coins. Or a murderess, perhaps. What was it her mother always said? Nothing but trouble right from the start.

Then it was down on her knees on the freezing garden path, scrabbling scrabbling, scraping together whatever dirty snow she could. Shovelling it through the letter box, handful after handful, hoping for the best. Until the rag lay smothered, not in turpentine this time, but with grit and slush, earth from the gravelly flower beds, blue flames dying out with nothing more than a hiss.

When Margaret looked up again, the two small faces had gone and she'd grabbed the first thing that came to her hand instead. A brick abandoned on the garden path, lobbed with fury against the large front pane. Smashing its way through the window. Splinters of wood, of metal and of glass flying through the air. Someone inside shouting, 'Call the police!'

Margaret threw something else too, as the clamour started up, just because she could. One of her Christmas clementines, tossed into a room painted the colour of the sun. It landed next to where a man had appeared, standing bemused amongst a sea of shattered glass. Happy Christmas, she'd thought then as she walked away. And a Happy New Year too.

Now, standing on that same garden path as though nothing untoward had happened, the ashen-haired woman held out her arms in a gesture reminiscent of a priest. 'No harm done,' she said. And they both knew what she meant. Even Margaret Penny was getting washed clean now.

Margaret indicated the bundle on the doormat. 'I brought your coat back. You left it in the cafe.'

Draped over a chair next to a small, stained table spread with a life Margaret had once imagined might be hers.

'Really, I thought . . .' The woman stopped. Seemed to decide that enquiry led down a path best left untravelled. 'Well . . .' She picked up the coat and unfurled it. 'I appreciate you keeping it all this time.'

The stolen coat was the colour of a tomato ripening beneath an Italian sun. Margaret was sorry to see it go. Somehow it had brought her luck.

'Yours is nice,' said the woman as though making social chit-chat. 'Where did you get it?'

'Oh, here and there.' Margaret ran a hand across the coat she was wearing, the colour of mulberries foaming in a wooden vat, cuffs worn thin. Mrs Walker's parting gift to the woman who had resurrected her. Protection of a sort.

The woman with the ashen hair stroked her own coat where it hung over her arm. A warning flag perhaps. Danger. Keep out. Margaret didn't tell her about the photograph hidden in the pocket. Two silver-haired children grinning in crumpled Technicolor. Home at last.

'Well, I suppose I'd better . . .' Margaret indicated the dark street, big cars lined up. They sparkled in the rain, winking at Margaret as though they had a message to impart. She turned back. 'I don't suppose you have a black car, do you?'

The woman frowned. 'No.' As though Margaret must have known everything about this woman's life, but chosen not to look.

'Oh.' Margaret wasn't sure whether to be sorry, or relieved. No pursuit from the south, then. A man with hair dark as slate in the rain coming after her to beg or to accuse. So this really was it. Right here and right now. Salvation, of a sort. 'Well, goodbye then.' Margaret turned to go.

'Oh, hang on.' The woman suddenly disappeared back inside the house.

Margaret waited in that rectangle of warm light, not certain whether to follow or hurry off down the street. Somewhere she knew that two silver-haired children might be watching. Maybe even a husband, lurking somewhere in the shadows. But in the end it only took a moment before the woman appeared once more, this time with a big cardboard box in her arms.

'Would you like this?' The woman held the box out to Margaret. 'I heard you might need one.'

Margaret reached out to take the box, uncertain what she might find inside. Another replacement coat, perhaps. Or a bomb to blow her out of existence for good.

'I found it in a skip down the road,' the woman went on. 'But it's practically brand new.' Margaret stared down at where the brown cardboard flaps folded one over the other. The woman started to close the door of her family home. 'It's a juice machine,' she said.

On the cabinet beside Barbara's hospital bed a clutch of tiny green-and-white flowers drooped over the edge of a plastic NHS cup. An illegal offering from Mrs Maclure, left to cheer Barbara up. How was it, Margaret wondered, that certain people always managed to subvert the rules?

Inside the bedside cabinet, bundled inside a yellow plastic bag like a whole coil of gut, lay the clothes Barbara had been wearing when they first brought her in. Large pants, a huge bra, trousers with an elasticated waist and a polyester top into which Margaret could have fitted twice. Margaret sifted through her mother's clothes piece by piece, remembering the things she had lifted from another woman's chest of drawers only a few days before. One old lady with nothing but ice on the inside of the bathroom window, another with a wipe-clean roller blind. Two sides of the same coin, ne'er the twain shall meet. But Margaret was starting to understand just which one she would prefer to end up as herself.

She moved all her mother's clothes into a pile and added the new things that she had insisted DCI Franklin stop for on their way over. A crumpled dressing gown in a shade that had once been pink. A pair of reading glasses. The TV guide. And a half-bottle of rum from under the kitchen sink. Emergency supplies should Barbara ever revive.

At the bottom of the bedside cabinet, Barbara's sizeable handbag stood firm as a monument to the dead. Margaret heaved it onto her lap and undid the clasp, *snip-snap*, to check if there was anything important inside that her mother might need. *Be prepared.* Wasn't that what Barbara always said? Though Margaret didn't want to think now about exactly what she might have to prepare for. After all, she'd only ever looked inside Barbara's bag to get at her purse before – a five-pound note here, a few pound coins there, enough for a hot sausage roll or a bottle of cheap wine. Never to rummage through what might turn out to be her mother's last relics of life.

A handkerchief, ironed and folded.

Lipstick worn to a brown stub.

Keys for the house.

A tortoiseshell comb.

And right at the bottom, hidden amongst the detritus of a life, a photograph of two dead sleeping children, back in the light at last.

A nurse rattled in with a trolley. 'Going to brush your mother's hair?' he asked, nodding towards the comb discarded on the bed.

Margaret looked at the comb, then back at her mother, hair depleted as though she had been the victim of some terrible radiation attack. Perhaps that explained why Barbara had joined every church within the vicinity. Cancer. Running through her body like some kind of bad spirit, dancing its way through the lacework of her bones. The fine strands of Barbara's hair reminded Margaret of the contents of the envelope she had given Janie. Some other little relics of the past, once lost, now found again. Blonde. Mousy. Dark. She tried to remember what colour her mother's hair used to be when they were both young. Brown, perhaps, maybe lighter. But she couldn't recall.

Her mother was just her mother, after all, not someone who had deserved attention until it was all too late.

Margaret reached out and placed her hand over Barbara's where it rested above the blue wrinkles of the hospital blanket. She was amazed to find how neatly they fitted, like two silver spoons, the bowl of one curved around the next. What was her mother dreaming of, tucked up in this hospital bed? A cherub with a sliced-off arm? A box room crammed with junk? An old Edinburgh flat where all you could hear were babies crying through the wall? Or a Brazil nut with the Ten Commandments etched into its shell?

Thou shalt not.

Next to the bed a monitor flipped its little signal – heart, heart, heart – as Margaret picked Mrs Walker's Brazil nut from the cup of her mother's palm. The nut was warm. The promise of new life, perhaps. Or a story that was yet to be told. Margaret bent her cheek towards Barbara's mouth, skin to lip, and listened for her mother's breathing, heart racing with all the things Barbara had never told her and all the things Margaret had never thought to ask.

For a moment she heard nothing, and her heart flipped to nothing too as she caught the thought skipping through her brain: *This could be it.* Then it started up again with a swift drumbeat against her ribs. For there it was, thin as a whisper, like a secret sent around a circle and back. Barbara was still breathing. Wasn't that what counted, just as DCI Franklin had said?

1963

It was late on a hot summer afternoon when Barbara Penny came to a London hospital to see what she could see.

'Penny, Ruby,' said the nurse on duty in reception. 'Room number twenty-four.'

'Thank you,' Barbara said, gloves on, hat on, handbag with its thick gilt lip. Then she headed straight up to another room at the top of the building instead.

At the end of a long corridor on the hospital's highest, furthest floor, Barbara peered through a wall of glass onto row upon row of cots lined up along the other side. One hundred babies (or thereabouts), all staring back.

'Which one are you, dear?' A nurse in a sensible white uniform appeared by her side.

'Penny,' replied Barbara, gazing at the tiny faces.

The nurse disappeared, then appeared again a moment later behind the glass this time. She walked up and down the rows glancing at each cot until she stopped beside one and reached in. A bundle. A small hand waving above the institutional wrap. The nurse held the baby up so that Barbara could see. There was a plastic band tight around its ankle, a name written across the middle in miniature script. Barbara couldn't read the writing through the glass, but she knew what it said. *Baby Penny.* So much for the Walker roots.

The baby wasn't pretty, nor was it sweet. Its face was round like a piglet, red and contorted. Its eyes not startling, but a commonplace shade instead. The nurse jiggled the crumpled infant in her arms, lifting one small limb to wave it at Barbara through the glass. Barbara smiled and touched the partition with her fingertip. The baby was perfect. It was just like her.

Half an hour later, on the floor below in the corridor outside Ruby's room, Barbara sat on a chair while a doctor, tall in his white coat, gave her the information he thought she wanted to have.

'Lost a lot of blood. Bit of a nightmare really, between you and me. Were you with her when it began?'

'No,' said Barbara.

'Should be fine though in a few days, maybe a week.' The doctor looked down at a chart attached to a clipboard. 'We can't get much sense out of her at the moment. Ever had that problem before?'

'Yes,' said Barbara, handbag on her knee.

'She keeps asking for someone called Clementine. Do you know who that is?'

'No,' said Barbara, feet flat against the polished linoleum.

'Oh well.' The doctor flipped his chart closed. 'Come back tomorrow at the same time and we'll see what we can see.'

Barbara stood up. 'What about the baby?'

'Oh, yes.' The doctor smiled. 'She's fine. Lovely. No problem there at all.'

Two days later and Ruby still had not risen from where she lay, sweating and writhing amongst the rumpled hospital sheets. The doctor seemed more agitated than before.

'We found her trying to get out of bed,' he said. 'Had to sedate her. Ever had that trouble before in the family?'

'Yes,' said Barbara.

The doctor nodded as though this told him all there was to know. 'We'll keep her on drug therapy. Knock her out for a bit.' He still had his chart and clipboard under his arm. 'She needs a rest, poor thing. Time to recuperate.'

On the fourth day, Barbara arrived to find a lanky young man standing on the wrong side of the glass. He was holding one of the hundred babies in his arms, and though Barbara couldn't see the little plastic tag, she knew straight away which child it was. Damp boarding houses, a curtain covered in small blue sprigs and a future Barbara had always wanted but never seemed able to get. Nye Junior. Come to see what he could get too.

Unnoticed in her sensible coat and gloves, Barbara watched as William Nye Junior dipped his head to Baby Penny's face. The baby gazed back at him, eyes huge, small limbs wrapped tight. Between Barbara's legs a sanitary towel pressed against the inside of her thigh, hot and thick. This time she was determined to get whatever might be coming, before anyone else took it first.

They met back on the correct side of the glass, Baby Penny consigned to its crib once more. 'Oh, hello.' Nye Junior stood before Barbara, colour racing up to stain his cheeks. 'I didn't expect to see you.'

'No,' said Barbara, her hands cool inside her gloves. 'I didn't expect to see you, either.'

William Junior's gaze darted along the corridor as though looking for an escape. 'I won't be here for much longer.' He lifted a finger to his forehead for a moment. 'Going abroad soon.'

Barbara's heart set up a little pitter-patter beneath her matching jumper and skirt. 'Abroad?'

'Yes. An adventure.' The young man let out a sort of gurgle, a laugh garrotted at birth. 'That's what my father calls it.'

'Oh.' Heat prickled up through Barbara's skin where a man's fingers once pressed into her arm. She gripped harder at her handbag. *Be prepared*. Wasn't that what Mrs Penny had taught her? 'Where are you going?' she said.

'Not sure exactly.' The young man was sweating all the way along his top lip. 'My father has made the arrangements. But I've a few things to sort out first.' Nye Junior turned his head for a moment to glance through the glass partition, one hundred babies staring back.

'What sort of things?'

'Oh, this and that. Luggage and so forth.' William Junior put a hand up to his mouth as though to quell the lie the moment it got out. But Barbara could read it in the colour that burned all over his neck. He was going to take the baby. Whether his father liked it or not.

Her heart beat quicker than ever then beneath her twinset. 'Will you be gone long?'

William Junior pushed his hair away from his face. 'Oh, I shouldn't think so. A few months. Maybe a year.'

'Right.' But Barbara knew already that it would be a lifelong thing. Heads to the north. Tails to somewhere else. To a land where cars were as big as boats, perhaps, and kitchens came with floors in which one could see one's face. Take me, she thought then, all of a sudden. Over the hills and far away. To somewhere we can start afresh. But as Nye Junior turned to go, she knew that he would not. For someone had got between them right from the start. Dancing on those curtains. Dancing across that wallpaper. Dancing over the narrow frame of a bed. After all, if Barbara could never forget Ruby, why should anyone else?

The very next day, no time to waste, Barbara sat opposite a large mahogany desk in an office just off Ironmonger Lane. Across from her a young woman with bony knees sat behind three large phones. Neither of them spoke. On the mantelpiece a stuffed stoat winked at Barbara in the low light. Through the wall came the sound of a bell. The young woman coughed. 'Mr Nye Senior will see you now,' and she reached behind her to open a door made of books.

In Nye Senior's office Barbara sat in a very upright chair, while the father-in-law she would never have advised her on what she must do next. 'It isn't difficult, my dear. It has been done before.'

'Has it?' said Barbara. Despite drudging in a solicitor's office, she realized Mrs Penny had been right: Barbara knew nothing of life really. But she was determined to find out.

'Oh, yes, dear.' Mr Nye turned his eyes to a folder in front of him tied with a ribbon dip-dyed pink. An admissions form. Adoption certificates. The deeds for a house. One family transformed into another with just the dotting of some *i*s and the crossing of some *t*s.

'I don't have any money,' Barbara said, shifting in the uncomfortable chair.

'Not to worry, dear,' said Mr Nye Senior. 'I'm sure there is something we can sort out between us.' He leaned up against the edge of his desk where he sat, right in front of Barbara, one elegant leg draped across the next.

'Like what?' Barbara had declined his offer to remove her coat. She knew from Ruby where that could lead.

Mr Nye Senior glanced towards his wall where a thousand naked women gazed back. 'I believe your sister owns a painting.'

Ruby with her legs thrown out. Ruby laid out on a chaise. Barbara gave a little twitch of her nose. 'That small brown thing. Is it worth a lot?'

'Oh, no, dear.' Mr Nye Senior slid himself further towards Barbara along the precipice of his desk. 'I shouldn't think so. Sentimental value only.'

'I might have seen it,' Barbara said, eyes sliding towards the gap on Mr Nye Senior's wall. 'But I'd need to check.'

'Of course, dear. No hurry.' Mr Nye Senior leaned forward and touched her for a moment on the shoulder, just as once he had touched her arm. Barbara felt the way her skin began to tingle. 'But the first thing we must do is arrange the paperwork. Then we'll see what to do next.'

The day after that, Barbara registered the birth herself, on Mr Nye Senior's advice. Rule number 3 – no unnecessary surprises. Though even as a child Barbara had thought, isn't that what a surprise is meant to be?

The Chelsea Old Town Register Office was not the

place for surprises either, just somewhere to get the job done. Barbara arrived a little before closing with all the documents she might need. Her birth certificate. Her proof of address. And a letter from a solicitor, just in case.

'What is your name?' said the woman behind the desk.

'Barbara Penny.'

'And you are the mother.' It wasn't a question, so Barbara did not reply. 'And what name do you want?' The woman was writing as fast as she could now that home time approached.

Barbara was flustered for a moment. 'I'm sorry?' She had a name already; why would she need another?

'For the baby.' The woman held her pen poised above the ledger, which once completed, with its dotted *is* and crossed *ts*, would be sacrosanct in every way.

'Oh, yes.' Barbara had wondered about that. There was Clementine, of course, Ruby's first choice. But why name a baby after someone who was irretrievably lost? And Dorothea seemed so ancient, apart from the fact that it was already inhabited by a ghost. Which left Mrs Penny. But Barbara wasn't even sure that she knew what Mrs Penny's first name was. For a moment Barbara was uncertain. How did one name a child when all the rest of the family were absent or dead?

The woman in front of her coughed and Barbara looked up. Beside the woman, on the table, was a handbag much like Barbara's. Next to that a pair of gloves much like Barbara's too.

'What's your name?' Barbara asked.

'Margaret.' The woman sniffed.

Margaret, thought Barbara. That will do.

'It won't be for long.' That was what the doctor said, sitting behind his desk as Barbara sat before him. 'A month or two, perhaps, maybe six. We can review it at regular intervals. See what you think.'

'Yes.' Barbara nodded. She understood exactly what he meant.

'There's no need to be concerned. We have all sorts of new therapies now. All sorts of drugs.'

'Yes.' Barbara was still wearing her hat.

'Runs in the family, I understand.' The doctor put out his hand to hold down a buff folder with the name *Walker* inscribed on the outside. 'Your solicitor mentioned it. Though not everyone succumbs.' He bent his head in Barbara's direction and she gave a slight nod of acknowledgement in return.

'You'll be taking the baby, of course.' It was not a question either. 'Probably best, under the circumstances.' Barbara waited while the doctor wrote something on his notes. Then he pushed a piece of paper towards her side of the desk. 'We have the admissions form here. It's just your signature we need now.'

The last time Barbara came to visit Ruby she brought a suitcase containing everything her sister might need. It used to belong to Mrs Penny, before Ruby stole that too.

Barbara laid the suitcase on the end of Ruby's bed, her sister sitting in a chair to the side, still wearing her hospital gown. Ruby's body was slumped, all folded over at the neck. Dark lashes curved against her cheeks as though she were eight years old once more. Her breathing came shallow and swift and her skin was a sort of ghostly blue, like a new mother's milk. Her eyes were half closed, veins running hither and thither across pale-violet lids.

Barbara pressed her thumbs to the suitcase's little metal clasps. *Click-clack* and that's that. Opened up the lid.

A slip.

A skirt.

A jumper worn at the elbows.

A teaspoon with a tiny apostle soldered to the end.

And an old green dress.

It wasn't much, but Barbara knew that Ruby only ever travelled light. She took each item from the suitcase, laying them one by one into a drawer. Then she closed the suitcase. *Clack-click.* That's it. And turned to leave.

'Help me, Barbara.'

Barbara turned to where Ruby sat in her chair. Ruby's body might be tranquillized, but it appeared that her mouth still worked.

'Help me, please.'

Ruby's fingers fell open in a loose curl on her lap. In her palm was a Brazil nut, all scratched and worn. Barbara went over and picked the Brazil nut out of Ruby's hand.

Thou shalt do no murder.

Thou shalt not commit adultery.

Thou shalt not steal.

'There you are,' Barbara murmured. 'I wondered where you'd gone.' She turned the nut in her hand, then put it down on the bedside cabinet. 'I always wanted this,' she said. 'But I think you need it more than me now.'

There was a knock on the door and a matron entered, carrying a syringe in a metal dish. Behind her came a nurse carrying a baby swaddled in a hospital blanket. And behind the nurse, a man cradling a camera and twirling one of the buttons on his black pea coat. *W. H. SYMMONS & Co. Est. London 1933.* Next generation along.

'All ready then?' The matron put the metal dish down on a table by the bed.

'Yes,' said Barbara.

'Help me, Barbara.'

'Now, now, dear.' The matron went over to Ruby and laid a firm hand on her arm. 'Your sister's come with your things.'

'She'll have to sit up a bit,' said the photographer, fiddling with his camera. He was a young man, impatient, determined to drag his father's business away from contracts such as this.

'We always like to take a photo, just in case.' The matron rearranged Ruby's gown so that it covered as much of her bare legs as it could.

Barbara didn't need to ask in case of what. A lot of babies left this hospital without the woman who first brought them in.

The matron tried to smooth Ruby's hair, sliding her into a more upright pose. 'Come on now, dear. Got to look your best.' But Ruby just rolled her head away, hair all a tumble across the shadows of her face.

Barbara stood back in the doorway as the photographer took up his position. 'Right, first on her own and then one with the baby.' And he lifted the camera to his face.

'Wait!' Barbara suddenly moved forward, hand held out, touching the photographer on the shoulder to make him stop.

'Yes, dear?' The matron frowned. She was anxious to continue. Ruby Penny had taken up far too much time already in this hospital. She was looking forward to getting this particular patient moved out.

In Barbara's palm lay a small brooch, five starry points, a drop of red at its heart. 'Could she wear this, please? She had it as a child. It will remind her.'

The matron picked up the brooch. 'I don't see why not.' She went over to the chair and pinned the brooch to Ruby's gown. 'There, lovely.' The matron patted the brooch where it sat sharp against Ruby's breastbone.

Across the room the baby wriggled in the nurse's arms and let out a small cry. Ruby lifted her head for a moment, confused.

'Smile, please.'

And the photographer pressed the shutter.

But it was Barbara who was smiling the next time the button was pressed down, holding the child up herself for all the world to see. For the baby was not beautiful. Its eyes were not startling. It was ordinary, just like its aunt.

That night, Barbara woke sometime after twelve and knew that it was done. Ruby always had left a hole in the world, one way or another, gone without saying goodbye. Taken from her bed in the nursing home to one much further away than that. *Good riddance to bad rubbish.* Wasn't that what Mrs Penny always said?

Out beyond the curtained alcove a baby was crying, its

small wail piercing the night. Barbara lay still, listening for a moment, and wondered if it knew too. After a few seconds she slid herself from the bed, standing in the middle of the cold room for a moment before going over to gaze down at the baby where it lay tucked into a drawer. The baby's cheeks were all aflame. Brow creased. Its mouth a big dark O.

Barbara bent down to pick the baby up. She held her close, feeling the warmth from that little body seep through into her own, nothing between them but a thin layer of someone else's genes. For a moment she stood there in the darkness, uncertain how she should begin. Then, as the baby cried on, she began to sway, bare feet on a thin rug, nightgown falling to just above her toes. 'There, there,' she said, burying her nose in the baby's hot skin. 'Don't cry. I'm your mother now.'

PART FIVE

Six Orange Pips Sucked Dry

THE SCOTSMAN
5 February 2011

FUNERAL NOTICES

The Funeral of Clementine Amelia Walker, late of Edinburgh, formerly of London, will take place at 2.15 p.m. on Wednesday 5 February 2011 at the Small Chapel, Mortonhall. All welcome. Join us in saying farewell to our sister Clementine, once living, now gone. Flowers welcome too.

2011

As I went down to the river to pray
Studying about that good ol' way
And who shall wear the starry crown?
Good Lord, show us the way.

O sisters, let's go down
Let's go down, come on down,
O sisters, let's go down
Down in the river to pray.

The indigent funeral rota swayed up the path towards the crematorium chapel like something out of New Orleans. A cluster of umbrellas hovered above their heads, but that was for the Scottish weather, not because of the sun. Rain had come to Edinburgh. The longed-for thaw at last.

'Where's the Reverend McKilty?' Margaret whispered to her mother as they congregated in the holding bay waiting for the coffin to arrive.

'Not his turn.' Barbara wheezed, trailing two grey NHS sticks now as she clung on to her daughter's arm. Barbara's heart was not what it used to be. But just like her, it hadn't given up yet.

'Who's he then?' Margaret jerked her head in the direction of the big man going around shaking hands with everyone he could find. His skin shone rich and earthy in the grey Edinburgh light.

'Oh, that's the Pastor.' Barbara gave a little wave of one of her sticks. 'Evangelical wing.'

Pastor Macdonald had brought a choir to sing Mrs Walker out. Three women almost as large as him, each dressed in their Sunday best. Three men in neat suits, their shoes glittering like jewelled brogues in the early-February rain. When Margaret saw them arrive in their sharp white shirts and perfectly coordinated hats she was pleased that she had purchased a new pair of shoes to go with her new stolen coat. Her remittance for services rendered had not gone far, but it had gone as far as that.

Margaret looked down now in satisfaction at where her toes tapered to a smart point, ankles criss-crossed with two straps fastened by neat buttons on either side. The shoes weren't practical (Barbara had already pointed that out). But there was something about them which Margaret felt had been fashioned just for her.

All around the crematorium holding bay a host of people Margaret had never met before crowded in. There were far too many of them for the space – a little square shelter with see-through walls where each funeral gathering waited for the one before to end. The day was damp. The people were damp. The air they all breathed was damp too. Yet nobody complained. It was Edinburgh, after all.

Instead, in every corner of the tiny, heaving space, people were smiling and chatting and shaking hands, nodding their heads in acknowledgement of an acquaintanceship or perhaps something more. Nobody seemed to be particularly mournful. Either the indigent brought out the best in them, or it was just that the deceased was unknown to anyone who had come to say goodbye. Only Barbara looked upset. But Margaret knew this was as likely to do with the rudeness of the taxi driver en route, as with some deeper wound to her mother's soul.

One by one, smiling and nodding, the mourners came and shook Margaret by the hand where she stood at the edge of the throng. It was as though they knew that she was somehow responsible for it all.

'Oh, it's lovely to meet you at last.'

'I've heard such a lot about you.'

'Your mother's so pleased that you're back.'

Margaret took each hand when it was offered as though she was pleased to be acquainted with its owner too, despite the fact that she had never heard anything of them before. Something about the occasion must be rubbing off. She caught a glimpse of Pati laughing and talking somewhere in amongst the throng, and dipped a hand into her pocket to finger a little matryoshka doll nestled amongst the mulberry-coloured wool. She wasn't the only stranger then.

Once the handshaking had ceased, Margaret leaned in towards Barbara and said, 'Who are all these people?'

'What's that?' Barbara's heart might still be beating, but ever since she'd returned from hospital her hearing seemed to have gone awry.

'Where are they from?' Margaret enunciated a little louder this time, right up against her mother's ear.

'Oh, all around, all around.' Barbara gesticulated with one of her sticks as though this answered Margaret's question. 'We asked for a representative from each group and they all came instead.'

Episcopal. Catholic. Evangelical. Friends. Here in the holding bay, crammed in damp and tight, was Edinburgh's indigent funeral rota. Representatives of all the city's faiths (and none), gathered together for a celebration of some unknown person's life.

Outside on the tarmac, umbrellas held high, the choir began to tune up once again, a humming and a thrumming, a line of a melody thrown out to show the rest the way. Everyone in the holding bay suddenly hushed and turned towards the door. Margaret peered through the misted Perspex wall. The cortège must be approaching. Pastor Macdonald was already at the front, shoulders and head held high, eyes beaming across the crowd. 'Now, ladies and gentlemen,' he declared, his voice rolling around the plastic walls like a drum before the clash of a cymbal. 'Your attention, if you don't mind. Our sister Mrs Walker is on her way.'

Janie had called Margaret two days before the funeral and asked her to collect the deceased's effects.

'Why me?' said Margaret.

'Who else?'

Full Name. Date of Birth. Place of Birth. Religion. Everything was in order.

Except . . .

'There was one thing,' declared Janie, and Margaret held her breath. 'Any reason why we should bury rather than burn?'

But there was no more time for Mrs Clementine Amelia Walker. Dead and cold in a fridge for weeks, dead and cold in an empty flat for weeks before that. Now dressed in emerald and ready for the off. Margaret had done her job, and done her job well. She had provided the

paperwork and sorted the proof. They had Mrs Walker's
birth certificate, so now they could issue one for death.
Janie had called up the indigent funeral directors in Leith
and now she must sign Mrs Walker off to the fiery pit.

The effects didn't amount to much. A photograph
showing a woman wearing a star-shaped brooch. Some
small scraps of paper. A receipt for jewellery long since
lost. And a Brazil nut with the Ten Commandments
scratched into its shell. Margaret looked at the things
laid out in a plastic bag on Janie's desk. 'What about her
clothes?' she said.

'They'll be sent to charity. The council's very big on
recycling.'

Margaret nodded. A sheet of newsprint turned into a
makeshift vest.

Janie pushed the plastic bag across to where Margaret
sat. '*Ultimus haeres* confirmed there was no value in the
estate.'

The last heir — receptacle of ownerless property (as
though there could ever be such a thing). All that remained
of Mrs Walker. Not even enough for a bouquet.

'Bereavement services will cover the funeral costs.'
Janie nibbled at the tip of her biro. 'There's still a budget
for that.'

A minister, a hearse, the cheapest of coffins and a few
members from the indigent funeral rota to sing the
deceased on their way. It wasn't what Margaret called a
good send-off.

Janie flicked her eyes towards her computer screen. 'Of
course, Mrs Walker's funeral will be a bit more extensive
than normal.'

'What do you mean?' Here was something Margaret had failed to discover.

'There's been a donation.'

'A donation?'

'Yes. Anonymous. Came through a solicitor's firm in London. Nye & Sons. Ring any bells?'

A stuffed stoat. A thousand naked paintings (or thereabouts). A woman with bony knees. Margaret had promised Jessica Plymmet she would never tell exactly how it was she got her hands on the Walker file. She coughed and shuffled in her chair. 'What does it mean? The donation . . .'

'Oh, flowers, shiny hearse, better coffin and a stone perhaps, or some sort of memorial.'

'Do the rest not get a stone? The indigent, I mean.'

'No, we just write them down in a ledger at the crematorium. Well . . .' Janie shifted in her seat. 'A computer ledger now.'

Christ, thought Margaret when she set off home again, Brazil nut and photograph in her bag. All that effort to find someone, then they're just cast back into the pit, nothing but a line on a computer screen. At The Court she complained to her mother. 'All that work resurrecting her and that is where it ends.'

'What, dear?' Barbara was watching murder on the television.

'Mrs Walker.'

But Barbara just turned up the volume with the remote. 'Somebody paid,' she said. 'That's all that matters. Let the woman rest.'

Swing low, sweet chariot
Coming for to carry me home.
Swing low, sweet chariot
Coming for to carry me home.

I looked over Jordan and what did I see?
Coming for to carry me home.
A band of angels coming after me.
Coming for to carry me home.

Outside the crematorium chapel the shiny hearse pulled up, Mrs Walker's coffin resplendent inside as though it had suddenly sprouted flowers. Margaret couldn't help noticing that the coffin was much grander than the one used for the indigent funeral she had attended only a few weeks before. But then that funeral had been ordinary, whereas this one was turning out to be exceptional in every way.

The communal throb of the choir rose up as the coffin was lifted from the hearse by five black-clad men and Micky, wearing a sombre but well-tailored suit. The anthem about Jordan and its river rolled on, accompanied now by the indigent rota's finest and some who perhaps should have kept their mouths shut. Margaret bent her head towards her mother as the choir (and others) intoned in every sort of key. 'Who chose the songs?' she said. Calling them hymns didn't seem quite appropriate.

Barbara looked away. 'No idea,' she said.

The choir sang on as the coffin was carried into the chapel while all the mourners waited respectfully outside. Once the deceased was in, Barbara made a sign for Margaret to help her forwards, into the chapel and then right to the front. Margaret gripped her mother's arm, holding Barbara back.

'What are we waiting for?' Barbara urged her daughter on.

'What do you think?' Margaret hissed into her mother's ear.

'I have no idea.'

'Any family, of course.'

Barbara clattered with her sticks then stabbed one towards the toe of Margaret's pristine new shoes. 'Don't be silly,' she said. 'You found her, didn't you? We're her family now.'

They stood, they sat, they sang, they laughed and they wept. It was a good sending-off indeed. In a chapel full of colour and of praise, Mrs Clementine Walker had the goodbye she deserved. Somewhere between the eulogy ('We didn't know Mrs Walker, but we feel we know her now') and the readings ('Suffer little children to come unto me'), Margaret leaned across and whispered to her mother, 'I read somewhere that death comes to a person twice. Once when it happens, and once when everyone who remembers them has gone too.'

Barbara pressed a crumpled tissue to her eyes, her face all damp and squashed. 'What do you mean?' she wheezed.

'Well, if that's true, maybe it means Mrs Walker has been reborn.'

'What?' Barbara stopped with her wet tissue as though someone had slapped her.

'Well . . .' Margaret sat back. 'There was no one to remember her before. And now there is all of us.'

As the coffin was prepared for its final journey, down into the depths of the fiery pit (or at least the crematorium's waiting room), Margaret turned the lucky coronation penny in her pocket and thought of all the other dead Walkers who had gone before. Dorothea and Alfred. Two little twins. Now their older sister Clementine, off to join them at last. She wondered then who might remember her when she was gone. Nothing but hair stuck to the sofa and a scattering of bones. A man last seen standing in a room surrounded by broken glass? Or an ashen-haired lady lifting a photograph of two silver-haired children from the pocket of her coat? There was Janie, of course, with her bubblegum sweaters. Or even Micky, murmuring endearments as she applied make-up to whatever remained of Margaret's face.

Heads or tails. Perhaps it was all random chance after all.

Margaret looked out across the grey heads of the indigent funeral crowd to find Pastor Macdonald watching her. He was singing as though it was the coming of the end (which of course, for Mrs Walker, it was). His voice flew out, resonant and true, soaring over them all on its way beyond the chapel door. Margaret was amazed at the hugeness of his mouth, the shine on his teeth. Surely not someone who came from Scotland, with teeth that perfect and straight. Pastor Macdonald winked at Margaret then, and in that flustered moment heat ran all up and down her body. Perhaps he might remember Margaret too.

Almost at the end (but not quite) Pastor Macdonald invited them up one by one to say a last goodbye to the dead before they all got on with life.

'What does he mean?' Margaret bent to her mother who was already rummaging away inside the pocket of her turquoise suit.

'You'll see,' said Barbara, who always had been prepared in a way that Margaret was not.

One by one the members of Edinburgh's mourners to the indigent stood up and stepped away from their wooden chapel chairs. They queued in a very Edinburgh way, orderly and polite, shuffling forwards to the coffin one by one to touch its surface in a gesture of farewell. Some people left small gifts – a pebble or a leaf, a clutch of crocuses from Mrs Maclure as though she had gathered them only that morning from a local park. As Barbara arrived at the front, accompanied by Margaret and two grey NHS sticks, she reached out her fist and left a Brazil nut with the Ten Commandments etched into its shell on the surface of the coffin. The nut skittered on the polished wood as Margaret started and fumbled in her own coat pocket. Sheep stealer. Peddler of fake coins. Trouble. Wasn't that what her mother had always been, right from the start?

But there was no time for Margaret to snatch back her mother's offering, so that she could offer it up herself. For now it was Margaret's turn to leave some sort of gift to the dead. The queue waited patiently as she put her hand into the pocket of her coat once more and wondered what she might present. Some scraps of paper covered in discombobulated girls' names? Maybe the coronation penny that had turned out lucky after all? Or six orange pips, frail and skeletal, sucked to within an inch of their bones. But in the end it was the miniature matryoshka doll that Margaret placed on the end of Mrs Walker's coffin. The baby of the family. A daughter to replace the one Mrs Walker never had in life.

Beside Margaret, Barbara's chest gave a great heave as she stared at the little wooden child, before she shuffled back with alacrity to her place in the front row, rather like a crab scuttling into its hole. Margaret followed, her own eyes surprisingly swimmy for a woman she'd only ever met in death. Then the choir began to sing once more. A humming and a thrumming topped with a single spoken voice – Pastor Macdonald's eulogy to a stranger none of them had ever known but who was part of their lives forever now. 'We say farewell to our sister Clementine Amelia Walker. Lost to the earth, to the wind, to the sky. Lost to the seas, to life and all it brings, both the pleasures and the pain. Lost to those who knew her once. But no longer lost to us.'

As he spoke the button was pressed and with a small shudder the coffin began its slow descent. The throb of the choir swelled up to fill the tall, high space and all around, hankies appeared from pockets, from handbags, from little packets stashed in readiness up sleeves. Out at the front three large women and three neat men began to sway, a deep, sombre movement as they sang Clementine Amelia Walker to the grave.

As though by magic, the indigent rota began to sway too, urging Mrs Walker on, not quite in a churchyard, not quite on a hillside, but to somewhere that would eventually be marked with a stone.

O sisters, let's go down
Let's go down, come on down,
O sisters, let's go down
Down in the river to pray.

'I always wanted a sister,' Margaret said then as she and her mother swayed with the rest in a very non-Edinburgh way.

'So did I,' said Barbara. 'But life's like that, sometimes. It gives with one hand and takes away with the next.'

The coffin continued its slow descent, watched by every one of the indigent funeral rota, eyes to the front, and Margaret was uncertain whether this was the end of something or the beginning of something else. It was then that it happened. A door opening at the far end of the chapel. A voice rising above the lament.

'Wait!'

1944

The light was almost gone from the sky when eight-year-old Barbara left the house in Elm Row. She closed the front door with a soft click and walked quickly away – from Mrs Penny in the scullery, from Tony by the stove. And from Ruby in their bedroom on the highest, furthest floor. Nobody saw her leave.

Down each shadowy street Barbara stumbled and scurried on her way towards the Underground, outdoor coat buttoned up to her chin. The blackout was already on, heavy curtains drawn across each of the neighbours' windows, grown-ups hurrying past too, heads held low against the possibility of a raid. They ignored the little girl as she made her way towards the trains, hugging railings and dodging from porch to porch, disappearing into a station entrance as everyone else was trying to get out. They were determined to get home before any rockets started to fly. But the Warning hadn't sounded yet. Barbara knew there was still time.

Back at 14 Elm Row a chicken roasted slowly in the oven, skin turning a gentle shade of gold. Mrs Penny had bartered six packets of Clementine's cigarettes and a quart of Tony's rum, amongst other things, to get it there on time. All ready for the rich American Clementine had promised to bring home that night. The chicken was nearly done, fat bubbling around it in the pan, smell rising up through the house. Past the scullery where Mrs Penny was hanging the weekly wash. Past the parlour with its green chaise longue. Past Tony's den with its box of treasure hidden under the bed. Past Mrs Penny's bedroom where a Brazil nut sat in the middle of the mantelpiece. Past the cupboard on the landing where a photograph of two dead children languished on a shelf. Up, up until it reached the highest, furthest floor, where eight-year-old Ruby was waiting and waiting for Clementine's sign to appear.

Except . . .

Ruby had already missed her chance. For it was little pig Barbara who had spied first what their sister Clementine had left.

Only that morning, while Tony scraped out the black insides of his pipe and Mrs Penny beat the weekly wash to a frothy pulp, Barbara had stood at the kitchen sink, cardigan sleeves rolled up, and slid the first clue from its cup. She had been doing the chore that Ruby was meant to complete: side plates and saucers, knives, teaspoons and cups. It had been Ruby's turn to do the dishes that morning, but as usual it was Barbara who'd had to fill in when her sister had been bad.

Clementine had gone before anyone else was even awake, nothing but a leftover cup of tea to show that she had been there first.

'Better be back in time for dinner.' Mrs Penny put down her butter knife and glanced over at the sideboard where a chicken lay, naked and dimpled, in its dish.

Tony sucked breakfast tea up between his lips. 'She'll be here.'

'You can never be certain of that.' Mrs Penny was still wearing her dressing gown. She felt tired. A whole day's

washing awaited her in the scullery. Then a dinner to prepare for six people, including a guest. She reached across
to slap at eight-year-old Ruby who was trying to stick a
finger into a small pool of jam spilled on the table top.
'Get off, disgusting child. I've had about enough of you
already this morning. Go and sweep the shelter. Barbara,
you do the dishes instead.'

Barbara tried not to drip suds all over Mrs Penny's
clean floor as she washed the dishes. One plate at a time,
one cup, dipped into soapy water then placed with care on
the rack. Barbara completed her chore in a diligent rou-
tine. Hers and Ruby's. Tony's and Mrs Penny's. Before
reaching for the cup that Clementine had left behind.

Inside, on the dregs of Clementine's tea, a tiny orange
pip circled like a miniature boat. Barbara stared down at it
with a frown. No one had eaten oranges for breakfast. No
one had eaten oranges since the secret oranges Clementine
had given them that night in her room. Barbara tipped
the cup up and the pip sailed over the china lip and into
her palm. She touched it with one of her soapy fingers,
remembering an exchange of secrets on a black-and-white
marble floor, miles below. Clementine and her lover Stanley, swapping oranges as though they were kisses. Then
some of those too. It wasn't only Ruby who saw things she
ought not.

'Barbara! Barbara! Come and help me with this sheet.'

Out in the scullery, cold and damp, Mrs Penny was
already manhandling the laundry in and out of the tub.
Helping with the washing was Ruby's duty too that week,
but Barbara knew there was not going to be any chance of
that. She swilled out Clementine's cup and placed it on the

rack along with the others, pulling the plug from the sink and watching the dirty water swirl away. Then she slipped the orange pip into the pocket of her skirt and went to the scullery to help.

'I hope that girl comes home in good time tonight.' Mrs Penny poked at the sheets in the copper with a set of big wooden tongs. 'Took me an age to get that chicken. Don't want it ruined because she's running late.'

Barbara stood by the mangle waiting for the first sheet to be fed her way. 'If Clementine marries the American,' she said, 'will we have chicken every week?'

Mrs Penny snorted. 'Don't hold your breath. Always likes to do things her own way, does your older sister.'

'What things?'

'None of your business. Husband and children probably the last thing on her mind.'

'Did you ever have any children, Mrs Penny?'

Mrs Penny stopped stirring for a moment and gazed at Barbara's small round face. 'I've got you, haven't I.'

It wasn't a question. It also wasn't what Barbara meant.

The sheets turned lazy circles inside the tub as Mrs Penny looked down into the grey, steaming suds. 'There was one once,' she said. 'But it wasn't to be.' She poked at a sheet as it ballooned towards the surface like the throat of a frog. 'Life's like that, sometimes. It gives with one hand and takes away with the next.'

Half an hour later, in the airing cupboard off the hall, Barbara discovered two more little orange pips waiting to be found. She was collecting fresh sheets ready to go upstairs into each of the rooms – Tony's bedroom, Mrs Penny's, the room under the gable that she shared with

Ruby, then Clementine's last. The pips were nestled on top of the pile of sheets that fitted Clementine's bed.

'What are you doing, Barbara?' Ruby stood in the passageway, a smear of mud from the shelter across the front of her skirt.

Barbara turned towards her sister, back against the airing cupboard door. 'Nothing.'

'Nothing is as nothing does.' Ruby giggled. Rule number 103.

Barbara frowned. 'Mrs Penny said not to do that, Ruby.' Ruby often tried to sound like Mrs Penny, especially if Mrs Penny might be near enough to hear.

There was mud on Ruby's knee, too. Barbara watched as her sister licked a finger and rubbed at it. Then licked her finger again and wiped it on the bottom of her skirt. 'You'll turn into Mrs Penny if you don't watch out,' Ruby said and headed up the stairs.

Another half an hour, all the sheets delivered but two, and Barbara knelt on the first-floor landing, one eye to the keyhole in the old nursery door that was Tony's den now. The door had never been locked before, not as far as Barbara could tell. But as she laid Tony's sheet on the floor beside her, she could tell it was locked tight now.

Inside, Barbara could see Tony sitting on the bed. And Ruby sitting on Tony's knee. Tony, with his black pipe, with his jokes and the way he let Barbara wet her lips with his rum. The only person in the household who'd ever winked at Barbara, even though she had never learned how to wink back. Barbara knew that she and Ruby were much too old to sit on Tony's knee. But still, as she watched, she wished that it could be her.

Downstairs Mrs Penny rattled her pans in the kitchen, while through the keyhole Barbara watched Tony put his hand on Ruby's leg. He had his lips to Ruby's ear too, a whisper passing between them just like the whispers that had passed between Ruby and Clementine beneath the huge dome of St Paul's. A real secret. Something Barbara was not supposed to hear. Something Ruby had never divulged, not even to her twin.

Barbara shifted then, small knees cramped and stiff, and the floorboards on the landing gave out the tiniest of creaks. Inside Tony's room, two faces turned all of a sudden to the door, Barbara's heart all pitter-patter in her chest until they turned back. It was then that Tony did it. Pressed his thick lips against Ruby's little mouth.

Two minutes later, upstairs on the highest, furthest floor, Barbara put her eye to another hole. Not in a door this time, but a mattress that she and her twin sister shared. Barbara knew this hole was one of Ruby's secret places, one of several Barbara had discovered over the years. For biscuits stolen from the tin. Or coal from the grate. For powder puffs from Mrs Penny's drawer. Or pennies taken from Tony's pocket without even asking first. It was dark inside the mattress. But unlike the door to Tony's den, this hole did not require a key for all its secrets to be revealed.

Squeeze, wriggle, poke. Inside, in a space just big enough for a child's finger and thumb, something was shoved in tight. Barbara prodded at it with the tip of one finger. 'Ow!' She pulled her finger out. Something inside the hole had pricked her. A trap, perhaps. A warning.

Barbara wondered if Ruby had done it on purpose, just because she could.

Carefully she wriggled her finger and thumb in once again and this time she caught something else – the edge of a small furl of cloth. She gave it a tug and out the secret slipped. A roll of dark serge falling into her hand, the same fabric that Mrs Penny used to patch their skirts. Barbara looked up for a moment to make sure nobody was near, then slowly, slowly she unravelled the dark cloth to see what she could see.

A piece of orange peel, perhaps.

One of Clementine's cigarettes.

But inside was something more precious than that. Barbara's very own apostle spoon (or so she thought), taken from a hole she had dug beneath the stump of a dead tree.

Barbara picked up the spoon and stared at her own reflection in the curve of the bowl. She looked funny, her features distorted. Trust Ruby to want everything, even when she hadn't got there first.

Except . . .

The spoon wasn't the only treasure rolled up inside Ruby's dark patch of serge. There was something else. Small and star-shaped, a pulse of red at its heart. Barbara stared, eyes wide, as the glittery thing was revealed. A love token. A promise. The sealing of a pact. Clementine and Stanley's secret treasure, fallen into Ruby's thieving hands.

'Barbara! Ruby!'

From down in the depths of the kitchen Mrs Penny started up with a cry, voice drifting up the staircase as though she was summoning the sisters from across a great expanse.

'Barbara! Ruby! Come down here at once.'

Barbara froze, heart drumming like a snare against her ribs. Then she heard a scuffle on the floor below, the sound of feet running across uncarpeted boards. The turn of a lock in a door. She held on to her breath as best as she could, counting *one elephant, two elephant*, just as Clementine had taught, until she heard Ruby jumping down the stairs two at a time in response to Mrs Penny's request.

Quickly she rolled up the piece of cloth and pushed it back, deep into the mattress. *Leave no trace.* Wasn't that what she had been taught? Then she touched the three orange pips in her pocket. There was another secret somewhere on this floor and Barbara was certain now that she knew where to look.

The real secret was murder in the family. Down in the scullery, feeding sheet after sheet through the mangle, Mrs Penny had told Barbara everything important there was to know. 'Like a cancer . . .' she'd said. 'The need to do wrong. Your whole family's got it. You'd better watch out you don't get it too.'

Thou shalt not steal.

Thou shalt not covet thy neighbour's goods.

Barbara held on tight to the sodden sheets and remembered a tin pig stolen from a child next door, not because she wanted to play with it, but just because she could.

Honour thy father and thy mother.

Love thy neighbour as thyself.

Barbara wondered then whether her veins ran as clear as they should. Or if it was already too late.

Mrs Penny turned the heavy handle. 'And Clementine,' she said. 'Bad example to you both. Wrong from the moment I arrived.'

Flattening out all the wrinkles from the linen.

'And before that, of course.'

Squeezing out all the life.

'According to Mrs Jones, that is. Trouble of the worst sort.' Mrs Penny heaved on the handle once more before turning to look straight into Barbara's little pig-like face.

Thou shalt do no murder.

'That's what you Walker girls have always been. Trouble, right from the start.'

Stockings hanging from the back of a chair. Kirby grips scattered on top of a chest of drawers. Cotton wool balls all stained with lipstick. And a small pile of orange peel discarded in the wastepaper bin along with a fourth little pip.

Across the landing from the bed she shared with her twin, Barbara stood in the middle of Clementine's room staring up at the top of a wardrobe where a suitcase lined with blue-and-white-checked paper was supposed to live. But the suitcase was gone now. Vanished. Nothing in its place.

Except . . .

A fifth little orange pip lying in the middle of Clementine's bed, just waiting for Ruby to bring a new sheet. Next to the pip was a piece of paper folded in four. On the outside Ruby's name was written in a bold and curving script. On the inside, cradled between the folds, was a sixth pip sucked dry. And a set of instructions ending with rule number 12 – the one that everybody in the Walker family knew.

Tell no one.

So that was what Barbara did.

That evening, as dusk fell all around, Barbara travelled straight across the heart of the city; racing beneath its maze of streets into the gathering dark. When she came out of the Underground at the other side, she hurried as best she could towards where a great cathedral stood alone amongst a wasteland of rubble. All the way her feet kept up a pitter-patter on the pavements to match the pitter-patter of her heart.

In her pocket five little orange pips danced and jigged. One from Clementine's teacup. Two from the airing cupboard. One from the rubbish bin and another from inside Clementine's bed. The sixth pip was clutched in Barbara's hand, along with a set of instructions and a bundle she had made up for herself. A nightgown, two pairs of pants, a handkerchief folded and ironed and a tortoiseshell comb taken from Mrs Penny's drawer, just because she could. Barbara knew exactly where she was heading. Reupholstered bras. Shining kitchen gadgets. Cars as huge as boats. The promised land, at last.

Up, up in the sky searchlights criss-crossed the dark as the Warning began its wail. Barbara was mostly alone in the streets now; everyone else hurried home or huddled into the bowels of the earth. Away across the river Barbara could hear the rockets beginning, the whistles as they flew in, then the clap and crump as they fell. Ahead of her, out of the black, the old cathedral loomed large, its huge dome rising above her in the night sky.

Barbara's heart trilled as she arrived on the edge of the desolate landscape and stood waiting where she'd been instructed. It felt like a lifetime before she saw the little pool of light coming her way. Darting across the rubble, navigating its way towards her over the shadowy ground. Barbara held her breath and counted as Clementine had taught. *One elephant, two elephant*, all the way to a thousand. Then there she was. Clementine Walker. Come to take her sister Barbara away for good.

'Where are you?' The call came quiet at first, a single question in amongst the darkness.

'I'm here!' Barbara called back, her voice small in the great emptiness of the night. She heard the stumble of footsteps getting nearer. Then a torch beam shone straight into her eyes. Barbara lifted a small arm to protect herself against the glare. 'It's me,' she said, heart racing like a train on a circular track. In the distance there was the *WHEEEEEE* of a rocket, then a sudden silence before it fell towards the earth.

'What are you doing here, Barbara?' Clementine hissed. She did not sound pleased. 'I was expecting Ruby.'

What was it Barbara could say? Ruby was ill. Ruby was indisposed. Ruby was sitting on Tony's knee right now, licking rum off Tony's lips.

'Ruby couldn't come,' Barbara lied, squinting into the brightness.

'Why not?' Clementine didn't let the torch drop.

'Because.'

'Did she tell you to meet me here?'

'No. Yes. I'm not sure.'

Cancer. Running through the Walker family every which way.

'God!' Clementine swore under her breath. She turned away then and Barbara blinked, everything black all of a sudden, before the grey shapes around her returned. Clementine was crouching a little way in front, small brown suitcase on the ground with the lid flipped up. She was holding the torch in her mouth now, its beam pointing down at nylons and knickers, an underslip thin as a ghost, a bottle of toilet water scented with lavender and, underneath, an ID card with her name printed in red. Inside that: the one remaining ticket for a boat.

Barbara watched as Clementine touched the ticket as though to make sure it was still there, then lifted it out and slipped it into the pocket of her jacket. She looked back at Barbara where she was standing in the dark with her jaw hanging down. 'Have you got the money, at least?'

'Money?'

Tony's share of blackmail. The proceeds from the very first Penny Family Business – all Clementine's hard work. A thousand dollar bills (or thereabouts), locked up inside a wooden box and hidden beneath Tony's bed. Alongside whatever else he could get his hands on. Watches and promissory notes, silver tie pins and coins of all sorts. No way for Clementine to get it back unless some small person purloined a key from Tony's waistcoat pocket while he was occupied doing something else.

Barbara shook her head. 'No,' she said. For the note hadn't mentioned money.

'Christ!' Clementine's voice cut through the inky blackness like a scalpel. 'Bloody hell.'

And Barbara couldn't help it. 'You shouldn't swear, Clemmie,' she said. 'It's bad. Mrs Penny said so.' Even in the vast wilderness of London at night, Barbara still managed to sound prim.

Clementine laughed then, a hollow thing thrown up into the sky, empty of everything Barbara had expected or hoped. 'For God's sake, Barbara. You shouldn't believe everything that Mrs Penny says.'

Somewhere to the south a plane sputtered and droned, the last of a mission to the east returning home injured and late. Its engine dragged nearer, a grinding, high-pitched sound. Both girls looked up. Something was not right. Suddenly, Clementine crouched close to the ground and closed up the lid of the suitcase. *Click-clack*, that's that. She shone her torch into Barbara's face again. 'You should go home now, Barbara. It's not safe.'

Barbara raised her arm to her eyes once more. 'But what about . . .'

'Don't argue. Just do as you're told.'

Barbara squinted, tried to make out the shape of her sister behind the dazzling beam. 'Aren't I coming too?' Small bundle hanging by her side.

'Don't be silly. Why would I take you?'

It wasn't a question.

'But you were going to take Ruby.'

'No, I wasn't.'

At least, that's what Barbara thought her sister said. For suddenly the torch was gone and Barbara was enveloped – by shadows and dark things, obstructions looming up at her out of the night. In front of her there was a scuffling. She put out her hand, touched nothing but empty air, stepped forwards and hit her toe on the edge of a stone or a brick. She stumbled, dropped her bundle, fell back. When she scrambled up again the torchlight was already six feet away, maybe more, a small pool darting this way and that as it travelled rapidly in the opposite direction over the destroyed ground. Twirling hair, shiny gadgets, the scent of orange peel in the night. Barbara Penny's promised land walking away forever into the dark.

She called out, 'Wait!' Stumbling after the light. 'Wait, Clemmie. I brought you this.'

A love token.

A promise.

The seal on a pact.

The torch beam stopped then for a moment, Clementine's voice ringing out in the darkness hard and cold as a bomb casing dropped on a concrete floor. 'What is it?'

'Ruby stole it.'

Ruby, hands all over the insides of a suitcase.

Ruby, folding stolen treasure into a small square of serge.

'I'm late now, Barbara. I don't have time for your silly games.' Clementine's voice was cool, like the bottom of an ocean where a million sailors had sunk slowly to their deaths. 'If anything happens it'll be your fault.'

'But I got it back for you.' Barbara waited, until at last the torch began its dance back to where she was standing. Two girls, two sisters. One nearly nineteen and all grown now. One with all her growing still to do.

Together they stared down into the small cup of torchlight illuminating Barbara's hands. A red eye glittered back, surrounded by five sharp points. Clementine's star-shaped brooch, where it belonged at last.

Clementine spoke first. 'She didn't steal it, Barbara. I gave it to her.'

'But Stanley . . .'

'It isn't from Stanley. It's from Tony.'

Ruby sitting on a bed.

Ruby sitting on a knee.

Ruby letting Tony kiss her: a promise to her older sister made and kept.

'He gave it to me ages ago.'

A small girl locked in a cellar, eyes rimmed with soot.

'It's nothing but a trinket.' The torch beam swung away again. 'Have it if you want.'

The pool of light danced off once more, quicker this time. Now here. Now gone. Now here again. Then lost. Hurrying, hurrying into the darkness, over piles of rubble, over huge blocks of broken stone covered in weeds.

Barbara watched as it vanished into the black, then appeared again even further away than before. 'Don't leave me, Clemmie,' she called out as the light got smaller and smaller. 'Wait!' But her voice was nothing now, a tiny echo calling to no one but herself.

Disorientated in the darkness, she stumbled first this way then that, bruising her knees and holding her arms out in front as though to ward off the worst. She wasn't certain whether to wait or to follow. Or whether just to go home. There was no one to tell her what to do now. Not Tony or Mrs Penny. Not Ruby or even Clementine. Not any more.

Ahead of her, across the wilderness, Clementine's torch was nothing but a tiny winking star. Barbara watched it disappear for the last time as she began to cry. Above them, a pilot, almost nineteen and not long to live, spotted it too. He locked onto the pinprick of light dancing on the ground. Home at last. Then set his final course.

An explosion of light. A tsunami of hot air. A wave of splinters and of brick. Dust rolling across the ground towards her like an enormous desert storm. But what Barbara remembered most before the cataclysm came, was the silence. Her life suspended for a millionth of a second, as though it might take a whole other turn.

Alfred returned from the hills.

Dorothea resurrected.

Two little twins crawling from their hideaway with grass seeds in their hair.

When Barbara opened her eyes she found herself gazing at stars, a whole sky of them gazing back. A thick layer of dust had covered her body like a blanket, from the very top of her head right down to the soles of her feet. Her bundle had vanished, tossed away somewhere by the blast, as she had been tossed too, up into the air, landing out of sight of anything she recognized. Her skirt was all crumpled. Her hair all this way and that. And the pin from a star-shaped brooch had got stuck sharp into the centre of her palm, reminding Barbara of everything she had tried to do right. And everything she had managed to get wrong.

Barbara got up, legs wobbling as though a wardrobe really had come tumbling down on her head this time. She unstuck the brooch from her hand and sucked at the little bead of blood that took its place. Then she wiped her hand on her sock to try to get it clean. She attempted to wipe dust from her coat as best she could, but just made it worse. Mrs Penny would not be pleased. Then she looked around to try to find her sister, Clementine.

At the edge of the wasteland, a huge fire roared. There was shouting and the sound of a siren blaring. An enormous arc of water falling into a void. Smoke hung thick and choking all about as Barbara stumbled towards the place where Clementine and her little beam of light had disappeared into the dark. Then she stopped. For in front of her there was a crater. And inside the crater, there was nothing at all. The suitcase and all its treasures vanished forever into a fiery pit. Clementine blown away forever too. Nothing left behind but a charred ID card, just waiting for the authorities to discover it and return it to the family stamped: *DECEASED*.

What was it Clementine had said? If anything happened, it would all be Barbara's fault.

There were two things about 14 Elm Row that were different when Barbara made it home. Number 1 – there was a hole opposite their house where someone else's house had once been. Number 2 – Ruby was sitting in the middle of the street.

'Help me, Barbara. Help me, please.'

The only time Ruby had ever asked her twin that.

Ruby's skirt was all rucked up around her waist. Her hair ribbon was torn. Her legs were folded beneath her at a funny sort of angle that made Barbara's stomach flip.

And in Ruby's hand, nestled in the palm, was Clementine's lucky coronation penny. Not so lucky now.

Barbara meant to say, 'Ruby, it's me.'

She meant to say, 'Don't worry.'

She meant to say, 'I'm back.'

But what she said was this: 'You know we're not allowed outside when the Warning goes.'

Badness. It ran through the Walker family like mercury through a silver tube, just as Mrs Penny had said.

2011

Clementine Walker Shaw was worth a fortune – at least, that was what she said. A fortune in oranges, growing like weeds by the side of the road. 'Florida,' she said when Margaret enquired. 'USA.' As though Margaret might not know of it. The promised land indeed.

Eighteen, nearly nineteen, twirled hair all scorched, suitcase blown from her hand, covered in dust from mortar and bricks, from rubble and earth, from all sorts of disasters, before she managed to resurrect herself and squeeze onto a boat. Clementine had promised herself then that she would only ever look forwards, and never look back. But promises had never been something Clementine Walker Shaw felt the need to keep.

Over eighty now, but tall still and straight, hair like a silver river flowing from the crown of her head to the tips, Clementine Walker made her way down the aisle of the chapel unaided but for a cane inlaid with tortoiseshell, tip-tapping on the cold tiles as she walked inexorably to the front. Her eyes, as they landed on Barbara's disbelieving face, were as startling as they had been the day her sisters were born, six little orange pips sucked dry pushed deep down the side of their crib.

In the face of her approach, everything stopped. The choir faltered. Pastor Macdonald stared. The indigent funeral rota turned as one to look, shuffling and gawping in a very non-Edinburgh way. Even the coffin's descent was halted before it disappeared forever into the irretrievable depths. The funeral had already been a special occasion, but now it was about to become something even more extraordinary than that.

Amongst the clumsy hats and sensible windcheaters of the Edinburgh crowd, it was clear that this woman did not belong to the Athens of the North. She was much too well dressed for that. Her coat was as black as the darkest Edinburgh night. Her gloves as close-fitting as a second skin. Her shoes were fastened each side by tiny ebony beads. And her legs, old now and riven with veins, were clad in the thinnest of gossamer tights.

'Am I too late?' the old woman demanded as she processed to the front of Edinburgh's small crematorium chapel leaning on an elegant black stick.

On the contrary, thought Margaret, staring at the new arrival. You have timed your entry to perfection, for maximum effect.

Beside Margaret, Barbara sagged as though punctured, almost dragging her daughter to the floor. Her face had turned as bloodless as the remains of Mrs Walker, laid out now inside her wooden box. As the new arrival gazed at Barbara with those startling eyes, unmistakable despite all the years that had passed, Barbara let out a small moan as though mortally injured through the heart. Her chest set up a great wheezing and wailing as if it were Barbara who was about to descend to the underworld with nothing but a small trail of orange pips to keep her company at the last.

On the woman's elegant lapel, pinned above her heart, was a brooch, star-shaped, the red stone at its centre like a tiny drop of blood. It winked at Margaret in the low chapel light. Even so, Margaret had to ask.

'Who are you?'

All the murmurings and the susurrations of the indigent funeral crowd fell silent then, as though a bomb were about to drop. The woman gesticulated with her cane, pointing its slender tip towards Barbara, or perhaps the coffin; even afterwards Margaret could never be sure. Then she said it.

'I'm her sister, of course.'

The funeral ended in the same confusion in which the dead Mrs Walker had existed for the past few weeks. A mishmash of exclamations and gasps, chatter and excitement, shuffles, whispers, even the occasional shout. The organist struck up with a hymn, 'Abide with Me', as the choir picked up the River Jordan for its last few beats. Pastor Macdonald attempted to finish his eulogy, voice straining as he exhorted his congregation to praise the Lord in the face of this obvious sign of deliverance from the west.

But no one was paying any attention. All eyes were on the stranger arrived from out of the Edinburgh mist, sitting now in the front row alongside Margaret and Barbara Penny as though by some divine right. The old woman clad in elegant black was silent as all around her the indigent funeral crowd thrummed with excitement, craning to get a good look. She sat poised and composed like an artist's model, staring resolutely towards the coffin at the front, occasionally gazing up at the small coloured windows positioned high beneath the chapel's roof.

The choir sang its way out as the organist lumbered to a close and Pastor Macdonald repeated *ashes to ashes* several times, as though to make sure the thing really was at an end. It was only as the coffin started once more on its inevitable descent that the old woman stood all of a sudden and stilled the demented crowd. They fell into silence as she moved slowly forwards to leave a gift all of her own on the surface of Mrs Walker's last abode.

A love token, perhaps.

A seal on a pact.

But it turned out to be neither of these things. Just a plain old orange of the kind one might buy in the street. The last thing any of the funeral crowd saw as Mrs Walker's coffin descended at last into its final berth.

Outside in the damp February rain, after the funeral had come to its chaotic, unruly end, Mrs Walker's long-lost sister explained. 'I eat one every morning for breakfast,' she said. 'From my own personal crop.'

Peeled and segmented, displayed like a wheel of fire on a blue stone plate. A reminder of sun burning in a prairie sky. And of a small girl sitting alone on the bottom step of a narrow stairway, waiting and waiting for her father to come home.

What more proof did Margaret need that this was indeed a relative of the dead? Still, it would have been a dereliction of duty not to ask. 'What's your name?' she said. It was a genuine question.

The lady with the long velvet coat, dark as midnight, smiled. 'You can call me the other Mrs Walker.'

And amidst all the confusion and the windcheaters, the general pandemonium, that was how it was left.

At the front door of the chapel, Barbara was wheezing now as though she might expire right there on the steps, no need for further hospitalization or even a residential home for the terminally old. 'Take me home,' she whispered to Margaret, squeezing out the words as if they constituted her dying request. She refused to look at the startling stranger.

'I can give you a lift if you want?' The other Mrs Walker's voice was a strange combination of old England and new America, something irresistible in its tone. She made her offer as a car, black and glittering with raindrops, glided to a halt in front of the chapel doors.

Margaret frowned. 'Have you been following me?' she said, even though she knew it wasn't entirely polite.

'Of course,' the other Mrs Walker said, as though it was an obvious fact rather than a mystery only just solved. 'How else was I to discover where my sister might live?'

'So lovely to meet you. Hope to see you again.' Barbara's voice was faint as she uttered the standard pleasantries accorded to a stranger. Say one thing, mean another. The Edinburgh Way of bringing something to an end.

'But what about the wake?' said Margaret. Sandwiches made of soft white bread. Rum in dark bottles. And three kinds of cake. All laid out in the kitchen at The Court. She didn't want this stranger to miss out on that.

'I'm sure she's got other things to do,' Barbara gasped, tugging at Margaret's arm as though to steer her towards the waiting taxis.

'Oh no,' replied the other Mrs Walker. 'That was why I came.'

Despite its bulk, the black car only had room for one other passenger. Or so the old woman said. 'Shall we toss for it? Heads or tails. You choose.' And from a small purse hanging from her wrist the other Mrs Walker produced a silver dollar, shining in the low February light.

But for the first time since Margaret had returned to Edinburgh, she got there first. There in her palm, held out for anyone who wanted to see, was a lucky coronation penny. Britannia on one side wielding her trident. A king who should never have been a king imprinted on the reverse. For a moment there was silence as two old women stared down at the flat brown thing. Barbara's eyes bulged beneath the brim of her lilac hat. While the other Mrs Walker just began to laugh. Let the king decide.

So he did.

'Heads,' said Margaret.

'Tails,' said Barbara.

And the other Mrs Walker flipped the coin into the air.

Up, up it went, everyone watching, mouths open, breath held as it made its lazy turn. Then down, down, plummeting towards the wet ground, bouncing once with a chink on the cold stone before rolling off towards the chapel door. Margaret pursued the coin as it faltered and toppled into the shadows.

'Heads,' she declared from inside the chapel.

Of course.

The inside of the black car was as luxurious as Barbara's box room was not. Leather, soft, with the dull sheen of money, large enough for plenty of passengers should that have been what the owner desired. Margaret stroked the seat as she clambered in, tucking little paws and a fox tail inside her lapels. As the car set off with a soft purr, gliding away from the chapel, she looked back out of the smoky glass of the rear window to see Barbara standing at the front of the indigent funeral crowd, jaw dropped down. She was propped up by two grey NHS sticks and Mrs Maclure.

'You'll get her home, won't you?' Margaret had whispered to the small woman as the other Mrs Walker instructed her driver where to go. 'It's just . . .'

'Of course.' Mrs Maclure bobbed and bowed. 'I understand. Family comes first.'

Black hands. Black feet. Hair stuck to the back of an armchair. This was the first opportunity since Margaret had arrived back in Edinburgh to actually get to know something of her client in the flesh.

'But . . .' Mrs Maclure had gripped Margaret's arm before she climbed into the back seat of the car. 'Don't forget, dear. The past is a dangerous country. Things there aren't always what they seem.'

As it was, in the car now, the other Mrs Walker wove a story in response to Margaret's request that was all about her rather than her sister. Of a troopship sailing away from an English port, full of the wounded and anyone else who could inveigle their way on board. Of crowds waving, handkerchiefs all aflutter, hats lifted, scarves trailing like banners in the breeze. Of a young woman standing alone on the other side of the boat, gazing towards a new horizon and at the cold, choppy waters still to be crossed.

'I came from the wrong side of the blanket,' the other Mrs Walker told Margaret. 'Not in the official records, so to speak.' And Margaret felt the thrill of a connection she had never quite considered for herself.

The old woman described how for the whole of the

journey she only ever stood at the prow, never in the stern, leaving behind a Britain where one rasher of bacon had to last for three weeks. And roast chicken cost a quart of rum. Where eggs came in powder form. And oranges were a luxury only the lucky could afford. She arrived to re-upholstered bras and shiny gadgets. To cars as big as boats. To a kitchen with a red floor that shone like a mirror right from the start. At least, that was what she said.

'I was a war bride, before the war was even out.' And the other Mrs Walker laughed then as though all the arrangements had happened just like that.

Mrs Walker to anyone who asked. Mrs Walker Shaw before a year passed. Confetti fluttering over her head as she walked down the steps of a clapboard church to a lifetime spent on a wide-open plain.

'Freshly picked beans! Tomatoes as big as my hand! You can understand, dear . . .' the other Mrs Walker said, her hand in its fine glove pressing Margaret's knee, '. . . why it was I never came home.'

The other Mrs Walker dipped inside her small bag then and took out a photograph. A man surrounded by four children, all of them grinning, a Polaroid bleached in the hot American sun.

'My husband, Stanley. Dorothy, my eldest. Stan Junior the next. Then my twins, Alfie and little Clemmie.' The other Mrs Walker pointed a fingertip towards the small girl in the picture. 'My own little gem.'

Margaret gazed at where a girl stared back, grinning with perfect little teeth and startling eyes, dark hair all about her face. She knew then that the other Mrs Walker was who she claimed to be. The names told that story, if nothing else. But also because the girl in the photograph was as small-boned and as startling as her ancestor lying now inside a wooden box.

So here they were at last, the deceased's relatives that Margaret had been searching for all along. Not a madwoman in a lunatic asylum, or two dead children sleeping in their grave beneath a holly bush. But a sister from the wrong side of the bedcovers, and all her descendants, returned from their hiding place across the sea.

Margaret felt in the pocket of her new stolen coat for a photograph of her own, just to be sure. A woman sitting in a chair looking bewildered, wearing some sort of gown. 'Is this your sister?' she said.

The old lady removed her glove to take the photograph from Margaret. She looked at the image for a long time before she said, 'Yes. That's her.' Then she lifted her hand and touched the surface of the picture, right where a small ruby stone was pinned above the woman's heart.

'Do you know what she was doing in Edinburgh?' Margaret asked.

The other Mrs Walker paused for a moment. 'Perhaps she was heading home,' she said.

'But she came from London.'

The old woman turned to look at Margaret. 'So do you,' she replied.

There was an awkward silence for a moment, before Margaret decided to push on. Who Dares Wins (and all that). 'Do you mind me asking how you found out she had died?' She couldn't imagine Janie's indigent funeral budget stretching to adverts in America.

'Serendipity,' said Mrs Walker Shaw. 'And a letter.'
'A letter?'
'From a representative of the dead.'

Clementine Walker Shaw was a widow of twenty years' standing living amongst the Florida groves when her life took its next turn. No longer dreaming of oranges but of something else instead. Rooms painted with distemper. Cold iron grates. A kitchen table covered in flour. And a mother singing 'Oh my darling', as she brushed and brushed her daughter's hair. Every time she closed her eyes, she saw them all again. Men in uniform leaning towards her from out of the shadows. An asylum rising from its grounds. And two little girls sitting on the edge of a bed with dirty ribbons in their hair.

Suffer little children to come unto me.

Wasn't that what the chapel window had said?

Clementine Walker Shaw knew that she had broken most of the Ten Commandments before she was even grown. She had lied. She had stolen. She had slept with them all. But was it too late to make up, now that she was old? She had pressed her hands to her face then, sticky with juice and age, and prayed to whoever might be listening. *Help me, Jesus. Help me, Allah. Help me, God.* After all, she had been buried once before and survived. Perhaps now was the moment for Clementine Walker to rise again.

She sent the black car out like a probe into the darkness of the past, just in case, chasing Pennys of the right age and name. Followed by letters to a solicitor's firm that had worked so hard to obliterate her past. Her reward came on an unassuming Florida morning, dropped into her mailbox as she ate an orange laid out on a blue china plate. A small thing, crumpled and lumpy, stamped with the imprint of a psychiatric unit somewhere in England.

Dear Mrs Walker . . .

Containing a brooch, small and star-shaped, with a dot of red at its heart.

Also a note. From Nye & Sons, solicitors, of London.

Your sister asked me to send you this when the time came. Deepest regrets.

Jessica Plymmet paying her debts at the last.

'I felt it then, dear,' the other Mrs Walker said, taking Margaret by the wrist. 'As though my final moment had come too.'

A pitter-patter inside the old woman's chest, the suck of her breath loud inside her head. Counting, *one elephant, two elephant*, all the way to a thousand, just as Alfred had taught. Nothing spiralling through her brain but a father who whistled as he walked away. A mother left swaying on a bed. Two small children crawling from their latest hideaway. And a girl with eyes as startling as her own, breathing out a promise to do whatever Clementine said.

Tell no one. That was what Clementine had made the little girl promise.

So that was what Ruby Walker did.

Back at The Court, surrounded by as many of the indigent funeral rota as could fit, the other Mrs Walker sat peeling an orange while all around her people whispered and watched. The stranger's fingers never faltered as she parsed the skin away from the fruit in one continuous curl.

'My orchard is beautiful,' she said, holding out a segment to Margaret. 'You should visit one day.'

'I'd like that,' Margaret said. But she knew it wouldn't happen. Apart from Margaret having no money, the other Mrs Walker hadn't told anybody where precisely she lived.

Teacups and rum glasses, sandwiches carved into fingers, three kinds of cake – Margaret busied herself in the kitchen replenishing refreshments for all of their guests. She could hear the other Mrs Walker spinning her story once again. Beans piling up in a colander. Tomatoes as big as her fist. Unlike Barbara, stories were something the other Mrs Walker appeared to do best.

On the side in the kitchen was a bottle of cheap rum, screw top loose. Standing next to it, a bottle of whisky of a very expensive brand. 'Duty-free,' the other Mrs Walker had said as she handed it over. 'What a wonderful thing.'

Next to the two bottles was Barbara, tumbler filled to the brim. 'But what did she say?' Barbara had been interrogating Margaret ever since she and the other Mrs Walker had arrived back at The Court. The liquid in her glass trembled and shimmied to match the tremor in her hands.

'Why don't you ask her yourself?' Margaret took some Bakewells from a box and placed them one by one on a plate as though they were the rays of the sun.

'Where has she come from?' Barbara didn't want to speak to the spectre at the feast. At least, that was how it seemed.

'America.'

Barbara's chest gave off a sort of whimper. 'America?' The promised land, of course.

'She was a war bride. Married someone called Stanley. Never came home until now.'

'But how did she know about the funeral?' Barbara lifted the tumbler towards her mouth with both hands, teeth chattering on the glass.

'Mrs Walker's solicitor got in touch. Jessica Plymmet? You know her, I think.'

Barbara's hand jerked and rum spilt all down the front of her turquoise suit. 'What does she want?' she said.

Margaret frowned at her mother. 'What do you think? To say goodbye, of course.'

From out in the living room where the other Mrs Walker held court, a great laugh gusted up from the indigent crowd, followed by a smattering of applause. 'I never knew she had a sister.' Barbara's voice was plaintive now, as though she was still a child herself.

'Who?'

'Mrs Walker.'

'No,' said Margaret. 'Neither did I. But then that's life, isn't it? It takes with one hand and gives back with the next.'

Margaret stood back to admire the tray of tea and cake ready to go out into the midst. She reached for the bottle of duty-free the other Mrs Walker had contributed to the wake. 'I think I'll have a whisky. Seeing as it was what Mrs Walker drank.'

'Me too,' said Mrs Maclure, appearing suddenly in the kitchen and moving in behind Barbara as though to catch her should she fall.

Barbara made a feeble stab at one of Margaret's new

shoes with the rubber tip of her grey NHS stick. 'How do you know that?'

'Nineteen empty bottles,' said Margaret, moving her foot away. 'Lined up in the deceased's flat.'

'Nineteen?' Barbara swayed for a moment, as though remembering her own cluster of bottles lined up beneath the sink. 'Was she ill?'

'Pain relief, I think,' replied Margaret. 'She only had a few weeks to drink them in, but she drank the lot.'

'My, my,' said Pastor Macdonald, chuckling from where he had come to stand in the doorway. 'It's one way to celebrate the coming of the end.'

Pastor Macdonald was even bigger close up, his face glowing with evangelical zeal and spirits of a different kind. 'How nice to meet you properly at last,' he said, clasping Margaret's hand in his enormous palm. 'Welcome back.'

'Nice to meet you too,' she replied. 'And where are you from?' She hadn't meant to say it. It just popped out. The Edinburgh Way.

Pastor Macdonald laughed and endowed Margaret with his most brilliant smile. 'Pilrig,' he said, 'by way of Leith. And you?'

'Edinburgh, by way of London.'

'Ah. And are you a London girl at heart, or a creature of the north?'

'I'm not sure.' Margaret looked over to where her mother was trying to squeeze past Pastor Macdonald, wheezing and panting on her way to salvation in the loo. Barbara was holding a grey NHS stick aloft in one hand, a tumbler of rum splashing and dancing in the other.

Margaret peered down into her own glass, a small slick of amber liquid smiling back. 'I haven't decided yet,' she said.

But she had.

Ten minutes later, through a crack in the box-room door, Margaret watched as two women, both old, one fat, one startling in every single way, confronted each other across a blue-and-yellow lilo. From the living room she could hear Pastor Macdonald leading the rest of the indigent flock in prayer. *Help me, Jesus. Help me, Allah. Help me, God.* But despite his entreaties, Margaret had made her excuses and left. There were other secrets she was more interested in than those that would only be revealed on death.

'I came to say goodbye.' The other Mrs Walker obviously had no time for prayer meetings either, standing in the box room propped up by her elegant stick.

'You're supposed to be dead.'

At least, that was what Margaret thought she heard her mother say.

The other Mrs Walker laughed, a lark surfing the low ceiling of the box room. 'I'm like Lazarus,' she said. 'You can't keep me down.' Then she held out her hand with its tangle of veins and its skin like crumpled greaseproof paper. 'I thought you might like this.'

Not a love token.

Or the seal on a pact.

But a star-shaped brooch with a drop of ruby at its heart.

The two old women stared down at the small, glittery thing in the cup of the other Mrs Walker's palm, while from outside in the hall, Margaret's heart set up a great thrumming against the wall of her chest. It was Barbara who spoke first.

'What for?' She seemed to have forgotten all her previous exhortations to be polite to the relatives of the deceased.

'To say thank you, of course.' The other Mrs Walker continued to hold out the brooch, red stone winking. 'For giving my sister the send-off she deserved.'

Barbara was silent for a moment, not making any move to take the gift. 'What do you want?' she said.

'What makes you think I want anything?'

Barbara rubbed at her face. 'Because.'

The other Mrs Walker shrugged then as though it was of no matter to her what Barbara thought one way or the other. 'Perhaps your daughter would like it instead. For looking after my sister, when no one else did.'

From her hiding place beyond the door, Margaret held her breath. Suddenly she wanted more than anything to hold that brooch in her hand. Something passed from a sister to a sister – or from a dead client to her handmaiden, at least. But before she could reveal herself, push open the door and snatch up the star-shaped brooch to pin to her breast, her mother interceded, as only Barbara could.

'Have you offered it to her yet?' Barbara's face had taken on that same look Margaret had seen when she first arrived back from the south. Fear, or something like it. As though whatever might follow could only mean one thing.

'No.' The other Mrs Walker closed her hand over the small gift. 'I wanted to see what it was worth to you first.'

Barbara's chest gave off a long, painful groan then as though something important might be taken from her unless she decided to fight back. 'Everything,' she said finally.

There was silence for a moment as the two women stared each other out. One still towering despite her age, the other crumpled now despite her bulk. Outside in the hallway, Margaret waited with her heart in her throat to see what might be revealed next.

Then the other Mrs Walker shifted slightly. 'There is one thing,' she said, 'that might make it worth my having come all this way.'

And for a moment both women glanced towards something propped up against the box-room wall. Small and brown, dirty in more ways than one. Once of sentimental value, but worth considerably more now. At least, that was what Jessica Plymmet had suggested, when Clementine Walker Shaw enquired about an estate.

Barbara's chest gave a great wheezy sigh like the last note of an accordion playing its final lament. 'Yes,' she said. 'Of course.'

The other Mrs Walker smiled and nodded, as though a deal had been struck. Then she tapped at the box-room carpet with the tip of her cane and said, 'Your daughter's a credit to you.'

Barbara exhaled as if she too knew that some promise had been made and would also be kept. 'I tried my best . . .' she said, growing larger all of a sudden. 'To keep her safe.'

From through the crack in the door, Margaret saw another expression settle on her mother's face now. Something she hadn't seen since she was a six-year-old child being picked on in a cold Edinburgh close. Determination. That whatever belonged to Barbara, would stay exactly as it should. And the knowledge that her mother would fight for her only child, to the death, if that was what it took. Margaret stared at Barbara, then beyond her to the painting leaning casually against the box-room wall. Something Margaret had only ever glanced over before, never really studied in the way she studied it now. The painting was of a woman, impossibly young, limbs spread all about in a muddy splash of oil. Greys and browns. No other colour except for something hanging over the young woman's breast. Not a fox's small paw or a head eaten away by mange, but a dot of the brightest green, like the eye of a cat. Or an emerald necklace, listed on a crumpled jewellery receipt.

What was it Jessica Plymmet had said as they stood, hidden away at the end of a long gallery corridor, beneath a painting just like this? That she wrote to Barbara before Christmas with news of a mutual acquaintance, long lost. Someone Barbara feared coming through her front door. Only to discover it was her long-lost daughter who had returned instead.

Margaret rolled back against the wall of the hall, heart kicking up thunder beneath her funeral dress, breathing *one elephant, two elephant* as she realized all of a sudden something that she'd missed. Mrs Walker wasn't just a refugee from the south, washed up in Edinburgh because it was any old place. Mrs Walker had come to Edinburgh for the same reason Margaret had arrived back. To reclaim something that she'd lost. Something misplaced, perhaps.

Stolen, even. Worth nothing once, but considerably more now. Mrs Walker had come to Edinburgh to see Barbara Penny.

Except . . .

Margaret had got there first.

From across in the living room a loud incantation rose up. The members of the indigent funeral crowd, buoyed by excitement and enlightenment of all kinds. Margaret turned for a moment towards the boisterous prayer, only to find Mrs Maclure tugging at her elbow. 'I need your help,' the small woman exhorted, pulling Margaret away from the box room with an insistent grip. 'They've had a little too much to drink, I think.'

Margaret glanced back towards the two old women, bending their heads together now to speak in whispers across a blue-and-yellow divide. 'I just . . .'

But Mrs Maclure was nothing if not persistent. 'It has to be now,' she said. As though it was a matter of life or death. 'Or who knows what might happen.'

And Margaret went with her. How could she not? It was the way Barbara had brought her up.

When Margaret returned from sorting out the indigent funeral crowd, sending them on their way one by one, she found her mother lying on the lilo in the box room like a whale washed up on a beach. Barbara's mouth was agape, her flanks heaving as though she had just escaped from being harpooned and dragged up on deck to be sliced and diced.

Help me, Jesus. Help me, Allah. Help me, God.

(And, in the end, they had.)

Margaret couldn't help noticing how the blue-and-yellow plastic sank beneath her mother's great bulk. She could just imagine how uncomfortable it would be to lie on now, assuming she ever managed to get her mother back up and onto her feet.

In the end that was achieved with the aid of Mrs Maclure, the last member of the indigent funeral crowd left standing after a send-off that had become an Edinburgh legend before it had even run its course. 'Here, dear,' she said, appearing once more in the box-room doorway as Margaret tugged at her mother's thick arms with little success. 'Let me help.'

Together they hauled and cajoled until Barbara was sitting up once more, wheezing out a final demand. 'Is she gone?'

It wasn't really a question. But all three of them knew who she meant.

For the other Mrs Walker had disappeared just as suddenly as she had arrived, vanished somewhere as surely as the dead Mrs Walker was gone too. One into the embrace of the crematorium's gas jets, the other to some place back across the ocean. Over the hills and far away, perhaps. Or somewhere much further than that. Margaret searched every inch of her mother's flat in the hope that she was mistaken. But she knew even before she began that it was a hopeless case. The other Mrs Walker had left a hole in the air when she went. Nothing to mark her strange passing but a curl of orange peel discarded on the floor.

'I needed to talk to her,' Margaret said to Mrs Maclure, eyes wild with everything that she'd missed.

'That's a pity,' said the little wolf-like woman, pinion-

ing Margaret for a moment with her own eyes like small
bits of jet. 'But some questions are best left unasked, don't
you think?'

There was one thing, however, that did appear out of
nowhere once the stranger from the west was gone for
good, discovered in Barbara's hand as Margaret helped
her up. A tiny translucent limb, severed at the elbow and
veined with cracks. The long-lost arm from a grubby china
cherub. Home where it belonged at last.

EPILOGUE

Springtime in Edinburgh, 2011

They measured the box room the day after the wake, Barbara seemingly recovered from her confrontation, all her faculties just about intact. The room was long enough for a daybed, if they threw plenty of stuff out.

'What's a daybed when it's at home?' Barbara leaned against the doorframe, propped up by one of her two NHS sticks. She wasn't wholly complete yet, having been to death's door before turning back. But she was still standing. And there was something triumphant in that.

'It's like a chaise longue, but more comfortable,' Margaret said.

'What do you need that for?'

Luxury, Margaret thought, the first time she lay down on it. Of a first-class kind.

They tidied the room together, Margaret lifting each item of junk, Barbara giving a shake or a nod of her head. The pile for the charity shop grew and grew. As did the pile for the tip. A heater with a broken dial. An iron with a frayed flex. The box room appeared to increase in size as the recycling heap grew ever larger and the stash of things to keep remained small. A mangy fox fur. A blouse scented with linseed oil. And something in a large cardboard box.

'What's that when it's at home?' Barbara enquired.

Margaret opened the lid and held up a shiny gadget for her mother to see. 'It's a juice machine,' she said.

There was also an old Christmas tree, its bendable silver branches folded up inside its tube as though they had been folded up all year. 'What about this?' Margaret said.

'Oh, that old thing.' Barbara gave a shrug.

'Why didn't you put it up this year?' Though Margaret already had an inkling of why that might be – was just waiting for her moment to strike.

Barbara shrugged again. 'Past its best,' she said, gathering up her sticks as though the chore of clearing the box room was suddenly complete. 'I'll keep it though.'

'What for?'

'Next year, of course.'

Later that evening Barbara and Margaret sat together in the living room indulging in a final toast to the dead. 'To Mrs Walker.' Margaret raised a glass of wine, dark as bull's blood, filled to the brim. *Be prepared.* Wasn't that what her mother had always taught?

'Whoever she was.' Barbara raised her glass too, just a single finger of rum covering the bottom of her tumbler.

'She was here,' said Margaret. 'I think that's what counts.'

'And now she's not.' Barbara smiled, then drank her measure down in one gulp.

Margaret smiled into her glass too. Contrariness was buried deep in her mother's bones, but still Margaret could tell that something was different. Ever since the epic funeral it was as though Barbara's life had taken on a subtly different hue.

On the living-room mantelpiece the china cherub stood in pride of place now, all its limbs complete. It had been polished and filled up with small flowers to mirror the green shoots appearing across the ground outside. Spring rampaging all over Edinburgh, a city putting on its best possible face.

Next to the cherub was a photograph. Two dead, sleeping children retrieved from the depths of Barbara's handbag, back in the light at last.

'Gave me the creeps when I was young.' Margaret shivered.

'We don't have to keep it,' said Barbara.

'But we should. They look so peaceful. And we don't have any other photographs to put in its place, besides the one of Mrs Walker.'

Barbara coughed then, a small wheezy thing, put down her rum glass and pulled a cup of tea towards her from where she'd left it balanced on top of the TV guide. Margaret wondered if now might be the time to bring up the missing painting, a picture that seemed to have vanished just as two dead, sleeping children finally rose from their grave.

But as though to forestall any questions that could only ever prove awkward, not to mention revealing, Barbara took something from the pocket of her dressing gown instead. A silver teaspoon with a very thin handle, a tiny figure attached to the end.

Margaret spluttered, red wine sprinkling the front of her cardigan. 'Where did that come from?'

St Andrew, patron of women who would be mothers. An apostle spoon just like the one in Mrs Walker's kitchen drawer.

Barbara stirred her tea with the spoon, the small chink of silver on china. 'Inheritance,' she said. 'From my mother.'

'You don't have a mother.'

'Everyone has a mother,' Barbara said, disappearing behind the rim of the cup. 'If you only know where to look.'

Margaret knew then that now was the moment. Who Dares Wins (and all that).

Except . . .

It was her mother who dared first.

Barbara put down her cup and pulled something else from her dressing-gown pocket. 'You might as well have this,' she said. 'No point waiting till I'm dead.'

Margaret couldn't remember the last gift she had received from her mother. Unless she counted the blanket with the torn satin trim handed over on the first day she arrived home. But there it was, held out in her mother's hand. Another photograph, of a newborn baby this time.

'Who is it?' Margaret said.

'Can't you tell?'

And then, of course, Margaret could. For holding the baby up so that the whole world could see was Barbara, smiling as though, at just that moment, all her dreams had come true.

Margaret gazed at the photograph, something inside her shifting. A mother and her baby, in her hands at last. 'Thank you,' she said. 'It's . . .'

But Barbara wasn't finished yet. 'Did you get the note?' she said.

'The note?' Margaret was confused.

'From Mrs Maclure.'

And there it was, in the pocket of Margaret's cardigan. A small piece of paper folded over several times. Margaret held the note in one hand, the photograph of her and Barbara in the other. She knew now where paperwork could lead. Then she opened it.

LOST, it said. *CAN YOU HELP?*

Acknowledgements

Thank you: Clare Alexander and everyone at Aitken Alexander; Maria Rejt, Sophie Orme, Claire Gatzen and everyone at Mantle and Pan Macmillan; my fellow writers in Ink Inc. with particular thanks to Pippa Goldschmidt, Theresa Muñoz and Sophie Cooke; Kate Tough; Brownsbank; Ivan Middleton; Jamie Reece at Mortonhall Crematorium, Edinburgh; Frank Davie, formerly of the Edinburgh City Mortuary; James O'Reilly of the Procurator Fiscal's Office, Edinburgh; Dr Robert Ainsworth of NHS Lothian and Edinburgh University; DI Willie Falconer and PC Emily Noble, formerly of the Edinburgh Enquiry Team; Christina Paulson-Ellis; Peter Brunyate; Audrey Grant and all my family for their continuing love and support. It goes without saying that any and all mistakes (and inventions) are, of course, my own.